THE
SWISS
ACCOUNT

Novels by *Leslie Waller*

THE
SWISS
ACCOUNT

by Leslie Waller

DOUBLEDAY & COMPANY, INC.
GARDEN CITY, NEW YORK
1976

For *Lee Barker* in memoriam

All the characters herein are fictitious and any resemblance to actual persons living or dead is purely coincidental.

Library of Congress Cataloging in Publication Data

Waller, Leslie, 1923–
The Swiss account.

I. Title.
PZ3.W1557Sw   [PS3545.A565]   813'.5'4
ISBN 0-385-09661-5
Library of Congress Catalog Card Number 75–6274

PART ONE

Monsieur Voltaire, it is said that you have written against the Lord; that is bad, but He will forgive you. Be careful never to write anything against the Swiss: they will never forgive you.

—Letter from the Bailiff
of Lausanne, c. 1755

CHAPTER 1

Swissair 821 is a suitable flight for someone who wants to get lost in the crowd. The female passenger waiting to board the economy class was traveling with a forged Austrian passport in the name of Berta Hütsch. She wanted to get lost in the crowd.

The DC-9 leaves London before ten in the morning, usually with at least two thirds of its seats filled. Its passengers arrive at the Basel-Mulhouse Airport at about eleven-thirty with more than enough time to make a luncheon meeting in either the Swiss or the French city.

Most are bound for Basel, which, depending on their nationality, they spell in that fashion or Basle or Bâle. Most are in banking or pharmaceuticals. They take a quick look around the Heathrow departure lounge in London and, if none of the faces are familiar, bury their noses in that morning's copy of the *London Financial Times* or *Neue Zurcher Zeitung.*

Most are men. The rare woman will be a secretary, a business associate or, occasionally, a wife. Never, at that hour, a mistress.

Margit Staeli carried both the pink-paper *Times* and the staid *Zeitung,* as well as yesterday's *Wall Street Journal.* Her only luggage was a small flight bag made of a golden-tan leather, supple and soft to the touch, with a shoulder strap of the same leather. Her maid, Elfi, had packed the dark sable coat and the rest of the clothes Margit had worn during the past week in London and carried it back to Basel the evening before.

As a sable substitute, more suitable for getting lost in this particular crowd, Margit wore what she privately called her *algemeine Ur-Lodenmantel,* one of those immensely depressing dust-green cloth coats with bone buttons and metal buckle straps beloved by

3

German, Austrian and Swiss hausfraus. The coat is heavy enough to camouflage not only fat breasts and bellies but thick thighs as well.

None of these were Margit Staeli's problem. Her small, pretty face was. It was far too recognizable. She had carefully arranged a plain silk scarf over her head so that its edges concealed her cheeks. Large Dior sunglasses and a turned-up collar completed the job of turning her, she hoped, into just another passenger on Swissair 821.

She looked up from the *Zeitung* and watched her faint reflection in the plate-glass window of the departure lounge. The loden coat sat there with a life of its own. One could hide a Sherman tank beneath it, Margit thought. She saw that her calves, which showed beneath the edge of the coat, were too slender and long. But wearing chunky *après-ski* boots had been an inspiration of disguise.

So had the Berta Hütsch identity, a remnant of her youth in Switzerland in the years before she had gone away to the States. It was risky, carrying a forged passport, but the forgery was an expensive one, extremely well done, and the alternative to carrying it was even riskier. Under her own name, Margit could count on attracting unwelcome attention wherever she went and, lately, she had been traveling quite a bit—Brussels, Frankfurt, Beirut—making the same sort of personal contact with the local banking fraternity as she had just completed in London.

Even in Switzerland, her home, there was little chance of moving freely under her own name. As the Austrian Berta, however, she had on a number of occasions kept the Staeli name out of the newspapers after some notable scrape, usually engineered by her fiancé, Erich.

He would not, of course, be meeting her at Basel. Even if she had actually needed him at the airport, Erich would simply forget to show up. It was a matter of some concern to her aunts and female cousins that Erich Lorn was so unreliable a fiancé. Not to Margit.

Nor would she be met by her Uncle Dieter, who temporarily headed the business interests of the family. Since her father's death, Margit had been urged by Dieter to look upon him as her surrogate parent, but this trip to London, in fact all her recent visits to European banking cities, remained a secret even from her uncle. It was especially not to be revealed to his fish-faced son, Walter. Some first cousins are charming and, when one is an only child, they become the brothers and sisters one never had. Not Walter.

No, Margit simply didn't want to be met in Basel, either by one of the family Mercedeses or one of the bank's Rollses. She wanted to slip into Basel as Berta Hütsch, age twenty-eight, national of Austria, born in Bad Ischl in the Salzkammergut, and that was that.

She could count on the perfunctory customs inspection to pass her as Berta Hütsch. No guards along any of Switzerland's borders were much interested in what visitors carried in with them. It was assumed—a basic assumption of all the Swiss—that what one carried was one's own business, especially if it were gold bars or large bank notes.

Swissair 821 opened for boarding of First Class passengers via its front entry hatch. Margit watched two men who knew her get on the plane. As a tourist-class passenger, she would be boarding the DC-9 by its rear hatch and could easily avoid being seen by either of the two men, which was just as well. One, a cousin of Erich's who worked for the Lorns' family bank, had known Margit since childhood, as had Erich. The other, a ranking minister in the federal cabinet at Bern, knew her only socially.

As far as either of them knew, Margit Staeli had been skiing in one of the small Styrian villages where Swiss and Austrians went these days to avoid both the Americans and the Germans, who clogged the ski lifts and sent prices ridiculously high. Although the price of anything at all was well within her means, Margit Staeli, like all Swiss, demanded value for what she paid.

A social column in one of the canton newspapers controlled by the Staeli clan had, in fact, printed an item about Margit's Austrian ski trip. An Italian scandal magazine had even commented on how lonely she looked in Styria without her fiancé rumored in Vienna "with a young starlet." It was a mark of the general reliability of such magazines that (a) in over a year Margit had not been within a thousand kilometers of Styria, (b) the photograph accompanying the item had been snapped two years before in Vail, Colorado, and (c) Erich happened to be ensconced in his own bed that weekend with the wife of the cabinet minister now returning to Basel in the First Class section of Swissair 821.

Margit didn't bother to keep abreast of common gossip, but she liked to have all the information she needed to run her own life.

The boarding lounge was almost empty now. Margit stood up and collected her newspapers and tan leather bag. Only she and one other passenger remained, a slight man in an oyster-tan Burberry who, like Margit, was collecting his possessions. He watched her board the plane but refrained from following her. He watched for a while until the gate closed down. Then he made the long trek back to the main lounge to wait for the next Paris flight, on which he was already booked.

Margit settled herself into a seat near the window, adjusted her scarf to hide even more of her face, and relaxed as the DC-9 rumbled down the runway, shot aloft at a sharp angle and soared out over the Channel toward Basel and home.

The Staelis had always been based in Basel, even though the family also had power bastions in Zurich and Geneva. Over the centuries it had been in Switzerland, it slowly branched off from other families of similar name, including Staelins and Staelingers.

Originally the family had descended from the Staël-Holstein line of Danish aristocracy into which the Swiss banker's daughter, Germaine Necker, had married at the end of the eighteenth century. Margit had inherited a strong interest in her ancestor, the talented and often scandalous Madame de Staël. Margit's father had counted this a mixed blessing. His daughter's affinity for the long-dead woman had given her a useful bent toward politics and history. But it had also instilled in her an independence of spirit and thought. In a Swiss woman, this was bad.

Margit's mother had died when her daughter was not yet four years old, after bearing Margit's brother, who lived less than a week. The brother was to have been the heir to the Staeli fortune.

Remembering, Margit stared out at the cloud cover spread over France like the innards of a goose-down comforter. If only her brother had lived, neither her Uncle Dieter nor the rest of the male clan of Staelis would now be impatiently waiting for her to marry Erich and accept her destiny.

Swiss girls have only two fates, Margit thought: whore or wife. Most of us make poor whores.

For one of her class, marriage was even more of a foregone conclusion because, when her brother died, control of the clan resided in Margit. It hadn't been planned that way, of course. She had been at Harvard, earning her M.B.A., when her father, Lucas Staeli, had died—of mysterious causes—leaving all his personal holdings to her. His lawyers—who were also his brother Dieter's lawyers—had done what they could to hedge the inheritance, delaying conveyance of it so that Dieter controlled it until she was thirty years old, or married. Their fond, almost desperate, hope was that marriage would come before her thirtieth birthday.

No one in the vast Staeli clan was under any illusion that the bonds, stocks and directorships had actually been left to a woman. Lucas might have been a disturbed man at his death, but he had still, after all, been Swiss. His daughter was only the custodian of his immense power and wealth, nothing more than the vessel by which it would be conveyed to her husband, as soon as he became her husband.

Yes, it was a pity the husband would be Erich. His family's holdings were modest by comparison, but strategically positioned to complement the tremendous Staeli holdings in chemicals, banking and steel. That was to the good, but Erich's character was to the bad. It wasn't that he had sowed enough wild oats to fill a prairie, or that he was forever risking his neck on skis or in racing cars. It was that he simply *wasn't serious*. It was almost as if— although his family had been Swiss as long as the Staelis—almost as if Erich Lorn weren't really Swiss.

Nevertheless, he was male and could be talked to and brought around. Or bought off. The moment he was married, the moment he and Margit had children, his penchant for oat-sowing would become a distinct liability to his freedom of choice. As a bachelor, even engaged to marry Margit, he was more or less blackmail-proof. But married . . . ? One way or the other, even if blackmail was required, the Staeli holdings would remain intact. Swollen by the Lorn holdings, they would become even more powerful in the great world. Of this Uncle Dieter had no doubt.

The corner of Margit's mouth crooked up again in that faint smile. Uncle Dieter would have been desperately interested in her recent meetings with bankers. Her London trip would have fascinated him.

She may have traveled there as Berta Hütsch. But it was as Margit Staeli, the future head of the great Staeli clan, that she had been welcomed into dimly lighted walnut-paneled board rooms of London's City where, as she glanced occasionally out the window at the pure green pleasure of Lincoln's Fields or New Square, a variety of extremely interesting contacts had been made—as in the other banking capitals she had visited. The merchant bankers with whom she had scheduled these secret meetings now knew the face behind the Margit Staeli name.

It had been a thoroughly satisfying week. She had flirted quite decorously with the younger bankers, single and married. They, in turn, had kept her busy evenings at the theater, at restaurants and in Annabel's. Knowing this about the English male, Margit had packed her most charming Paris and New York dresses for the evenings, alternating between two very sensible suits for daytime meetings.

They had made effortless small talk, spinning on for hours about such a silly thing as the way her first name was pronounced. Since Basel was part of German-speaking Switzerland, most Swiss would have called her *Mar-geet,* but the older Basler families, including the Staelis, often spoke French among themselves. To them she was *Mar-gee.* The Englishmen had usually settled on the total mispronunciation *Margaret,* but that was the English for you.

And, knowing even more about the English male, she had made sure that Elfi, her maid, slept in the second bed of her suite at the Connaught. Even so, the English continued to be fascinated by the knowledgeable young Swiss woman who would soon inherit control of Staeli Internationale, GmbH., the clan's overall holding company.

No deals had been discussed, of course. One didn't operate that way with the British or, this early in the game, with any international banker. The sole purpose of these meetings over the past months had been personal contact. In a world grown wildly more mechanized, in which electronics equipment concluded deals in less than an eye-blink, it had become even more important for bankers to know each other on an eye-to-eye basis. Soon now, every banker of importance in Europe, the Middle East and America would have met Margit Staeli. Soon, too, she would reach her thirtieth birthday.

Thinking about it now, Margit smiled to herself. Once thirty, she might even consider marrying Erich. She had always liked him. He was difficult not to like, being handsome, good at making small talk and having fun. Margit had never regretted the oriental manner in which her family had betrothed her to Erich almost before either of them had graduated from dancing school.

She had observed in him, as had so many other women, a fatally attractive streak of self-destruction. Knowing Erich as well as she did, she knew he played on this chord in his character, a surefire song of seduction. What woman could resist the challenge of keeping him from doing himself in?

The faint smile left Margit's face. Through breaks in the cloud cover she could see the first snow-topped range of mountains below, not the Alps, these, but the Vosges. Some of the peaks loomed sharp and cruel through the clouds.

It wasn't her fault, she mused, that she liked Erich well enough —but didn't love him at all. It showed a calculating streak in her character, true. But this was perhaps a result of her own study of Madame de Staël, who threw everything away for love not once but many times, only to learn in the end that love, like money, has to be maneuvered, disguised, withheld and made to pay its own way.

A hard lesson. Margit frowned at her face, reflected in the Plexiglas window. She realized she could well become a hard person.

The only problem, she thought now, was that if someone came along with whom she could allow herself to fall in love, what sort of person would she be by then? After so many years of hardness, would she even know what love was? Or what to do about it?

These were the problems of the well-to-do, Margit realized. Not the problems of most of humanity, just of a tiny corner of it. Her maid, Elfi, for example, had no such questions of life.

If one were to look at them standing next to each other, there would be a moment of confusion because they resembled each other quite a bit. Elfi was as tall as Margit, easily 173 centimeters, or as her new friends in London would call it, 5 feet, 8 inches. This was tall enough for an English or American woman, but unusually so for a Swiss. In heels, neither Margit nor Elfi could readily find that many appropriately tall escorts from among their countrymen.

They were the same age, twenty-nine, and their coloring was

alike, brunette, with the high flushed cheekbones of a race that inhabits mountain peaks. In her own way, Elfi was attractive, but Margit had no idea what her private life was like. She was not part of the live-in staff at Schloss Staeli. It would have been no life for a young woman shut away in the country as Margit was in her ancestral home.

As she stared out the window now, the mountainous teeth below her seemed unfriendly, menacing. For many people it was a hostile world. There had been an amusing young Socialist lord in London who kept himself busy as a merchant banker, but kept his mind free of the usual cant bankers believed in.

"The big slaughter's about to begin, you know," he'd told her. "For at least half the people in the world, there simply won't be enough food. They're starting to die now. By the end of the century, we'll have killed them off."

Margit frowned and pulled from her tan flight bag a plain exercise book in which she now and then made journal entries.

"Check famine statistics," she wrote now. "Has increase in price of oil put cheap fertilizers and pesticides out of the reach of underdeveloped countries? Is it all made from oil?"

She stared at her own writing. Then: "Whose responsibility?" she scribbled. "Oil producers quadrupling prices? Affluent nations using all the oil? Big manufacturers monopolizing world's supply? Big banks financing monopolists? Staeli Internationale GmbH.?"

She started to close the journal, then decided she was taking the word of a charming Englishman for too much. "Check population statistics," she wrote. "Check whether increasing mechanization makes redundant nearly half the people on earth."

She put away the exercise book and continued peering out at the unfriendly landscape below. A world too hostile to live in was something she and Erich had never known. And never would.

But how horrible if it existed for other people. And if Staeli were in some way responsible for it.

The touch-down at Basel-Mulhouse was smooth and imperceptible. The DC-9 taxied toward the terminal. Margit remained in her seat until First Class passengers had left the aircraft and disappeared inside the modern tan-brick building. She wondered if Erich would by now have returned his lady of the weekend to her home well in advance of her husband's arrival.

Knowing Erich, he was probably just now telephoning for the taxi to take his inamorata away. He liked living dangerously and, it seemed clear, so did the lady.

Margit stood up and took a steadyingly deep breath. And, in my own calculating way, she thought, so do I. It's a reaction to the dullness of being Swiss.

Berta Hütsch, carrying her golden-tan flight bag, was one of the last passengers to leave Swissair 821.

CHAPTER 2

Nineteen hours was a damned long time to inhabit any aircraft, even a jumbo 747. Matthew Burris paced slowly in a tight circle he had laid out for himself on the blue carpet of the First Class lounge that lay just behind the cockpit of the immense plane.

At any moment the pilot would signal everyone to belt up. They would be landing at Paris.

It was at times like this, Burris reflected, that he toyed with the idea of pretending to be a cripple so that he would be met at airports by an attendant with a wheelchair. Nineteen hours in the air was just too damned long.

The only bright spot was landing at Orly, instead of Charles De Gaulle Airport, which had been closed by some local strike. At least, Burris thought, I won't have to shuttle from one to the other to get my flight to Basel.

He'd boarded Air France 273 in Tokyo. A dozen members of his staff had come with him to Haneda Airport to see him off, including both Iko, his secretary, and his male assistant, Tanabe. They had all seemed sorry to see Burris go. It wasn't always easy to read a Japanese face, but a few had even wept.

The bank for which Burris worked, United Bank and Trust Company, known around the world and in its native New York as UBCO, insisted on its foreign offices being staffed as fully as possible with natives of the country. In fact, after his second year in Tokyo, Burris had been the only American in the office. He'd sent his U.S. associates on to other assignments once he'd trained Japanese for their jobs.

He'd spent, all told, nearly four years representing UBCO in Japan, four years in which the tiny country had force-fed itself into becoming a world power in finance and industry. He'd seen the planning of what was called "Japan, Inc." shove the rest of the country ahead with the rough pressure of a cop hustling an unwilling prisoner. And he'd seen the lethal mixture of inflation and fuel shortages start to bring the whole proud effort to its knees.

Burris stopped pacing. He stood in the exact center of the empty lounge and tried to pull himself together. Japan was behind him, finished, gone. His memories kept tumbling together good and bad in a confusing way.

He loved Japan. He hated it. The Japanese never showed emotion. Neither did Matthew Burris. But his secretary and his assistant had both been tearful at Haneda Airport as they put him aboard the 747. Burris had felt like a stick of wood, unable to summon any of the outward trappings of sadness to match theirs.

Had he really been beloved? Did he have that much claim on their loyalty and affection? Strange that he had felt none of it until it was time to say good-bye.

He rubbed his gritty eyes, then decided to wash up for his arrival in Paris. Standing before the mirror in the lounge lavatory, his husky frame filling the tiny compartment, he stared into his square face, the mug of a fullback or a heavyweight fighter, wide chin squared off to meet any blow, mouth drawn into a tight, wide line, blue eyes squinting against the glare, dark-blond hair rumpled. Burris-san Number One Tough Customer.

He shook his head violently. Japan was over, done with.

He had, for his hard work, been promoted. At least that was what the UBCO high command called it. He was being put in charge of something new and quite suicidal. He was to be a one-man task force in Switzerland charged with nothing less than infiltrating Swiss banking and establishing UBCO as a major competitor *within* the system.

Burris saw the RETURN TO SEAT sign flash. He walked down the spiral staircase, sank into his seat and buckled the strap. The Swiss will treat me like smallpox, he thought. They have always tolerated a few UBCO branches in Switzerland because the offices were mere conveniences, not real banks. But once the Swiss realize UBCO wants a slice of the real pie and won't settle for a thin slice, either—they will close ranks and kill us. Me.

There were a lot of advantages to working for the largest and best-known commercial bank in the States, Burris told himself now. But in a situation like the one he was stepping into, he would have given anything to be representing a much weaker, relatively unknown U.S. bank. That way the Swiss wouldn't take his campaign seriously. But as UBCO's representative, he would be watched closely at first, suspected at every turn, feared, and then hated and, finally, balked by every means known to the Swiss.

He watched the Paris skyline bank steeply as the big plane made its final turn and approach. The early-morning light was leaden. Only the faint green of the French earth marked a horizon for him to see. He heard the landing gear thump down in place. The pilot gunned the engines up to landing speed.

The picture of Iko, his secretary, her face wet with tears, flashed across Burris' mind. He had never touched her in four years. Strange to see her cry. Had she really felt anything for him? Living among the Japanese had, for Burris, been like living inside a deep freeze. Any emotional involvements, if that was what they were, had been with Americans. He'd had only two affairs in that time, each with the wife of an American Air Force officer. Of course he'd become something of a regular patron of the same geishas who served three or four of Japan's top industrialists and financiers, but that could hardly be called an emotional involvement.

He'd hoped, through the geishas, to get insights into the minds of these leading members of "Japan, Inc.," the informal group-think arrangement of business and government leaders who really ran the country by secret arrangement. The geishas had been amusing, often exciting, but always discreet. Burris had finally reached the conclusion that "Japan, Inc." had learned a lot more about him from the geishas than he had about them.

The ground began to fly by his window. He felt the Air France plane touch gently down, then link solidly into the ground and trundle forward, decelerating strongly. Burris felt his upper trunk tilt forward as the plane's speed dropped.

Four years of the Orient, he thought, and now God knows how many more of Europe. He hardly knew what was happening in the

States any more, except in financial and business circles. He had almost forgotten how American women dressed on their own soil. His slang was four years out of date. None of his native land was real to him any more.

There had been an excruciating moment on his flight when Air France 273 had landed for refueling at Anchorage, Alaska. They'd had half an hour to stretch their legs and Burris had wandered alone around the terminal building, picking up strange, baffling clues to the land of his birth. Something told him Anchorage was not an accurate reflection of the States, but he also knew that it represented the future of the country in the same spooky way the entire West Coast did.

Whatever the West did today, he knew, the tight-ass Midwest and East would do in five years, be it high divorce rates or outdoor luau barbecues, breast-implant puffery or drive-in crematoria.

He'd been away so long, and with so little desire to return, that his curiosity at Anchorage was compounded partly of guilt. Although he had never been a rah-rah patriot, his life as an exile occasionally gave him misgivings. It was as if he should take more of an interest in home. As if, in fact, the States were "home." As if, to put it bluntly, he had ever really felt at home in his native land which, for as long as he could remember, he had not. Nor had he among the cheap gimcracks and vinyl ugliness of Anchorage Airport.

And Paris was already restoring Matthew Burris' equanimity. If, for example, this had been New York, he would by now have grown almost inarticulate with the strange guilts and anxieties to which he was subject.

No one knew, of course, that hard Matt Burris had a soft side, full of unsureness about who he was and what he was doing as an exile. Not even any of his mistresses, though they, too, were exiled Americans. And certainly not anyone in UBCO, where Matthew Burris was considered something of a strong man, a troubleshooter who could be depended on to tough his way through to success.

Burris was sure that was why he had gotten the Swiss assignment, that and the fact that he had a powerful patron in the UBCO hierarchy. The man was no longer chief executive officer, as he had been in the years when Burris had first joined the bank. As a matter of fact, Palmer was semiretired. He had been elevated, at his own request, to honorary chairman of the board, and was living somewhere in Switzerland, at last report.

Palmer had been Burris' protector for strange reasons, but nothing Palmer did ever seemed to follow a straight line. He had himself been a third-generation banker, socially connected in Chicago and New York. But Palmer had always gone out of his way to help those of UBCO's junior officers with no social background whatsoever. It was almost as if he felt the bank needed new blood that was red, not blue. In Burris he got damned close to peasant stock, since the name had originally been Brzyck and as dumb-ox Polish as only a Southern Illinois miner's son could get.

Matthew Burris allowed himself a grim smile as the aircraft locked into its gangway and the steward's voice welcomed him to Paris in French, Japanese and, as a last thought, English.

He gathered his briefcase and topcoat and stood up to his full height of over six feet. He'd often wondered about Palmer's interest in his own career. The old boy wasn't that old, really, just a shade over fifty, not even fifteen years older than Burris, hardly a father-son relationship.

Maybe it was guilt. Burris had become a bit of an expert on guilt. Maybe Palmer had begun to feel guilty at the dry-rot damage done to UBCO by generations of tennis-playing lightweights, Wasp sons, nephews and sons-in-law. Time for a house Polack, a little touch of heavy street-savvy, of balls, of whatever it was that the Palmers of the world had lost.

Burris felt his face growing red. Christ, if he hadn't learned anything else from the Japs, hadn't he at least learned to control his temper? And why the hell was he bad-naming Palmer? Hadn't the old boy gotten the bank to pay his tuition at Harvard Graduate School of Business Administration, and then promoted him?

Making his way out of the plane, Burris forced himself to smile at the stewardess. That might not be the Polack way, he mused, but it was surely the way a Japanese would behave, putting a smile on his face, whatever questions lay behind it.

Ahead of him, marching almost in formation, walked three Japanese, each carrying identical large, hard-sided attaché cases with combination locks. Burris didn't remember seeing these three in

15

First Class, but here they were disembarking with him. Probably they'd been sitting ahead of him so that only the backs of their heads were visible.

Only the fact that they were traveling First Class made them at all interesting to Burris. Normally, Japanese businessmen, at least in the middle echelons of management, paid homage to the national predilection for appearing to be economical and traveled Economy. The fact that these three had coddled themselves, as Burris had, for the long flight, said that they considered themselves somewhat above the common horde.

Burris quickened his pace and easily passed the three Japanese. As he got on the moving sidewalk ahead of them, he stopped, put down his briefcase and leaned against the moving rubber handrail. He casually glanced around and in the process tried to get a look at their faces. One he recognized, only one, a Colonel Somebody he'd met at a party a year before, some sort of mystery man who, like a few other Japanese business types, was rumored to have strong links to the underworld. The other two were strangers.

Burris frowned. He had worked in the Orient long enough to have turned his face away from the three men before he allowed it to express any emotion. Then the frown cleared. Japan was not his concern any more. Switzerland *was*. To hell with mysterious tycoons.

He stepped nimbly off the moving sidewalk and, as he was about to board the next, he heard his name being called. He stopped and turned. Jim Dauber, UBCO's Paris branch manager, was running toward him. Effete little Ivy League tennis player. Burris closed his eyes and gritted his teeth. Behave yourself. Dauber got on the moving sidewalk with him.

"Jim, how's the boy?" Burris forced himself to say through almost motionless lips.

"You look terrific." Dauber stood back a second, still pumping his hand in welcome. "Damned if your eyes aren't starting to slant."

Both of them broke into standard good-old-boy guffaws. Burris found himself wondering if Dauber's laugh was as phony as his own. Ah, what difference did it make? Be civil. The guy met you as a token of hospitality. He didn't have to take time off to do this.

"Nice of you to meet me, Jim."

"We don't get to talk enough," Dauber said, relieving him of his briefcase and piloting him off the moving sidewalk. "I reserved a room for you here in the airport hotel. You can sort of shower and shave or nap till your plane to Basel."

"Damned thoughtful of you."

"Nothing's too good, Matt, for the man who's going to walk into the lion's den and pull all the gold out of his teeth."

CHAPTER 3

Because it was nearly noon, Bunter let the telephone ring several times. Normally, as butler to Erich Lorn, Bunter would instantly snatch the telephone from its receiver in the morning so as not to disturb the master's sleep. This was especially true on those mornings when the master did not sleep alone.

But, it being almost noon, Bunter had made the mistake of assuming that Herr Erich and his current lady were, if not actually out of bed and getting dressed, at least awake and considering the possibility of ringing for breakfast.

Bunter was horrified to hear the telephone ring a second and a third time. He quickly picked it up and, in the odd way he had, which always amused Herr Erich, he greeted the caller in the little-used Romansh dialect. *"Bun di."*

"Bunter," an irascible voice rasped, "put me on to Herr Erich at once."

"Is it Herr Staeli?"

"At once," Walter Staeli snapped.

Bunter frowned as he pressed the button that would buzz in his master's bedchamber. For a young man, hardly older than Herr Erich himself, Walter Staeli presumed on his family's position to speak in such peremptory fashion to someone else's man. After all, this wasn't Germany, where the masters drew real joy from humiliating servants, nor Italy, where servants were treated as junior members of the family, nor the United States, where they were deferred to as proud and sensitive friends.

No, Bunter reflected, this was Switzerland, thank God, where

17

everyone was the same and even the Staeli billions did not qualify a young snip like Walter to order around a man twice his age who was equally as thrifty, God-fearing, hard-working, discreet and righteous as any rich young cub, if not more so.

Bunter heard his master come on the line, voice clogged with sleep. *"Süss Gott, Bunterli, was gibt noch?"*

"Erich?" Walter's voice cut through.

"That's not my Bunterli."

"It's Walter Staeli. Don't tell me you are still in bed?"

Bunter carefully, and noiselessly, hung up the telephone, went to the small kitchen and proceeded to load a breakfast tray with coffee and heated croissants. In the less than five minutes it would take for him to deliver this tray, Bunter hoped, the lady would have retired to the dressing room and his master would have ended what promised to be a highly unpleasant telephone call.

It was very plain to Bunter, as it was to most Baslers, that in as big a family as the Staeli clan, there had to be a few bad ones. One would have expected that Dieter Staeli's rather pleasant personality would have somehow imprinted itself on his son, Walter. But the mother had not been a Basler. In fact, Bunter remembered, she probably was not even Swiss, only passing as one.

He made a face as he carried the tray out of the kitchen and up the flight of stairs of the Lorn bachelor house. Living room and library shared the ground floor with the kitchen. The next floor up was all bedroom with two baths and two dressing rooms, a thoughtful touch considering how many female guests stayed the night.

The top floor was a sort of office-cum-den which Bunter was never supposed to clean. He did, of course, otherwise it would have looked like a sty.

He mounted the stairs, hearing even at a distance through closed doors, his master's shout:

"Why in hell should I know where she is?"

The shout had been reduced to a mutter when Bunter knocked at the bedroom door. "Come in, Bunterli," the master called. Then, into the telephone: "So she is my fiancée. She's your cousin. Why should I know Margit's whereabouts any more than you?"

He gestured to Bunter to set up the tray on the table near the window. The dark-haired form beside him in bed was turned

stomach-down with a sheet drawn over most of her face. Bunter knew her, of course. Everyone knew the Herr Minister's lovely wife from the society pages of the magazines. It showed a certain breeding of her to cover her face, however. It also showed, in Bunter's severe opinion, a certain lack of breeding to be still in bed.

". . . where in London?" the master was asking. "Who saw her there? With whom? At the Mirabelle? Good. It's the best damned feed in London."

He paused, listening, his thin face hard to see in the darkened room, black hair sprawled all over his high forehead. Bunter arranged the breakfast and hid the tray behind a screen. He started to leave.

". . . watching the airport? *Mein Gott!* You are too much, Walter. Who?" A stunned pause. *"Scheiss!"* Erich Lorn slammed the telephone back on its receiver. "Bunterli, get the car. You're driving the lady—" He stopped. *"Liebchen, achtung."* He glared at Bunter. "Never mind the car. Get a cab, *schnell!"*

Bunter closed the door behind him as his master began prodding his lady love awake. The last words he heard were: ". . . idiot husband of yours has returned a day early."

Making his way down the stairs, Bunter allowed himself a smile. He of course did not approve of the scandalous life his master lived. No honest Swiss could, naturally. But, after all, the man was still a bachelor, although long betrothed. And the scrapes he kept getting himself into were very comical, to say the least. Life with Herr Erich was a constant series of surprises.

The telephone started ringing again, evidently an offended Walter Staeli calling back to demand more news of his missing cousin Margit. Bunter picked up the instrument and let it drop back in place, breaking the connection silently. He then lifted the telephone and called for a cab.

As he hung up, the telephone began to ring. He hoped Miss Margit, as his future mistress, would appreciate the discretion with which her fiancé, Herr Erich, treated her private life. Walter Staeli might pry and spy, but Herr Erich was a forgiving man, very Bohemian in his feelings, very *gemütlich,* very human. Bunter hoped Miss Margit would give her future husband as much leeway as Herr Erich was prepared to give her.

It was even now a very modern arrangement, of course, and not to be countenanced by a God-fearing Swiss. And yet, Bunter reflected, this freedom was a very ancient tradition among the European aristocracy, was it not?

The telephone continued to ring, unanswered.

Bunter was quite aware of the fact that of all the well-to-do Swiss for whom he had worked in his forty years as a butler, Herr Erich was the most cosmopolitan, the most traveled, the most European. With his lack of concern over business—he neglected the family bank most shamefully—and his attraction to women and wine, he was almost Austrian, in Bunter's considered opinion.

That faint trace of *Schlumperei* in the master's character was Austrian or Italian, either one, but definitely not Swiss. To be told that his fiancée had been seen in London's finest restaurant with another man, that would have quietly infuriated a true Swiss. He would have arranged, very discreetly, of course, to learn everything about the event and everything leading up to it. He would then use this information to redress the grievance and put the woman in her woman's place.

Bunter smiled again, this time at his own feelings about his master. The young man was shocking, of course, shamefully so, and yet one couldn't help being tickled at the things he did and the way his mind worked. Bunterli, he was called. Bunter's real name was something else. He was, in fact, one Albrecht Mütfäng.

Ten years ago, when Herr Erich had reached twenty-one and come into his grandmother's bequest, he had bought this house and interviewed for a man. "Mütfäng?" he had muttered, glancing over the applicant's letters of recommendation. "With only two umlauts?" He pondered for a moment. "I have always wanted a man named Bunter," he said then, "like Lord Peter Wimsey's man. And Bunter is not necessarily English, is it? I knew a Bunter in Zurich. Fine old Swiss name."

So it had been Bunter for ten years, and the idea of it titillated Bunter even now. At home, at church, in his neighborhood social club, Albrecht Mütfäng still lived, drank white wine, played *jass*. But there was something secretly pleasing to know that in another part of Basel, the great city of high finance, of politics and amorous adventures, Bunter was a man of some distinction.

The whole thing set him apart as someone special, Bunter knew.

Like his occasional use of Romansh. Most native Baslers spoke the Baseltütsch dialect, which was so obscure not even other Swiss understood it. But Bunter had originally come from east of Basel and he liked now and then to underline the fact that he was more solid, more stable, indeed more Swiss, than the flightier Baslers.

Scandalous, of course, to go through life with two identities. Bunter reminded himself that the situation was purely temporary. No honest Swiss would let it go on forever, naurally. One day . . .

The telephone stopped ringing.

At that moment the cabby rang the front-door bell. Bunter glanced up the stairs and saw his master hastily wrapping a silk dressing gown around him as he ushered his fully clothed lady out of the bedroom. Bunter opened the front door and, with a lifted finger, bade the cabby wait.

Then Bunter retreated to the rear of the ground floor, where he produced a series of clinking noises in the kitchen to assure the Madame Herr Minister that he was not watching her exit and had no idea of her true identity.

No God-fearing Swiss would have done less.

CHAPTER 4

Walter Staeli glanced cautiously around him before hanging up the telephone. Although he was entitled to an outside office overlooking the Aeschenvorstadt—an office like his father's on the front wall of the anonymously gray stone building, with a window box of red geraniums—Walter preferred an inside office.

There were several reasons for this and it was typical of Walter that he knew all of the socially important ones without once taking account of any of the trivial or human ones.

For instance, Number 17 Aeschenvorstadt was an old building with thick walls, but its windows still let in most of the street noise from below. The Aeschenvorstadt was one of Basel's main streets with a double car line along which the electric trams sped, bells clanging. For someone with his father's mind—the mind of a sharpshooter with an extremely fine-tuned target rifle—the noise of the Aeschenvorstadt was unimportant. To Walter it would have been highly distracting.

But these reasons he failed to recognize. Instead, if asked, he would tick off much weightier ones, speaking of a profound knowledge of management, business, diplomacy, human nature and other highly acceptable qualities Walter liked to draw up about him.

He would cite his strong desire (enemies might call it a morbid need) for privacy. But this was a *sine qua non* for a banker, yes? The second floor of Number 17 Aeschenvorstadt was certainly not beyond the reach of telephoto lenses, was it? Certainly not. And the Aeschenvorstadt was, after all, Basel's street of banks, little ones, big ones, cantonal ones, national ones, banks for savings, for investment, for loans, banks for union members, postal employees, farmers.

Why, there was even a small street-level branch of a foreign bank right across the street, the ubiquitous UBCO of New York. And the second floor of the Staeli building was by no means impregnable. Nowadays there were all sorts of spying mechanisms, bugs, taps, hidden records, parabolic reflectors, God knew what.

Walter might also cite his feeling for democracy (or a misreading of it), which held that if all Swiss are equal, then none should have corner outside offices even if they were the boss's son and heir. He felt, too, that he possessed the knack of instilling efficiency and loyalty (or waves of suppressed hilarity) in employees by making certain they all saw him hard at work out in the common area with the rest of them.

The fact that there was a wide *cordon sanitaire* of empty space around Walter's desk that gave him freedom from being overheard, especially if he kept his voice down, was not part of his thinking.

In further explanation of his high motives, Walter would definitely refer to his concern for economy (some called it stinginess). If an executive of the highest echelon like himself were to have a private office, the walls would require something rather expensive in the way of decoration. Surely a number of high-priced paintings by modern masters of some repute would have to be bought, possibly including a Klee or two (since Klee was, after all, a Swiss). The frames would also be quite expensive.

Walter, like all the Staelis, eschewed the distressing American practice of writing off such personal expenses against a company account. Certainly not. He, like his father, would have to pay for such costly decorations out of his own pocket. No, thanks. Then, too, the Staelis, like most well-to-do Basler families, donated large sums each year to such cultural institutions as the city's famed Kunstmuseum, which had one of the finest art collections in the world. Naturally, this was a corporate gift and, thus, a corporate deduction, and more than enough obeisance paid to art, thank you.

Finally, in describing his behavior, Walter would certainly cite his sensitivity to office gossip (a few called it simple nosiness). What is hidden is talked of. Working out in the open, even at a remove from the rest of the executives, indicated to the world that Walter led a blameless existence, that everything he did was open to scrutiny and that everyone else should have as stainless an exterior as his.

This was Walter Staeli, who had gone to nursery school with his cousin Margit and to all the other schools with her fiancé, Erich Lorn. Of all the things Walter might explain about himself, the one he would keep silent about would be his fond hope that he was being groomed by the rest of the male Staeli clan to ride herd on the feckless Erich once he actually married Margit and thus controlled the vast Staeli-Lorn empire.

Or as Margit's Uncle Dieter had often put it to his son, Walter: "Once Erich mounts her, my boy, you saddle Erich and ride."

Glancing around the office now before he replaced the telephone, Walter made sure no one had seen him place the same call a third time. It was damaging enough to his prestige that Erich had hung up on him the first time and again, silently, the second time. It was typical of Walter that he had waited until half the executives had left for lunch before placing even the first call. Privacy above all.

He hung up the telephone and glanced at his watch. Almost time for his own luncheon appointment.

Damn Margit. The information from London had been unequivocal. She had been seen dining with some young Britisher in the Mirabelle and later dancing at Annabel's. At the time she was supposed to be skiing in Austria. As soon as his London source had so informed him, Walter had put a watch on the Basel-Mulhouse Airport, but no one had seen Margit come through customs. Certainly not.

The whole thing made Walter very nervous. There was no knowing how Margit's last will and testament read. Being a Staeli, she should be counted on to leave her holdings to the family. But being a headstrong woman full of neurotic ideas, she might just as readily have left everything to some foundation for female rights.

It was not that Walter cared for his cousin or wished her a long life. It was simply that he wanted her married to Erich and his thumb securely pressed down on Erich. Then Margit could drop dead in the Aeschenvorstadt for all Walter cared.

It absolutely galled Walter Staeli that there was even the faintest possibility of his cousin Margit truly taking control of Staeli Internationale, GmbH. Her double-damned father, Uncle Lucas, had been a madman, that was certain. To have left his controlling interest in the clan's holding company to an unmarried woman was insane enough. In a way, of course, he had little choice, she being his sole heir. But to leave it to someone with such irrational, modern ideas as Margit was more than mad, it was suicidal.

Walter glanced around the half-deserted executive area. The walls were unadorned by art of the creative kind, but here and there a framed photograph reminded the men who worked here in the holding company of what Staeli meant in Switzerland and the world.

Banking, of course, went without saying. Walter had been trained since secondary school to handle the various banking services provided by the many kinds of Staeli banks. Like any Swiss banks, these were utterly free institutions, providing anything and everything from normal checking or savings accounts to the intricate mysteries of currency arbitrage, forward gold speculation, proxy battles for corporate control, leasing of factories, and even securities trading and the writing of insurance.

But banking made up not even a third of the Staeli holdings, nowhere near a third if one thought only of profits. Perhaps as much as half the clan's corporate profit came from its chemical operations.

24

Like other immense Basler operations, these were divided roughly into pharmaceutical and industrial production. There were very few people in this world, Walter reflected proudly, who didn't rely regularly or occasionally on Staelipharm pain killers, tranquilizers, drugs that altered mood, that helped lose weight or gain it, that preserved youth, that did anything at all to help people avoid reality.

And these drugs were only the most profitable, not the most commonly produced. Back of such money-making pills stood the bulk of Staelipharm production: antibiotics, vitamins, germicides, hormones, anesthetics and the rest of the millions of vials of ethical pharmaceuticals required by the world's doctors and hospitals.

Staelichem, on the other hand, dealt not in vials but in 200-liter drums of acids, alkaline reagents, pesticides, defoliants, alcohols, fertilizers and farm-animal feed. A subsidiary, Staelibel, produced a broad variety of consumer products ranging from hair sprays and deodorants to perfumes and soaps.

And, of course, there was Reiger, S.A., little-known subsidiary which, because it produced explosives and the main ingredients of such exotica as nutrient media for germ-warfare cultures, nerve-gas carrier liquids and alternate substitutes for napalm, cautiously did not bear the Staeli name in its corporate identification.

The same shyness was responsible for the Staeli clan calling one of its subsidiaries Pietrasassi, Ltd. This was a company licensed in thirty-two countries of the West to handle, for legitimate medical uses only, of course, vast quantities of morphine base and raw opium shipped via legal channels from Turkey, India and what had once been Indochina. From this, Pietrasassi concocted the regular morphine and heroin used in normal medical practice, codeine and other fractions of opium alkaloid useful in pain-killing medicines, and several highly successful products used to control diarrhea.

Walter shifted restlessly at his desk and glanced at his watch. He was still a bit early for his very important luncheon appointment.

To think that a woman—and a fractious, strong-minded bitch like Margit, to boot—would have even a remote chance of controlling all this.

His glance fell on a rather large photograph, hanging from the

25

wall nearby, of the newest Staelifer mills near the Austrian border. Staelifer was not as profitable as banking or chemicals, but in many ways more solid. This new mill, for example, produced only the finest grades of high-quality tool steel, from high-carbon to vanadium and molybdenum alloys.

What had begun over two centuries ago as an enterprise devoted to making swords, bayonets and razors, had now expanded until Staelifer was not only making the steel but the weapons, instruments, apparatus and machinery itself. Scissors, yes, but also rocket launchers. Kitchenware, of course, but also chronometers.

Very little made from steel was not produced by Staelifer, whether it was heavy-duty electric motors, or the large electric trains that used such motors, together with the valves, meters, brakes, signals, track and everything else needed to run a railroad. At the same time, it was Staelifer that manufactured the turbines, generators and transformers that helped create electricity from either water power or steam.

A tiny corner of Staelifer had recently gone into electronics, producing desk-sized computers, telephone equipment, large display clocks and the like. His father had ordered Walter to familiarize himself with this small part of the great Staeli holdings as being one with growth potential. Even a sniff of electronics had given Walter some very ambitious ideas about the future of the business.

It was a man's natural duty, a man's inborn masculine skill, that gave him this "nose" for business opportunities. What woman, Walter asked himself now, could ever hope to be as successful in business? If Margit were *his* wife . . . !

It was a pity that first cousins didn't marry these days. Not that he coveted her. Certainly not. She was attractive, of course, in the thin neurasthenic modern fashion, like some English or American model in the fashion magazines, small of breast, buttock and thigh.

Walter grimaced. And yet the real solution to what the rest of the male Staelis referred to as The Problem, would have been for Walter to marry Margit, if he had been allowed to. Useless to speculate.

He sighed unhappily and got to his feet. Making his way to the

26

men's room he used with the other vice presidents on the floor, Walter passed the empty desks of his fellow executives. His fingers twitched slightly. He may not have been aware of this involuntary movement.

The fact was that his fingers itched almost constantly to rearrange the desktops of his colleagues, to move a pad nearer the edge or a pen-and-pencil set to the center or a tiny electronic calculator to the right, or to hide a picture of a wife and children in a drawer or straighten up the edges of a pile of correspondence or . . .

Inside the executive washroom, Walter dabbed at his face with a plain towel dipped in cold water. Better. Soothing. He eyed his reflection indirectly in the mirror, never facing himself head on. He adjusted the wave in his blond hair and urged it a few millimeters forward over his brow. He knew his pale-blue eyes had a furtive look. This was not real, certainly not, only a result of the fact that he was eyeing himself sideways.

With his pale complexion, fair hair and almost colorless irises, at some moment in the past dozen years that he had worked after graduating from college, Walter had come to be known behind his back as The White Rat. On several occasions he had heard this phrase when eavesdropping on the unguarded conversation of co-workers who didn't know he was in the vicinity.

Although he had heard the phrase clearly and correctly on these occasions, it had become changed in his mind to The White Fox. There is practically no similarity, in German or the Schweizer-deutsch dialect, between the words for rat and fox, *Ratte* and *Fuchs,* but perhaps he had overheard the conversation in French or Italian or Romansh.

Walking downstairs to the street, Walter nodded this way and that to various nodding and smiling clerks and tellers who were all equal, honest Swiss under God, but who believed in toadying to the boss's son. The dark-gray Mercedes was waiting for Walter as he emerged from the side door of the bank. No point in everyone knowing that he was being chauffeured to a restaurant quite far from the office. Certainly not.

In point of fact, the Mercedes lost itself rather thoroughly in noontime traffic as it left the Aeschenvorstadt and crossed the

Rhine over the St. Alban Bridge, then moved slowly along the Schwarzwald Allee and doubled back over the Rhine again on the Drei Rosen Bridge, heading toward the French border via Elsässerstrasse. The car passed through border control almost without stopping. Herr Staeli's car, after all, was well known to both the Swiss and the French guards.

The Mercedes pointed toward Mulhouse along the airport road, then turned left suddenly and took a side road to the Belfort highway. The gray car turned right then and proceeded rather quickly due west to a small inn-restaurant just before Altkirch. As it pulled into the parking lot, Walter was pleased to see the rented Peugeot already there, its uniformed chauffeur sitting behind the wheel, asphyxiating himself in a cloud of cigarette smoke.

Good, Walter thought, they have already arrived. It didn't do to seem overanxious with any business associate, particularly a Japanese. Certainly not.

Walter waited for his chauffeur to open the Mercedes door and escort him to the gravel. He got out and drew in a breath of cool air, surveying the inn. The food here was rather good and the inn itself was just a bit too far from Basel for anyone to lunch there. It was more frequented in the evenings, usually with a mistress. The availability of seven or eight bedrooms over the restaurant made it more of a dining than a lunching place.

The inn had been built rather recently, Walter knew, because he had been involved in approving the loan for purchase of the land and the mortgage for the structure itself, a mock-Norman château with pointed arches and brown half-timbering sunk in white cement, the whole topped by an immense round tower whose conical spire was roofed in overlapping slabs of slate.

Walter was immediately shown to a private dining room. On the whole, he congratulated himself, the utmost in privacy had been achieved, consistent with impressing the Japanese by feeding them extremely well. It wouldn't do to skimp on such details now, when he was so close to getting their signature on a contract of extreme delicacy and promise. Certainly not.

No one in the Staeli clan yet knew of this, not even his father, Dieter. Nor would they. Not until the whole project was ready for the world at large. Then, and only then, would the business communities of Basel and Switzerland and, more important, of the male Staelis themselves, see and wonder and know that it was not mere idle praise that had earned Walter the sobriquet of The White Fox.

CHAPTER 5

Matthew Burris slept for almost two hours. His big body lay motionless on one of the rather hard mattresses in a room at the small hotel that occupies part of the main air terminal at Orly Sud. The hotel stands near the international transit lounge where the duty-free shops can be found.

In his dream, Burris was coming home from football practice in Carbondale, Illinois.

The big seventeen-year-old had a bruise under one eye and a lame knee. His mother was going to cream him but, of all the Brzycks, she would know that football was important to him. Being able to play it well could make him the first in the family ever to get into college. Pa might sneer at college, but Ma did not. So a few bruises were okay, right, Ma?

This was the old house on Douglas Street behind the I.C. tracks, loud with engine noise, filthy with soot, haunted at night by the hoarse, lonely whistles of the through freights. The sidewalks along Douglas Street were packed dirt. The few trees grew stunted and short.

Three men stood on the earthen sidewalk. They would not let Matt Brzyck pass.

He was tired and he ached. He was hungry and he wanted to get over his mother's scolding and on into dinner because it was Saturday, the night they had meat, chunky kielbasa slices in steaming onions and cabbage, potatoes dripping with the taste of pork fat, and these three little men wouldn't let him pass.

He faked right, then swiveled left, but there were three of them and, even though they were small, they were all over him. It was a strangely bloodless encounter, without contact. There seemed to be a space around each of them, an invisible shield that kept them from colliding with the big teen-ager. Then he saw they were Japanese. Three of them.

He awoke, sweating.

At first he had no idea where he was. His big body rolled sideways and his long, muscular legs were halfway off the hotel bed toward the carpeted floor when he remembered he was no longer in Carbondale. Where, Japan?

Then he remembered the three Japanese on the plane. Funny that they'd stuck in his head. Not that there had been anything really sinister about them, but just unusual enough to stir his curiosity. Or to stir something deeper inside him that returned when he was asleep.

He grunted mournfully and sat up on the edge of the bed. What had there been about the three Japanese that could wiggle its way down into his dreams? Had he subconsciously recognized one of the others? Did something hidden inside him know something the top of him hadn't figured out yet?

In the stall shower he alternated warm and cold blasts. But no matter how hard he ran water over his head he still felt he was missing something. As he toweled dry, he checked his watch and saw that the visitor Dauber had promised to send him was late.

"One of our people," Dauber had said as he'd left him to enjoy a brief sleep, "has some material for you."

Burris shaved and had just put on clean underwear when he heard the knock at his door. The man to whom he opened it was an even slighter fellow than Dauber, about the same age, mid-thirties, weedy of frame with thin blond hair raked sideways over his skull and a too-casual air about him as he strode into the room, pulled off his oyster-tan Burberry and slung it on the bed.

"You're Matthew Burris?"

Burris nodded. As he did, the other man produced a wallet with an UBCO identification card showing his face in full color and a description of him. Five-ten, Burris noted idly, age thirty-six, name Curtis. Who the hell needed all this rigamarole?

Burris sat down in an upholstered armchair and began pulling on fresh socks. He eyed Curtis from time to time and decided he was just another lightweight tennis player. Standing up, Burris put on a shirt, buttoned it partway and sat down again. "What's the briefing?" he asked then, not bothering to sound friendly.

Curtis began checking the room, opening and closing closets, dresser drawers, and looking behind pictures on the wall. He examined the headboard of the bed and looked under the box spring. He investigated the bathroom in similar fashion and inspected the two sets of heavy draperies over the windows. Then he sat back down.

"Did anybody bother to tell you who I am?"

"Number 007?" Burris guessed.

Curtis' thin mouth quirked up at one side. "I work for Bill Elder," he said then. "Internal Security for UBCO."

Burris nodded. "You going to issue me cyanide tablets or something?"

"Just a lifeline," Curtis responded. "The only thing I want now is to let you see my face and give you some phone numbers and addresses for me. And impress on you that when you need me I'm always available."

Burris thought about this for a while. He didn't need this kind of help, especially from an obvious weak sister like Junior here. "I need a different sort of help," he said aloud. "I need social contacts. I need financial information. I need business background. I don't need gumshoes, even UBCO's own."

Curtis nodded. "I figured." He reached inside the breast pocket of his sports jacket and brought out a folded packet of Xeroxed sheets. Handing them to Burris, he said: "The financial and business stuff is all there, at least for the Big Three banks and about a dozen of the next largest ones. When you need more, call me." He gave Burris a slip of paper with several numbers on it for Paris, Rome, London and Frankfort. "Whichever you call, they'll know the city I'm in."

Burris paged quickly through the sheaf of papers, then looked up. The other man still looked like a lightweight to him. That shirt. Wide stripes. No tie. Corduroy trousers. Loafers. What the hell kind of Joe College were they saddling him with?

"As for social contacts," Curtis went on, "you've got whatever our resident manager in Basel can give you. Mostly second- and third-echelon stuff, plus whatever the American Consul dreams up. We've primed him to be very social on your behalf. And you have Woods Palmer's contacts, of course."

Burris frowned. "Palmer? He doesn't live near Basel."

"Nowhere in Switzerland is far from anywhere else."

"Palmer." Burris thought for a moment. "He's mostly retired by now. I have to drop in on him. We haven't seen each other in four years."

Curtis cleared his throat. "Palmer likes to give the public impression of being retired. Actually, anything UBCO does in Europe goes through him. This whole new Swiss project is his idea. He swings an awful lot of weight still. And, as for social contacts, he's the king in your suit of trump. He knows everybody and everybody knows him."

Burris glanced at him, sensitive to any suggestion that he was Palmer's boy and the recipient of favors he hadn't earned by hard work. But the thin man was watching him with absolutely guileless eyes. "Of course," he added then, "you also have a hidden Ace."

"Is that so?"

Curtis nodded solemnly. "You have personal entrée into the highest social circles of Swiss banking."

"How did I get so lucky?"

"It was six years ago at Harvard Business School."

Burris stared at him. "Don't tell me—"

"I am telling you."

"How in hell did you dig that up?" Burris demanded.

"My business," Curtis replied. "You said you didn't need a gumshoe? On this assignment you'll need every help you can get." He paused. Then, delicately: "How was it left with the young lady? Everyone friends?"

Burris picked up a tie. "I suppose this story is spread all over UBCO by now."

The other man sighed. "I dig things up. I don't publicize them. As far as I know, the story isn't widely known." Then, with an edge to his voice, "Why should you care?"

"I don't like my personal life being traded back and forth."

"When somebody starts doing that, I'll let you know."

Burris fingered the tie, thinking, "So she's living back home in Basel. I didn't know that."

"She's been in London a week, secret talks in the City," Curtis said. "She took off for Basel this morning."

"You've been tailing her?"

"Yes." Curtis stood up. "Once I picked up the connection to you, I had to know what she was up to."

"Ancient history," Burris grunted.

"I don't know if you're aware of it, but if she reaches age thirty unmarried, the whole corpus of the estate goes to her in her own name."

Burris was knotting a tie. He stopped for a moment and looked at the other man in the mirror. "When does that happen?"

"Next year."

"But there's a fiancé."

The slight man produced one of his wrinkled smiles again. "And there is you."

"We don't mean anything to each other," Burris said, his glance locking with the other man's in the mirror. "We never even wrote after we left Cambridge. The whole thing lasted a year."

"It meant something," the thin man said. "She hasn't had too many other flings since. None of them serious."

"Stop kidding me," Burris insisted. "She doesn't even remember my name."

"They're not going to try for any publicity on your arrival, so she may not know you're in town. On the other hand, Basel is a network of gossip. She may just phone you."

"She may just not."

"Then you phone her."

"Do I have to get your permission?" Burris asked sarcastically.

"You already have my blessing. I've seen the lady. She's, uh, nice."

Burris finished knotting the tie and turned to face the slight man. "Is this Palmer's idea, saddling me with a gumshoe?"

"If you don't ask for me again, this is the last you'll see of me."

"Could be, then."

Curtis shrugged. He picked up his raincoat. "I'm not all that crazy about you, either." He went to the door.

"Hey."

"You've been fighting me ever since I showed up here."

Burris nodded heavily. "I admit it. I'm . . . what the hell, disoriented." He grinned slightly. "Not a bad pun. Disoriented and sleepy. And not too eager to let the Swiss hack me up into fondue strips."

Curtis let go of the doorknob. "If you work the Staeli connection right, they won't lay a hand on you."

"How much do you know about Margit?"

"Not very much."

"I don't think she'd be interested in shielding me." Burris sat down in the upholstered armchair again. He watched the other man sit in a plain chair next to the desk. "She's sort of a hardheaded number."

"Stubborn?"

"Cold. Lives up in the head. More of a banker than you, me and Palmer rolled into one."

"Cold but . . . not frigid?"

Burris took his time answering. He tried to remember how it had been and find something reportable about it, something not snide, something one could say about a woman and still be a gentleman. He was beginning to warm up to Curtis, but he still had him pegged as a Wasp lightweight who would, of course, set great store by being a gentleman.

"N-no. Not frigid. Sort of scientific, if you know what I mean."

"Not spontaneous?" Curtis asked.

Burris laughed softly. "There is nothing spontaneous about Margit Staeli, not then and not ever. It's been bred out of her. It hasn't existed in her family for dozens of generations."

"I see. No sudden phone calls when you arrive in Basel."

"She may not be home to me when I call her."

"But you will phone."

"Will you get off my back?" Burris exploded.

The other man let a long moment go by in silence. Then, calmly: "I've seen the lady. It shouldn't be that much of a hardship, calling her."

Burris sat watching him, trying to calm himself and match the other man's casual impartiality. He wondered what bothered him more, being told to call up an old girlfriend or the realization that she was possibly more than an old girlfriend and he'd never allowed himself to admit it. It hadn't seemed necessary, over the past six years, to analyze an old affair. But, now that it had become necessary, he found himself no longer sure of the pigeon-hole in which the whole thing had been filed away. Nor why, in fact, he had so busily hidden it from himself.

"No," he said then. "It's no hardship."

"Then you'll phone?"

"One more time," Burris said, trying to keep the anger out of his voice. "Get off my back."

CHAPTER 6

The arrival a day ahead of time of her maid, Elfi, had alerted the other servants in the house that their mistress was returning. By now none of them were under any illusion that she had come back from a ski-week in Styria.

Elfi was loyal to Margit Staeli, but she was, after all, only human, and the whirlwind London week, with all the gowns and frocks in constant use, the maelstrom of famous places, the young men with titles—one even heir to a dukedom!—made the whole adventure too juicy to keep to herself. Like Elfi, the rest of the servants—eight in all—were honest, God-fearing Swiss, each equal to the other and to any other Swiss under the sun. But they did love that touch of titled aristocracy so conspicuously absent from their Alpine republic.

The old house lay to the east of Basel, situated on several hundred hectares of greensward and birch copses that from a height led by gentle curves down to the banks of the Rhine itself. The house faced north toward Germany across a lazy loop of river.

Since the nearest town, Bad Rheinfelden, lay as far to the east of Basel as the airport had been west, Margit had directed her cab driver to avoid the city and take the cutoff toward Pratteln. There she left the cab and watched it head back to town. She stopped for a stroll and some window shopping, then walked to the Bahnhof and entered one of the cabs waiting there for passengers off the trains. It was in this cab that she arrived at Schloss Staeli.

The gatekeeper recognized her at once, of course. She had

removed the all-shielding scarf and Dior sunglasses, but old Wolf-Dietrich had known her since she was born. Not even the heavy Ur-Lodenmantel could have disguised her from him.

"Mein Gott, Fraülein Margit," he said. "If we had only known when, we would have sent the car for you."

"Machts nichts," she called. As the cab gathered speed again, she blew him a kiss.

The long, curved gravel drive had been laid down in the time of four-horse carriages and *fiakers.* No succeeding Staeli had bothered to widen it so that two automobiles could pass each other. In any event, this being a carefully restricted thoroughfare, two cars never did pass each other, not as long as Wolf-Dietrich could telephone the house in advance, as he was now doing.

The gravel had been bordered by needle cypress sometime in the mid-eighteenth century. The trees, some of them replaced as the years went by, now towered nearly fifty feet into the air. At their widest, a third of the way up, they were still less than six feet in diameter, so closely were they pruned by the gardener and his assistant. There were so many of the trees that in the schloss's garage stood a gardener's truck with an attachment brought all the way from Ottawa, Kansas, a hydraulic lift that elevated a man fifty feet in the air to prune the daggerlike trees. Margit could remember the day it arrived by special barge and was unloaded at the schloss's own river landing. It had five ladders stacked on top of it. They interlocked automatically. The gardener refused to let her ride on it but she even recalled the name, in English, a "Dual-Drive Sky-Hook."

The curve of the path and the tight shield of the cypresses as the cab moved along the alley made it impossible for Margit to see the schloss. Not that it was a real fortress or castle. In Switzerland, where everything was small—even the names and words, ending as they so often did in the "li" diminutive form—a house of such a size, regardless of the fact that it was designed somewhat along Palladian lines with a touch of Biedermeier, automatically became a schloss.

Now the cab cleared the last of the cypresses. The house came instantly into view with the same flash of recognition that a traveler might get when he stepped through the dark-red stone wall at Agra and stood precisely where the architect of the Taj Mahal had planned him to be, at the foot of the reflecting pool seeing the amazing creation at its best.

Margit sincerely doubted that the various local architects employed by generations of Staelis to concoct this schloss had ever bothered to set the stage for it as the Taj Mahal designer had. For years, in fact, ever since she could remember, Margit had had a love-hate relationship with the ancestral keep. Seeing it again stirred the same conflicting emotions.

It still hugged the crest of its hill with a Palladian balance that no later excrescences could shove awry. The basic design of a central three-story building with two lower wings could not, after all, be altered drastically except by bombing. Nor could the Fontainebleau façade of windows and curving carriage drives between topiary shrubbery leading to a broad stairway be entirely ruined by the hundreds of terra-cotta urns with their pleached dwarf fruit trees which some Staeli had added rather impetuously around the time Franz Josef ruled the Austro-Hungarian Empire.

The cab had, in fact, already started to make the turn into this overly landscaped curve of drive when Margit stopped the driver. "Back up and take the turn to the right, please."

She directed the cab to the side entrance, under a two-story porte-cochere that led to the wing in which she lived by herself since her father's death. At one time, when she had been struggling her way through puberty without the help of a mother, Margit had been more or less coerced into serving as hostess for the few parties her widower father gave during the year. In time she had come to like these large, gay dinners, preceded and followed by extremely good chamber music played by a quartet from Zurich or, on special occasions, imported all the way from Munich.

But her father had, over the years, fallen into a different frame of mind that no longer welcomed visitors. He had begun to show signs of turning away from life at about the time Margit had gone off to Paris to earn her baccalauréat at the Sorbonne. Her years in the United States had more or less finished the job of turning the once energetic and social Lucas Staeli into something of a hermit.

He had gone to his office several days a week during that last year of his life, Margit reflected as the cab drew to a halt under the porte-cochere, but most of the business had been conducted from his study here in the schloss.

After his death, the family doctor had taken her aside and used such nineteenth-century terms as "melancholia" and the like. To Margit it seemed quite clear that if she had stayed home and played for him the role her dead mother had once undertaken, Lucas Staeli would still be alive, energetic and social.

As it was, his sudden death at the age of fifty-five, of an embolism, was considered emotionally shocking and medically unlikely. No one, of course, even whispered the word "suicide," although they may well have been aware, as Margit was, that in the immense mansion there existed enough medical paraphernalia, including hypodermic syringes and needles, for her father to have done almost anything he wanted with his life.

She was walking up the short flight of steps to the double doors that formed the side entrance when the thought "self-administered air bubble" crossed her mind.

So it was that when Elfi and Uschi, the housekeeper, rushed out through the doors to greet her, they found Margit Staeli as still as marble, one foot poised to take the next step up, a slight frown wrinkling the skin between her eyebrows, a look of unconscionable shock around her mouth.

"Liebchen, was ist los?" Uschi called.

Abruptly, the look disappeared. The brow smoothed over. The foot advanced to the next step. Margit Staeli was home.

CHAPTER 7

Having brushed and folded away Margit Staeli's woolens, handwashed her underthings and examined her gowns and dresses for any sign that dry cleaning was needed, Elfi surveyed the long room which her mistress used both as a sittingroom and an office. The wall of windows faced the river and, on this spring day, a somewhat wintry sunlight made the wavelets shimmer in the distance.

Elfi did not like either this suite of rooms or the immense house in which they were located. However, she liked her mistress, the pay was certainly good, there was a great cachet to working for the Staelis, and her mistress's clothes fitted her perfectly, which made for a nice bonus in expensive dresses, sweaters, skirts and slacks which Margit Staeli no longer fancied wearing.

Elfi checked the room again, drew on her coat and ran down the back stairs to the kitchen area where Bodo, the under-chauffeur, waited to drive her back to town. He had chosen, as always, not one of the big autos but the VW Bobbibus station wagon.

It was Uschi, the housekeeper, who planned such things and she nearly always combined Bodo's taking Elfi to Basel with shopping errands. For a house this size, even though one wing was sealed off and the other scarcely used, material had to be bought in large containers: drums of detergent, heavy five-liter carboys of bleach or a dozen new brooms at a time. It did nothing for Elfi's prestige in the neighborhood where she lived to be delivered home in what amounted to a light truck, like just another article of household goods.

But, on the other hand, like every Swiss, Elfi was well aware that arriving in a Bobbibus was a sign of real status. Only the very rich didn't give a damn about appearances. More than that, only the very rich took pains to disguise the scope of their wealth. In Switzerland, where everyone's bank balance was a secret guarded by severe penalties under the criminal code, privacy was everything. If anyone doubted Elfi's status as the servant of an extremely wealthy heiress, they had only to look at the chic hand-me-downs she wore, hardly used, almost like new, to understand the profundity of the Staeli wealth.

Bodo drove the Volkswagen like a madman as usual, trying to beat the evening rush-hour traffic in and out of Basel. As usual, too, he tried his normal approaches with Elfi, who was a year or two older than he. The two of them jounced along on the front seat of the Bobbibus.

"London war prima, nicht?"

Elfi gave him a small frown. "It's a city," she said in what she hoped was a cutting tone. Under-chauffeurs had no claim on privileged information, even cute ones like Bodo.

"A city," he mimicked, cutting out into the opposite lane and speeding around a haywagon drawn by a tractor. "A city like Basel?"

"Bigger."

This reduced Bodo to helpless giggles for a moment. "Come on, did she have herself one or two of those milords?"

Elfi's mouth pressed shut. Her dark-brown eyes watched the road ahead.

"I hear they are all homo," Bodo continued undaunted. "That would make Ma'moiselle very frustrated, yes?"

Elfi permitted herself an icy half-smile. "For a *Lausbub* who is still making love to goats," she said with cruel pleasure, "these comments are laughable."

Bodo nodded. "And there isn't any nannygoat that wouldn't make a better lay than you, darling."

"Oh, you've given up billygoats?"

This sent Bodo into such peals of laughter that he nearly let the VW slip off the road onto the shoulder.

"Elfi, when can I show you how to live?"

"You? Never."

"I don't have to be back at the schloss until dinnertime. We have hours."

"Forget it."

"Such hours as you have never known before," he rhapsodized.

"Put it out of your mind."

"Your flat is empty. No one's there. It would be simple for us."

Elfi shook her head. "My roommate returns from the office precisely at five o'clock."

"What's his name?"

"She. Her name isn't any of your business."

Bodo patted Elfi's knee. "I know her name. She won't be home from the bank for two hours. Two hours in which you will be transported beyond your wildest dreams of ecstasy."

"By you?" Her laugh indicated scorn, but did not demonstrate total lack of interest.

"Elfi, it's a waste of a good apartment. What do you say?"

The Bobbibus was careening into the eastern section of Basel now. "I say slow down or they'll arrest you."

"Not for thinking." Bodo stroked her thigh beneath the smooth coat. "Say yes."

"Absolutely no."

A sharp sigh escaped Bodo's lips. "You and your mistress are two of a kind. You've picked up her tricks."

"I beg your pardon."

"You're both teases. She won't marry a perfectly good example of a hot-blooded male, and you're turning down a man who's even better in bed than Herr Lorn."

Elfi's faintly plucked eyebrows rose slightly. "Really? You've had a contest? With judges?"

Bodo broke up, pounding the VW's steering wheel and shrieking with laughter. "You're a riot, Elfi. Come on, invite me upstairs."

He had pulled the Bobbibus to the curb in front of a tall, modern apartment house in Kleinbasel, the section of the city east of the Rhine. Small but efficient terraces decorated the side of the ten-story building that faced south. Elfi glanced out the window.

"We'll be having a party, my roommate and I, for *Fasnacht*. We'll have a dozen or so friends. I'll invite you then, Bodo, not before."

"*Fasnacht?* It's ages from now." He had her hand and was stroking her fingers. "And your roommate's friends will all be people she works with at the Staeli bank. Bloodless tellers and clerks. They're not our kind of people, Elfi. You and I like a good time."

"That's what *Fasnacht* is for."

Bodo was silent for a moment, digesting this. Elfi was as aware as he that the Basel *Fasnacht* could get even more riotous than other Mardi Gras holidays. The normal Basler demeanor was so restrained that, when it was licensed to cut loose, it went to extremes.

So wild did the *Fasnacht* become that petty crimes committed during the four-day holiday were usually let off by the police and judges without even a fine. Infidelities and indiscretions committed during *Fasnacht* were universally overlooked. And no one expected anyone to show up for work in any shape to do a job. All in all, Elfi felt, inviting Bodo to spend *Fasnacht* with her was a great deal more than he deserved, at this stage of their relationship. But he was cute. And persistent. And not without appeal.

"I accept!" Bodo shouted suddenly. He pulled her hand to him and kissed her palm fervently. Then he broke into laughter again. "But remember, *Liebling,* this doesn't mean that afterwards you and I have to fast for Lent."

"You can always go back to your goats."

She escaped from the VW and ran into the entrance hall of her apartment house, pausing for a moment to wave to him before she disappeared inside.

The flat was small for two people, she thought as she let herself inside and took off her coat. But it was too expensive for one. She could have done with a somewhat livelier roommate. Christa was small and high-voiced and timid, like a mechanical doll that no one has bothered to check for run-down batteries. But she kept to herself in the evening, rarely going out with men and never bringing one home for a drink. There were advantages to a roommate as self-effacing as Christa Ruc.

Besides, it was really Christa's apartment, which she had been able to get, despite a long waiting list, because of her father, who also worked at the bank. Elfi merely paid her share to Christa every month, but the lease was in the name of Christa Ruc and, technically, Elfi was there illegally. Aside from sharing the rent, Elfi knew, she was useful to Christa in other ways. Any man the girl went out with had been introduced by Elfi, who was much more social than her roommate.

Of course, most of the men she knew were at the Bodo level, crude, untutored and talking of nothing but sex. That there were other, smoother, more sophisticated men, Elfi was well aware. And she would interest such men, of that she had no doubt. But in the closed-off society of Basel, she was doomed to a succession of Bodos. It wasn't that she disliked the Bodos in her life. It was only that she knew there were other, better things in life than bantering about sex with Bodo.

Elfi had seen quite a bit of the great world. She didn't think of herself as a party girl, far from it. No one of that character could hope to hold a job with the Staelis. But in the two years she had served Margit Staeli she had visited all sorts of cities and resorts. And her mistress had no objection to Elfi finding her own amusement in such places.

She was not an overbearing mistress. She was, in fact, quite liberal with free time, once the basic work was done of keeping her wardrobe and effects in order. She didn't demand that Elfi do her hair or nails or dress or bathe her, none of those rather demeaning body-servant jobs that Elfi had been called to do often enough by earlier employers.

42

She stood now in the tiny entrance foyer of her apartment and carefully smoothed the sleeves and collar of her coat before hanging it away in the front closet. It was a good coat, cashmere, of a rather swaggering cut of camel's-hair color that her mistress had handed down to her this past winter.

In such a coat one did not trade sexual insults with a Bodo. This was a coat for innuendo, for intrigue, for finesse. It was a coat one wore with suave men, men of breeding, of rank, of background.

In such a coat, one went forth to live a new and different life.

In such a coat, film stars lounged about on Alpine decks sipping hot drinks. In such a coat, international adventuresses swept through the lobbies of de luxe hotels to assignations in royal suites. In such a coat . . .

Elfi's mouth tightened into a straight line. No daydreaming. The coat was warm and almost new. Forget the rest.

And yet, once one has seen the great world . . .

CHAPTER 8

"Bunterli," Erich called. "Warm up the sports car, yes? I've got calls to make for the rest of the day."

He watched Bunter leave the dressing room, where he had been laying out clothes, and move quickly down the stairs to the servants' part of the house in the cellar.

Erich finished the last of his coffee, folded the newspapers Bunter had brought him, and moved into the dressing room. It had taken him years to teach Bunter that Erich Lorn did not, except perhaps for board meetings or funerals, wear the medium-gray suit with the medium-gray vest, the plain white shirt with the starched collar and the discreet dark-blue tie.

Instead, Erich donned a broadly patterned shirt, pulled on brown suede trousers, linked and fastened a leather belt as wide as his head, knotted a foulard around his neck and wiggled into a pair of soft leather boots whose uppers were slightly higher than the current chukka fashion.

He tilted the pier glass slightly to catch all of himself in the mirror. His Uncle Dieter had given him the pier glass years ago when Erich's engagement to Margit had been formally announced. The glass was English, probably Georgian, and by now quite valuable as an antique whose provenance was a matter of record.

Dieter did not give small gifts, certainly not to the man who would one day be both his nephew, once removed, and the titular head of Staeli Internationale, GmbH.

Erich's thin face was put together mainly from a group of V-like formations, as if a cartoonist had drawn it with a series of checkmarks. Above his sharp chin two V's were sketched in by the pad of flesh under his lower lip as it merged into his chin and by the small, pointed dip in the center of his upper lip. The tip of his nose, too, was V-like and the faintly darker areas under his eyes, the skin only now, after years of dissipation, beginning to wrinkle, were V-shaped, giving him the look of an apprentice clown who has just begun to learn his real make-up. Erich's dark-brown hair came to a widow's peak which, as it pointed down the center of his forehead, seemed to scrape up a series of identical furrows in his brow.

A clown, he thought. Yes, of course. If there is one universal criticism of Erich Lorn, it is that the poor chap is *not serious.*

Somewhere in Erich's boxes of memorabilia—old menus, labels from wine bottles, women's gloves—was a caricature of two young men, he and Walter Staeli, that had appeared in one of the Austrian ski magazines during the mid-fifties of the century, when both had been eighteen-year-olds.

The caricaturist had drawn the two of them coming down the slopes. He had given Erich's figure a V-like snowplow stance for his skis, with his poles flung up and out behind his back making yet another V to match the series in his face.

Erich's eyes, fastened unseeingly on the image in the pier glass, blinked at last. He knew his habit of regarding the world without blinking was abnormal. Friends had complained of it. "It's like sitting across from a television camera, old man." Women had faintly admitted that they were hypnotized by his unwavering regard.

The fact was, Erich reminded himself now, blinking was usually the sign of some inner turmoil, of being serious. How often had he sat in the lounge of a plane or train and watched someone blinking as he unreeled, in the private cinema of his mind, some serious epic film of ingratitude, frustration and missed opportunities.

Erich rarely felt frustration. And as for ingratitude, he never expected thanks from the world. It simply wasn't one of the rules.

He turned away from the pier glass and left the room, half running as he descended the stairs to the entrance hall. Close shave earlier today, he remembered. He hoped Helene had gotten home ahead of her husband. But she was resourceful enough to invent an overnight visit with a girlfriend. In any event, it was the money Helene's family brought to the marriage that paid for the Herr Minister's expensive career in politics. He would believe whatever story Helene told him.

And that, Erich reminded himself, is one of the rules. Don't bite the hand that feeds.

Switzerland was a country addicted to rules: about God, about family, about marriage, politics and neutrality, too. For a country whose central government was kept deliberately weak so that its cantons could rule themselves, Switzerland seemed to have too many rules.

Perhaps this was a symptom of the self-control every Swiss so proudly exercised. After all, how many countries of Western Europe issued a gun and ammunition to every male citizen over the age of twenty, to be kept in his home, instantly ready to defend the national borders? If such a thing had been tried in any other country, half the population would now be dead, mowed down on drunken Saturday nights. Imagine letting the Russians or the Americans loose that way?

And yet, Erich knew, the rest of Switzerland thought the Baslers a bit wild. Their proximity to France and Germany made them suspect, apparently, and Baslers had a reputation for being a bit eccentric, a reputation they little deserved. Basel was as dull and hypocritical as any other place. Only by Swiss standards could it be thought a bit less dull.

Erich opened the front door and walked out onto the street, which fronted on the Rhine. He gazed across the fast-flowing river at the old part of Basel and grimaced slightly. He was about to tackle something unpleasant.

Bunter had started the sports car and driven it out to the curb. He waved good-bye as his master gunned the small antique roadster and sent it purring along. The car had been bought at auction in England some ten years before and was so ancient an MG that it still bore the predecessor name of the L-2 Magna, built in the 1930s but already showing the long bonnet and cutaway doors as well as the spare tire mounted over the rear boot. It had been painted a bright orange.

Rules, Erich recalled, pulling the short car into a hard right turn to produce a sound he loved, rubber yowling and stuttering against smoothed cobblestones. Some people, he thought, wanted fewer rules. Rules make hypocrites, they said. But that wasn't it, Erich was convinced. Hypocrites made rules.

He had studied the character of his fellow Swiss quite thoroughly over the years, beginning with his mother and father and two younger sisters. His mother, he remembered, made sure to show his sisters the right and wrong way for a knife to face on a table setting ("Edge in, girls. Otherwise it tells your guests you want to cut them."), and she also developed rules about how far from the edge of a plate food could be pushed ("Three centimeters, girls, and not a millimeter less. Let the Austrians and Italians mess food about all over their plates. We are Swiss.") and what was more, she rigorously enforced such nonsense.

To this day, as grown women, his sisters continued to push their food into a small muddle at the precise geographic center of their plates. Their children, too, were already brainwashed to keep their food in the center of the plate.

He took a left turn and entered the Aeschenvorstadt. Normally a busy thoroughfare lined with banks and other business buildings, the street was even busier now, at two in the afternoon, as those clerks and executives who lunched late hurried back to their desks. Basel was the most densely populated city in Europe, Erich knew, and yet even here there were no pushing hordes, only desperate pedestrians obeying the rules.

The business of rules, Erich knew, was a symptom of something much deeper in the Swiss character. He couldn't be sure whether it was the original teachings of Calvin and Zwingli that had first given the Swiss their viselike grip on Right and Wrong. But once a people is convinced it knows one from the other, the rest of the hypocrisy is inevitable.

He braked to a halt at the curb. This was a no-parking zone, of

46

course, at least until the close of the business day, but police were rare along the Aeschenvorstadt. And they knew the tiny orange Magna, its cloth top usually folded down, and knew Herr Lorn was good for a five or a tenner. Swiss police are incorruptible. But they overlook my car, Erich thought, not because they are corrupt and take anybody's bribe, but because they have somehow convinced themselves that *my money is not a bribe*. Marvelous.

He got out of the car in the same way he always did, lifting one long leg over the cut-down side of the closed door and deftly hopping onto the pavement. He had business with his future Uncle Dieter, or rather, Dieter had business with Erich.

The Staeli clan did not normally conduct business with the Lorn clan via Erich. His father, yes. His Cousin Werner, yes. Even his idiot brothers-in-law. But no serious businessman would transact anything of substance through Erich, despite his title of executive vice president and chief operating officer of Lorn et Cie.

So Dieter's topic today could only be Margit.

Erich surveyed the gray stone building of Number 17, bright red blots of geraniums vibrating slightly in their second-story window boxes as the breeze shook them. Very pretty. Hectic dabs of color on the prison-gray face. His eyelids lowered very slightly, as close as he ever came to blinking.

He disliked this interview with Dieter Staeli because, as Margit drew closer to her thirtieth birthday, the pressure from the Staeli clan to force her down the aisle and into marriage would begin to build to almost intolerable strength. So far they had used words, arguments, promises. During this next year they would, if they felt panicky enough, apply other forms of pressure, business pressure that Lorn et Cie. could not withstand.

He entered Number 17, gave his name to the aged male receptionist and was immediately ushered upstairs. Dieter was standing in the doorway of his office, all smiles.

Dieter Staeli was now past sixty-five, but an extremely hale sixty-five. He skied, still, Erich knew. He also played around, but never in Basel. Never in Switzerland, for that matter. That made it easier for him never to admit, even to himself, that he played around.

Watching the older man as he sat down in his office, Erich couldn't help but remember the one who would have been his

47

father-in-law, Lucas Staeli, Dieter's younger brother. He had died so far ahead of his appointed time that it was always amazing to see the older brother still very much alive and full of tricks. Erich had often wondered exactly what business dealings prior to Lucas' death had left the younger brother in charge of the Staeli empire, but so firmly in command that even from his tomb he could keep Dieter from seizing control.

Erich would have to sound out his father on this subject, assuming the old bird would talk. These Basler merchant-bankers were a close-mouthed lot. The bond of secrecy between different, often competitive, bankers was stronger than between father and son. Or, in the Staeli case, between brothers.

". . . nice piece of business for the Lorn bank," Dieter was saying. He had been churning up social and business chitchat for almost a minute now, larding the discourse with great chunks of unwarranted praise for Erich's business acumen.

"You're not the scamp most people think," Dieter went on flatteringly. "You know when to pounce and profit, eh? Most amusing."

Erich smiled softly. "Coming from you, sir, that is the highest of compliments."

"*Na, na, na,*" Dieter said, wagging his forefinger, but returning the smile. "Don't try to outflatter an old-timer. When we want to spread it on thick, you know, nothing makes us blush."

Erich's smile broadened. If this hypocrite thought he was winning confidence, let him persist in his error. "My experience, sir, is that nothing a true Swiss does will ever make him blush."

Dieter's almost perfectly round face began to resemble a sun. A noon sun, Erich decided, so effulgent with self-satisfaction and the pleasure of thinking he'd fooled someone that he was in danger of exploding from sheer spontaneous combustion.

"In that case," Dieter said suddenly, "when in the name of Christ are you going to marry my bloody niece?"

Erich kept the grin plastered on his face. He had several ways of parrying this unexpected thrust. Possibly a cool response would calm the old bastard.

"Bloody?"

The sun eclipsed. Dieter's face crumpled, but was not yet extinguished. He smoldered for a moment. His full, small mouth

48

framed and rejected several fresh starts. Then: "I apologize, Erich. She is a very attractive young lady. I am her devoted slave. I know your feelings for her are of the tenderest. I was unforgivably rude. I beg your forgiveness."

Mein Gott, Erich thought, these old-timers really didn't blush, did they? Shameless hypocrites, thoroughly dangerous because they could toady and bluster and toady again, all in the space of a minute or less. He made a gesture of brushing away some unfortunate crumbs that had fallen on the desk between them.

"But, Erich, you have a responsibility to yourself, to Margit, to me, to your parents, and to all our families," Dieter said then.

Erich shrugged. "Margit is a Staeli," he said then. "She is also the bride-to-be. She and her family set the date, do they not?"

The sun hid itself behind a convenient cloud. Dieter seemed to think for much longer a time than Erich had felt he needed. Then the older man nodded in agreement. He nodded only once, Erich noticed, but this single gesture was more forceful than a dozen of his son Walter's meaningless head-bobbings. *"Touché,"* Dieter said then. "As we have grown so candid, Erich, tell me, one man to another, why Margit has delayed so long?"

"You must know."

"I?" He touched the edges of his gray jacket, piped with a faint line of black leather. His big, stubby hands resembled those of a butcher or a mason, not a man who used his fingers to push around a pen. "Please have mercy and throw even a scrap of this to me. Why must her uncle and guardian and protector be the last to know?"

Erich paused a moment. Uncle, yes. Guardian, never, since Margit was of age. Protector, not bloody likely. "What can I tell you?" he asked then.

Dieter Staeli held up one meaty hand and ticked off points with the fat forefinger of his other hand. "She could have married you a year after your betrothal. She did not. She could have married you on her return from Harvard. She did not. She could have married you at any time in the six years since. She has not. It is beginning to seem that she has no intention of marrying you."

"Not until she's thirty, no."

Dieter's blue eyes widened so alarmingly in his sunlike face that the skin around them, normally smooth over its fatty padding, grew deeply wrinkled with effort. "So that's it."

"I can't believe this is news to you."

"I know the situation as well as you," Dieter cut in brusquely. "And I know every line of my late brother's last will and testament. With the best of intentions he managed to do us all the most grievous injury of which a man is capable from beyond the grave."

Erich listened to the theatrical phrase rumble around the room for a moment. He liked play-acting as well as the next person, but not enough to play uncritical audience to this performance.

"I may as well tell you, then," he said, without bothering much to choose his words carefully, "that although she hasn't said a word of it to me, I'm quite sure she will wait until her thirtieth birthday before she marries. That way she inherits directly, in her own maiden name, with no husband interfering between her and control."

"It is not a question of interference," Dieter assured him. "A husband has the full power of the law behind him."

"Not for long."

"They will not enact this monstrosity, which they so cleverly call a reform," the old man stated.

"The *Abschaffnung des Patriarchats?*" Erich responded. "It's a reform, all right. And it will be enacted."

"But not for years."

"Perhaps."

Dieter's round head shook from side to side. "I am not a fool, Erich. I know what kind of trivial issues excite the voters. I knew that once we gave women the vote, the *Abschffnung* would not be far behind. But we still have time."

"We? We men? We God-fearing Swiss males?"

The head kept shaking, slowly, as if in grief. "You miss the point, Erich. It doesn't matter what happens after the *Abschaffnung* becomes the law, as long as you have already married Margit."

"And you miss my point," the younger man snapped back somewhat tartly. "Margit's lawyers have, I feel sure, given her reason to believe that if she inherits her Staeli holdings in her own unmarried name—that is, at the age of thirty—she will be free of any control by any husband who might come along later. This may not be what Lucas Staeli's lawyers intended when they wrote the will, but it is nevertheless what will happen."

Dieter said nothing. The room fell silent. Not even the traffic noise from the Aeschenvorstadt penetrated to Erich's ears. He shifted restlessly in his chair. He had two other appointments today and this fool was delaying him.

The round head began to shake from side to side now in a monumental display of nay-saying. "Erich," the voice quavered, no longer razor-sharp nor honeyed but shaking with age and betrayal. "What are you telling me, Erich?"

"That which you have already prepared for."

Dieter looked genuinely surprised. He dropped the quaver. "What?"

"Tell me, then," Erich asked, "why is Margit already an assistant vice president, the only female of that rank in the entire country? Hasn't this been your way of preparing her for what we all knew would be her inevitable role?"

Dieter's plump mouth opened and closed twice, like a tropical fish against the glass of an aquarium. He seemed to be trying at the same time to spew words and suck air. He pushed his chubby body back from the desk and let his butcher's hands move up and down the leather piping of his jacket.

"Now look," he said then. "She demanded these jobs. All I could ever do was delay giving them to her. But anyone who thinks that, in time, the Staeli fortune will be ruled by a woman is a fool."

"Margit believes she will."

"Damned, meddling, neurotic fool!" Dieter spat out. Then, hastily: "I love her, this girl, like a father. I adore her. But she is destroying herself with this American foolishness. It is all part of the whole democratic *Scheissdreck*," Dieter said in a somber tone. He made a disgusted face and flapped his heavy hands twice. "Most amusing, eh? They infect her brain and export her back to Switzerland like a . . . a . . . a typhoid carrier," he spluttered. "It is too much."

Erich got to his feet to cut short any further flow from the less-ventilated sewers of Dieter's mind. "So you see," he said, "there isn't a thing I can do. Margit will marry when she pleases."

When he spoke again, Dieter's voice had gone cold and businesslike. "She has made a great mistake, this headstrong girl. Her attorneys have ill-advised her. The law of the *Patriarchats* has been on the books for many centuries. It has always protected the husband's supremacy in *any* family decision. His is the last word . . . *by law*. Whether she inherits before marriage or after, her husband's word continues to be law."

Erich stood there for a moment, towering over the older man. "Don't be too sure of that."

Dieter scrambled to his feet. He was a head shorter than Erich, so he remained behind his desk. "The law is the law, Erich. As her husband, your word must be obeyed. The *Patriarchats* protects your rights in this. And, if you need them, I will put my best lawyers to work on breaking her hold, whatever my brother's will says. Of this you may be sure."

You may be sure, Erich thought, you already have. And devised a dozen sneaky tricks. He reached for the butcher's right hand. "Margit evidently doesn't feel that way," he said in a pleasant voice. "Perhaps her attorneys have given her good reason to feel so."

"*Her* attorneys?" Dieter burst out, his round face glowing again, this time with anger. "She has no attorneys that are not on my payroll. Do you think I let her that far out of my sight?" Dieter's hand had clamped over his like a large squid, not cool and slimy, but hot and dry. "We all love her, Erich. We worship our little Margitschen. There is nothing I would not do for that lovely girl."

Or *to* her, Erich added silently. He extricated his hand and went to the door of Dieter's office. He eyed the older man unblinkingly. "She's lucky to have you looking after her," he said, and left the room.

CHAPTER 9

Walter Staeli stood in the courtyard of the inn waving good-bye to the chauffeured Peugeot carrying his three Japanese business associates back to the Basel-Mulhouse Airport. He let the car recede into the distance before getting into his own dark-gray Mercedes and ordering the driver to return to the office.

He glanced at his watch. Two-forty. But it couldn't be helped, Walter excused himself. When The White Fox is tricking his way to new victories, schedules mean nothing. Of course his colleagues would give him odd looks when he returned nearly an hour late. Of course they would grumble to themselves about the boss's son. That, after all, was their function: by being small-minded and petty, to set off magnificent business acumen like Walter's. By contrast to further glorify him. By their inescapable lowness to elevate him to new heights.

He smiled and nodded several times. Walter, who considered himself acutely aware of all his reasons for doing things, had never realized that one of the things he did—to an excessive degree that amounted almost to a tic—was to nod his head, an eternal yes-saying and, considering his rather negative disposition, an eternal lie to the world.

But he was in a good mood today. He had totally bilked the Japanese. They might know production. They might even know financing. But they didn't understand marketing and Walter did.

He had just concluded what was, in the beginning, a rather small deal for Staeli Internationale GmbH. But there were larger considerations. Like all loyal Swiss, Walter had for some time been worried about his nation's watchmaking industry. Except for a few extremely high-priced lines of watches and chronometers, everything else was suffering, especially the medium-priced and cheap watches. These had been more or less swept off the counters of the world's shops by Japanese watches that were a bit cheaper and just as good. Or better.

Although every honest, God-fearing Swiss is covered by unemployment benefits of sufficient scope, idleness is a venial sin and poverty the chief of the cardinal sins. No able-bodied Swiss can stand himself when he is without work. And no Swiss can contemplate with equanimity the fact that some of his own loyal countrymen are, in fact, idle and poor, or about to be if the watch factory for which they work goes out of business.

So. Walter sat back in the rear of the gray Mercedes and watched the lovely spring countryside of Alsace roll by. To the north, the Vosges peaks loomed against the horizon while, toward the east, in the direction the car was moving, Walter could just barely make out the Jura range of mountains, beyond the valley of the Rhine.

This was a very old part of Europe. In this valley, Walter knew, on the banks of this broad river winding toward the sea, man had done business since before Christ. The Romans, he knew for a fact, had settled the area just east of Basel, where Schloss Staeli stood, about half a century B.C. The Latin name of the town, Basilea, was first mentioned in Roman histories only four centuries later.

It was fitting that here, in one of the oldest areas of both Europe and Switzerland, in his country's second largest city, that the honor of his countrymen should be vindicated at one clever stroke by the dashing wit and cunning of The White Fox.

What the Japanese had signed today after the extremely good meal at the inn, complete with a liter for each man of a '73 Moselle that defied comparison with any other Riesling under glass, was an agreement to supply the innards, circuits and digital readout arrays for one of the newly popular hand-held electronic computer devices. So much was routine. But it was also an agreement by which they committed business hara-kiri.

Which they never suspected, Walter thought as his car sped east toward the city. The tiny solid-state circuits were to be programed not only for the typical add-subtract-multiply-divide calculations, but also a special series of additional functions that included straight-line percentage, percentage on a diminishing principal, metric conversion and several other tricks uncommon for these handy little gadgets.

The little calculator was tailor-made, in fact, for use by banks, brokerages and other financial institutions.

The Japanese had agreed to keep the transaction secret. They waived the imprinting of either their own company name on the circuitry or, what was much more important, the legend "Made in Japan." Negotiations with two very prestigious Tokyo concerns had already broken down over just this point. They had insisted on the "Made in Japan" imprint. Walter had continued looking for a Japanese company that would agree to such terms and, finally, had found one. The fools.

Walter watched the highway as his car neared the three-country meeting point where a piece of modern sculpture stood, vastly resembling an aluminum SST aircraft with stubby but sharp winglets, needle nose sniffing God straight up, tail exhaust port buried in concrete. This was Basel's Rhine Port, where Germany, France and Switzerland met. As always, Walter frowned slightly at the wing decoration on the sculpture, concentric rings similar to, but not identical with, the old British RAF insignia.

In the smoggy middle distance, giant gantries and smaller cranes lifted freight on and off low-lying ships. Donkey engines chugged along railroad tracks on the river's edge, shunting freight cars here and there, sending short puffs of black smoke into the air.

One of these days—rather soon, Walter felt—some of these ships would be carrying something new and unique to the markets of the world. Walter's head bobbed up and down for a moment, then stopped. No. His marketing plans called for air freight. Ships would be too slow. For what he had in mind was nothing less than a worldwide marketing plan for the tiny new hand-held calculators with special functions designed for bank use—and on them the legend "Made in Switzerland."

The idea was really quite simple, like all brilliant schemes. Walter sat back as his Mercedes slid past the city limits of Basel and into the western part of town, called Grossbasel, on this side of the Rhine.

No longer interested in confusing onlookers, as he had been when he'd left for lunch, Walter had given the driver instructions to take him directly back to the bank, which he now did by driving down Kannenfeldstrasse and into Missionstrasse.

Ahead loomed the Spalentor, which everyone called one of the best medieval gates in Europe, but which Walter found rather squat, even with its upswept pointed cap of diagonally laid tiles. The crenelated towers on each side of it were not to his taste, either. He checked the clock face on the Spalentor. Ten to three. Not bad. The Mercedes followed the old streetcar tracks to the right around the gate and moved on along the Spalenvorstadt. To his left, over the three- and four-story buildings, Walter could see the fussy twin spires of the Münster cathedral, lacy gothic stone as ventilated and insubstantial as the dream-spires of the Duomo in Milan.

The Western mind, he told himself, and especially the Swiss

mind, that could conceive of something as complex, yet as simple, as a Gothic cathedral, would be more than a match for the most devious of oriental minds. It could spin a scheme so simple as to defy understanding. He giggled under his breath, not wanting the chauffeur to hear him.

A simple scheme that the Japanese had not even suspected, Walter told himself now as the chauffeur turned into the Aeschenvorstadt. The unemployed Swiss watch craftsmen, adept at this kind of work although they perhaps did not have the delicate fingers of the Japanese, would be put to work in secret factories south of Basel. There they would produce metal-and-plastic cases for the tiny computers, install the Japanese circuitry, test and adjust the mechanisms, box and crate them and send them forth to the world with the trade name "Staelicomp" prominently displayed on each box and case, next to the "Made in Switzerland" line.

Walter's head began bobbing up and down again. This was the penultimate step in his scheme for rehabilitating the watch industry and making a fat profit while doing it.

The Staeli name on the hand-held calculators would be the keystone of an advertising campaign addressed primarily to banks around the world. "Good enough for Staeli" might be an appropriate slogan, Walter thought. It didn't have the ring of some lines his advertising people might create, but he was far and away more creative than any of them. Perhaps "Good enough *even* for Staeli." Would an exclamation point help it? "So good, it bears the *Staeli* name!" Or "For *Staeli,* nothing but the *best!*" More exclamation points? "If it's *Staeli,* it's *got* to be the *best!!!*" Let the creative boys fool with it. They were paid good Swiss francs to play games with words.

The dark-gray Mercedes slowed to a crawl. Walter's head stopped bobbing. The penultimate stage of the scheme, he thought, would be to sell these computers to banks, insurance companies, brokerage houses, all the special offices for which its special functions were designed. The Staeli name carried considerable weight in financial circles. But this was not the final stage.

This alone could not guarantee domination of the market so that computer sales provided enough work for former watchmakers. But the pricing did. Walter began to nod more violently as he thought of his scheme, something only a really astute Swiss business leader would have created.

He would "dump" the computers worldwide at cost. Their retail price would be below what competitive Japanese instruments sold for. He would, in effect, carve out a large chunk of the miniature-computer market by stealing it away from the country that had invented it, Japan. And with their own circuits!

The combination of low price and the Staeli name would be irresistible. Once established, the price of the calculators would rise to a profitable level. People expected that. Prices always rise.

He would have no real manufacturing expenses except the nominal labor costs of having Swiss workmen put cases on Japanese innards. He would himself finance the buying of the Japanese circuitry at extremely favorable interest rates. Thus, the entire scheme could show serious profits by just a small price rise, predicated on volume. It was a scheme dear to any businessman's heart and especially Walter's, the application of strong leverage from a favored position. The Japanese might never, in fact, tumble to how they had been outfoxed by The White Fox himself. If they did, it didn't really matter. An air-tight contract bound them to continue supplying the electronic innards of the calculators for at least three more years. For three years they would be forced to continue cutting their own throats! Walter laughed out loud. Then he quickly composed himself.

The Mercedes slid to a halt before Staeli Internationale GmbH. and Walter left the car with a certain gravity, a certain weight that would have been natural and expected in a man of sixty, but unusual in one yet to reach his thirty-fifth birthday.

The weak spring sunshine made his blond hair and light eyes look even paler. He glanced at himself in the glass doors of the bank in the instant before the doorman swung it wide open. The White Fox? The White Knight! With his fingers, Walter brushed his hair sideways to make up for the fact that it was already thinning, at his age.

As he did so, he caught sight of Erich's orange Magna sports car illegally parked a few meters down the street. Walter frowned. Playboy and wastrel and worse. Libertine. Adulterer who, by an accident of marriage-to-be, was to take the Staeli interests out of Margit's hands.

Never mind. Once the results of today's lunch became known to the rest of the family—and Walter would take care to spread the news widely—everyone would know once and for all who the real ruler of the clan was destined to be.

CHAPTER 10

Now that she had returned from her secret week in London, now that the life of Schloss Staeli had gathered around her and the servants had all come in to bid her welcome and slyly hint at the joys of the big city, the fact of being back home settled down on Margit's shoulders like the heaviest of leaden *lodens*.

It was more than being back in Basel, she told herself as she sat at the desk in her study. Listlessly she went through a week's accumulation of personal mail and office memoranda.

This had once been her mother's bedroom, a long room lined with immense casement windows that looked out on the Rhine and, beyond its sparkle, the dark clumps of distant fir that signaled the borders of the German Schwarzwald.

Here her mother had played with Margit as an infant. Here she had taken to her chaise longue—the same one that still sat in one corner of the room—during the difficult pregnancy that led to the ill-fated birth of Margit's brother. The doctor had ruled out parties, even those without dancing or music. He had ruled against leaving the Schloss at all. The idea of an Rh-damaged fetus was not new to science even then, a few years after World War II. The doctors had all agreed that when there was a danger of it—Margit's mother tested Rh negative—it was with the second child, not the first, that danger was to be feared.

Margit's own family doctor had concurred with the local obstetrician and also with the eminent gynecologists who had been summoned from Paris and Zurich. Quiet and rest, preferably horizontal, were indicated.

So it had been here that Margit's mother had spent the last seven months of her life, with few companions other than Margit herself, a baby of less than four years. And it was here that she was laid out by the undertakers, Pfäffli und Sohn, after she had died at the *Frauenspital* the day following Margit's brother's death in childbirth.

And from here, dressed in a long white chiffon gown, dark hair bound in a bun, carefully rouged face fixed in iron lines of peace, Margit's mother had been buried. The four-year-old girl had followed the coffin, her hand clamped in her father's, the one-mile walk from the Schloss to the private burial ground next to the ancient Staeli chapel.

In the next few years after the awful day, the room with its adjunct bath and dressing room had sat in silence, locked against the world. Then Margit's father had caused it to be opened and painted and repapered and paneled in fairly modern taste. It became Margit's room and it remained so even after she left home at eighteen for college.

All her mother's furniture had been thrown away by order of Lucas Staeli, all but the white wicker chaise longue in the corner, which Margit had insisted on keeping. In her mind it had somehow become her mother. It had even taken on the reclining shape of the woman, full of life and bursting with death.

Margit looked over her shoulder at the chaise longue. The cushions needed reupholstering again.

It all seemed like the day before yesterday, she having just learned so many new things, her mother so delighted with her progress, teaching her new words, daring her to climb on chairs, push the tea table around. She had begged to be her mother's maid, bringing meals, opening letters for her. But her mother had needed her more as someone to whom she could talk. Good God, what hadn't she talked of! The river, the forest, the grass, the people of another age who had lived here, her own girlhood in Geneva, her plans for Margit and Lucas. The child inside her was to be a boy and he was to be named after his father. He would be Lucas Staeli III. Or was it IV?

Margit's eyes misted over. The chaise longue grew dim and streaky. She turned back to the desk and watched the letters and memoranda swim before her eyes. *Muti, schöne Muti.*

She blinked and sniffed and made a face, a stern face not unlike one her father used. As much as she wanted to forget them, they were both still with her. As much as she was determined to be herself, parts of them were still inside her.

She wondered about her feelings toward them both. Had anyone ever had such a childhood? A father who carefully explained to her when she reached puberty that it had been Margit's gestation in her mother's womb, the interaction of Margit's positive Rh factor with her mother's negative one, that had later triggered off the dread mishap which had killed both brother and mother? Did many fathers have such stories to tell their only daughter? More to the point, if anyone had such a story, would he be mad enough to tell it? To place the blame for two deaths on his daughter? To leave her with such guilt? And then, ten years later, to sink into melancholia and, perhaps, kill himself, perhaps out of grief, perhaps . . .

Too many indefinites, Margit decided. Too many gray areas. Had Lucas Staeli wanted her to be his wife? Not in bed, perhaps. But in every other way, yes. But perhaps also in bed?

Perhaps.

She stood up and went to the window wall, staring out at the river. Even at this distance, a quarter of a mile, she could see the sun glinting on small waves as they moved rapidly past. Who among her friends had endured such a childhood? It was one thing —and not that unusual among her childhood acquaintances—to have the money to fulfill any whim, buy anything from a dress to a house that attracted one's attention. Many of her friends came from families almost as wealthy as the Staelis. But none of them bore this weight. They had living brothers and sisters to help them share the gravid, dead weight of parents filled with God-fearing Swiss guilt.

An only child has advantages, Margit reminded herself. When the parents are loving, love doesn't have to be shared. But the disadvantage of loneliness more than outweighs it.

Early in life, at the age of nine or ten, Margit had begun to keep a diary, but gave it up in her teens. Then, in her mid-twenties, she had started an informal journal. Sometimes there would be no entries for weeks, then a series of short comments. The journal filled the role of a confidante, especially for an only child not used to confiding in others.

Erich had been impressed by the idea and occasionally begged for a peek at it. He'd even talked of keeping one himself. "When one has the sisters I have, and the so-called friends, one needs a real confidante," he'd said. Then, hastily: "Other than you, dear Margy."

Margit watched six loaded dumb barges, pulled by a tugboat, make their way around the bend of the Rhine. This bend had been chosen with exquisite care by the Staelis who were contemporary with Madame de Staël herself. Just to the west of the Schloss lay the ancient town of Augst, in whose ruined Roman amphitheater Margit had run and played as a girl. Immediately to the east stood the small medieval town of Rhinefelden, with spas established by the famed Paracelsus, so it was said, and romantic promenades along the river's curve.

Between lay the Staeli fief, walled off from visitors, a private preserve in which trees three hundred years old could be found. An early Christian chapel from the year 600 had been restored for family use. As a child Margit had explored archeological digs on the property that had since been sodded over to keep the government from expropriating Roman relics and the bronze weapons of the Alemanni barbarians who had swept through this land like a plague in the third century.

To have that kind of power, Margit told herself now, was not unusual among the families of Basel. But the insolence to authority that said, in effect, "If it means depriving the world of these relics to protect our privacy, so be it," was typically Staeli. No other family had that recklessly direct a feeling for power as to place itself on a par with governments or, if the truth were known, above them.

Lucas Staeli had caused the archeological digs to be camouflaged. He had caused sod to be laid and watered, shrubbery to be grown. Nature had done the rest. The servants who had helped were all gone. No one was left who remembered that period except Margit herself and the housekeeper Uschi. Some had been fired, some enticed away, some had died. Uschi would probably not remember the event because, for her, no importance had attached to it. Only Margit remembered. Only Margit wondered at the hubris of her dead father.

And always will, she thought now, turning from the window. He was mad or a genius, or both. But his determination had left her now with the entire Staeli empire well within her grasp. And whether Lucas had meant it that way or not, there was enough of him in her to make sure she held onto it.

She sat down at the desk, a long, dark walnut refectory table, and at once the feeling of depression knelt on her shoulders again like a weighty demon, one of those malicious gargoyles from the waterspout of a cathedral, all talons and teeth and leer.

Margit shook her head to dislodge the demon. A persistent devil. Not for the first time in her adult life, Margit wondered what it was like to be mad. Not eccentric or neurotic. Insane.

She picked up the week's correspondence from her office. For several years now she had held a series of executive posts with Staeli Internationale GmbH. that seemed suited to a woman.

Her first assignment had been to head a department that was to develop a limited credit plan for married women who held jobs. Until that point in Swiss history, no woman could get credit except in her husband's name and on his signature. Now, on the strength of a job, minuscule line of credit was being extended only in the conventional area of retail purchases. It was hardly more than a department-store charge card, but perhaps half a faltering step forward into the twentieth century for Swiss banking. A full credit card was yet to be proposed, but Margit had one in mind.

Having successfully established this new Staeli department and nursed it until it began to show a profit, Margit had been promoted by her Uncle Dieter to the post of assistant vice president, the first woman officer in any Swiss bank since the dawn of time. With the title went a new job of determining whether there were any profit for the bank to be made in financing such high-risk businesses as couturier shops, the mushrooming youth-clinic business and other female-oriented industries.

She stood up and went to a locked cabinet in the corner, which she opened. Inside lay the most recent exercise book in which she kept her journal. She paged through it until she reached the blank section. Rarely did she reread her entries. The mere setting down of thoughts was usually all she wanted from the habit of keeping a journal.

She read through the entry she had made on the flight about famine. She frowned and brought the journal back to the refectory table, where she added it to the pile of correspondence. In a pen with an extremely fine point she wrote:

"May 26. London trip useful. Some strong initial contacts. Must redo study. Place has grown too melancholy. Hard to sit here without remembering. Wallpaper? Or cut into two rooms? Or abandon? Move records to the office at Number 17 Aeschenvorstadt? So Dieter can pick the lock of my desk? Must ask Erich if Helene made good her escape this morning before Herr Husband noticed her absence. It's all right for Erich to take his own chances, but she is a fool."

She paused, started to write something else, then stopped and closed the exercise book. She stared for a moment at its cheaply printed cover. Perhaps she was outgrowing the journal? Perhaps she could begin to confide in someone else? But who, other than Erich? And why dignify their curious relationship by such a move at this late date?

She put the book aside and spent the next fifteen minutes going through business correspondence, making notes, writing out brief letters for a secretary to type and mail. The office deluged her with pieces of paper. Here was a new loan proposal, a memorandum on checking accounts for unmarried women (out of the question!), another on a perfume company's stock prospectus.

Margit stopped suddenly. She had grown abruptly tired of paging through endless office memoranda. She pushed the folders aside and continued looking through private mail. She had no idea why she did this. Most of it was bills or advertising or publications of one kind or another. It was almost as if the demon on her back had forced her to postpone the business mail for the personal mail.

She stopped, fingers frozen in position. The letter was long, airmail-striped, with a twenty-six-cent U.S. stamp and a return address from Harvard Graduate School of Business Administration, Cambridge, Massachusetts. Her fingers felt numb.

She opened the letter and glanced at the clever counterfeit of a signed personal letter being sent her by the alumni office, some notice of a reunion dinner and the usual request for contributions. Why had she known this letter was in the pile? Why had the devil on her shoulders told her to look for it?

She threw the letter in the wastebasket, together with most of the personal mail she had already looked at. Then she sat back at

63

the long walnut table and stared out at the river again. The barges were gone. But the sparkle remained on the swift-flowing water.

The Charles River had been straight and just as broad, bordered by the skyscrapers of Boston across the water, the wavelets sparkling in the sun of late May, a few dinghies already scudding across the river in short tacks, scooting back and forth like waterbugs before a stiff spring breeze.

Where was he now? Tokyo, someone had said.

Funny to think of his big body surrounded by Japanese. They had been attracted to each other first because both of them were tall. There weren't that many men who looked right walking with Margit. In heels she could be an inch or two short of six feet.

Where was he now?

Why had her fingers gone to that envelope? She hadn't thought of him in months. The demon scraped his long talons across the skin of her neck, sending a shudder across her shoulder blades and down her spine.

What nonsense. Margit stood up and rang for Uschi. It was two hours past lunch and she hadn't eaten since breakfast in London.

But still and all . . . where was he now?

CHAPTER 11

As he arrived at Basel-Mulhouse Airport the aroma was distinctly that of sour grapes, or so Matthew Burris thought as the UBCO car sped along the broad international highway that led east from the airport. The road was flanked by guard-wire fencing fully twenty feet high.

At this hour the highway was almost empty in the direction of Basel, but the other lanes leading west were filled mainly with cabs carrying people to the airport after a day of transacting business. A big chauffeur-driven Peugeot swam past, heading in the direction of the airport. In its back section three Japanese sat immobile, upright.

Burris blinked. Not possible. Lack of sleep and the long, punishing flight had started him seeing things. Those were not Japanese, nor were they the same three he'd disembarked with at Orly this morning. Not possible. Good night's sleep.

He glanced at, but did not see, the stubby-winged monument at the three-nation post on the Rhine, except to spell out the name of the corner, *Dreiländerecke,* and pronounce it under his breath.

He knew as little German as Japanese, but he'd been warned that Germans tended to combine small words into big ones. He felt in the pocket of his coat for the miniature red dictionary he'd bought in the lounge at Orly and, after painstakingly picking apart the word on the sign, he realized it only meant three-country corner, which was a piece of information he did not really need.

He was still a bit upset at the bank's sending one of its undercover spooks to load him up with information he also did not really need, although there were two or three typewritten pages just on the Staeli interests that showed pretty good sleuthing. Curtis might be a lightweight, but he did do his homework.

Matthew Burris leaned back against the hard cushion of the car, a four-door Audi he was sure wasn't the best vehicle in UBCO's Basel fleet. And why the hell hadn't the manager been at the airport?

The sun was behind him now, starting down toward the western horizon as the car reached the city limits of Grossbasel. He had the name of UBCO's resident manager in Basel, a fellow with the improbable name of Shelter, but it was after 4 P.M. and Burris had hesitated to telephone him from the airport. He had, instead, questioned the driver, only to find that the man spoke no English.

Everything seemed to point to Shelter's nose being so far out of joint at having to welcome his successor and new boss that he had neglected even the routine amenities. Burris habitually thought in terms of finding where conflicts lay so that he could meet them head on. He felt fairly certain Shelter was so angry at Burris' appointment that he was retaliating in this petty way.

"Driver," he called, "how soon do we reach the hotel?"

The man's face turned very slightly, but his eyes remained on the road. *"Bitte?"*

Burris started to page through the German dictionary, then shoved it back in his pocket. Fortunately, he had been given the German name of the hotel, the *Drei Könige,* which he had been able to convey to the chauffeur. Watching the city passing by on either side, Burris decided he knew what *drei* meant already. He made a face and retrieved the dictionary. The name of his hotel was The Three Kings. Okay.

He knew he was being petulant. And he knew that having Shelter stiff him at the airport was only part of the reason he felt this way. The other part of it was Curtis.

He understood that UBCO was only trying to help by giving him his own private spook. But having someone like Curtis on hand was a two-edged sword. You could tap him for accurate information, yes. But at the same time he was accurately spying on you for UBCO. Yes, again.

Whoever had decided to stick him with Curtis, it would have to have been cleared with his old patron, Woods Palmer. Of that, Burris felt certain. As soon as he got settled in his hotel, and even before he started looking for a flat, he'd have to phone Palmer and make a date to visit him.

The Audi was moving more slowly now as it passed through the Voltaplatz and entered Elsasserstrasse. The afternoon rush hour was on. Burris knew that Swiss banks closed later than in the States, sometime after four o'clock. He assumed that the crush of pedestrians and cars at this hour was caused either by people going home from work, or customers making a mad dash to the bank before closing time.

The car was moving along another street now. In the block ahead of him, on what looked like a row of tall medieval houses backed up against the very rim of the Rhine, Burris could see the discreet entrance of a hotel. He glanced around him and saw a street sign that read *Totentanz*. The car paused for a moment in traffic. Burris checked through the dictionary again. He looked up several entries, but before he could put the red-covered book away in his pocket, the Audi was at the hotel.

Burris wasn't sure at first that it was, in fact, the Drei Könige, as it had been described in all the various brochures and booklets UBCO had sent him. All the hotel's signs proclaimed it to be *Les Trois Rois,* but when Burris tentatively pronounced its German name to one of the doormen, the answering *"Ja wohl, Mein Herr!"* seemed conclusive enough.

The odor of sour grapes disappeared as doormen and bellhops swarmed around the car, lifting suitcases from the trunk and show-

ering Burris with a fine rain of *"Bitte, Herr Burris"* that at the very least confirmed the fact that they were expecting him. Shelter, or someone in the UBCO office, hadn't forgotten to make the reservation. When the driver gave him a form to sign, Burris realized that the Audi was a rental car. So someone had laid that on, too.

Nor had Shelter stinted UBCO's expense account on the suite of rooms, three of them, all fronting on the Rhine itself. After Burris paid off the two baggage men, he pulled open a window in the big sitting room and leaned out to look at the river, moving swiftly before him from right to left.

To his right a bridge loaded with autos and trucks led across to the other part of the city. Between him and the bridge lay a landing at which a small pleasure steamer was moored. Nobody seemed to be getting on or off. To his left, attached to an overhead cable, a tiny ferryboat moved steadily across the Rhine, its body twisted sideways by the swift current.

Burris pulled his head back in and went to the telephone. "Any messages for Burris?" he asked the concierge. "Any mail?"

"No, Herr Burris," the man responded instantly. "We would have given them to you when you registered, sir. May I send anything now? Refreshment of any sort? Cold beer?"

"No, thanks."

Burris hung up. Shelter was running in form. It was not, after all, carelessness or stupidity. It was a definite slur. He was being ignored on purpose.

Topcoat still on, Burris sat down in a comfortable armchair and stared for a long moment at the small oriental rug on the floor. Was he being overly touchy? Had four years in super-polite Japan spoiled him for the West?

He shook his head and jammed his hands into his coat pockets. After a moment he withdrew the tiny red dictionary and dropped it on an end table. *Totentanz.* Dance of Death. Funny goddamned name for a street.

Matthew Burris got to his feet and began pacing the room. Something was wrong. He could feel it. Not knowing what it was made him jumpy. Not knowing the town or the people or even the language made him even jumpier.

He strode to the telephone and asked the switchboard operator for the UBCO office on the Aeschenvorstadt. The telephone rang at the other end. After a dozen rings, Burris hung up.

He opened his briefcase and pulled out a file folder. Inside it he found the sheaf of papers Curtis had given him, found Palmer's address in a small town near Lugano and gave it to the hotel operator. Then he started pacing again. The room was big, almost thirty feet long, but Burris seemed to cover the distance in four or five strides.

After ten minutes he whipped off his coat and threw it on the bed. When another five minutes had elapsed, he picked up the telephone and asked the operator what had happened.

"There is no answer, Herr Burris."

"Have room service send up a cold beer."

The feeling that something had gone wrong was now almost a certainty. No resident manager. No answer at UBCO. No messages. No Palmer. His glance fell on a note Curtis had written on one of his sheets of information. "Fraülein Margit Staeli, Schloss Staeli, Basel-Land." He had added a telephone number.

Burris turned on his heel and strode toward the windows. He shoved back the curtains and stared down at the river. A line of barges was moving downstream. The traffic over the bridge had come to a standstill. No one honked his horn, of course. It was a completely silent traffic jam, Burris noted.

He wasn't going to call her. That much was clear. Something had gone wrong with the reception committee. Either they thought he was due in on another day or this bastard Shelter hated his guts and didn't mind letting him know it.

Burris tried to take long, calming breaths. He was not going to telephone her. Until this was all squared away and he had his feet firmly under him and his base was secure, he was not going to open up old love letters. Even then he might not call her.

He watched the little cable ferry tie up on the far shore of the Rhine. Then he sat down in the armchair and contemplated his shoetips. Any minute the telephone would ring and Shelter's apologetic voice would begin the litany of excuses. Well, why not. Goddamn it, this was no way to welcome a full UBCO vee-pee, your new boss and the man who was going to set Swiss banking back on its tail. Any minute the call would come.

Totentanz. He shook his head as if trying to dislodge something.

If only he had something in front of him that he could shove. Burris was not geared for deft infighting, nor was he the man for fading back and chucking a long pass to an unsuspected runner. His idea of strategy was to hit the center of the line as hard as possible and crack it.

He knew this was the wrong approach. Years in the banking business had shown him how to softshoe his way past tacklers, outflank them and score big, the way he once had in college. How the hell else could Matt Brzyck of Carbondale, Illinois, ever have landed a scholarship at Northwestern, except on the gridiron? But the bull-like kid who'd once made All-American fullback had finally learned enough to stop hitting the center of the line.

Burris felt better. The sense of something unknown closing in on him had begun to fade. There had been that momentary panic and he'd wanted to smash through, plunge straight on, stiff-arm whatever it was, smear it out of the way and knee it in the jock as he rumbled past.

Okay. Fine. Back to normal. He glanced around the room and decided he liked it. Perhaps he might stay here longer than a week or two. Perhaps the monthly rate was reasonable. He liked the view. Think positively.

Three Japanese in a Peugeot.

Not possible. Why were imaginary Japanese bugging him? Maybe it was something else rattling around in his head, unfinished business he'd left behind in Tokyo?

He sat back in the armchair, relieved at being about to do some positive thinking for a change. What had he left undone in Japan? Not the affair with Marian because that had been over for several months. Had he transferred all his personal things? Did he owe anybody money? What about his own bank accounts? Then what was it? Something hidden.

Always much more going on than met the eye. He'd made a mistake, thinking he could crack "Japan, Inc." No outsider could, especially not an American. But it had been the secret consortium of a few key business and government leaders nicknamed Japan, Inc. that had forced the nation's economy forward at a hellish pace and was now, with inflation eating the heart out of the yen, facing the prospect of a bust as big as the previous boom.

Burris found himself smiling. There was still a bit of Pearl Harbor virus in the American bloodstream. We wanted them to succeed, our yellow brethren, but we weren't above smiling when they tripped and fell on their faces.

Japan, Inc. would now begin to bolster what it had by conventional means and strike out in new and unconventional ways to recover its lost momentum. Knowing the "face" they had lost in the current economic setbacks, Burris wouldn't have been surprised to learn that the secret masters of Japan had grown reckless in reaching for more.

Burris knew that for the Japanese there are no such things as bygones. Past coexists with present. It may have had to do with ancestor worship, their religion, or their reverence for clan and national honor. But the fact was that Japan, Inc. still sweated with shame at the memory of Pearl Harbor and the ultimate, ignominious defeat in fire and hell at Hiroshima.

That alone, he decided now as he sat in the armchair, would be enough to guarantee that Japan, Inc. would keep trying—even in ways that were wildly extreme—to redress economic disaster and rekindle national pride.

Funny, he thought, to sit here and contemplate such terrible things about the Japanese. He had liked them. They were friendly to him, even though he stuck out like a Labrador pup in a kennel of kittens. He had made genuine friends of a few, which was more than he could say for his relations with Westerners in Tokyo.

He knew that the ruthlessness of Japan, Inc. was not typical of all the country's businesses and business leaders, just of an important handful, a handful in which dreams of national honor still smoldered.

Did anyone suspect what insane things were being dreamed? The handful of dreamers had reached out in every direction for power, upward into the highest echelons of Japanese industry, downward into the tightly controlled underworld of organized crime. To most people the massacre at Lod Airport, carried out by Japanese gunmen in the name of Palestinian liberation, looked senseless, irrational.

Only later, when the Arab states began to sign preferential oil agreements with Japan in return for major Japanese industrial involvement, did the hand of the dreamers show more clearly.

Burris sighed unhappily, wondering if even his Japanese friends suspected such things or whether they were as innocent as the rest of the world when it came to understanding their own business leaders.

A few would have their suspicions, just as he did. He'd never mentioned them to anyone at UBCO, of course. Over the years Burris had become too adept at the game of corporate advancement to single himself out as a Cassandra. Nobody wanted to hear nasty things that couldn't be proved. The bearer of such tidings was set aside as some kind of nut.

Burris nodded slowly to himself. Play the game the team way. No negative thinking.

And stop worrying about Japan. Switzerland is your problem.

He reached across for the sheaf of papers Curtis had left him and riffled through the pages on Staeli Internationale, GmbH. The unusual thing Curtis had developed for him—which would have taken Burris months to do on his own—was a description of how the various parts of the Staeli empire related to each other.

He saw, for instance, that banking had been kept quite separate from the chemical and steel interests. Even though the Staeli bank financed a lot of Staeli manufacturing, it had other major clients. And the Staelis had gone to some pains to make sure their manufacturing interests were partly financed by banks other than their own.

All of this was simply good business, dispersion of risk. But it had other advantages. The fantastic profits of the pharmaceutical divisions, for instance, ranging far above the 50 and 100 per cent level, piped cash that could be used by the Staeli bank for lending purposes. But the fact that the Staeli factories also got financing from other banks was a master stroke of business acumen. It told the other banks: be good to us, boys, and you get more of our business.

A lovely come-on. Sitting there rereading the Xeroxed pages, Burris quickly added up some of the chemical and steel volume figures and decided he'd be happy if through some stroke of sheer good luck he could get to handle even 10 per cent of their financial needs through UBCO.

He paused and looked up, his eyes unfocusing, as he fantasized about such a major business coup.

For that, after all, was what he had been sent to Basel to do.

Palmer could talk grandly of overall strategy. But the day-to-day tactics of carving out a chunk for UBCO lay in being considered a prime financial source by the big business interests here.

Until now, UBCO and the other American banks in Switzerland had been kept pinched and skinny by the big Swiss banks. They were being limited to consumer financing and small, short-range business loans. The big stuff was reserved by the Swiss for themselves. One could hardly blame them for trying to limit foreign banks to this minor role.

With the tremendous freedom any Swiss bank had to invest as it pleased, as soon as its volume reached a respectable level the entire bank turned into a gigantic money-making machine. It wasn't just that money made money, or that more money made more money.

No, there was a critical mass to money, just as there was to plutonium or U-235. Before it grew to this weight, it was just a heavy metal. But when it reached critical mass it became something else, wildly powerful. An A-bomb, the guts of an H-bomb, as it spewed forth immense, endless shafts and showers of energy.

Building UBCO until its volume reached critical mass would give the bank Swiss entry into the financing of gigantic multinational companies, the colossi that ruled the world, the faceless giants who decided which governments reigned and which fell, who lived and who died.

UBCO already financed many of these global enterprises, but not through a sizable Swiss subsidiary that enjoyed Swiss banking freedom. Once Burris had raised such a subsidiary to critical mass, what couldn't UBCO do? It was already funding such corporations. Now it could also operate their cash arbitrage, safeguard their secret slush-fund accounts, handle payoffs to generals and prime ministers, supervise the corporations' marketing cartels, underwrite their speculative securities, administer their Eurobond issues, sequester their gold reserves, manage their control of patents and franchises, provide Swiss-franc accounts for multicurrency payrolls, discreetly hoard each executive's personal holdings, transfer and hide the deposits of corrupt government and military officials, expedite currency exchange at the most favorable rate of the hour or the day, execute forward contracts in cash and commodities—

And put its men on the board of directors of each customer corporation. Becoming privy to the inside thinking, becoming part of the planning apparatus . . . this was the final weight that triggered a critical mass of money into an explosion of superprofits. To achieve this, a bank would—

Someone knocked at the door. Burris practically leaped out of the armchair, as if something hidden inside it had ejected him. He made for the telephone, stopped, blinked. Good Christ! He shook his head and went to the door. Cracking up.

The waiter placed the small tray on the end table. It held a glass and an opened bottle of beer. "Shall I pour it, Herr Burris?"

"No. Thanks." He handed him a one-franc piece and let him out of the big sitting room.

Burris sat down and stared at the open bottle. "Warteck Tambour Helles Starkbier," the label read. Burris' lips moved, mouthing the words under his breath. He'd definitely have to pick up German.

The label and the trademark included a drawing of three clowns pounding on drums. Three-country corner. Three kings. Three clowns? Three languages, too, not just German, but French and, down where Palmer lived, Italian.

Three Japanese.

He picked up the cold bottle. He poured the beer. As he settled back to sip it, he realized he'd made a mistake not bringing Curtis with him.

CHAPTER 12

The orange Magna jolted along the gravel path between the tall needle cypresses. It cut around to one side of the house and pulled up at the delivery entrance of Schloss Staeli. Erich got out without opening the door, jumped up on the loading platform and pounded on the kitchen door.

"Uschi!"

The housekeeper opened the door and allowed Erich to capture her hand and kiss it several times. This pinkened her complexion sufficiently to rob her of the power of speech.

"Up in the office?" Erich said, indicating the floor above by raising his eyebrows.

"Does she expect you, Herr Erich?"

"Didn't Wolf-Dietrich telephone from the gatehouse?"

Without waiting for an answer, Erich made his way through the immense kitchen, counters topped with zinc, copper pots high overhead hanging from ancient black-iron S-hooks. He ducked out through the butler's pantry and took a shortcut to avoid going through one of the dining rooms to reach the stairs. This was not the formal staircase that visitors used. It was the back stairs the servants and family employed when they were in a hurry.

Erich was, indeed, in a hurry. The interview with Uncle-to-be Dieter had taken twice as long as he'd expected. And he had to be back in Basel before six o'clock to dress for his very first dinner with a certain Madame Michele, who promised to be quite a bit more than just an enjoyable dinner companion.

"Margit?"

He stuck his head into her office-sittingroom and saw her put down the telephone. Either old Wolf-Dietrich was slowing up, or he'd driven the Magna faster than he realized. His fiancée had just been informed of his arrival. She managed to smile and put her cheek up for a kiss. Erich decided to do a thorough job of embracing her and kissing both cheeks.

"Is that how the English kiss?" he asked then.

Margit's face went dark, rather than pale. As Erich watched her with his unblinking gaze, he realized that he had never seen her grow pale when surprised or angry. From somewhere deep inside, blood suffused her face and darkened her skin ever so slightly. Fascinating.

"English?" Her brown eyes had darkened, too. Storm warnings. Erich patted her arm and sat down on the edge of the long walnut refectory table.

"Your loving cousin Walter," he said then, "had the audacity to awaken me this morning with some churlish demand for your true whereabouts. His spies had reported you at the Mirabelle in London. Is the saddle of lamb as good as ever?"

The dark eyes regarded him as steadily as he watched her.

"Since when do you run Walter's errands?" she asked. Her voice sounded husky and Erich could see faint signs that her eye make-up had been patted rather too quickly. Had she been crying?

"I am no man's errand boy," he promised her. "On the other hand, if it's a woman . . ." He tried one of his sharp, V-like smiles, turning his face into Harlequin for a moment. It usually amused Margit, but not this afternoon. "You're angry at me," he said then. "And it's I who should be angry at you."

"For what?"

"For not taking me with you to the Mirabelle."

This time she smiled, but faintly. "What else did Walter tell you about me?"

"Nothing. I was supposed to tell him things. Fortunately, I knew nothing of interest."

"Wouldn't you rather keep it that way?"

Erich nodded. "Definitely." He glanced at the welter of papers on the desk. "Catching up?"

"That reminds me. We've been invited to the Noulli dinner on the fourteenth. Can you make it?"

He frowned. "You received one invitation for both of us?"

"Like everyone else," Margit said, "Beata Noulli would like us permanently merged as one social unit."

"To hell with Beata Noulli."

"Then I'll refuse. Or will you make your own apologies?"

"Dear God, Basel." Erich watched his fiancée with what seemed to be his usual staring intensity, but his thoughts had started to move sideways. He blinked, getting back to business. "No, let's go. The Noulli table is five cuts above the best restaurant in town. And Georg believes in a well-stocked bar."

"*D'accord. Et tu, chérie? Ça marche?*"

Erich shrugged. "*Lentement.* I would have been here sooner, but my long-postponed quarterly interrogation by Uncle Dieter was held today. As a matter of fact, this was the Christmas interview which I managed to delay until just now."

"This is the year of decision," Margit said in a dark voice that matched her look. "Do you know what my family calls me? The Problem."

"Your spy system is still working, I see."

"I've always known what they called me behind my back," she

said. "And I've long ago stopped spying on them. There's no one I can trust to do the work for me."

"I am, as always, your faithful errand boy. You know that." He produced one of his Mephistophelian grins, all V's, which normally made her laugh.

This time the smile was a real one. She patted his cheek and sat down at the table. She was looking out the windows now at the Rhine. It was that hour before dusk when the almost horizontal sunlight cast a long black shadow to the right of every tree and turned the air orange. Erich watched the view. It would not be all that bad when they were married. There would be moments of peace as long as they respected each other's right to live separate lives.

"You won't mind it that much," Margit said in a low voice, reading his thoughts.

He got up and stood behind her. "How's this pose? Formal enough?" He laid a hand on her shoulder, mimicking a photograph from the previous century. "I could wear my hat."

"The better to cut and run every evening." She stroked his fingers for a moment as they lay on her shoulder. "It will be a very Basler marriage."

"Aber ganz richtig."

"You mean, consummated?" she asked. *"Natürlich.* There must be an heir. Tell me, Erich, do you make boys or girls?"

"What?"

"The sex of the child is determined by the father's genes. Well?"

"What do you take me for? This isn't the age of the Hapsburgs. I haven't left a trail of bastards across Europe."

"No? A tribute to modern contraceptives, then."

He went around the table and sat down across it from her. "I can guess what you want. A girl."

"Why do you say that?"

He merely shook his head slowly from side to side by way of answer. Then: "You're very hard for other people to read, Margit. But you have never tried to mislead me, nor I you. I read you."

"Yes." She thought for a moment and then laughed out loud. "Do you remember Vienna?"

"What?"

"That time we checked into the Sacher on a Saturday night? You *do* remember the female pharmacist?"

"Remember? That moment gave me my most surefire technique for picking up women in strange cities." He nodded. "Your period came on suddenly and it was Sunday morning and I had to trudge along the Kärtnerstrasse trying to find a pharmacy that was open. But there was one near the Opera, remember? And when I asked the girl for what I wanted, it worked the most amazing change in our relationship to each other. I was no longer a stranger off the street, perhaps with a toothache or an upset stomach. I mean, it suddenly worked wonders."

"I waited hours for you. I was sure you'd been run over by a car."

"That episode opened my eyes," Erich said. "It works. It never fails. London, Paris, Rome, even New York, where very few female pharmacists are worth looking at twice."

"Erich, you will never change, will you?"

"Never. I can't tell you how grateful I am to you for leading me to this ploy. I mean, it's so simple. With a brief request one opens up doors. One's immediately on an intimate basis with the girl. The only loose end is whether she can get away from the pharmacy for a while."

"Eventually, I'm sure." She watched him for a moment. "Let me tell you, Erich, that the same surefire technique, if divulged to another man, wouldn't work. I mean, give yourself some credit."

He turned to look at the river. "Then why doesn't it work between you and me?" he asked in a different voice. "Vienna, you'll recall, was supposed to have been a trial run for us."

"Which got me so upset my period came on early."

"Ending the trial run." He swung back to face her. "But there's always something to help you fend me off. Why? You're not a virgin. What are we saving each other for?"

She burst out laughing at this and Erich watched her grow less wary, more at ease. The dark look had gone. Her eyes were almost hazel. "What, indeed."

She made a helpless gesture, as if trying to dismiss her hands from her body and let them fly away on their own. "It's been such a blameless engagement," she said then. "There has never been anything between us that I couldn't confide to my journal."

"You're still keeping it?"

"Why not? To whom can I confide any girlish qualms?"

"You? Qualms? Nonsense."

"I have them," she insisted. "And I have no confidante—the Americans call it a girlfriend—to exchange confidences with. I'm even wary of my journal. Did you ever try keeping one?"

"Now and then. I generally forget." He gave her his Satanic smile again because she was showing signs of growing depressed once more. "So," he said in a mock-villainous voice, "I'm your only confidant, eh? Very interesting. No psychoanalyst? No lover? *Tr-è-es intéressant.* The solemn responsibility of it is too heavy for my shoulders, you know."

"All responsibilities are too heavy for you."

"Exactement. Je ne suis pas sérieuse."

"Never serious about anything."

"Except you, my dear."

She smiled cynically. "But of course," she said with sarcasm.

"I must be. Your family demands it.'"

"Of course they do, the swine."

"Dieter's weight is beginning to bear down harder on me," he told her. "This year the pressure will become unbelievable. Already I feel it. And so will you."

He watched her with his usual wide-open stare. She seemed oddly distracted, not really listening that closely to him. "Your mind's elsewhere, is that it?"

She shook her head. "I had been sitting here all afternoon thinking about old things. The old days. Even an old lover." Her face grew grave.

"Which old lover?" Erich pounced.

She got up and moved aimlessly about the room. "Everything will happen with us, Erich. We will marry. We will have sex. We will have a child." She stopped abruptly in front of the wicker chaise longue.

"Eventually?"

She failed to respond. He watched her for a moment, her tall body motionless, her short dark hair with its slight curl reflecting the orange glint of the late sun outside the window. After a while he got up and went to her.

He put his arm around her. He could see that she was staring down at the chaise, as if hypnotized. But the moment she felt his arm she moved sideways, spell broken, and turned to face him. "Yes?"

"Everything all right?" he asked.

"Perfectly." Her face was white. A tiny muscle at the corner of her eye kicked twice. He heard the very faint tremor in her voice.

Their long friendship was based on maintaining a certain distance. He was perhaps pushing too close. "Good," he said, hoping it sounded sincere.

She flashed him a small, quick conspirator's smile, as if agreeing to keep the distance between them. "Erich," she said then, "what do you know about famine?"

His eyes widened slightly, like television camera lenses trying to pull in more light. "Personally, as much as you. Nothing."

"There was a Britisher fellow who said we had started to starve out the redundant people of the earth and by the year 2000 we would have done it."

Erich shrugged massively. "What is redundant? There are people who would say you and I are redundant, *chérie.*"

"He meant technologically redundant. People idled by mechanization. The trend toward mechanizing everything, even agriculture. That sort of thing. He was very persuasive and very, ah, what is the word . . . dour?"

"Sounds like a Bolshie."

"Yes, and also a hereditary earl, I believe. Fully as redundant as we."

They giggled guiltily together for a moment. Then Margit sighed. "I wish I could simply put the whole thing out of my mind. But, you see, he holds that the industrial nations are responsible, particularly the big industries. And, of course, the banks who finance them."

"Ah."

"Don't say 'ah' as if you'd suddenly learned I had a clubfoot."

"Nothing so obvious," he teased. "You have a social conscience, and, in the end, that's even more crippling."

"Yes, but Erich . . ." She paused and thought for a moment, her eyes fastened on him. "Look here, if we are redundant and they are redundant, why are we alive and healthy and why are they dying?"

"Questions like that," he said, "will eventually do one in."

"How so?"

"Tempt one to redress the inequity."

"How?"

"Oh . . ." He laughed softly. "Suicide?"

CHAPTER 13

"They haven't the slightest idea of what I'm up to," Walter assured his father.

The two men were sitting in Dieter's office overlooking the Aeschenvorstadt. Beyond the door to the open executive-desk area, everyone had left for the day. Dieter's round face had cooled in the presence of his son to the pale color of a full moon as it rises over the horizon, flattened slightly like a pumpkin. He had put on the pince-nez which he needed in order to read, but which he usually kept hidden from the rest of the world. Through the two round lenses he examined his son's face and found both vanity and foolishness there, as always.

"How does it come," he began in a sententious tone, "that a man grows up a Staeli and he still is able to tell himself he knows the mind of a business adversary, especially an Oriental?"

"Papa, this is *narrischkeit*. I can read these Japanese as much as I have to. I know what makes them tick."

"You hardly know their names."

"It's their affiliations that count."

"One of them," Dieter pointed out, "is still anonymous to you."

Mulishly, Walter shook his head from side to side as deliberately as he usually nodded up and down. His whitish face and hair looked washed out in the afternoon light. "He is a Colonel Sato," he said then.

"Colonel of what?" his father demanded. "Army? Police?"

"I got the distinct impression it was, ah, security forces."

Dieter Staeli removed his pince-nez and put them in the inner pocket of his leather-piped jacket. He had seen enough to know that Walter was still Walter. "In business," he said then, "a distinct impression is no substitute for verified identification."

"But that is—"

"Why is a Colonel involved in this?"

"It's only a mat—"

"And why have they capitulated on the use of their name? Why have they suddenly allowed it and the 'Made in Japan' legend to be removed?"

"I told you they—"

"When the previous two companies refused point-blank to do so?" Dieter cut in again. "This is a point of national honor with the Japanese. To see them forego it is to see something very strange indeed."

"If you would only—"

Dieter stood up. *"Genug!* Commit the whole plan to writing and bring it before the board on Friday."

"You don't understand, Papa. I have signed a letter of intention that is binding on me as it is on them."

"Nonsense." Dieter made shooing movements. "We will decide on it Friday. And unless I am very mistaken, the board will turn it down. One cannot be too prudent with the Japanese. On your way out," he added heavily, "find Ruc and send him up to see me at once."

"Ruc? He'll have gone home by now."

"Not Ruc. He is a late-stayer, like me." And as you should be too, the father added by his tone of voice.

Walter backed out of the room, happy to get beyond range of his father's usual dressing-down. Dieter watched him go. Foolish contract to sign with the Japanese, he thought. It did little for Switzerland except to employ out-of-work watchmakers. Why should this be a concern of the Staeli clan? Let the watchmakers rot in idleness.

When he arrived, it was typical of Ottokar Ruc that he stood a bare two inches inside the open doorway of Dieter Staeli's office and waited silently, as if the great man's antennae alone were enough to warn him of the arrival of an underling.

Ottokar Ruc was a permanent underling of the type that Swiss banking relies upon, even though Ruc himself was only second-generation Swiss. His family had emigrated around the turn of the century from Slovakia, where the name rhymes with swoosh. After two generations in Basel, Ottokar now unfailingly pronounced it to rhyme with book.

Whether because of his once-foreign origins or some other ingrained feeling of total inferiority, Ottokar Ruc was the perfect bank underling, arriving early, working late, scrupulous in his accounting, thorough in his records, never asking for more money, barely taking as much vacation time as allowed, cheerfully watching younger men get promoted over his head, gladly breaking them in to the new job, accepting any increment in salary, no matter how small, with gratitude and God-fearing loyalty. He had become more Swiss than the Swiss.

After nearly five minutes, during which Herr Staeli had neglected to look up, Ottokar Ruc cleared his throat, the tiniest of dry noises that the chirp of one cricket could have drowned out.

Dieter looked up. He had known of Ruc's arrival from the moment it occurred, but he had waited more or less as a matter of policy to allow the underling to imagine the worst. Instant dismissal. Jail sentence. Dieter knew the guilts that lurked beneath the placid surface of many Swiss, especially the naturalized ones.

"Roosh, come in." He watched the little man advance. They were the same age, and Ruc was perhaps as plump as Dieter, but he walked with a slink. He had hastily thrown on a rusty black alpaca jacket and the collar was still awry. "Fix your collar."

"I beg the Herr Staeli's pardon?" Blinking eyes, red-rimmed, rabbity.

"Your collar, Rooschl."

The eyes flared wide in horror and the hands flew to adjust the offending jacket collar. "Wh-what does the Herr Staeli wish?"

Dieter listened to the third-person in Ruc's form of address. "Your daughter, Christa, is still in Foreign Accounts?"

"Yes, Herr Staeli."

"And has been for nearly three years?"

"Yes, Herr Staeli."

"Is this all you would wish for such a well-trained young woman?"

"Yes, Herr Staeli."

Dieter bit down on his impatience. "We have had our eye on

this girl for some time. She might do very well in Gold Deposits, at a good increase in salary."

The reddish eyes blinked, blinked. The head nodded a bit to one side, as if Ottokar Ruc was testing the air for a trap, or hadn't really understood what was being offered or that there was an "if" hanging in the air.

"But she must merit such an advance, Roosh."

"Yes, Herr Staeli."

"I understand she lives apart from you, with a suitable young woman as roommate?"

"Yes, Herr Staeli."

"I want you to get in touch with your daughter this evening, Ruck." Dieter squinted slightly to make sure his changed pronunciation had gotten through. "I want no one to overhear what you have to tell her. I especially do not want her roommate to know anything of this, Ruck."

"Yes, Herr Staeli."

"Tell your daughter to report to my office before work tomorrow, at eight-fifteen. Right here in this room. I have a confidential project for her to undertake. The nature of it is confidential even from you, Ruck. But I want you to explain to her that if she performs this job effectively, the position in Gold Deposits is hers."

"Yes, Herr Staeli."

"Goodnight, Roosh."

Like Walter, Ottokar Ruc backed out of the presence. Most people did.

Dieter glanced at his watch and saw that he still had time to stop by his club for a beer or two before going home. He smiled and his face once again resembled a refulgent sun. Dieter, who normally examined and tested his motives much more honestly than his son ever did, failed to distinguish tonight whether he felt so well because he was about to enjoy good beer or because he enjoyed twitting Ruc about his name or had just set in motion, with extreme gravity and power, the whole Ruc matter.

It was imperative, during this crucial twenty-ninth year of Margit Staeli's life, that he have an eye and ear into her boudoir. If the Ruc girl were clever she would easily tease out of her roommate, Elfi, all the superficial dross of Margit's personal life. And if Elfi proved as clever as Christa Ruc, she too could benefit from Dieter

Staeli's generosity. A cash bonus every month would not be un-welcome, would it, for a few additional tidbits of information?

The information might be trivial, useless. One never knew. Or it might be something Dieter could use to prove what an irre-sponsible girl his niece really was. The whole weight of Swiss tradition, the *Patriarchats,* the very law of the land, was his first bastion against Margit taking control of the Staeli empire. But it was a bastion with cracks in the walls. Any year now the *Abs-chaffnung* might be passed by the legislators. For the first time in Swiss history, a wife would have an equal say in family decisions with her husband, a grown daughter with her father, a niece with her uncle. The power of having the last word in a decision would be removed from the Swiss male. A crack this wide in the wall of a bastion was a serious threat indeed.

His second line of defense was to make sure she was married before her thirtieth birthday. She would thus inherit from her fa-ther as Margit Lorn, not Margit Staeli. It was a fine point, but bat-teries of expensive attorneys had assured him it would hold firm and that Erich would have real control of the Staeli holdings. But this defense, too, had flaws. It could lead to a protracted and public struggle through the Swiss courts, for one thing. For an-other, Erich showed little promise of being co-operative.

Finally, therefore, Dieter had a last-ditch line of fortification.

It was a tricky proposition. If he could collect enough damaging material he might be able to win a sort of silent showdown with his niece, perhaps in a private session of bargaining. He would show her the evidence and calmly clip her wings. The tricky part of the problem lay in the fact that she might not sit still for clip-ping. She might dare him to do his worst with the blackmail evi-dence, whatever it might be. It was very difficult to know how things would turn out, since he did not yet know what the evi-dence was. Or even if any existed.

No longer smiling broadly, Dieter straightened his desk, locked its drawers, closed and locked his office door and left the bank. As a last ditch, blackmail was awfully chancy. But, in trench warfare, what wasn't?

He managed a grim smile as he left the building and stepped into his waiting car. He had not forgotten the problem with Walter, but he had managed to keep it toward the back of his mind. One problem at a time and, these days, all of them involving his family.

He sat there, staring at the back of his chauffeur's neck, wondering what the Japanese had up their sleeves. He harbored no illusion that Walter had the acumen to outsmart anyone except, possibly, himself.

CHAPTER 14

At the end of Orly Sud's international lounge, opposite the corner where the terminal hotel is found, stands a bar that is well-stocked with things to drink, although what it offers to eat is usually the French idea of a sandwich, cardboard-dry white bread coated with oleo and hiding a paper-thin slice of desiccated ham, the whole designed to foster thirst.

None of the three Japanese was eating. Air France 274, the transpolar flight to Tokyo, was slightly delayed but would be leaving soon and dinner would be served aboard. It was the prospect of Air France food on the long flight that had tempted the three away from their own national airline. However, the JAL flight had left long before their shuttle plane from Basel, so it was with a clear conscience now that they anticipated the good French dinner awaiting them in First Class, preceded by the usual caviar and Stolichnaya vodka. The luxury would more than make up for the fact that, by the time they reached Tokyo, they would have been in planes or cars or at meetings a total of thirty-six consecutive hours.

They had ordered three bottles of Kirin beer and slowly sipped the Japanese brew at one of the round tables near the bar that overlooked the main concourse of Orly. All three kept their heavy, locked attaché cases on their laps as they sat in silence and sipped the pleasantly strong beer.

Finishing his Kirin first, one man reached into the pocket of his jacket and brought out a small flat black plastic hand calculator. He glanced at his watch, punched a few figures into the computer and read the result on a row of tiny lighted red figures.

One of the other Japanese reached over to take the calculator from him. He read the row of red figures and handed the instrument to the third man, who put down his beer, erased the figures, glanced at his watch and punched up the equation again. He got the same result and nodded. It was thus that they always worked, as a team, checking each other at every step of the way.

Then he turned the calculator upside down and opened a slide in its back. He removed some penlight batteries from a cavity, then carefully eased open the two halves of the case as if shucking an oyster. Inside, held in his two hands, lay a miniaturized array of tiny silicon chips in printed circuits of thin copper lines etched onto a plastic wafer the size of a playing card. Silently, the other two Japanese bent over the gutted instrument as if scrutinizing the entrails of a sacrificial chicken.

The man who had opened the case took a ballpoint pen from his outside breast pocket and gently touched the plastic wafer with it. The other two shook their heads negatively.

He then indicated the discarded batteries with his pen and again the other Japanese shook their heads. Then the man with the pen inserted it under the wafer and slowly levered up the plastic sheet.

Beneath lay more electronic circuitry, further layers of amber plastic wafers imprinted with copper lines. The pen tip hesitated for a moment, then lightly touched a shiny black plastic capsule in one corner, hidden before this by the topmost layer of circuitry. The capsule resembled a pill that might be used to treat a large horse. Both watching Japanese nodded affirmatively in what was evidently another form of rechecking their work as a team.

Face impassive, he tweaked the black capsule out of the computer's innards. It came away neatly, as if it had merely been plugged in. He closed the computer's plastic case and pocketed the big capsule. Then he handed the calculator to the man who had first produced it. This he carefully stowed in his jacket pocket. The three men sat motionless for a while. Then the man with the computer patted his pocket and nodded sagely up and down several times.

Whether this gesture was a comic one meant to mimic Walter Staeli's habitual movement, or not, it had the effect of sending all three men into equal laughter.

PART TWO

Here I stay, in this town where I have been bored
for the past ten years.
　　　　—Letter from Switzerland, sent by
　　　　　Mme. de Staël to Mme. Récamier, 1811

CHAPTER 15

The little orange L-2 Magna produced a snoring noise halfway between a rasp and a rattle as Erich Lorn shifted into third gear forward and forced the vintage car up a sharp rise in the road leading south from Basel.

It was much earlier in the morning than Erich was used to, barely nine o'clock. The fact that he was out of bed and miles from home was a tribute to a new woman in Erich's life. Last evening with Madame Michele had been exciting but tantalizing. Her long black Lincoln limousine had called for her on the stroke of midnight and, like Cinderella, she had vanished from Erich's arms as he kissed her goodnight under the tiny canopy of a discotheque.

He had done everything right, he reflected now. The dinner had been the best Basel could offer, the wines carefully chosen in advance to avoid the usual discussion with the sommelier, which Erich considered too French a scene to be anything but vulgar. The disco had been small, the music loud enough to make it necessary to whisper in one's companion's ear, but not so loud as to produce physical pain. Nevertheless, Madame Michele had not dismissed the black limousine when it arrived. She had, instead, permitted the goodnight kiss . . . and vanished.

Erich smiled slightly, his eyes staring wide open at the road ahead, the smile faintly lopsided with a certain cynical appreciation for a professional job of teasing.

Everything about Michele was professional. What she had worn last night, modest and also revealing, was like her conversation, intimate and also impersonal. She had been very good at emitting simultaneous signals of "come closer" and "keep your distance."

And, of course, he reminded himself now, she was too experienced to fall victim to any of his more practiced approaches. Knowing this, he'd fallen back on being more or less himself, not very serious, much the way he was with Margit. He hadn't yet decided—but he would someday soon—which approach was going to land Michele in his second-floor bedroom. The effort would be worth it.

Consider the advantages of such a woman, he thought as he wheeled the antique sports car down a long slope, the morning sun pouring in on him from the left, touching his ear and cheek with warmth. To begin with, she was attractive. She didn't have Margit's lean, clothes-horse look, but Erich really didn't care that much for the type. Cosmopolitan he might be, but he was still Swiss enough to like a rounder woman.

Michele was rounder. She had legs almost as long as Margit's, but a shorter torso, full breasts and a slight swell to her rear that Erich itched to run his hand over. Her face was not round but broad, with a wide chin and Magyar cheekbones, the kind of face that never aged.

Which, considering Michele's profession, was just as well.

Madame Michele's profession was youth. Even after a long evening in her company, and after listening to the gossip about her that had flown around Europe over the past few years, Erich had no real idea how she'd started her career.

She was rumored to be a doctor with a legitimate medical degree from a prestigious teaching hospital in Vienna. It was also whispered that she had been nothing more there than a nurse, if that. She was said to be Hungarian, no, Dutch, no, Italian. They were certain she'd been married twice at least, or three times. That her last husband's name had, in fact, been Michele. Or else it was the Christian name with which she'd been born. She was rumored to be well over forty, no, thirty-six, no, forty-eight.

Erich's cynical smile broadened unevenly. When there is that much mystery about someone's private life, the mystery is self-stimulated. This much Erich knew, that Michele retained two extremely expensive public relations concerns, one in Paris and one in New York, to make sure she remained to the public the same tantalizing mystery she'd been last night to Erich.

But about her spas, her clinics and her treatments, there was no such mystery. There was, in fact, the opposite, an avalanche of publicity. Originally it had begun to pour down through women's magazines which Erich rarely saw except in the boudoirs of his lady friends. The emphasis of these breathless articles had been on rejuvenation through a variety of means, physical, chemical, psychological. If the youth-producing results of Madame's treatments might be in doubt, there was no denying the magazine prose was juvenile.

But lately her message had been carried by other media: news magazines, journals of science written for laymen, newspapers, even television documentaries. The lever used by her publicity people had been controversy.

Somehow—Erich had no idea how these things were arranged —a prominent British physician and geriatrist had been induced to attack Madame Michele's reputation on an early-evening interview show over London television. Erich supposed now, as he steered the Magna along the road, that the scientist had been as incorruptible as anyone else, but had been lured into the attack in much the way one attracted a chicken to the place one chopped off its head, by a trail of tidbits along the ground.

There was something basically simple-minded about honest British scientists anyway, he decided. They spent so much time perfecting their absent-minded professor act that they truly became the artless gulls of all time.

Once launched, the rather wild attack on Michele's reputation instantly drew an overkill counteroffensive of heavy explosives, sniper fire and poison gas from dozens of her former patients (or were they clients? Erich didn't know the legal requirements of the situation and neither did anyone else), many of them not only prominent, but beloved and, in some cases titled.

Film stars of international magnitude sang her praises. A former Archbishop of Canterbury had benefited mightily from her ministrations. Distant galactic brilliances were invoked by discreet mention of such names as De Gaulle, Pius XII, Picasso, and other prodigies of creative longevity.

Whatever the honest British doctor had thought he was unlocking, what escaped this particular Pandora's box had been an almost overwhelming tidal wave of publicity geared not to self-praise but to self-defense, always a more admirable posture.

In the distance, touched by the flat rays of the morning sun as they swept across the low hills, Erich could now see the grouping of buildings large and small that made up Michelebad, flagship spa-clinic of Madame Michele's network. Much of the area was devoted to hush-hush research work, but here every weapon in her arsenal of age-defying treatments was also to be found.

Erich had no idea why Michele had invited him to visit her this morning. If it was for the purpose of further impressing him, she had no need. If it was to continue their flirtation, the clinic was not Erich's idea of a suitable locale.

If it was anything else, he was at a loss to know it, any more than he could have correctly guessed her age. She could look and act younger than he, and occasionally had last night. That she was older than he seemed certain, but by how much he couldn't tell. Five years? Ten? Appearance was no clue. Conversation told him little, except to verify that her experience with the opposite sex was easily equal to his. But experience can be crammed into a few years. So he was left with the mystery, as she knew he would be.

The Magna snored up another incline. Michelebad was surrounded by a high wall of dressed fieldstone, random sizes and colors of rock that had been squared off to fit neatly together into a row the height of a tall man. Thick wrought-iron uprights studded the top of the wall at one-meter intervals.

The spaces between were filled with thinner wrought-iron rods welded into a kind of heraldic "M" that effectively barred entrance. At this distance, of course, it was impossible to see the barbed wire carefully entwined in the top level of ironwork, but an uninvited visitor might learn of its presence all too painfully.

Motoring up to the entrance, seeing the enclave for mile after mile as the road wound toward the gate, Erich got a feeling of unbroken space. The wall was formidable but not institutional. It had been designed to keep people out, not to hamper an escape from within.

In some ways the place reminded him of Schloss Staeli, which occupied an estate somewhat larger and, of course, much more lavishly landscaped. But where the Staeli mansion dominated the land, here there were several buildings, none overpowering in size. Two were modestly large country homes. The rest were one-story brick affairs set in their own little copses of birch, poplar and hemlock. The effect was that of a small, exclusive village rather than one central abode, not unlike the Hameau that Marie Antoinette had caused to be laid out on the grounds of Versailles, pleasant, quiet, and costly.

A very small sign which nevertheless presented the same instructions in four languages, told Erich to pull to a halt several meters in front of the gatehouse. He watched his front wheels roll over a kind of trigger plate in the pavement.

Immediately the red lights on two small television cameras went on. The long lens on one seemed focused on the Magna's license-plate area, the other on the entire car. A guard in cornflower-blue uniform, something on the order of what a chorus boy might wear in a musical comedy about the Franco-Prussian War, stepped outside the gatehouse.

He stood for a moment, eyes fixed on Erich, as if waiting for some signal. It came finally. Even at a distance Erich could hear the high-pitch triple beep. The guard stood aside and, with a flourish as if swishing an invisible cape, indicated that Erich could drive on into the spa proper.

As he steered the little car around a winding road somewhat longer than the *allee* to Schloss Staeli, Erich found himself wondering whether the television-computer control room at Michelebad was as well-equipped as it seemed to be.

It was not easy for even a well-financed company like this to suborn the God-fearing Swiss officials in charge of motor-vehicle registration and get a copy of all license-plate identifications. Considering how many visitors to Michelebad were from other countries, the acquisition of such a list was not even terribly useful. Even more to the point, many guests (clients? patients?) came in hired limousines from the airport, so identifying a vehicle registration number would be valueless. Or would it? More likely, Erich decided, a sharp-eyed observer watched the TV monitors in much the way that a floor manager at a gambling casino watched incoming customers (clients? guests?) and passed or rejected them on the basis of appearance.

The cynical smile now cut a new V in Erich's face. He appreciated highly skilled chicanery perhaps more thoroughly than any other Swiss would admit, even to himself.

He guided the orange car between broad Corinthian columns that supported a large porte-cochere. As he switched off the engine and prepared to leave the car in his usual manner, by legging it over the side of the unopened door, another guard in musical-comedy blue appeared, touched the black leather beak of his kepi and said: *"Herr Lorn, bitte?"*

Erich handed him the keys to the Magna and walked up a broad flight of stone steps. Damn. They did indeed have a vehicle registration list in the security-monitor room. Everything about this woman was impressive.

A third chorus boy in cornflower blue swung open the immense doors, beveled edges of plate glass set in polished brass. *"Will-kommen, Herr Lorn."*

Erich stopped to survey the place, his eyes adjusting from the morning sunlight to the rather darker interior of the immense entry hall. Double curving stairs led up to a second floor and Erich could see by the workmanship that they were of another century, effectively redone, as the walls had been, in a muted off-white that managed to convey a slight undertone of blush.

Erich had never seen such a color. It was white enough, as befitted a spa-clinic, but it was not a white he had ever before experienced. The admixture of a faint peach-rose undertone gave the staircases and walls the look of a young virgin's cheek after being told an only slightly improper joke.

He glanced at the long rows of wall sconces, each double, with flame-shaped blubs of low wattage shielded by round shades. The light produced by these lamps was of the same blushing white. Since there were hundreds of the bulbs, the final effect was shadowless, a bath of youth in which even a disinterred mummy would have looked desirable.

Across an expanse of softly blond floor formed by random widths of oak that glowed pinkish yellow under their coats of varnish, a great thin slab of rosy marble seemed to float at table height off the floor. As his eyes grew accustomed to the sourceless, shadowless lighting, Erich saw that Lucite legs supported the marble and the elbows of the attractive young woman who sat at what was obviously an arrival desk. He walked across to her.

"Guten morgen, Herr Lorn," she began as he crossed an invisible perimeter barrier about two meters from the rose marble. "Madame is looking forward very much to your visit."

She got to her feet, a petite girl barely twenty, with short brunette hair and a face absolutely scrubbed of make-up. "Unfortunately," she went on in a voice that handled such concepts without betraying any feeling for their content, "there has been a research problem in Laboratory Three this morning which requires Madame's personal attention. She will be a bit late for her appointment. Until she is free, which should not be too long from now, she hopes you might care to take a look at what Michelebad has to offer. If this is agreeable to you, Herr Lorn, we can leave on our tour at this time and I shall be pleased to serve as your guide. My name is Henriette." She extended her doll's hand, which Erich took, temporarily at a loss for words.

He had met this type of girl before, whose inflections had nothing to do with what she was saying, and who could coolly announce the death by forced rape of a convent of nuns in the same carefully polished tones as she offered a cigarette.

"Is it a long tour?" he asked then, still holding her cold hand.

"It is as long as you wish," she countered, letting her hand go even deader in his grip.

He dropped her hand and glanced at his wristwatch. Nine-thirty. If the tour were half an hour and his talk with Michele (about what?) another hour, could he be back in Basel for lunch? Erich had last evening made an appointment with his fiancée to lunch in one of the better-known hotel dining rooms precisely at twelve-thirty as a public display of togetherness that restated their undying devotion. Both had deemed it politically useful in case further word of Margit's London escapades continued to leak into the business-banking community.

"I would very much like the tour, Henriette," he said then, giving her name the same French pronunciation she had used. "Lead on."

She turned to a door in the wall behind her and opened it. "This coat please, Herr Lorn," she said, extending a plain white laboratory coat to him.

He shrugged into it and buckled the fabric belt, feeling foolish at looking like a pharmacist or dentist or whatever he was supposed to be. "I take it this is absolutely necessary?"

Henriette's eyes widened slightly under carefully combed short black bangs. "This tour," she said then, "is rarely given to anyone, not the press and only rarely to visiting scientists. We will be passing through areas where patients (ah! Erich thought, not customers!) are being treated. It is a deception, of course, but we feel it less alarming to their equanimity if you were to appear to be one of the staff."

Erich found that he liked short girls who used long words like equanimity. One could overlook her mechanical-doll voice and find her rather piquant, in a somewhat dull way. He frowned slightly at such muddled thoughts and decided to keep himself pure in mind for Henriette's employer.

He realized he had been staring at her in his usual unblinking way. Now he saw that Henriette was returning the stare, but absolutely laundered of meaning. "This way, Herr Lorn."

He'd been wrong about the length of the tour. Almost an hour later, he was back in the main building even more impressed with Madame Michele. The woman had a gold mine here, and damned if she'd left an opportunity unturned.

The tour had begun with some of the smaller outlying buildings, many of them laboratories in which banks of caged guinea pigs and white rats chittered and nosed about as Erich passed through. He was never quite certain from Henriette's cool tones and overly polished delivery whether these animals were there for researchers to experiment upon. In all the time Erich stood about watching bearded young men in white coats peering through microscopes and shaking test tubes, he got the strong feeling of watching another act of the same musical comedy to which the Franco-Prussian uniforms belonged.

It was true that Erich had no scientific training—or any other kind, for that matter, since he'd carefully flunked himself out of half the prestigious universities of Europe—but he hadn't seen any of the things with which films and magazine articles had familiarized him, the instruments used to kill, dissect, section, microtome, freeze and otherwise torture and kill little rodents.

There were none of the flat Petri dishes for culturing bacteria. None of the cages had proper identification tags on them. If one were to start looking for a particular rat, it might take all day and an intimate familiarity with rat physiognomy to find the rodent of one's choice.

On the whole, the cages had underimpressed him and, since Henriette had warned him not to talk to the researchers, there was no way to allay his suspicions that he was simply passing through a rat zoo.

On the whole, the vitamin-mineral laboratory was more impressive. Here great chemical balances, sealed inside dustproof glass boxes, were being manipulated by white-coated girls with long white gloves. Centrifuges whirred with impressive silence, whispering of expensive bearings. Vacuum pumps exhausted chambers through which ruby laser beams lanced hotly, impinging on targets where minute samples were reduced to ash.

At one end of the lab a large cloud chamber was being monitored by two young men who tracked the passage of various heavy atomic particles through the mist, snapping dozens of sequence pictures by means of strobe lights and motor-driven Nikons. Cathode tubes glowed greenly as oscilloscopes traced the tormented wave forms of substances or processes about which Erich hadn't a clue. In another corner a massive supersonic vibrator caused various powdered materials to coalesce into molecular mixtures of infinitely discreet separation and dispersion.

In yet a third laboratory the apparatus was primarily nineteenth century in nature, some of it reminiscent of early film versions of *Frankenstein,* with their miles of glass tubing in coils and bends, extremely serious Tesla coils emitting rising violet sparks, and giant copper hemispheres out of Captain Nemo's laboratory aboard the *Nautilus.* A Van de Graff generator turned ceaselessly, feeding static charges into a Leyden jar that a lab assistant periodically discharged with a crack of lightning not unlike the snap of a .22-caliber pistol.

Erich was a little sorry they'd felt it necessary to show him the Karloff Museum of Horrors. None of those ancient instruments had anything to do with anything, did they? Dimly, Erich remembered some of them from his secondary-school physics classes. But in a modern laboratory? What purpose did they serve except to impress gullible visitors, the ones so "rarely" taken on this tour?

And Henriette's cool line of gibberish had finally begun to annoy him, too. He hated being taken for a fool.

". . . unique combination of natural approaches to the problem of aging," had been one of her pivotal phrases, repeated several times as the tour progressed. As nearly as Erich could understand it—which he told himself with some arrogance was a hell of a lot more than most people would—the Michele system took advantage of every scrap of rumor, solid fact and experimental theory known to the worlds of both science and superstition.

Thus, for example, imbedded in the overall regimen, which featured honest vitamin supplements and low-fat meals, were little gobbets of medievalism, including placenta tissue from newborn calves and such long-outmoded substances as royal jelly from queen bees, gland extracts from horses and cows, and mysterious essences from fertilized eggs and rose hips.

The laboratory devoted to the extraction of such substances from natural sources produced such a mélange of odors that Erich had to hurry through it, cutting short his instant acquaintance with overpowering attars of apple, beech bark, ginseng root, sassafras leaf, rauwolfia serpentina, camomile and foxglove.

Henriette also made frequent references to secret natural ingredients, control of which rested exclusively with the Michele laboratories, mysterious essences found in nature that conferred not only a youthful appearance, but the boon of restful sleep and the perhaps doubtful gift of greatly improved memory.

From all this, as the hour progressed, Erich got several impressions he felt certain he was not supposed to get, inferences he should not have drawn. One was a composite picture of the typical patient. Despite Henriette's warning, they had not really broken in on any intimate patient-staff relationships, unless a ten-minute visit to the gymnasium counted.

Here women of various ages over forty, clad in leotards of the universal cornflower blue, practiced in small groups the ageless precepts of Yoga, while others worked out on rowing machines, stationary bicycles and other mechanized instruments of torture. Erich found the combination of Tantric wisdom and electrical apparatus, if not reassuring, at least charming.

By and large, he came to see, the entire place catered to women in fairly good health who could be pummeled and starved into a better figure, made to feel livelier by vitamin-mineral therapy, and jazzed up with some of the mystery ingredients which Erich took to be the usual dexedrine derivatives or perhaps one of the procaines. Such women would leave Michelebad looking and feeling younger, for as long as they held down their weight and kept taking the magic pills.

When, as it had to, the whole thing sagged and fell, they would be back at Michelebad again. Some of them were on their third or fourth visit, Henriette had proudly explained. Just as proudly, she had several times made a point of the fact that surgery had no place in the Michele system. Whether this was out of some deeply felt sense of community with nature or simply that licensed surgeons and back-up medics would be too expensive, Erich never completely determined. About the only thing one could say for Michelebad was that, of all the myriad ways of promoting the look of youth, face-lifting was the only technique not used.

In fact, Erich mused on the walk back to the main building as Henriette led the way between neatly barbered shrubbery, since Nature was the resident goddess of Michelebad, cosmetic surgery would have made a mockery of the rest of the treatment. So much homage had been paid to Nature—such emphasis had been placed on "natural" substances and methods—that recourse to the scalpel would have given the whole game away.

But that, in the end, was what finally impressed him.

The system obviously worked, for a while, and because it rarely flirted with anything even vaguely resembling medical treatment, it stayed clear of the law. Not that Swiss law was hard to evade. In this area, as in so many others, the law of his native land was permissive in the extreme, much more so than in any neighboring country. The smallest corner pharmacy in Switzerland could, and did, sell across the counter substances that anywhere else required a doctor's prescription or were forbidden to be sold under any circumstances.

Nevertheless, Madame Michele was impressive by her shrewd decision to create the appearance of youth "naturally." The word was very much in vogue these days, Erich knew, and carried enough overtones of ecological good as to make it socially acceptable in anyone's home.

A woman freshly returned from Michelebad was someone who could babble freely about her feasts of rauwolfia salad, beech-bark brownies and ginseng soufflé. Since no one had told her precisely what the other mystery ingredients were, she had no idea that she was taking mood-elevating drugs or the procaine derivatives whose effects were still unproved and largely unknown. All she knew was that she felt wonderful. She credited all of this to Nature . . . to Nature and Madame Michele.

Erich removed his lab coat and, as Henriette hung it away in the closet behind the rose-marble reception desk, he glanced at his watch. Well past ten-thirty. Considering the long drive back to Basel, he was starting to run late for his lunch with Margit. And he still had no idea what further mystery Michele had summoned him to discuss.

"It's up the left-hand stairs," Henriette said then. "Turn left again at the top, the double doors at the far end."

Erich eyed her for a moment, his glance wide open. "I beg your pardon?"

"Madame will see you now. Her chambers are up the lef—"

"I see," Erich interrupted. He reached out to shake her hand and found it strangely warm, the palm almost hot. "Thank you." They shook hands and Erich mounted the curving stairs to the left.

On the second floor the walls were a slightly deeper shade of blush, as if a naughtier joke had been whispered in the virgin's ear. Erich turned left. The double doors at the far end were quite large, extending from the floor to the ceiling some four meters above him, curved so that together they formed a gigantic arch through which a Roman legion might return in triumph, bearing slaves and loot.

Erich found himself frowning at the turn of thought in his mind. He reached the double doors and swung them in to open them.

The bed was even wider than the doors, not King size but Imperial, fit for a Caesar. She lay back on a scattering of small pillows in shades ranging from pale pink to an orangey salmon.

She had pulled up her pale, reddish hair, French-chambermaid style, and tied it with a cerise ribbon. That was all she was wearing.

"Close the doors and lock them," she called in a soft, low voice.

CHAPTER 16

It was your typical Japanese throne room except that instead of your typical Emperor, upper teeth stretching his lip in a broad but guarded smile, you had three Emperors in flowing robes embroidered with long-tailed birds of golden thread and sparkling sequins for eyes, flashing white and ice-blue and steel-gray, warning lights, rotating like beacons atop police cars.

Each of the three Emperors talked gravely and well in unison, but each spoke in a different tongue, all of which Burris understood.

The three Japanese seemed to find nothing wrong with speaking together in three languages. Now and then, like motors faintly out of sync, the words they spoke seemed to correspond and run together into one word that was the same in all three languages, in German, in French and in Italian, and that word was Burris' name. His real name, Matt Brzyck.

"Brzyck!" they shouted in unison.

Burris' big body lurched sideways. One heel hit the floor of the hotel room with a thud that opened his eyes. He glanced around the bedroom of his suite in the Drei Könige. The telephone was ringing, a funny, rasping sound like a giant cricket. "Brzyck. Brzyck. Brzyck."

Burris pulled himself back on the bed and sat up on the edge of the mattress, planting his feet on the floor. All his movements were slow, heavy, unsure. "Brzyck, Brzyck." He moistened his dry lips and picked up the telephone.

"Yes?"

"Herr Burris?"

"Yes."

"Moment, bitte."

The receiver next to his ear emitted a series of small clicks. Then: "Matt, is that you?"

The voice sounded familiar, but Burris was as yet in no shape to place it. He felt drugged with sleep. "Yes," he said.

"It's Woods Palmer, Matt."

Burris sat up straighter on the side of the bed and cleared his throat. "Hey! Good morning," he managed to croak. "A friendly voice at last."

The older man's voice, when it began again, spoke in the common accent of their native Midwest, the *r*'s as hard as rocks, the *a*'s as flat as pie plates. "I know this sounds insulting, Matt, but did I wake you up?"

"Did you ever." Burris managed what he hoped sounded like a

chuckle. This man, although retired, was still powerful in UBCO and still, after all, the reason for there being a Matt Burris at UBCO. "Listen, I tried to phone you yesterday evening when I got here but . . ." His voice died out.

Burris' glance swept the room and found a glass half full of what looked like a urine specimen. He reached over and sniffed it, found it was beer and sipped some to relieve the terrible dryness in his mouth and throat. The warm beer had a metallic chemical taste.

"Matt," Palmer was saying, "I think I owe you an explanation. I take it nobody met you at the airport?"

"Dauber did, in Paris."

"I mean in Basel?"

"No. What happened to What'shisname, Shelter?"

"It's a little hard to explain . . . over the phone," Palmer said after a moment. He paused again. "I think you'll have to conduct yourself from here on in as if all your conversation was in need of, uh, Six-Twelve."

Burris frowned and felt the movement of his forehead settle into horizontal furrows. His head felt fuzzy with sleep. What the hell was that remark supposed to—? Then he remembered Six-Twelve. It was the U.S. trade name of a bug repellant. He groaned slightly. "Already?"

"That's the way I read the Shelter situation, which is why he is now the recipient of a Section Eight."

Burris groaned again. Section Eight, a discharge for the good of the service. With Palmer talking in All-American code, it was going to be a hell of a day. Burris glanced at his watch and almost yelped in pain. The time was half-past eleven. He had slept twelve hours straight through without feeling anything but horrible.

"Matt, are you listening?"

"Section Eight," Burris echoed grimly. "This is a great way to start things off."

"Shelter's assistant is a Swiss named Ingo Huffel," Palmer went on. "We're extremely fortunate in having Huffel with us," he went on in a tone so Pollyannaish and so unlike Palmer that Burris was instantly alerted. "He's hard-working, reliable, utterly trustworthy and thoroughly execrable. You'll enjoy lunch with him today."

"Today?" Burris repeated the word mainly to give himself time to remember what "execrable" meant.

"Yes," Palmer went on smoothly, "I've taken the liberty of making the date for you with him. He'll be downstairs in the dining room at the Drei Könige at half-past twelve. I know you'll have a wonderful time talking to him, Matt. He'll remind you a lot of Ben Arnold. Remember Ben?"

"No."

"Maybe you recall his buddy, Major André."

Burris nodded. Benedict Arnold. Lovely. Huffel turns out to be a traitor and his boss had just arranged lunch with him. "In that case," Burris said, "I'll let him pick up the tab."

Palmer laughed quietly for a moment. "You do that. Did Curtis see you in Paris?"

"Yes."

"Good. Look, Matt, if you can be at the UBCO office on the Aeschenvorstadt around three today, I've sent a courier through by car. He left here this morning with a written report on the situation. He's seen your photo and he'll hand the report over to you at the bank."

"Terrific," Burris said in a dull voice.

"That's what I like," Palmer commented drily, "real enthusiasm."

Burris sighed. "Listen, give me a chance and I'll get back to you with some real laughs."

"You have to come down for the weekend with me, just as soon as you get settled in there."

"Say a year or so?"

"Come on, Matt, it's not that bad."

"In between the Six-Twelves and the Section Eights, I'm beginning to feel Eighty-Sixed already."

"Matty, it's only the first quarter of play," Palmer told him. "A good fullback is just hitting his stride. I know you can do it. What do they say in Japan, *sayonara?*"

"Yeah. And *auf wiedersehen* to you, too."

There was a click and the line went dead. Burris hung up the telephone and got unsteadily to his feet.

He was now supposed to assume that all his conversations would be bugged. Shelter had defected to the Swiss and left his assistant, Huffel, to spy on Burris. The only thing that remained to finish off the whole sorry mess was to find out how much Palmer or anyone else had told Shelter about the master plan. If he'd been told a lot, Burris' mission had gone from almost impossible to a condition that could best be characterized as Instant Pre-Defeat.

Which left him where? Burris picked up his watch and saw that he had to be downstairs for his lunch with Huffel in forty-five minutes.

He got into the shower and, after a quick soaping, began to do his usual hot-and-cold rinse. As a kid in college, even after four quarters of bone crushing on the football field, this alternate hot and cold spray had always picked him up. It did nothing for the drugged feeling in his body now.

Rubbing himself with a towel, he padded out into the bedroom and looked around him for the first time. Had he left the place in such a mess the night before? It looked as if someone had raided the joint.

Had he really flung underwear and socks about? He didn't even remember unpacking. Then why were all the bureau drawers open?

Slowly, Burris realized that he was looking at someone else's work.

He sat down in the armchair and carefully checked over the place. He'd arrived with a briefcase and two suitcases. The rest of his stuff was coming air freight from Tokyo next week. Both cases had been rifled. The briefcase, too, had been gutted of papers. He tried to see if the wad of Xeroxes from Curtis were anywhere on the premises and finally found them under his pillow.

Now it came back to him. He'd finished his first glass of beer, poured a second, undressed and slumped onto the bed, intending to reread Curtis' report. Instead he'd zonked out cold.

Moving cautiously, he got to his feet and went over to the glass of beer. He sniffed it and got the same chemical smell he had tasted a few minutes before when he'd sipped some. Yet, last night it had tasted fine.

Last night it had been ice cold. But it had arrived with the cap off.

His body movements slowed down to a crawl, Burris picked around in the mulch of underwear someone had strewn over his bedroom floor, found a pair of shorts and pulled them on. Then he picked up the telephone and ordered a pot of coffee from room service.

While waiting for it to come, he began looking through the debris to find the slip of paper on which Curtis had written the telephone numbers where he could be reached.

If somebody wanted to search his luggage badly enough to slip a mickey in his beer, then it was time to call for help. Curtis might be a bit light for the job, but any help was better than none.

CHAPTER 17

From the second-floor window of Dieter Staeli's office at Number 17, Aeschenvorstadt, he could stand behind the fine marquisette curtain and look directly across the street at the small storefront office of UBCO in Basel.

Dieter was, in fact, standing there when the bells in nearby churches began to tell the noon hour. As he always did, Dieter glanced at his own watch, then moved ponderously toward the antique tavern clock on the wall opposite his desk. It was nearly two centuries old, the work of a Silesian horologist named Gustav Becker. Its eight-day movement was controlled by a regulator pendulum that swung quietly back and forth behind glass.

Dieter frowned as he cocked his head at the face of the clock and compared it with his watch. Then, his pudgy butcher's fingers moving stealthily as if to snap up an unwary fly, he gently touched the minute hand and edged it forward half a minute.

"So. It's absolutely correct now," he told the man sitting in the chair across from his desk.

"I like things absolutely correct," he went on, returning to his desk and sitting down. He allowed his round face to radiate goodwill for a few moments. "Even when they are valuable antiques, I like things to be absolutely correct. Don't you agree, Herr Shelter?"

Shelter's narrow frame, thin through the shoulders, even thinner through the chest, wriggled slightly, but whether with indecision or embarrassment Dieter couldn't tell. The man baffled him ever so slightly, as some foreigners did, especially those who, like Shelter, seemed prepared to sell out their own national interests.

Watching Shelter's pinched face for some sign of response, Dieter Staeli found himself thinking about Swiss national interest. Not for the first time, he made a pleasing discovery.

There was no such thing as Swiss national interest. It was identical with Swiss private interest. What was good for Staeli was good for Switzerland and vice versa. Which accounted, no doubt, Dieter mused, for the fact that there were so few Swiss turncoats and traitors. The God-fearing Swiss were too honorable to betray their own sacred trust. Whereas this decadent American specimen seated across from him, in return for a few thousands in a confidential gold bullion cache and the promise of a job in the Staeli Foreign Trading department, had been willing to turn his employer's pockets inside out like the traitor and thief that he was.

As if the job they'd give Shelter would last more than a few months. As if any Swiss could associate with an American turncoat. As if Staeli Internationale GmbH. could afford to hire anyone who had sold out one employer already.

No Swiss would have behaved as Shelter did. Thinking about him now as he waited for the man to make some routine, even social, response, Dieter Staeli wondered what terrible hatreds, what jealousies and frustrations lay beneath that nervous but unyielding face.

"About the bullion cache?" Shelter spoke up then.

"It has already been explained."

"But, you understand, although a U.S. citizen can own bullion, there is always the IRS. That my ownership is securely hidden before . . ." He let his voice die away.

Before you spit out the full story of what UBCO is planning, Dieter finished silently. "As we outlined yesterday, Herr Shelter, it's an air-tight plan. A Liechtenstein *Stiftung* or personal trust is opened up with you as sole beneficiary. Under Liechtenstein law, this fact remains a secret. In turn the *Stiftung* acquires ownership of a number of bars of gold bullion, .999 pure, valued, at the current exchange rate, at not less than ten thousand dollars. These bars are held in the vaults of a subsidiary of Staeli Internationale

GmbH. here in Basel, a subsidiary doing business as a commercial bank. The ownership of the bullion is, by Swiss law, secret. Thus the laws of two nations protect each link in the chain of ownership."

He stopped and waited impatiently. Dieter Staeli loved details. His life was made up of the most minute of them. But he did not enjoy explaining them to fools, especially traitorous fools, especially twice.

"But my guarantees," Shelter began in his thin, constipated voice, a tone produced no lower than his Adam's apple and channeled primarily through his nose to the outside world.

"The finest," Staeli snapped. "As good or better than anyone's."

"The documents of ownership."

Dieter began to realize that, in addition to being a turncoat and informer, the American might be mad. He did not seem to talk in complete sentences. True, they were conversing in English and perhaps Staeli wasn't used to such an elliptical style. But there seemed something so . . . so *subjunctive* about Shelter. Everything seemed, perhaps not contrary to fact, but certainly subject to grave doubt.

"The documents of ownership are here," Dieter said. He lifted a small pile of legal-length typed forms, one bound in blue, another in green, a third bound in an ecru color. "All there. All ready for signing."

Shelter's narrow face seemed to pull in at the sides. He was not more than forty, Dieter saw, if that, but his habit of trying to condense himself into invisibility had aged Shelter. "For your signature," Staeli added then. "And, may I add, with the arrival yesterday evening of the man, Burris, we must conclude this arrangement as quickly as possible and effect the fullest transfer of information immediately."

"What Huffel knows . . ." Again Shelter stopped before he had constructed a sentence.

"Is what?" Dieter Staeli urged him.

"Is . . ." Shelter waved a thin hand. "Is nothing. I alone . . ." Another misty wisp of gesture.

Staeli nodded. The man was beginning to bother him. "Precisely why you are being so well paid for your information."

"But if . . ." Shelter paused, shrugged. Suddenly he got to his feet, so fast Dieter Staeli blinked. "The pen."

"By all means." Staeli placed an open fountain pen in Shelter's hand and watched him scribble his name on the three documents. The man sank back into his chair as if the effort had sapped him of energy. Outside the last of the noon bells had just stopped pealing.

"Now, then," Dieter began in a low-pitched but businesslike tone, "I am going to turn you over to my son, Walter. You will talk to him. He will tape your conversation, of course, and also make written notes. It shouldn't take too long, Herr Shelter. I would say that unless it is terribly complicated, you will be out of here in time for a late lunch, and ten thousand richer for it, too."

"The gold."

"Yes?"

"It's current value?"

"*Mein Gott.*" Dieter tried to mask the annoyance in his voice. He pressed a button on his desk. "You can take all of this up with Walter. He is much better informed as to day-to-day fluctuations. Ah." The knock on the door was soft but audible. "Come in."

Walter's silky blond hair and milky blue eyes made him look more than ever like what they called him behind his back, his father mused. But if he is a White Rat, Dieter told himself, he is *my* White Rat.

"Herr Shelter," Walter was saying, shaking the American's flaccid hand. "A pleasure to see you again."

"Walter, Herr Shelter has signed the necessary documents for the transfer of ownership of the bullion. He is now prepared to transfer information to you. I don't think it should take too long, and I know," the emphasis was heavy, "you will tape-record everything."

"Quite. Herr Shelter," Walter indicated his desk out in the bullpen. "Will you be so kind as to take a seat at my desk for a moment? There is one matter I must discuss with my father."

The two Staelis watched the man's narrow frame insinuate itself through the doorway, slip past several desks and slump into the guest's chair at Walter's desk. "Strange man," the father said then.

"Father, about the Japanese matter."

"Was ist?"

"You remember I gave you a preliminary report on the portable compu—"

"Ach, ja. Walter, Walter." Dieter Staeli's face still radiated light, but it shook slowly from side to side. "What am I to do with you, Walter? The deal is a foolish one."

"I strongly urge you to—"

"Genug. I'll think about it." Dieter made a shooing gesture, as if driving a goose from his office. "Go, go, go. And squeeze that skinny little traitor like a grape until there is nothing left but skin. Let's see if there's ten thousand dollars' worth of information in him."

"And you'll reconsider the—"

"Go, go, go."

The father watched his son leave. What a morning. Spies on every side. He wasn't running a bank, he was running a private intelligence agency and he could trust no one, barely even Walter. Why, even before the start of the business day, he'd been in here talking to the Ruc girl.

A quiet, God-fearing Swiss maiden who knew her place—unlike his niece Margit—Christa Ruc was prepared to do what she was ordered to do. No fuss. No false modesty, either. A simple, straightforward Swiss trade, open and aboveboard.

In return for a better job at almost twice her present pay at the bank, Christa had agreed to pump her roommate, Elfi, for as much information as possible about Elfi's employer, Margit Staeli. She had also agreed, at a time in the near future when Dieter Staeli ordered it, to bring Elfi to him and arrange for Elfi herself to defect.

This second betrayal of trust would in no way change the bank's arrangement with Christa Ruc. She would still keep her new job and new salary, no matter what sums were also paid to Elfi. Straightforward. Cards on the table. Open. That was the way Dieter Staeli and every other God-fearing Swiss did business.

The effulgence that shone from Dieter's round face was almost luminous now. He reached for his private telephone and dialed a number. Picking up the instrument, he carried it on its long cord to the window, where he watched the UBCO branch across the street. After two rings, a woman answered, "UBCO, *guten morgen.*"

"*Guten abend,*" Dieter Staeli corrected her. "*Herr Huffel, bitte.*"

After a moment the assistant manager, Shelter's second, came on the telephone. His broad Basler accent made Staeli smile. "All is well," Staeli told him without bothering to identify himself. "Everything is signed. The transfers are proceeding now."

"I . . ." Huffel stopped for a moment. "*Sehr gut, mein herr.* I have to lunch now with Herr Burris."

"*Nein.*"

"*Aber ja.*"

"It would be a mistake, Huffel."

"I have no choice. The appointment was made by a higher power."

"God?" Dieter Staeli's laugh filled the telephone. "There are no higher powers. Huffel. You are dizzy. You have a headache. Did you know that? You must take the afternoon off and go home and get to bed and call the doctor."

"But, I—. Yes, yes, I do feel feverish."

"Tonight, where one plays jass on Sankt Wolfganggasse."

"*Ja.*"

"After dinner, Huffel. About nine o'clock, yes?"

Without waiting, Dieter Staeli hung up and returned with the telephone to his desk. He sat down behind it. Through the open door he could see Shelter leaning forward across Walter's desk while his son scratched hasty notes. Then Walter got to his feet and, carrying a small tape machine, escorted Shelter into a conference room and closed the door behind him. Good boy. Though his lust for power was too naked and his judgment so half-baked that perhaps not even time would cure it, nevertheless Walter was a Staeli and a good one.

Things were at last moving forward. The UBCO thing was under absolute control, thanks to Huffel who had been planted in the UBCO office two years ago precisely to subvert Shelter and get him to defect.

The surveillance of Margit's own boudoir was about to begin, giving her loving uncle the last tidbits of information he needed to manipulate the problem she represented and bring it to a successful conclusion.

And as for Walter's little fling with the Japanese. Well, why not? He was a hard worker. He followed orders. God knew he was loyal to the family. Why not throw him his bone? It wouldn't make a franc, might even lose a few. But how else was Walter to gain business judgment unless he was allowed to make a few inexpensive mistakes?

Let him have his Japanese computer deal. Let the boy learn. It would do him good.

Dieter's sunlike face radiated goodwill and understanding.

CHAPTER 18

Although the light-proof shades were motor-controlled, as were the pale-pink curtains, still, on a sunny day like this, a certain amount of raw light filtered into Michele's bedroom.

Not much, of course, not enough to waken Erich from the sleep into which he had finally fallen, but more than enough of the patented pale blush for her to watch his face in repose. All the V's had disappeared. He slept the way he made love, with great confidence, which was the only way.

Michele had propped her head up on one arm to survey Erich's face. The fabled Erich Lorn. Not bad.

She had been prepared for almost anything. Her experience with womanizers of vast renown was contradictory. Some were good, some dismal failures. She had half expected Erich to be put off by her frank approach. She had provisionally decided he was the type who had to make all the moves or the game was off. She'd been wrong. Fortunately.

Michele found herself wondering whether he was as good with his fiancée as he'd been with her. She was also wondering whether she should let him sleep or awaken him by ordering a little light lunch brought to the bedroom for the two of them. And, because Michele's mind was always able to handle several levels of inquiry at the same time, she was wondering how soon Margit Staeli would learn of the new liaison. And what she would do about it.

111

Finally, because whatever else she was thinking about with a new lover, this always lay at the bottom of her mind, Michele was wondering whether he could tell how old she really was.

The face, she knew, would never give her away, certainly not under this controlled lighting with its flattering mixture of flesh tones. The body might tell another story. She had had some trouble last year with the insides of her thighs leading to her pubis, the area a former lover had referred to, incessantly, as "God's Country."

The epidermis had lost its tone and neither massage nor astringents seemed to hold the subcutaneous layers in their usual silken smoothness. The surgeon in Madrid had suggested silicone replacement, which was radical advice. The Bucharest man suggested low-voltage galvanic stimulation. Her old friend Yaki, in Casablanca, had spent an hour lovingly examining the area and cooing over it before coming up with the course of action that sounded best to Michele: acrobatics.

Under a pseudonym, she had enrolled in a Paris salon where young men and women learned tumbling, splits, trapeze and high-ring work.

Within a week, she had nearly died of exhaustion. Within two weeks the inner surface of her thighs had firmed so successfully that she had taken on one of the assistant teachers as a new lover. He was twenty. Most of the students were sixteen. If Michele had celebrated a birthday last year it would have been her fifty-fifth.

Michele had learned to handle all the equipment used in the Paris salon. She had then caused a new gymnasium to be built at Michelebad, complete with trapezes and tumbling mats. Privately, after hours, while most of her patients slept, she continued to work out on the rings alone, swinging through the darkness, hanging from her feet.

The whole thing worked marvels, but none of it had yet been integrated into the official Michele system. It probably never would. Her patients didn't come to her for hard work.

Watching Erich deep in sleep, she continued to wonder how old he thought she was. She had carefully cultivated conflicting rumors about her age. Naturally, there were people alive in the world who could, if they wished, create a small sensation and report that little

Agnes Losch with whom they had gone to grade school in Graz in the late 1920s was, in fact Madame Michele.

They could tell this story but they would not be believed. It had already happened. Janos, who had married her in Budapest when she was fifteen, had come forward, badly in need of funds, to tell all. He had tried first to blackmail her with wedding photographs of a man who was certainly himself and a pudgy teen-ager who could have been any Magyar girl at all. She had told Janos to peddle his pictures elsewhere and he'd tried.

Stern had bought and printed them. She had denied the story. The whole thing had blown over. Janos had been the first of seven husbands and twenty regular lovers, but the only one to try such a trick. Michele supposed, on balance, that she'd been lucky.

One day, she knew, when she was perhaps in her mid-sixties, she would let the whole thing come out into the open. My God, what a shock it would be to that long, hard-breathing parade of lovers and husbands. My God, that poor little acrobat in Paris, young enough to be her grandson. This one here, this Erich. She had never been truly promiscuous. There had always been only one man at a time. Well, nearly always. All of them would feel as if they'd been hit over the head.

And no matter how many millions she would be worth at that time, her value and that of her name would double overnight. Triple.

She found herself smiling fondly at the fantasy. She wondered whether she would continue to look this good at sixty-five. Probably not. But why not?

Although she was much given to such thoughts, and was able to keep a number of them going at the same time, Michele had long ago mastered the art of not wondering about things that aged her.

For instance, and it was a significant instance, Michele had trained herself never to wonder what her purpose was in all this. To keep herself looking young and attractive to men was self-explanatory. But for what purpose was she amassing the already large fortune she now kept in various Swiss banks? What was the end of all this? To what goal would she address herself, once she was rich beyond all further dreams of avarice? Was there ever an end to such a dream?

None of this did she wonder about. She knew precisely why she had picked out Erich Lorn—aside from his reputation as a woman's man—for this rather complicated seduction and the extremely high-pitched affair that she planned as a sequel, an affair in which Erich literally disappeared from his normal haunts to spend most of his waking hours between her legs. An affair, in short, that would destroy both of them in fire, releasing them to step from its ashes into free new lives.

Michele smiled at her own romantic ideas. Erich was making love as much to her reputation as her body. And she was making love to him because he was engaged to marry Margit Staeli.

As if he had overheard her thought, Erich's lips moved. He grunted something unintelligible and came awake in a single opening of eyes, staring directly into hers, unblinking, steady.

"You," he said.

Michele nodded. Face propped on one arm, she continued to lean over him, observing. "Do you know what we have done?" Erich asked then.

"Yes."

Erich rolled away to look at the tiny clock on her bedside table, its face surrounded by a pale circlet of Florentine gold leaves. Michele did not ignore the fact that earlier, in the midst of everything, Erich had seen the clock and knew just where it would be later. He now stared at the face. "Woman," he intoned hollowly, "I have left my fiancée alone in the most public dining room in Basel."

"If you leave at once and do not pause for the Taittinger and a bit of caviar or some Scottish salmon and Danish brown bread and the prosciutto from Genoa and a terrine from Périgord and strong espresso with just a touch of Sambuca liqueur, if you refuse to stay for that, you can run to meet her, breathless, perspiring and late."

"Breathless, perspiring and smelling of you," he added.

"There is a shower."

"Never."

"You don't want to remove my smell?"

He rolled over away from the clock and buried his face between her breasts. She sank back on the bed and he began to run his tongue down into her navel.

"In fact," she said, lifting her knees up around him, "you want more of it."

"Not more," he muttered, "all."

CHAPTER 19

Shelter left Number 17 Aeschenvorstadt with the furtive air of an escapee from a prison camp. He glanced both ways along the crowded thoroughfare, then plunged suicidally between two long green streetcars coming in opposite directions, dodged across the street and dashed in the door of the UBCO branch.

The Swiss girl at the reception desk looked up with blank eyes. *"Guten abend."* She saw who it was and substituted a smile for her blank look. "Herr Shelter."

His small eyes shifted past her to survey the back of the office. "Where's Huffel? Still at lunch?"

"I'm sorry, Herr Shelter, he went home sick.'

"What?"

"Stomach," the girl reported with something very much like satisfaction.

Shelter went out the door onto the Aeschenvorstadt at a slower pace. He glanced up at the second-floor windows of Number 17 and saw that no one seemed to be watching. Walter Staeli had taped every word of his. It was only a matter of time, perhaps minutes, perhaps hours, before even Walter Staeli realized that what Shelter had given him was not worth ten thousand in gold.

If only he'd been able to scrape up anything in Burris' room last night. But the silly bastard hadn't been carrying a single clue. Shelter had gone to a lot of trouble—and a hundred francs to the room-service waiter—to make sure Burris slept soundly. Shelter's hand, in his pocket, closed over the duplicate key to the suite, which had to be returned to the Drei Könige waiter today sometime. To hell with him. He could wait. Dieter Staeli couldn't.

Shelter glanced at himself in the glass of the UBCO office. His dismissal had come through so recently, yesterday morning, in fact, that even the girl at the desk hadn't been told yet. How had Palmer caught on? There had to be a leak somewhere in the Staeli apparatus. Or had his own assistant, Huffel, turned him in? But that made no sense. Huffel was a Staeli agent.

Shelter grimaced at the reflection of the thin, miserable creature in the window. He straightened up and tried to puff out his chest an inch or two. He tried to erase the anxious look on his face. He straightened his tie and decided it was the best he could do.

But he and Huffel were in this together. The Swiss couldn't hide at home playing sick, not when things had reached a squeeze like this. For the plain fact, Shelter knew, was that when Dieter Staeli reviewed what his son had taped in the way of useful material from Shelter, the deal would be canceled.

Burris was the key. Burris knew the answers Shelter had been unable to provide. Burris would have to tell what he knew.

A Number 3 streetcar had slowed to a halt in front of Shelter. He ran for it and hopped aboard as the doors were closing. He had no ticket, but the inspectors rarely boarded any of the cars in the afternoon, only at morning and evening rush hours.

He sat down and tried to distract himself by glancing out the window as the car made its way silently through Basel toward the neighborhood where Huffel rented an apartment. Shelter supposed, in a way, it was pure foresight that he remembered where Huffel lived. He'd been there once before, a year ago, to pick up some books Huffel had taken home to work on over a weekend.

The Number 3 streetcar swooped down into the Barfusserplatz, picked up a load of college students and continued on its way past the music school toward the Spalentor gate that seemingly blocked its path.

Shelter stared out the window with a stony, blind look. He was in a bit of a corner, true, but with Huffel's help he could wriggle out. His life had been one kind of bind or another, starting five years ago when he'd transferred from a Chase branch in Manhattan to a Chase office in Paris. His knowledge of French had been a point in favor of the move, and so had the fact that his branch manager in Manhattan had wanted to get rid of him.

Shelter had no illusions about how other people felt toward him.

He knew he often made a poor impression. You'd have to be blind not to see how Dieter Staeli felt about him, for example. And seeing this made Shelter behave even less prepossessingly. Okay, he knew that. But he *did* have a banking background, and when UBCO needed an assistant manager in Basel three years ago, he'd spotted the ad in the Paris *Herald-Tribune,* applied for the job and got it.

Three years in this town, the last as full manager of the UBCO office, would have been more than enough for most people to put down roots, make strong contacts, friends. Shelter had done none of these. He was as rootless in Basel as he had been in Paris or New York.

He eyed the Spalentor almost without seeing it as the Number 3 car swung around it and moved off along Missionstrasse toward Kannenfeld Park. It was across from the park, or rather from the end of it where the outdoor-theater performances were held in summer, that Huffel's apartment house stood, one of a dozen like it, five floors, dark-maroon brick and weathered aluminum trim with a pitiful ring of grass around each to justify its proximity to the real park across the street. Shelter left the streetcar just before the Felix Platter Hospital.

The apartment house looked almost deserted at this hour, no one coming or going, no young mothers with baby carriages. It was too early for children to be returning from school. Shelter noted Huffel's apartment number on the directory downstairs and went up without buzzing first.

He knocked on the door and, when he heard shuffling footsteps beyond it, prepared to greet Huffel's wife. It was something of a surprise to see Huffel himself open the door. He looked fit enough. The two men stood there for a long moment, eyeing each other silently. There was a faint physical resemblance in that both were thin and had poor posture, but Huffel's face was sleeker, a bit better fed and infinitely more smug.

"They told me you were sick," Shelter began.

Huffel nodded once. "What will you want here?"

"We must talk. We have a problem."

"We?" Huffel shifted his weight slightly. He made no effort to invite him into the apartment.

"I can't talk out here in the hall." Shelter started to push past

117

his former colleague, but Huffel held the half-closed door firmly.

"We must talk," Shelter insisted.

"What is the problem?"

"Burris. We have to get information from him."

Huffel's small head was moving from side to side now. "We don't," he said, stressing the pronoun. "I don't," he added.

"Listen." Shelter heard his voice grow too loud. He tried to remain calm. "Listen," he hissed, almost in a whisper. "You and I are in a spot, Ingo. You know we are."

Huffel's head kept shaking. "I am in no spot."

"Maybe worse than mine," Shelter added.

"I am in no spot."

"We have to help each other, Ingo."

The door started to close. "You are on your own," the Swiss said. He had narrowed the opening to a slit barely two inches wide through which one of his eyes peered at Shelter.

"Ingo." Shelter shoved at the door and found it so firmly braced against him that all of Huffel's weight must have been poised behind it. "Goddamn it, you got me into this, you—" The door clicked shut.

"Ingo!" Shelter began to pound on the metal door. The sound was like a great base drum in a wilderness of echoing corridors. At last the noise died away.

After a while, Shelter turned from the door. Damned treacherous Swiss. Huffel had been on Staeli's payroll from the beginning. It had been Huffel who suggested that there was a lot of money to be made if Shelter defected with the new information. But the information was worthless without missing pieces Burris was holding.

It was a jigsaw puzzle and the key bits lay in Burris' hotel suite at the Drei Könige.

Shelter grimaced. He put his hand into his pocket, turned and walked away from the door to Huffel's apartment. In his pocket, his fingers closed over the duplicate key to Burris' hotel suite.

As he scuttled down the stairway to the street, his heels made fast, stuttering machine-gun noises on the steel treads. Then he slowed his pace. No sense hurrying, he thought. Calm down. Burris wouldn't possibly be back in his suite until later tonight.

He stood in the building's lobby for a moment, collecting his thoughts and trying to remain calm. He was in a spot, no denying it. Without a job here in Basel, the Swiss would revoke his work permit. The ten thousand in gold was his, as long as he could give Staeli enough information to justify it. But if he failed, it was leprechaun's gold. One false move and it evaporated in a yellow mist, never to return.

Worse, Dieter Staeli was a vengeful old bastard, everyone knew that. A man who tried to cheat him out of ten grand in gold could expect all sorts of trouble, official trouble, and not just over a work permit.

Shelter expelled a long breath of air, trying to exorcize his tensions. It was a bind, no question about it, a very tight place, squeezed between a big U.S. bank and a Swiss one. A man could be ground into butter with one turn of the machinery.

Although the lobby of the building was cool, he had started to perspire. He patted his forehead with a not very clean handkerchief. Hell of a spot, but he had at least one more chance to make it come out right. Burris didn't know what he looked like. A man with the proper disguise, nothing elaborate, just, say, a darkened room and a handkerchief over his face, couldn't be identified later if he used a fake voice. All he needed was a way to make Burris talk.

For the first time, Shelter smiled.

He strolled casually out into the sunlight and moved at a leisurely pace across a bit of new grass lawn. He would take a walk to his own apartment. It was less than fifteen minutes away. There he kept the .38 Special he had bought when he became UBCO's Basel manager. All perfectly legal, of course. He had a permit from the Basler police, a courtesy they almost never granted a non-Swiss, but were pleased to provide for a bank manager.

Quite legal.

Burris had looked big, asleep on his bed early this morning, at least a head taller than Shelter and much heftier. The .38 would make the difference. What did they call it back in the States, the Equalizer?

Shelter snickered. All, all quite legal.

CHAPTER 20

If it hadn't been for the fact that at lunchtime a lot of knowledgeable bankers ate here and would see Erich with her, Margit would never have agreed to this place. Normally she never ate here. It was too suavely continental, too filled with male expense-account wheeling and dealing. The long, dark-red room fronted on the river and was divided into several smaller areas. But, on entering, one first walked past an elaborate grill. Here bloody chunks of costly meat were variously charred, revolved, smeared with strange unguents and otherwise expensively tormented in imitation of some supermasculine caveman or hunter's semi-raw, still-bleeding meal, or, rather, the would-be hunter seeking to impress another male for business reasons. Margit disliked the whole thing, although the view of the river was occasionally interesting in summer, when the outdoor terrace was open.

Not that she yearned for something with frilled lampshades, but this dining room represented all too clearly the dominant element in Swiss life against which Margit found herself pitted. The place was redolent of people like Uncle Dieter and the rest of the crew Erich referred to as Hypocrites Internationale GmbH.

She glanced at her watch and found that, although she had arrived precisely at twelve-thirty and had been here five minutes, her fiancé was definitely late. She signaled the captain.

"Ja wohl, Fräulein Staeli?"

The man bobbed up and down like a well-made mechanical toy —Swiss, of course. Margit waited until the genuflections finally ended. "Does the bar have an open white wine?"

"A *Bordeau blanc '67* perhaps?" he suggested hopefully.

"Nothing good?"

"A *Piesporter Goldtröpfchen '71.*"

"One glass, please."

When it arrived within a minute, she held it up to the light and admired the straw color. She delayed sipping. That was how she

120

happened to see all the way across the crowded room to the table where Matthew Burris was sitting.

She put the wine down, untasted.

The gargoyle that sat on her shoulders drew a long talon across the skin of her neck. She shivered. "Let me alone," she muttered, then realized she had said it aloud. But no one had heard.

Probably not even the gargoyle. Certainly not the soft-talking group of Baslers at the next table. Surely not her waiter.

At the far end of the room Burris hunched a bit forward at a table for two, glancing impatiently at his wristwatch and twirling his finger around in the bits of ice that remained in his glass. He had probably ordered what he always ordered, a very dry vodka martini, except that nowhere outside of the States would Matthew Burris ever get it precisely as he liked it or as he once used to make them in his little apartment on the Charles River where he introduced her to such things.

He seemed to be waiting for someone, and that someone was late. It wasn't possible, was it, that a woman would keep Matthew Burris waiting? It had to be a man.

Margit sat back in her chair, relaxing her very erect posture to put other people's heads between her and Burris' line of sight. She stared hard at the pale white wine. Yes, standing there it was already covered with a faint coating of condensed mist. Yes, that airmail letter yesterday was from the Harvard Alumni Association. Yes, dear God, she was going mad.

She was seeing things. He was not in Basel. He was not in the dining room of the Drei Könige.

Margit sat up straight and watched him summon a waiter and talk heatedly to him for a moment, then hand him the glass. "Not so much vermouth," she could imagine him saying.

She found herself wondering if this were all a mean-spirited joke Erich was playing on her, hiring a man who looked like Matthew Burris. It had been Erich who had suggested the dining room of the Drei Könige. The restaurant of the Euler Hotel had, perhaps, better food. But it was more of an evening place, as was the best Basler restaurant, the *Schützenhaus*. This place, however, was better known at lunch. And yet, it must all be a cruel joke of Erich's. It had been years since he'd teased her this way, but the whole thing was typical of his strange sense of humor.

Unless, of course, Erich had nothing to do with this and she was going mad.

The terrible thing about insanity, she told herself, is that it takes no account whatsoever of reality. Matthew Burris, for example, in her own fantasy, looked no older now than he had in Massachusetts six years ago. Margit was staring, and knew it, but she had to find some sign of aging. If he had aged, he might be real. And if he were real, she was perhaps not going mad.

When the waiter returned with a fresh drink, Burris sipped it and made a face but decided to accept its dubious claims. He checked his watch and spoke to the waiter again, who this time went to the captain, standing not far from Margit.

She slumped in her chair again, but not before she heard the waiter speak Burris' name and that of another person. All right. Better. It was no hallucination, then? But if one can fantasize a man across a room, one can imagine a waiter has spoken his name.

Margit glanced at her own watch. Twelve forty-five. Erich was quite late. For an irresponsible fiancé, he was either punctual or simply didn't show up. This would be one of his disappearing days, then.

Vaguely, more to give her mind something to do than because she was really interested, Margit wondered who the woman was who had caused Erich to break his luncheon date with her. Then, before she could think of a name, she saw Matthew Burris rise impatiently from his table and make his way to the men's room.

Yes, thicker through the middle. Yes! A few kilos thicker! And a faint bit of extra weight to that square chin of his. Was that all six years had done to him? In six years he'd gained a bit and she'd lost a bit. Funny.

Not terribly funny.

She glanced at her wine and sipped it. *Bordeaux,* not *Piesporter.* The captain had tried to fox her. As if the faintly sweet smoothness of the Moselle wine could ever be mistaken for the raw acidity of the off-year French. She summoned the captain by crooking her finger.

"This is not what I ordered," she said in a casual voice.

"But I assure you Fräul—"

"Enough. Has Herr Burris' luncheon companion arrived yet?"

The man blinked, but responded quickly enough. "Not yet, Fräulein Staeli. I am having Herr Huffel's office telephoned."

"Ingo Huffel?"

"Of the UBCO Bank."

Margit nodded slowly. She reached in her purse and brought out a small notepad bound in red Morocco. She removed the thin pencil from it, scribbled a note and folded it twice. "When you report to Herr Burris about Herr Huffel, you will give him this note."

"*Ja wohl.*"

"And you will bring me the Moselle I ordered."

"A thousand pardons, but you see—"

"It is not the bar's open wine. Then bring a half bottle. And the menu."

Margit sat back to watch the developments. She felt a faint flush of accomplishment, putting the captain in the wrong, stripping him of information and setting in motion the one thing she had never expected to happen. She felt rather like a child who had carefully wound up a deliciously complicated mechanical toy and was now waiting for it to begin performing its advertised miracles.

No, she had never expected to see Matthew Burris again. Although banking had once brought them together, it could not have been relied upon to bring them together again. They moved in entirely different worlds. And yet he was here. He really was here.

She watched him return to his table, frown at his watch and sit down. He sipped the drink and his frown deepened. He pulled a sheaf of papers from his pocket and began reading them.

The captain, on his way to Burris' table, paused an instant next to Margit. "Herr Huffel is indisposed. He has gone home for the day." The captain's voice was produced something like a ventriloquist's, without moving his lips, so that it seemed as if a chair had vouchsafed this confidential information to Margit.

She watched him make his way between tables. The mechanical toy began to whirr. He bent deferentially over Matthew Burris. Burris' frown turned into a scowl, then disappeared. He sat back in his chair and nodded. Then the captain handed him the folded note.

Burris opened and read it in one quick motion. Margit had tried for a light touch. In these things, the light touch was wisest. "I think both our lunch dates have stood us up. Is that still the current U.S. slang?"

Burris' face looked absolutely blank. He glanced at the captain and said something. Discreetly, with a gesture not too many people could see, the captain pointed Margit out. Burris got to his feet like some immense redwood tree that has been felled and is now being hoisted slowly back into an upright position. He wavered for a moment, his eyes focusing down the room.

Margit lifted one hand slightly, another discreet gesture.

* * *

This whole town was *Totentanz,* Burris thought. This whole mission, all the malfeasance, misfeasance and nonfeasance—spooks like Curtis on his tail, missed appointments, managers who had been sacked, phones tapped, lunch dates canceled, even Palmer being mysterious and difficult—that one more goddamned cryptic message was one too many.

He saw Margit lift one hand slightly.

"That is she," the captain announced in his ventriloquist's voice, the words issuing from Burris' martini.

"That sure is," Burris agreed.

He pushed his chair back with the calves of his legs, picked up his martini and threaded his way between tables toward Margit, his mind suddenly blank. He banged his knee on a chair, ignored it and kept on coming.

He got to her table and smiled down at her, cool, a small twitch of the lips, meant to signify, "State your reason for this encounter" in an aloof way. To his horror, Burris found the smile degenerating into a big, fat, sloppy grin.

"Hey, look at you," he heard his voice saying, thick with pleasure.

"Welcome to Basel."

They watched each other for a long moment of silence. Burris eyed her face. In the old days she had been nice to take on dates, attractive without standing out. Now all that had changed.

"My God," she murmured in an undertone, as if telling it to herself, "you look exactly the same. And don't say I do, because I don't."

124

"You don't," he agreed, the grin widening. "You look a lot better."

"How better?"

"May I sit?"

"My God, of course."

Burris sat down so suddenly that the chair shot out backwards a few inches with a *thunk* that managed to cut through all the luncheon conversations around the room.

"How better?" she persisted.

"Thinner, svelter, more gorgeous." He could feel the unaccustomed strain on the facial muscles at the corners of his mouth. Was it possible to relax this silly grin? No.

"Keep talking."

"I'm serious," he assured her. "You used to be a big girl. Uh, well, not plump, just, uh, lotsa woman. Okay? I mean, more than okay. Terrific. But . . ."

"This is absolutely fascinating. Don't stop."

"But now . . ."

"Speak!"

"Now," he floundered, "well, the word is svelte. Sleek. Listen, don't get mad at me. At Harvard you were a big overgrown farm girl, healthy and solid. Now you're . . ."

"Ephemeral?"

"Ethereal. Sophisticated. Uh . . . sexy?"

"And not before?"

Burris began waving his hands around in a churning motion. He never knew what to tell women about their sexual attractiveness. As far as he was concerned, he felt damned if he did and damned if he didn't. "You were always sexy," he told her. "This is just a different kind of sexy."

"Sexier?"

"Listen, did somebody really stand you up?" he barged ahead, "because my lunch date went home sick. So, I mean, if you . . . ?"

"My fiancé is now half an hour late," she said. "This means he isn't coming at all."

"How do you know that?"

"It's his code. This way he sends me a message without having to hear a word of complaint from me."

125

Burris started to laugh. "That's quite a fiancé."

"It's quite an engagement." Her eyes, which had been fixed on Burris all this time, dipped slightly. "Quite a long-playing engagement, as they say in show biz. I was engaged to him when I was . . . at Harvard."

Burris looked up as the sommelier brought a bottle of wine and a stand with a bucket of ice in it. "Did you order this?"

"It needn't be opened yet." She smiled at the sommelier. "Let it cool, Herr Schnüffli. Bring me a very dry vodka martini on ice, almost no vermouth."

"Listen," Burris told the man, "here's how the barman can do it right. He pours a little vermouth from the bottle into its own cap. Got it? And then, from the cap, he lets one fat drop fall into the vodka. Okay?"

The sommelier's eyebrows went up and down several times during this. Then he turned to Margit without speaking. Equally silently, she nodded and watched him leave. "This is not Schnüffli's happiest moment," she said. "The barman will detest being told how to make a martini. He already knows how to make a martini, of course."

"Yes, he does." Burris' head started nodding.

"Equal parts," Margit went on, nodding in unison, "vodka and vermouth."

Both of them began laughing and, once again, glances throughout the room turned in their direction. "I get the idea we're making a spectacle of ourselves," Burris muttered. "Don't the Swiss laugh at lunch?"

"Baslers do. It's not the laughing," Margit explained. "It's that you're not Erich."

"Your late fiancé."

"You will like Erich," Margit said. "Everyone does. I do. It's really better to like one's fiancé." She stopped and made a small face. "Rather than love him. No, that's not why they're staring," she went on quickly. "It's because obviously I picked you up. Or you picked me up. They're not sure which, but this kind of gossip is too piquant to ignore."

Burris sat back in his chair and watched the waiter bring two new martinis. The bar had produced another one for him, possibly

126

recognizing him as the source of all the ridiculous fuss about the vermouth. He lifted the glass to Margit. "To seeing you again."

"To seeing you."

They sipped. Burris found the seldom used muscles at the corners of his mouth quirking upward again. "Right on the nose." He sipped again. "Perfect." He glanced at her. Her first sip had carried away half her drink. "Yes?"

"Yes, perfect." She brought the drink to her lips, and when she had finished only ice cubes remained.

"Hey, that good?"

"I'm nervous." She refused to meet his glance, staring at her empty glass instead. "When I saw you across the room, I thought I was going mad."

"The sight of me can do that to a girl."

Burris lifted his martini and drained it in one swallow. He remembered quite a few bars in Manhattan where the martinis were too big to be treated that cavalierly. But European drinks were smaller. Not that much smaller, of course.

"You didn't have to do that," Margit said, "just to put me at my ease."

"Sure, I did."

"I thought I was seeing an apparition," she went on, still not looking up, "and when you went to the w.c. I saw you had put on a bit of weight and somehow I was reassured. I mean, that I wasn't just hallucinating the whole thing."

"You really know how to make a fella feel great," Burris said. "How much weight?"

She glanced up with a faint look of malice. "A few kilos. Three or four."

"That's what? Eight-nine pounds?"

"Perhaps."

"It's twelve. I'm twelve pounds heavier than when we were at school," he admitted, "and every lousy ounce of it comes from here." Burris lifted the empty martini glass. He glanced up and found the waiter hovering nearby. He pointed to their empty glasses and held up two fingers.

"I don't normally drink much more than wine," Margit said. "It's easy to live that way in Basel, but in London, for instance, they all drink themselves silly and it—" She stopped. "At any rate," she went on more slowly, "I've been under quite a lot of strain."

"You?" Burris chuckled. "It can't be money."

"It is precisely money."

"I'd like to be under your strain," he told her.

"Matt, it's not lack of money. It's who handles it."

He nodded, remembering some of the information in the sheaf of papers Curtis had prepared for him, a few of which were even now in his breast pocket. "That would be your Uncle Dieter," he suggested then.

She sat back in her chair and eyed him with suspicion. "Why are you here in Basel?"

"Come on."

"Why, Matt?"

"Nobody's told you?"

She shook her head. "Nobody tells me anything."

They fell silent then. Burris watched her and, since she was no longer avoiding his glance, he knew she was aware of the close scrutiny.

He was very pleased with her, there was no other word for it. She pleased him, sitting there, looking trim and bright and wanting to be friendly with him. It was a change from anything that had happened to him since leaving Japan. It was the first upturn his life had taken on this *Totentanz* mission.

He was grinning again. He couldn't seem to stop it. His facial muscles ached and he even liked that feeling, too.

She looked vibrant and open in a way she never had before. There was a shine about her, not the glossy hair, a lighted edge to her face and throat, as if they were illuminated from within. She seemed more sharply silhouetted than the rest of the world, clearly delineated from everything else by this halo edge around her face. Damn it, she looked terrific.

"I take it," she murmured, "that you really do like what you see?"

The waiter brought two more drinks. Burris lifted his to her. "Shut up and drink your martini," he said.

"Big overgrown farm girl," she quoted in a low, husky tone. "We'll see about that."

CHAPTER 21

They got dressed at sundown and went for a stroll on the now deserted grounds of Michelebad. The patients (customers? clients?) had gathered in the dining room to chat over the sound of Telemann as they enjoyed lean *entrecôtes* and leafy green salads.

As Erich and Michele walked slowly along the broad gravel allee flanked by poplars, the baroque music filtered thinly across the grounds toward them, just the suggestion of music, unreal, the faintest plangent stroke of the harpsichord, the ghost of a cello bass note deep in the bowels of the music.

"Why wouldn't one grow younger here?" Erich asked, breaking the silence between them. "It's an enclave of peace in a money-grubbing universe."

"The universe? Money-grubbing?" She turned to face him directly. Michele knew she was always better head on. Not that there were any telltale folds in her chin line, not as long as she held her head as high as she had over the years. "Only a Basler banker would see the universe in his own money-grubbing city."

Erich chuckled. "My dear, you will never make me guilty about being a Basler banker, because, as you know, I'm not one."

"Then you're a changeling." She sat down on the long wrought-iron bench, enameled white. In the light of dusk it glowed faintly pink and it was a mark of Michele's particular intellect that she had aleady calculated the effect of the rosy twilight before suggesting the stroll.

"The gypsies stole the real Erich Lorn at birth. You are their agent, yes?"

"You're the first to penetrate my disguise."

"Tell me what is so rewarding about being a secret agent in the midst of Basler bankers? They're a dull lot."

"My mission is not to associate with socially brilliant Baslers," Erich confessed. "It's just too large a task, even finding some. My mission is to uncover the secrets of Basel banking."

She took his hand and stroked it softly, fondled it against her cheek and then turned it palm up. "What secrets?" she asked, absent-mindedly, her glance on his palm. When he failed to answer, there was a long pause. Suddenly, she looked up at him. "Your . . . your Mound of Venus is immense."

"Any other news?"

She smiled tightly. "But we don't need any more."

"The lines," he demanded. "The head line, the heart line, the life line, all that. I know you read palms. You're a witch."

She folded his fingers over his palm and let his hand go, realizing she'd already betrayed too much. "I know nothing about palms."

"Did you see something bad there?"

"Seriously, darling, I know nothing of palms."

He sat down next to her. "When a woman begins, 'Seriously, darling,' I steel myself for a spectacular falsehood."

"Nothing of the kind. You're interrupting my questioning of you. I must know more about the spy the gypsies left us."

He sat perfectly still, she noticed, as if debating whether to press the point or let her distract him. She'd been a fool to believe in the testimony of the hand, a bigger fool to let him guess there was more in his hand than she wanted to talk about.

Finally, Michele saw, he was wiser than she. He let the matter drop. "As to the gypsies," he was saying, "there are secrets buried in the vaults below Basel that the gypsies could use to shake the planet out of its orbit." He seemed to lose interest, glancing back at the main building. "Let's go inside."

"Soon, when they're finished dining." She circled his waist with her arm. "Keep me warm?" Then: "What sort of secrets?"

Erich gestured meaninglessly. "A figure of speech. Of course there are real hoards under Basel. Every rich man keeps his secret gold there. We have the Arab oil loot, the Pahlevi fortune, and all those numbered accounts. The usual boring exposé in the usual gossip journal."

"You have my gold, too."

"Do you bank with us? Lorn et Cie.?"

"I mean my funds are in Swiss banks."

"Good. Shall we go in now?"

He turned to watch the deep-rose color of the sky in the west darken rather quickly to a magenta stain. "What good?" she persisted. "What is so wonderful about Swiss banks?"

"You've asked the wrong man, my dear."

"On the contrary. I've asked the right one."

"Well, then." He seemed at a loss for words. "But I must ask you how much you know about banking in general."

"No more than anyone else."

"Because the Swiss system is unique only if you know the way banks in other countries operate." His arm circled her shoulder and she snuggled in against it. The evening had grown cool, but not yet chilly.

"In other countries," he went on, "they are heavily regulated. They do little without having to answer to some government bureau. Yes, of course, the bureau can be corrupted, usually is. But we Swiss don't need the bother. I think . . ." He paused for a long moment.

"I think this complete and open freedom is our real success. We do as we like. We are very much the inner government. Switzerland is its banks."

In the distance the faint music of the string ensemble shifted to a livelier melody, Mozart, quick-paced and bright. Michele listened to it. She had no real desire to know that much about Swiss banks. She wanted to distract Erich from what she had seen in his hand. Now that she had accomplished this, she got to her feet, and Erich with her.

They started back toward the main building of Michelebad, a darker mass against the darkening trees and shrubs, graceful in its balanced proportions, windows streaming with a rose-orange glow.

"It's *laissez-faire* carried to its ultimate," Erich was saying in a thoughtful tone that indicated he was puzzling it out more for himself than for her.

"We take a customer's money," he continued, "your money, let's say, and within the instructions you give us, we do as we wish. No limits. All in total secrecy because we needn't report anything we do except to you. It's a bond stronger than between a sinner and his confessor. The strength is no illusion, it's written into the law. One violates the secrecy laws at a high risk of punishment."

The music now was even livelier as they neared the main building. Michele had taken his hand. Dusk was darkening almost into night. A lone bird chirped fretfully in one of the poplars.

"Thus we attract every kind of secret, nasty or otherwise," Erich went on slowly. "Hoodlums use us. Defunct dictators. Thieves of all kinds. The flow of cash from those terribly holy statesmen who rule the West! Almost as torrential as the flow from their business colleagues in organized crime. If one wished, one could figure out who really owns these immense corporations. I can assure you it isn't the small stockholders, nor even the public stockholders who think they hold control."

Michele shook her head slightly, not enough to attract Erich's attention. He'd never been stolen by gypsies, she thought. He might loathe Basler society, but banker blood ran through him, always would. She felt sorry for the girl who would marry him once she herself was finished with him. Erich would give Margit Staeli a lifetime of trouble, not just the women, but his inner contradictions, a Basler to his soul, and hating it.

When he had been silent a while she said, in a light tone: "Thank you, Herr Professor."

"It's all corruption," he responded absent-mindedly.

"The lecture continues?"

"Anywhere there is this corrupt alliance," he said, "between businessmen and politicians, there is a steady flow of cash into our banks."

"Bribe money, is it?"

He nodded. "Political contributions. It's deposited in our numbered accounts, but it doesn't sit there." His voice grew almost melancholy. "In a day or two we get cabled instructions. Buy a thousand shares of this or that stock. Hundreds of these buy orders each day."

"And you moral Basler bankers ignore the orders?" she teased.

"We execute them and make our percentage on each." His sigh seemed to reverberate along the pathways of the park. "A nameless account then owns the shares. If one were the financial officer of a major corporation and one needed to know who owned so many shares of one's stock . . ." He stopped and shook his head. "The famous shield of Swiss banking secrecy can never be penetrated."

Neither of them spoke for a moment. "Do you wonder that I

132

detest all this?" he burst out then, squeezing her hand. "In the fullness of time, these faceless men with their Mafia enforcers and political whores end up secretly owning the world. Thanks to us."

There was a faint burst of applause in the dining room as the string ensemble ended its spirited playing of Mozart. Michele smiled in the darkness. "They adored your speech, *chérie*."

His unblinking eyes stared at her. Then his face cracked into V's of delight. "The part about political whores was a nice touch." He grinned Satanically.

She caressed his cheek. "Erich, you almost took me in. Almost, for a moment, you seemed . . . serious."

"Me? Never. It's my major flaw."

"It's your major attraction." She linked her arm in his and led them up the broad flight of steps to the entrance hall. They would make quite an impression on guests leaving the dining room. It didn't at all hurt one's reputation to be seen on the arm of perhaps the most eligible bachelor in this corner of the world, certainly not in Michele's business, anyway.

She glanced at him out of the corner of her eye and satisfied herself that he had forgotten about the palm of his hand. She already knew too much about Erich Lorn. He was, in fact, serious, and bleeding internally as a result. As for the hand, there was simply no point in telling him what she had seen there, now or ever.

CHAPTER 22

The *Lokal* on Sankt Wolfganggasse, in the old part of Basel, had been known for well over two hundred years as a place where Balser men met in their cliques to plan their forthcoming part in the Fasnacht celebration, or their outing next Sunday at a new place for target shooting.

In Switzerland, a man's family is the primary social structure, as it is in Italy and elsewhere. But where the Italian can look for support to his extended family, down to remote third cousins and phalanxes of friends joined to him not by blood but by being godparents or godchildren, the Basler need look no further than his men's clique.

This is a small group, often from his old neighborhood. They may even have gone to the same primary schools as he, or worked in the same office or factory with him. Whatever their original bond—and in the case of some cliques it can go back centuries to a time no one now living can recall—a man's clique is his extended family, ready to succor him in illness, find him a better job, wangle a position for his son, enforce a marriage for his daughter, hold his wife's repute above suspicion, relay valuable secrets, shun detested enemies, alert him to coming opportunities, bad-name his rivals, elevate his family name, support his electoral favorites, join in discreet public demonstrations of protest, listen sympathetically to his troubles, stand him to a schnapps, join in a variety of business and financial ventures, visit him in the hospital, hush up his peccadilloes, send flowers in sad moments and follow his coffin to the grave.

The cliques of Basel are especially strong, mirroring as they do the secular control of this city that medieval craftsmen's guilds once fought to take away from the powerful archbishopric. Some of the old guilds persist into the highly industrial present, giving their names to several ancient eating places. But the prime purpose of the modern cliques, after their function as an extended family, lies mostly in the fifing, miming and drumming that goes on during Fasnacht. It is for this that most cliques meet.

And to play jass.

While this card game is usually played directly after lunch or dinner as an acceptable *digestif* and an honorable method of delaying one's return either to the office or the bosom of one's family, there are some players who prefer to devote an evening to the game, after a dutiful dinner with wife and children. They then repair to the place in which the cliques normally meet and they play jass late into the night, often with men of rival cliques, since it is much sweeter to beat an outsider than a clique-brother.

By eight o'clock Bunter was ensconced at his usual table, having bought a new deck of cards from the proprietor, who was sitting with him for the moment, opening the deck and shuffling it expertly. Here in Sankt Wolfganggasse, his fellow devotees of jass knew Bunter by his legal name, Albrecht Mütfäng.

Bunter fanned out the new deck on the dark oak of the tabletop. There are thirty-six cards in jass, a game superficially like pinochle or bezique. One can play it with what the Baslers call a "French" or regular deck as used in bridge or poker. All the cards between the six and the ace are first stripped out. But the true Basler plays with the "German" deck designed for jass. For a few francs the landlord is always able to supply a fresh one.

The suits in the "German" deck resemble stylized roses, heraldic shields, acorns and round bells not unlike Christmas tree ornaments. The suits go by the name of *Rosen, Schilten, Eichlen* and *Schaellen.*

In the jass deck Bunter was staring at now, the face cards were different from the regular or "French" deck. Yes, one could play jass with the usual king, queen and jack, but there was something un-Swiss about it. Perhaps it was the queen.

Bunter frowned thoughtfully. He'd played with both kinds of decks, of course, but nine times out of ten it was with this "German" one. As made for jass, the deck had no queens of any suit. It had the *König,* of course, with and without beard, holding the symbol of his suit. There was also a jack, called the *Under,* full of fun, smoking a pipe or carrying a letter like a postman. But, between them, where the queen would be, was the *Ober,* a man smoking a churchwarden pipe or, in one suit, a cigar. No queen. For the utterly Swiss game of jass, never a queen.

Across the room, already playing with two men whom Bunter didn't recognize, sat Ingo Huffel, whom Bunter knew by sight but had never seen before in this place. From Huffel's easy familiarity with the cards, it seemed clear he had played as much jass in his time as had Bunter. But there was a somewhat distracted look to the man as if he were merely filling in time. His glance slid often toward the low door that led out onto the street. This lack of attention, it seemed to Bunter, had already cost Huffel two games.

Bunter stopped watching Huffel. The man was not a friend, hardly even an acquaintance. Basel was getting to be a big city, overcrowded with new faces. And even men of Bunter's age, who had spent many if not all their sixty-odd years in this place, could no longer count on knowing every face on the street. It had been ten years or more since Bunter could honestly say a new face was a surprise to him.

That had all changed. The new faces were not always comfortable to be with. They came from all over Europe, these strangers' faces. They bore the characteristics of half a dozen peoples. Their lines were unfamiliar. Their coloring was often strange. The way these new people dressed was not Basler, not even remotely so. But, what the hell, Bunter thought, Basel isn't Basel any more, either.

His slight, cynical smile attracted the landlord's attention. "What's funny?"

Bunter shrugged heavily, peasant-fashion, as if managing the gesture while holding a yoked pair of filled milk buckets on his shoulders. His master, Herr Erich Lorn, had never seen this kind of movement in Bunter. It did not fit the elegant manservant of perhaps the most elegant bachelor in Basel. But it fitted Bunter's mood now, here in this place where they all knew him for what he really was, a Mütfäng with two umlauts.

"I was thinking only that Basel isn't Basel," he said then. "It hasn't been for ten years. It's another place now, with all these new people."

The owner sniffed appreciatively. "Some of them aren't even Swiss," he added primly. "I get a new clientele here during the day."

"I know."

"This is part of the tourist zone," the landlord went on. "I get tourists on foot every hour of the day and night during the season. The damnedest collection of oglers and askers."

"But they are buyers, too," Bunter suggested slyly.

"Some are buyers," the owner demurred. "'The *Scheisspifke* have money," he added, using a private term for Germans, "also the Americans. But now even the Americans have no money. They take pictures, but they never buy any more than a beer."

"Only the *Scheisspifke* buy."

"Why not?" the landlord said with heavy irony. "Didn't they win the war?"

Bunter smiled slightly at this often repeated joke. At that moment the door to the street opened and a stranger came in. He was short, about Bunter's age, with a round face somewhat hidden by his loden coat's broad upturned collar, which he had pulled to ear level. Even so, and even before the stranger had turned away

136

toward the table where Ingo Huffel was losing another game of jass, even then Bunter had already recognized his master's soon-to-be uncle, perhaps the single most powerful man in all Basel, the Herr Dieter Staeli.

Bunter's eyes flickered sideways past the landlord's shoulder several times, as if silently urging him to look around. "You have a distinguished guest," he said in an undertone, his lips hardly moving.

Dieter Staeli had seen Bunter on the few occasions when Herr Lorn had held small galas at his town house. But the great Herr Staeli would not have noticed Bunter, any more than Bunter could have helped but notice the great Herr Staeli.

He watched the newcomer sit down rather heavily with his back to the room, nodding politely to both Huffel and his fellow players. The jass game ended quickly, and badly, for Ingo Huffel, who lost for the third but last time. His partners got up from the table and moved on.

After a whispered consultation with his new guest, whose back remained to the room, Huffel called to the landlord: *"Zwei Pokal Weisswein, bitte."*

Moving with unaccustomed speed, the owner slipped behind his tiny dark-oak service bar and quickly filled two large green glasses to the top with white wine. He carried them to the table without spilling a drop, even though the level of the wine reached the lip of each glass.

Bunter watched with some amusement. The landlord rarely moved that deftly any more, not after a long career of eating and drinking his own wares. Like any true, God-fearing Swiss, the owner of this place respected temporal authority as awesome as that of Herr Staeli, even though all Swiss were the same in the eyes of God. And, since this was the first visit of this prominent man to such a humble establishment, who knew whether alert service and a brimming glass would not bring him back again, perhaps as a regular customer.

Even the Staelis must have a place to drink white wine and play jass, Bunter thought, but wherever it might be, it wasn't in the tourist zone of Basel, or anywhere nearby, unless they could be protected from intrusion.

His years with Herr Lorn had given Albrecht Mütfäng a great

many things besides his name of Bunter. The chief lesson he had learned was the length to which the very wealthy went to preserve their privacy—even their anonymity, where possible—but always their privacy. He knew, for example, that his own master regularly assumed other names in the course of his escapades with women. So, for that matter, did his fiancée, Fräulein Staeli, except that she was widely known never to indulge in any escapades whatsoever.

Sitting alone now, covertly watching the broad, squat back of the most recent visitor to his *Lokal,* Bunter decided that he might strike up a game of jass with the men who had just left the table after defeating Ingo Huffel three times. They might have quite an inflated opinion of their prowess with the cards, these men, although Bunter was quite sure that Huffel had lost because his mind was not on jass at all but on the imiment arrival of the powerful and wealthy Herr Staeli.

And what would such a man have to discuss with a nobody like Ingo Huffel, Bunter asked himself. He idly reshuffled the new deck of cards as he thought. What did the *König* want with the *Under?*

Who, after all, was Ingo Huffel? Not even an *Under.* He worked for a very minor bank, Bunter recalled, a bank so minor he could not even recall its name.

Not that it was Bunter's business to keep such nonsense in his head. No true, God-fearing Swiss cluttered his head with such gossip. Now he recalled: the Basel branch of some American bank, hardly a bank at all, more of a storefront where an American tourist might cash a check, perhaps. A courtesy office. And Ingo Huffel, of such low business connections, was now locked in profound discussion with one of the most powerful men in Switzerland? It made no sense.

Bunter's clique was a small but select one. Herr Lorn, his employer, was not a member, of course. But it was never a bad thing for an employee to help his employer, was it? Of course not.

Bunter stood up and moved ponderously past the table at which the very private discussion was taking place. He rounded the dark-oak post that formed the corner of the yellowish stucco wall behind Ingo Huffel's back. He continued down the narrow corridor toward the toilet. But he stopped walking after two paces and listened. Eavesdropping? No, just a pause on his way to piss.

Herr Staeli's voice had grown suddenly louder. ". . . damn it,

138

this is precisely why I put you into this job two years ago, to—"
Staeli's voice lowered suddenly and Bunter could hear only murmurs. He backed up a pace, hidden from the two men by the corner of the stuccoed wall with its old oak crossbeams, pillars and braces showing through the creamy plaster.

". . . never learned any more about it than that," Ingo Huffel was protesting.

"Then we know nothing!" Staeli burst out.

"But Shelter has—"

"Shelter?" Dieter Staeli cut in coldly, his voice loud but under control. "He has what you have. Whispers. Rumors. Inklings. Put them together and they make a patch of fog. Someone has gone to a lot of trouble to envelop this operation in a smokescreen, Huffel. I depended on you to see through it."

Bunter stood there, poised on one foot, marveling not so much at what was said but at the fervor, the fierceness of the great man.

". . . bothered me at home today," Huffel was complaining.

"He's become dangerous, then," Staeli muttered. "Dangerous to us."

The sudden coldness of the man's voice sent a chill across Bunter's shoulder blades. Time to be moving along to the toilet, yes?

". . . cannot have been the new man, Burris," Ingo Huffel was saying. His voice had a peculiarly plaintive note to it, as if, whatever the words seemed to mean, they were actually a plea for his very life.

"I know that!" Staeli said, so ferociously that it whipped like a curse. "I recognize the trademark of this smokescreen," he went on then. "I know whose mind produced it."

"If he's here in Basel, I can—"

"He's not here in Basel," Staeli interrupted, almost snarling. "He's in Lugano." Then his voice dropped to a murmur and stayed there.

After waiting a while, Bunter continued on tiptoe to the toilet, urinated and returned nosily to the main room. Something about the intensity of what he had overheard, as well as the careful undertone in which the two men now conversed, made him uncomfortable at remaining here in his own *Lokal*.

He signaled the landlord, left a franc piece on the table, and went outside into the cool night. He stared up at the moon. It was almost full, another night or two lacking.

Its cool, merciless face reminded him of Dieter Staeli's. He shuddered slightly and walked toward the Rhine for a constitutional before heading for home and bed.

Such men struck chill into one's heart, Bunter told himself. Poor Ingo Huffel's voice had been shaking with fear. Not that Bunter's own master couldn't get angry. But with Master Erich it was a sudden storm and it passed. He grew angry, he shouted, he calmed down, he smiled. One could work for such a man and respect him as a human being and never fear him, never find oneself shaking in one's boots. It was very un-Swiss to fear an employer.

And yet Huffel had been in terrible fear of Herr Staeli. Well he might be. Bunter could gather very little from what he had overheard, but it was enough to know that Ingo Huffel had been entrusted with some secret undercover business and had miserably botched it.

Bunter took deep breaths of the air now as he stood by the edge of the fast-flowing Rhine. He had walked for a while now, pondering the matter. He stood just above the *Totentanz* area, not far from where the ferryboat left.

He could gaze along the river, downstream, and see the red taillights of autos, and the long, narrow double streetcars still crossing the main bridge at this late hour, still rattling over the Mittlererhein Brücke to and fro, that ceaseless scurrying between the two halves of the town that melded Basel into one great city, a city that had even now grown strange to him, who had lived here so many years of his life.

He walked down to a narrow end of the Rheinweg, the footpath that ran along the river, a few flights of stairs down from the *Totentanz*. The moonlit night was quiet. The *Feuerlöschboot* shifted peacefully in its moorings. In the moonlight one couldn't even see its bright-red paint. The ferryboat, too, lay at rest beside its landing. The fast-running river produced a tiny curl of foam where the stationary prow cut the water. At this distance, the flowerpots, filled with geraniums, looked flat and gray.

Bunter sighed and stared across the river at the Unterer Rheinweg, the street that ran along the river there, wider than the one he was on, with a pavement for cars and two sidewalks. The Unterer

Rheinweg was not the side of the river where the old, moneyed names lived. Most of them sat in their private, fenced-off parks in the Gellertstrasse section on this side of the Rhine.

But Bunter's master, Erich, lived in one of the houses across the river. From here, in the tricky moonlight, with his aging eyes, Bunter could not make out which one it was. *Gott,* he was getting old, not even able to distinguish by night the house where he worked all day.

Herr Erich loved living in the quarter across the river not because it was unfashionable—although this pleased him, too, of course—but because it was quiet and had the only good view of the city itself. And one thing more, no across-the-street neighbors to tattle on his comings and goings. Across the street from Herr Erich's house lay only the swift-flowing river, never the same from one moment to the next, and totally without interest in the amours of even as high-born a lover as Herr Erich.

A string of three barges towed by a tugboat was busily hustling upstream. Bunter watched it carefully thread its way under the narrow arches of the Mittlererhein Bridge. He glanced up at the moonlit sky and saw that the delicate traceries of the cathedral spires were silhouetted against bright clouds. Nearer, the shorter steeple of St. Martin's Church rose above the rooftop of the Drei Könige.

Bunter watched the Martinskirche steeple for a moment. It was then that he saw he was not alone in his study of the night. Some one hundred meters along the edge of the river in the direction of the hotel, a man in a dark-colored coat held a pair of night binoculars to his eyes.

He seemed to be watching the same steeple Bunter had studied. But then, from the angle at which he held the glasses, it seemed more likely that the man was keeping one of the suites in the Drei Könige under surveillance. Bunter judged it might be the suite at the end nearest him, where a single small lamp somewhere inside the room caused the corner window to be faintly illuminated. The room had a narrow balcony. Was there someone standing there?

Someone, or perhaps two people, Bunter couldn't tell, stood on the balcony looking at the moon. The idea of a hidden watcher, lurking in the shadows of the night, watching them, made him as nervous as had the scene in his own *Lokal* a few minutes before. It was so un-Swiss to spy this way, from a hidden place. Bunter hated the idea of it.

He turned and walked away from the Rhine toward his home. Basel was a city of many secrets, many intrigues, much spying. This he knew. All cities were that way now, and none more so than Basel, where so many business and financial secrets were safeguarded.

But this was no longer his city, Bunter mused unhappily. It was a strange city full of furtive conversations in which high-born, high-placed men demeaned themselves with petty sneaks. In which sordid men lurked in the night spying on hotel windows.

The *Unders* were spying on the *Obers*. Kings consorted with Jacks. Basel wasn't Basel any more.

CHAPTER 23

In the darkness of Burris' bedroom at the Drei Könige the breeze off the river parted the curtains for an instant, then let them softly close again, like the vertical iris of a cat's eye. Margit sat up in bed watching the window and wondering how much of this adventure had been alcohol, how much physical attraction.

And how much insanity, she added silently.

Of course it went without saying that both of them had to have been drinking to try anything as insane as this. In the heart of Basel, in a hotel teeming with people who knew her, after a highly public reunion, to have drunk the afternoon away and then—when? Six P.M., had it been? —to somehow sneak up a rear stairway and into Burris' hotel suite without being seen.

It wasn't possible not to have been seen. Some cleaning woman, some porter, someone had seen them.

Even the cat's eye of the window curtains was watching, blinking, watching.

Burris' regular, deep breathing was like the soft purr of a refrigerator late at night when one can't sleep, Margit thought, and one goes down to the kitchen for something suitable, a cup of hot chocolate, and one stands against the rim of the sink in the half-dark, with the house, the world and everything in it fast asleep, and only the mindless purr of the great refrigerator to keep one company at such a terrible hour of one's life.

Except that this man was not sent to her for the purpose of chilling things. That he had been sent, Margit had no doubt. She did not believe in coincidence, only in her own ignorance of what had produced what seemed to be a coincidence.

Burris had been sent, she mused now. And why?

She had already thought of how they had first met, six years before, and it had become clear to her that originally she had been sent to Burris. He had been terribly awkward, with a bad habit of turning truculent in the presence of people he took to be his social superiors. What made it worse was that he never once admitted their superiority, since, after all, he was an American.

At first he hadn't known who she was, in those long-ago days at Harvard. Just some foreign student or other. He had made a conventional pass at her and she had made the conventional response of an adventurous girl far from home. He had had no way of knowing he was her first affair because she displayed none of the outward signs of virginity. The inward sign, Margit amended silently now. Anyone who had skied as much as she could be said to be intact only in the technical sense.

Nor could he tell by her behavior in bed, because she had read widely and listened at length to the late-night confessions of college roommates whose post-adolescent fantasies were far steamier than hers.

By the time Burris had learned who she was it was too late for him to tense up, turn to stone and go into his poor-boy-from-the-wrong-side-of-the-tracks act. They were already lovers. She had been sent to smooth him out of his awkwardness. To smooth him upward to where he was obviously headed anyway, some high-ranking position where he would have to be able to hide his inbred hostility toward moneyed people. Judging from his behavior today, she had done a good job.

But, the second time around, why had he been sent to her?

She eased herself off the bed, careful not to wake him, and tiptoed to the window. The gentle breeze off the Rhine pressed the curtain against her naked body as she peered out at the river that had rushed and curved its way through her life, the river of her birth, her youth, and soon her middle years.

Behind her the comforting purr of Burris' breathing formed a kind of bass note to the scene below her, the rushing water, the muted single *clang* of a streetcar bell warning some tipsy pedestrian out of the way as it curved silently up over the bridge and down into Kleinbasel across the way.

Across the way, almost directly across, stood the small house Erich had bought some years ago as his bachelor quarters. It was in darkness now but Margit knew it would be only a matter of time, if she stood here long enough, before his little Magna pulled to a halt and he ushered some favored female into the house. Someone rather good this time, she decided, good enough to keep him from his luncheon appointment with her, so that her meeting with Burris might take place. Intricate plan. Worthy of the gargoyle, perhaps.

She sighed. The river wind was chilling her now. She stepped back from the curtains and watched their slit slowly close.

Burris mumbled something in his sleep, a collection of half-syllables. Margit found herself wondering if she really loved him or if it was just the way they were in bed. With him she had always been at the height of her—what to call them?—capabilities? Other men didn't bring all of her up and out the way Matt did. It was something to do with his having been her first lover, something she really didn't feel like analyzing. One just accepted some things, and it wasn't really all that hard to accept the fact that there was something special between them, something physical, that made everything go well.

She smiled crookedly at the lazy workings of her mind. She, who felt it necessary to analyze everything, was contentedly giving herself a leave of absence when it came to Matt Burris.

Perhaps it was because, in a way, she had initiated him as thoroughly as he had initiated her. But that had been six years ago and everything was quite different now. This drunken rendezvous, for example, was about the most dangerously spontaneous thing she could have done. If word of it ever got back to someone who wished her ill—someone like her dear cousin Walter or her devoted uncle Dieter—it could be used to destroy her.

In other words, she told herself now with the surgical clarity of her late-night mind, what I am doing now is disastrous, self-destructive, insane, and I knew it from the moment he sat down at my table. Even then I knew we would end as we have, in bed.

She recalled that she had even had a chance to escape this self-destructive trap when he'd left her for a while at the table to take care of a piece of business at his bank. And, like a lamb self-led to slaughter, she had sat there and waited for him to return. Amazing behavior for a woman who prided herself on her intelligence.

Strange that she should jeopardize herself for a man she really didn't know that well.

Not that Burris was unknowable. He had been programed somewhere deep in his American psyche to rise, to succeed, to mount ever higher in the system of which his parents had been victims, to rise from that level until he could control a piece of the same system and call it his own. That was the simple, economic Burris, but there was an emotional Burris, too.

Margit had studied the world around her for many years, rarely as a participant, nearly always as an observer, watching it as if through a magnifier that gave her the objective view only utter security could produce. She knew enough about the emotional Burris—from outside him, but using a powerful lens—to know that his strength was a passive one. By contrast, Erich was always in motion. Matt was usually braced in an impregnable position. Erich was an irresistible force. Matt was the original immovable object.

She sank into the depths of an upholstered chair, sitting sideways in it so that her long legs dangled over one arm.

Matt wasn't phlegmatic, she mused, but he was . . . stolid? He could be funny and, when the spirit moved him, he could be quick. He'd certainly shown no signs of hesitation or lethargy this afternoon. But his basic stance was a show-me one, testing each new bit of evidence suspiciously, like the banker he was, evaluating, holding back until the right moment. With Erich everything came out all at once. He really didn't give a damn. What happened next year or next month or in the next instant was of supreme indifference to Erich.

Matt planned. Matt rose. And Matt would rise higher. Even today, in the midafternoon, as they continued their tête-à-tête in the dining room downstairs, he had excused himself for ten minutes to

145

run over to his office and meet a courier. When it came to his job, Matt could keep his head about him. She admired that single-minded side of him in which he could drop her for a moment. He had never fawned on her and never would. She found her independence . . . intriguing. Which made it all the more fascinating now to Margit to know why he had come back into her life. Was the airmail letter from Harvard a warning, an omen? Or was she being insane again?

Not that he wasn't welcome. She shifted restlessly on the upholstered chair, thinking of the week in London and of her tentative, almost half hearted plans to strike a blow for her own independence, at last, from the domination of people like her uncle Dieter. Matt would be good that way. He would have good ideas. He had managed to rechannel his hostility into a sound sense of business maneuvering. Most successful men managed that shift. Matt would be able to help her a great deal, if she could count on two things: his loyalty and the secrecy of their relationship.

This would have to be the least-known affair in Basel. Already too many people had had the opportunity to see it begin, or begin again. Somewhere in this hotel there might be a chambermaid who held another clue to it which could be teased out of her someday by a Walter or one of his agents. After tonight, she and Matt would have to be much more careful how and where and when they met.

That they would continue to meet had not even been settled. That he would not betray her to the males of the Staeli clan was still problematical. That she was being foolish in trusting him even this far was the only sure thing in the renewed affair.

But, no, she chided herself. It was impossible not to trust Matt Burris. His disinterested feelings for her were the real basis of their relationship. He was still the same surly I-go-my-own-way person he'd always been. If he'd known, when he'd first seen her six years ago, that she was a Basler Staeli and heir to one of the great fortunes of Switzerland, he'd never have said hello to her in the first place.

Something stiff and unyielding had been designed into him when it came to wealthy people. It wasn't hatred, or, if it were, he had learned to dissemble the hatred very usefully. It was something else, more likely, perhaps pure distrust. He suspected the motives

146

of the well-to-do and he always would. It was this poor boy's chip-on-the-shoulder attitude that she had always found so irresistible . . . and thus trustworthy.

Matt Burris had obviously not wanted her for her fortune. Even then, in those days so long ago, Margit had been quite aware that she had been betrothed early in life to Erich as a simple protection against fortune hunters. The combination of wondering whether a new man might love her for herself alone, and the various other debilitating requirements of being a good Swiss daughter and fiancée, had kept her virginal for Matt Burris.

Over the intervening six years, neither of them had changed that much. He still wanted her just for herself. Her money only irritated him. He had been brought up to make his own. The fact that the woman he enjoyed sleeping with had more money than he would ever earn might have inflamed a fortune hunter to greater feats of bedroom daring. It only annoyed Matt. More than that, she realized, it probably kept them from ever expressing their feelings for each other more concretely than in hotel bedrooms, on the sly.

Dangerous business. All that happens in hotels is known.

She smiled cynically and thought: dangerous this may be, and I don't care. In the darkness of the room her smile grew more lopsided. If this is what love does to one's judgment, then love is the most dangerous game.

One grew vulnerable, spontaneous, changed, grew scheming. Already her mind was leaping ahead to such problems as where they might meet. Basel, for example, was out of the question. Any of the small towns nearby, even the farming villages, were equally useless. People noticed everything in such towns. They needed a fairly good-sized city where their comings and goings would pass anonymously in the crowd. Strasbourg was too far away. Perhaps Colmar, half an hour away by car. She had a good friend in Colmar who owned some apartments that . . .

But they'd need a car whose license plates could not be traced to her. Effortlessly, Margit's mind spun through the permutations of the problem. None of the vehicles belonging to the Schloss would do. Neither would a rented car, whose plates tracked back to a signed agreement. A broad deception was necessary . . . yes, Erich's orange sports car. It was his treasure, but he had let her use it before and he'd let her use it again. What were fiancés for, if not that? And wherever it stood parked, curious eyes, knowledgeable eyes, would instantly reach the wrong conclusion: Erich Lorn's car, eh?

That solved that, but the rest of the logistics were still formidable.

All the intrigue would be up to her. Matt Burris simply didn't understand this kind of scheming. Business, yes, but never in his private life. It would be her responsibility to find a place for them where they could meet and come and go in safety. It irritated her to think that she would have to bother herself with details the man usually handled, but this was her home ground, not his.

Would he agree to it? More important, would he realize the need to be cautious, the need for secrecy? And, finally, most important of all, would he continue to be loyal to her?

In Margit's entire life, as she sat back now, legs dangling, and reviewed it with that dark pessimism of the early-morning hours, had anyone ever been completely loyal to her? Other than servants, of course. Had anyone of her own class been loyal? In this context "loyal" meant something complete, without exception in word, in deed, at the level of the head and the heart. Had anyone been that loyal? Only one: Erich.

The gargoyle that sat on her shoulder made a hissing noise that only Margit Staeli heard, or ever would hear. It was as close as the gargoyle ever came to laughter.

Erich loyal? When he had betrayed their betrothal hundreds, perhaps thousands of times with other women? But if his sexual fidelity was meaningless to her, because she had no desire to possess Erich, then by her standards he was loyal and always had been. Even as children, whiling away the lazy summers together, with all the casual cruelties that children carelessly inflict on each other, even then Erich had been loyal.

The man asleep on the bed, who had once been the most important thing in her life when she was far from home, alone and glad to be, but needing someone to share her aloneness, this man had also been loyal to her. It was Margit who had broken up the affair, simply and swiftly, the day after graduation when, with trunks packed and air tickets in hand, she had made for Matt Burris a brief speech that was the equivalent of the American song, "It was great fun, but it was just one of those things."

148

Cold-blooded, of course, and he'd told her so. "But we both knew it had to end," she'd reminded him.

And he'd produced no comeback. No, "I don't want it to end." No, "I'll follow you to the ends of the earth." There had never been any rhetoric between them. If they had any meeting ground other than the physical attraction between them, it was that both of them distrusted rhetoric. And, of course, neither of them would ever beg, would they? Pride was important.

In a certain type of affair, she mused now, swinging her bare legs up and back in the darkness of the room, the absence of rhetoric eventually kills it. Damn the hours after midnight! One saw life too coldly clear at such times.

Erich would know all about the rhetoric of love. He would know, perhaps intuitively, that one had to say "I love you" even if "love" wasn't an accurate description. Even proud people needed that, perhaps more than anyone else. Erich would know that, at times, one had to say "I can't live without you," even though of course one always could. People had to hear these things, Margit told herself, or the affair was just—what had one Englishman called it?—organ grinding.

She laughed out loud at the thought. One organ grinding against the other.

Burris mumbled something incoherent and suddenly sat upright in bed.

"Hey."

They stared at each other in the half-dark. "How long have you been up?" he asked then, getting up off the bed.

"I started thinking how foolish we've been and it kept me from getting back to sleep."

He looked about the bedroom and then nodded slowly. He winced then and held his aching head. "But nobody saw us."

"Perhaps."

He shook his head gently. "I'm sorry," he said then. "There was something about seeing you again. I just fell in and drowned." He laughed sheepishly. "The way you looked. There was a . . . light . . . coming out of you."

Neither of them spoke for a long time. Margit decided it was up to her, apparently, to be the businesslike partner. "Are you really here permanently, Matt?"

"If a few years is permanent, yes."

The next part was hard for Margit to put in words. "You . . . what I . . . I want to . . ." She stood up and went to the window. Outside, the river sped past, broad, swift, utterly without interest in what was happening to her, now or ever.

"If we want to see each other again," she began at last, "we—"

"You must be kidding." He had come up behind her and she could feel his body pressed against her, warm with sleep. His arms went around her and she locked her arms over his. "Of course we do," he said.

"Then we have to be practical," she heard herself saying. She hated the sound of the word. What did "practical" have to do with "I can't live without you"?

"How practical?" he asked.

"Enough so that when we want to be together we'll be in a place where we won't worry about some chambermaid seeing us."

"Sure."

She waited for something beyond that, but he was silent again, accepting in advance whatever conditions she would set down. But she was damned if she wanted him that way. Instead of saying anything, she waited.

Finally, Burris said: "This is your bailiwick. You're known here. The only way we can swing this is away from Basel."

Margit felt a small sense of relief. At least he'd taken that much of a lead. But if she knew Matt, this would be the limit he'd go. He had never pursued her, not before, in the States, and not now. "That doesn't sound very comfortable," she told him. "How far away?"

"Christ, I don't know." He pulled her around to face him. "If it was up to me, we'd never leave this suite."

She smiled up at him. "It took you long enough to say that."

He touched her face. "But your life here has problems."

"More than usual."

His big shoulders moved almost convulsively, as if shrugging off some immense burden, or assuming one. "It doesn't matter what I have to do to keep seeing you. Whatever it is, I'll do it."

Because, Margit added silently, I can't live without you. I have to learn to translate what he means from what he says. "Even if it gets complicated?" she asked then, testing.

"I don't care." He started to say something more, then stopped

150

and made a balloon-bursting noise, as of releasing pent-up pressure. "I'm crazy about you and I don't care."

She was silent for a moment. "Nothing changes," she told him then. "We're six years older and we're not even a bit wiser. I think it's . . . touching."

"Um. Listen, it's cold by this window. Can we sort of . . . ?"

". . . get back to bed?" she finished. "You mean, in addition to everything else we ought to have learned at least that much?"

He took her hand and led her back across the room to the bed. "You always did like to analyze everything, didn't you?"

"I've given that up."

"No, you're still at it."

"No, I've stopped," she assured him. "I really have. Otherwise, I wouldn't be here. I wouldn't be planning ways of seeing you again and again and again. It's dangerous and it doesn't lead anywhere and a calm, rational analysis would show me that." She lay back on the bed and pulled him down beside her. "Which is why I've given up analyzing."

He began to kiss her nipples. "At least you haven't given up everything."

He started to make love to her again and this time there was something more ruthless about it. They had been relaxed before, the alcohol had seen to that. But he was pushing now, moving her along faster than she liked, forcing the pace. He had always been gentle with her, as perhaps a big man knew he had to be. But now she felt impaled, like something that had gotten in the way of his penis and was being rammed home with a fury completely outside of either of them.

"Matt."

"God, it's been so long," he was saying, his mouth against her ear. The insistent rhythm was quickening now. The bed shuddered beneath them with each thrust. "You have no idea how good you feel. How good it feels to be fucking you. There's something so—"

"Matt!" she shouted and an instant later felt herself turn inside out, the spasm shaking both of them with its force.

Her fingers dug into his buttocks, pulling him deeper into her. She could feel him thrust one more time and then his body lifted away from her, spine arched backward, connected to her at only one hot, streaming place. His mouth rounded into an O and he climaxed in utter silence. Then, after a while, he slid off to one side, curled against her body, his mouth open and gasping for breath.

Neither of them moved for a long time. She found a pillow and tucked it under his head. His breathing had calmed and slowed and grown more shallow. She could feel long waves rippling up her belly like pleasant electric shocks. There had never been anyone like this. It didn't matter what he wasn't.

She lay there amazed at herself for having been that out of touch with her body that she hadn't made it her business to find him long ago, wherever he was. Japan, she had heard. It would have been the easiest thing in the world to find him. What was happening now could have been happening all along.

It really didn't matter that on some things he was inarticulate. There are all sorts of ways of expressing oneself, she thought. She had gotten his message several times tonight without, until now, understanding it.

It was her damned background, her training, the fact that she lived so much in her head, studying, being the good Swiss daughter, scholarly, taking the cerebral approach, doing all the right things in her head and nowhere else. It focused everything in one place, the mind. And this now had nothing to do with the mind.

She smiled privately in the dark, thinking that if one couldn't sleep in these fearful early hours, there was at least one thing to be done with the time, and it was vastly superior to brooding about life.

"And you'll be in Basel," she heard herself say, "for a few years at least?"

He laughed softly. "At least."

CHAPTER 24

The thin man in the dark-colored coat stuffed the binoculars into his pocket. He eased himself back into the shadows of the shrubbery and moved slowly, quietly up a footpath to the street above. There he paused for a moment and glanced both ways. After a while he moved off along the street in the direction of Drei Könige at a normal pace, another pedestrian on a late-night stroll.

Before he reached the hotel he darted into the shadows again. A narrow entryway led down a steep flight of stairs to a landing halfway between the street above and the river below. He paused on the landing and tried the steel door set into the basement level of the hotel. It had been open last night. It should——. Ah. The knob turned.

Shelter eased himself inside the cellar of the hotel. He moved carefully but the binoculars in his coat pocket rapped against the door jamb as he came through. He froze. In the distance he could hear two men talking in low voices. After a long moment, he shut the door behind him and turned sharp right along a narrow corridor.

The service elevator off the kitchen area was poorly lighted. Nevertheless, Shelter paused again before moving from the shadows into the open elevator. He listened. The voices of the two men seemed much farther away. Somewhere deep in the kitchen a machine produced a steady thumping, sloshing sound. Shelter got in the elevator and pressed the button for the top floor.

The door closed loudly and the elevator began to climb. At the top, the door slammed open. Shelter stepped out of the elevator, pressed the basement button and let the door bang shut. In the little rear-landing space here the light was even dimmer. He felt certain no one in any of the suites had heard the elevator doors or, if they had, were not alarmed by the noise. It was late, but not that late.

He eased open the door to the main hallway and peered along its carpeted length. Burris' suite lay at the far end near the river. Between this back-elevator landing and his door stood only one other door. It led to the back stairs. In the days before elevators room-service waiters had used this stairway.

He moved quietly on the heavy carpeting now, edging his way past the door to the stairwell. Was this the time to pull the handkerchief up over his face? From his surveillance of the room he already knew that Burris had a visitor. This could have been bad, but the visitor was a woman, and in Shelter's experience a new man in a new town usually had only one kind of woman in his room.

Shelter paused, halfway between the stairwell door and the entrance to Burris' suite. The turkey-red figures in the carpeting seemed to twist slightly as he stared down at them. He blinked.

His head ached. It had all afternoon since leaving Huffel's apartment. Thinking had been difficult. His brain seemed clogged by the worries he had.

What to do? Burris alone would be easy enough. Burris with a strange whore in his room might even be easier. Christ, of course!

Shelter smiled faintly in the half-dark. What better plan? He had Burris in a perfect blackmail bind. And, for reassurance . . . Shelter felt in the other pocket of his coat and brought out the .38 Special, a six-shot, blue-steel Staelifer with a long-enough barrel to guarantee accuracy at any reasonable distance. The Basel police used a similar version.

Still and all, Shelter reminded himself, surprise was an important edge. He'd have to let himself noiselessly into the suite with his duplicate key. As he recalled, there was a small entry hall, then a rather large living room before one reached the bedroom. Neither Burris nor the whore would hear him until he was ready to be heard. He'd tiptoe to the doorway of the bedroom, switch on the lights and catch them in the act. Perfect.

Shelter moved along the dimly lighted corridor until he reached the door to Burris' suite. He held the .38 in his left hand while, with his right, he took the key from his pocket and gently inserted it, millimeter by millimeter, into the lock. He felt, rather than heard, it click into its final position. He started to twist it gently.

Behind him he heard a thin, disembodied squeak.

He whirled, .38 aimed at groin level.

*   *   *

Curtis had come through the door from the stairway. He paused now and slowly, gravely, raised his hands over his head.

He hadn't figured the man for a gun. Curtis himself never carried one, hadn't even thought, after the telephone call this morning from Burris, that he was hurrying down to Basel to run head on into some loony with a Ned Buntline Special of the sort Marshall Dillon used on "Gunsmoke."

The man with the gun backed him down the hall into the rear-hall elevator landing. "No funny moves," he said then.

American, Curtis thought. Well, we *are* a violence-prone people, aren't we? "Listen," he said then. "I don't know who you are, but my wallet's in my hip pocket. So if you'll let me—"

"Shut up!" Shelter rammed the muzzle of the .38 into Curtis' midriff. "You wake anybody on this floor, you die first."

Philadelphia, Curtis thought. Or maybe Baltimore. This monkey is the bank manager Palmer sacked yesterday, some creep named, uh, Shelter. "Isn't much in my wallet," he went on in a soft voice. "Hardly two hundred francs, but it's yours."

Shelter grimaced. "You're going to have to sleep this off," he muttered then.

Curtis backed up another step until his back was against the rim of the elevator door. He began to reach behind him for his rear pocket. "Two hundred francs and this is a Movado watch. You can have it, too, if—"

"Up in the air, dammit!"

Curtis' fingers, hidden by his body, had just reached the service-elevator button. He pressed it and instantly threw his hand over his head again. "Right," he said. "Right. Right."

"Turn around."

"Right." Curtis turned his back to Shelter. He hoped the man knew how to gun-butt somebody neatly. Otherwise the back of his head was going to get chewed up.

Neither of them spoke for a moment. He could hear Shelter's heavy breathing. Then both of them heard the elevator rising in the shaft. "Hey," Curtis said. "Company's coming."

He let the thought sink in one beat, then turned on his heel, arm cocked over his head and brought his wrist down hard on Shelter's outstretched arm. The man had been in the process of reversing the gun to hold it by the barrel.

The heavy Staelifer revolver dropped to the concrete floor. An instant later, the service-elevator door banged open. Curtis kicked the gun into the elevator.

He turned to grab Shelter's arm and twist it behind him. Instead, Shelter dived past him like a tackler, arms outstretched, falling headlong into the elevator. His fingers closed on the gun and he scrambled across the ribbed steel floor of the elevator to a crouching position. He had skinned his fingers. A drop of blood oozed out over the first joint of his index finger as he pointed the .38 at Curtis and took careful aim.

The elevator door slammed shut.

Curtis jumped sideways out of the rear-hall landing. He made it down the hall and through the stairway door. He paused, listening. He could hear the elevator's downward whine, faint but clear. He pounded down the stairs two at a time, wondering which floor Shelter would choose.

Dizzy, sliding, holding the rail, slipping off an extra stair tread accidentally, Curtis made it to the main floor and dashed past the reception desk into the lobby. He glanced around the room, then ran out onto the street.

Far down the block, parked half off the street with two of its wheels on the sidewalk, stood a beige Volkswagen. Shelter had already opened the door and was starting the engine.

Curtis ran toward him. The little car was in motion. Shelter put it into a tight curve and started to U-turn. He had wound down the window on the driver's side. He paused for an instant and leveled the Staelifer .38 at Curtis.

The noise filled the narrow street with a roar and a clatter of echoes. Curtis dropped to the ground. The searing pain in his left arm felt like a hot iron. He watched the Volkswagen disappear toward the *Totentanz*.

Those damned long barrels are accurate, he thought fuzzily. Then he blacked out.

* * *

At this hour the emergency room at the Burgerspital around the corner from the *Totentanz* was entirely empty of other patients. As a matter of fact, Curtis thought as he sat there answering questions being put to him by a sleepy sergeant of police, this was probably the first time the emergency room had been used in months. There were no emergencies in Basel.

He finished going over his story for the third time. The sergeant seemed unhappy with the sequence of events, but since Curtis had told it exactly the same way every time, he snapped his notebook shut and nodded politely before getting to his feet.

"You are correct?" he asked in his uncertain English.

"I'm all right," Curtis corrected him with a smile.

"May I drive you to your hotel?"

Curtis pondered this for a moment. He had come directly from the airport to the Drei Könige without checking into the hotel across the river where he had a room reserved. He had been the only one, as far as he could tell, to spot Burris and Miss Staeli cop a sneak upstairs at six that night. Curtis had spotted Shelter about an hour later and had devoted the rest of the evening to waiting for him to make his move.

"It's the Hotel Krafft am Rhein," Curtis said. "I can easily walk it."

"So." The sergeant stood up. "You are a man of luck, Herr Curtis."

"You're telling me."

"I *am* telling you."

He watched the sergeant leave. The man was absolutely right. Curtis' luck had been with him. The .38 slug had still been rifling in a smooth path, thanks to the long Staelifer barrel. It had not started to tumble. It had passed very neatly through the flesh of his left arm leaving a wildly bleeding trench less than half an inch deep in its wake. The intern had cauterized and closed the trench with four butterfly sutures, then taped everything with the thoroughness of an Egyptian high priest mummifying a dead king for his final journey in the solar boat.

Curtis flexed his left arm and made a face. A few inches closer to his torso and the slug would have drilled him through the heart. As it was, the bleeding had caused him to black out for a moment. No real harm done, except to his shirt and suit jacket. They had brought his oyster-tan Burberry raincoat to the Burgerspital from the Drei Könige where he had checked it earlier this evening.

He got up and began looking for someone to pay. The emergency room was deserted. He pulled on his Burberry and looked at himself in a windowpane. Pale but no longer bloody. Good enough.

Curtis walked slowly, thoughtfully, back along the Blumenrain to the Drei Könige. It was now two in the morning. The story he had concocted for the police was of seeing a man sneak out of the hotel's cellar exit with such a furtive look that he, Curtis, a mere passer-by, had hailed him as he got into his beige Volkswagen. The man had taken a shot at Good Citizen Curtis. Nothing more.

Leaving UBCO and Burris out of the story had been easy enough, Curtis thought as he paused before the entrance of the

Drei Könige. But would Shelter do the same for the rest of the night? Had he had enough or would he be back? Not likely.

Curtis winced at the ache in his left arm. He walked along the street to the bridge and slowly, conserving his strength, strolled across the Mittlererhein Bridge toward Kleinbasel across the way. The Hotel Krafft was a good, small place that faced the river. Pausing in midbridge, Curtis could see the Krafft's outdoor garden restaurant, closed now, chairs tilted against tables. In a little while, if they had held his room for him, he would be peacefully asleep in one of the rooms upstairs.

He turned and stared at the top corner windows of Burris' hotel suite. Damned silly idea, taking her upstairs. If this was the kind of control Burris had over his emotions, he'd last another twenty-four hours on the job before Palmer would sack him.

If he were doing his job right, Curtis told himself, he'd telephone Burris and tell him to get her out of the room fast. But he didn't want to blight love's young dream, after all, and he had the feeling his boss, Palmer, wouldn't have thanked him for breaking up the tryst. Nor would Burris have taken it kindly, the big stiff.

Still and all, he hadn't been pigheaded enough to refuse help. If he hadn't telephoned Curtis this morning in Frankfurt, he might have ended in the center of an extremely messy scene with a pistol-packing Shelter and a permanently compromised Margit Staeli. Close thing.

It seemed clear to Curtis as he rested for a moment on the railing of the bridge, that it had been Shelter who had doped Burris' beer and searched his luggage. Evidently the little creep didn't have enough information to satisfy Dieter Staeli. You had to hand it to Palmer, sitting there in Lugano, weaving his spider's webs. When he wanted an operation kept secret, he made damned sure of it.

Curtis felt his wounded arm again. The intern had been uncertain, perhaps a week before the dressing came off and a smaller one replaced it? Perhaps a few days? Curtis walked the rest of the way off the bridge.

A streetcar came up silently behind him and crossed ahead of him now, running swiftly into Kleinbasel. Curtis' glances followed it a few blocks and saw it pause as a car with a revolving blue light on its dome suddenly darted across the street.

Curtis walked faster now. He moved along the Greifeng toward the Claraplatz where the police car had silently crossed. When he got there, he saw two cars, rooflights still turning, parked at angles a block along the Claragraben near a large department store, windows dark at this hour.

He got within a hundred yards before he saw the beige Volkswagen parked neatly at the curb, both doors open, flashbulbs going off as police swarmed over it. Instinctively, Curtis stepped into a doorway, but not soon enough. The sergeant who had taken his statement less than a quarter of an hour before had spotted him. He came ambling over, big, good-natured, but absolutely deadpan.

"He was a *Landsmann* of yours, Herr Curtis."

Curtis frowned. "Is that the—? Is he—?"

"Dead."

The sergeant's eyes looked coldly alert as he snapped out the monosyllable, producing something that sounded like "debt."

"Good Lord. And you say he was an American?"

The sergeant's head nodded slowly, his glance still combing Curtis' face for information.

"And he just . . . shot himself?" Curtis asked then.

The sergeant's face jerked suddenly. He seemed to lose interest in Curtis. "Not shot," he said. He turned and escorted Curtis to the car, gently moving other police aside. "You see?"

Curtis peered inside the beige Volkswagen. Shelter's skinny chest slumped across the steering wheel. His face looked at peace, eyes open but not staring. There seemed to be no blood.

"Poor man," Curtis murmured.

"A bad heart, perhaps," the sergeant suggested.

"How long has he been dead?"

"Perhaps half an hour, perhaps longer. Did he have a bad heart, Herr Curtis?"

Curtis shook his head. The time of death gave him a perfect alibi. He'd have to waltz the sergeant around at least one more time tonight before he got to sleep, but he was in the clear.

"I wouldn't know, sergeant," he said then. "Any gun?"

"Wait over there, please?"

Curtis sat down on the fender of a police car and watched the routine photographing and fingerprinting continue for a while before they lifted Shelter's body out of the car and laid it on a canvas stretcher. Another sergeant covered Shelter from scalp to bootsole with an olive-drab blanket.

It was a strange scene, Curtis noticed, not because it looked that much different than any other street accident. What made it strange was that it was going on in dead silence. There had been no sirens, no horns. There were, thus, no bystanders. The police spoke in solemn undertones as if they were advance agents for the mortician.

They seemed determined to make things as dull as possible. With any luck, Curtis thought hazily, they could even put me to sleep.

He forced his eyes open. A pair of headlights had turned the corner into Claragraben, aimed directly at him. The car stopped. Then it quietly reversed itself and backed out of sight onto the Claraplatz again. The police had been so busy with Shelter that Curtis had been the only one to see this strange, but understandable, maneuver.

The car had been a Jaguar, of that Curtis was certain, as light-colored as his oyster-tan raincoat. Cream color, perhaps. An E-type Jag with a hardtop. The main headlights sat high off the ground and close together. The parking lights had also been on.

Hard to blame the owner of the Jag from reversing the hell out of the Claragraben, once he caught a glimpse of the police cars.

Curtis yawned. With the exception of the beige Volks itself and the police cars, the Jag had been the only vehicle he'd seen on Basel's streets. Oh, and the long green streetcar, of course.

He stared at one of Shelter's hands, carelessly allowed to fall against the cobblestone surface of the street. Heart attack?

Curtis suddenly felt like asking if they'd found a needle track anywhere on Shelter. Not that he'd seemed like a junkie. But the death had been so tidy. Even one puncture could make a difference. Your normal, all-purpose Sicilian embolism required only one puncture in order to introduce a few cc.'s of air into the bloodstream. A neat way to go and, apparently, someone had really wanted Shelter to go. Would the driver of the Jag know anything about that?

Curtis sat, quietly nursing his arm, and wondering if this were the finish of something, or only the start.

PART THREE

Free? The Swiss? What can't one make people believe!

—Goethe

CHAPTER 25

Once his chauffeur had piloted the car southwest out of Basel along Highway 18 toward the Jura, Walter Staeli began to hope for some relief from the unseasonable heat of late August.

The summer had been a busy one for him, what with his secret work on the production of the hand calculators, and no letup whatsoever in his normal routine at the bank. He had actually done the work of two men, Walter told himself, and done both exceedingly well. His father had no cause for complaint—not that this would stop him from complaining—and neither did Walter. It had been a very productive summer.

This quick trip today into the Jura was an example of the kind of time-consuming events that now filled Walter's working day to a bursting eighteen hours. Outside the watchmaking center of Neuchâtel, in a tiny village near the suburb of Valangin, the miraculous calculator project had been translated from dream to reality, but only by Walter's constant attention.

He leaned forward in the Mercedes now to order the driver to shut off the air conditioning and open the windows. Walter liked to be cool, and in the heat of Basel closed car windows and air conditioning were necessary, but not out here in the open Jura countryside, eh? The winds off the Jura were notorious, the winters deadly. The only people who could ever live here were the dour Huguenot refugees who had fled here from France centuries ago. Their close-mouthedness was notorious, an ideal place for a secret project.

All four windows of the Mercedes lowered in stately unison, their motors activated by the chauffeur. Instantly a hot blast of soggy air struck Walter in the face. Damned weather! He shouted to the driver to close the windows and switch on the air conditioning again.

There would be no relief in the August heat, Walter decided, until he was at the Lac de Neuchâtel itself. This rather uninteresting body of water, with its steep, vineyarded shoreline and scattering of small, wooded islands, could usually be counted on to lower summer temperatures by about ten degrees. It still had a relatively unspoiled coastline and fairly unpolluted water, a contrast indeed with Geneva's nearby Lac Leman, whose shores were not wholly in Switzerland and thus subject to foreign filth. But on such a day as today, Walter feared, the Lac de Neuchâtel would raise the local humidity far beyond its already unacceptable level.

Humidity was a problem at Valangin, he knew, in the abandoned watch factory he had caused to be converted to the assembly of electronic calculators.

The citizens of the Valangin area had been quite grateful, in their stony-faced way, for this small favor. Two or three smaller watch companies had already gone out of business—or merged into a larger concern and closed their factories, which amounted to the same thing as going out of business—and there was in the region, for the first time in decades, real unemployment. Men were actually out of work. Women, employed for the delicate subassembly and quality-control inspection jobs, were also out of work. Families were on government support.

The entire matter was a national disgrace and no one felt more ashamed than the Valangoise themselves, who, perhaps because of their strong French Calvinist background, were even more Swiss than anyone else in detesting idleness and shunning unemployment as Satan himself.

The mayor of the town and the officials of the commune had wanted to open the abandoned watch factory with a discreet public spectacle, a corps of drummers, perhaps floats depicting scenes from the life of the region. Walter had steadfastly refused such public honors.

He had also managed, so far, to avoid a testimonial dinner at which the elders of the area would salute him with hours of elaborate speechmaking leavened only by unlimited supplies of the local wine from grapes that clustered around the perimeter of the lake itself.

Walter, who considered his taste in food and wines to be vastly superior to most, had developed something of a fondness for the local Neuchâtel wines. There were two produced in the area, a good Pinot Noir red so light in color it could almost be called a rosé, and the region's own version of the universal Chasselas white wine that in other locales went by the name of *Fendant* or *Donn*.

Walter particularly liked one version that had a slight bubble to it which produced on the back on the tongue a delicate little *frisson* one could continue to enjoy silently during the most boring of public speeches. He had attended hundreds of such meetings. Bankers must. But he had found them a bit easier to take with copious additions of wine. Walter, it goes without saying, publicly condemned alcohol, as did every God-fearing Swiss.

Time enough for such wordy tributes after all the calculators were en route to the wholesalers' warehouses and the advertising campaign was under way. Not now. No sense letting whatever competition there might be know in advance what The White Fox had so cunningly created.

Walter smiled with satisfaction as the artificially cool air flowed over him again. The countryside was heavy with heat in late summer. It slid smoothly past the windows of the Mercedes like a thick tapestry worked in fat yarns, puffy trees, bulging shrubbery, white-walled houses bursting with sunlight, sharp-angled roofs burning bright earth-red.

When the time came, in a few weeks, he would let the eager Valangoise fete him. He would make sure everything was filmed for television, that the wire services got their invitations, that the leading magazines sent reporters. In this way the entire nation would know what The White Fox had done, what Staeli had done, for the faltering watch industry. In this way, too, the entire world would get its first preview of the new hand computer.

In actuality, the Staelicomp calculator was already in unannounced distribution. It was already being sold to certain "advanced elements and favored customers" in the global financial community. But until the Japanese had shipped the remainder of the circuits, Walter was delaying public announcements. He had no intention of letting the little yellow brothers know how he'd

165

outfoxed them until he absolutely had to. The master strategy was too important to upset by premature publicity.

It wasn't, Walter reminded himself now, as if the entire Swiss economy rested on its troubled watch factories. Timepiece production made up only about 10 per cent of the nation's exports. Far more important to the prosperity of the land was the export of industrial machinery, of drugs and dyestuffs and of electrical power, generated by hydroelectric plants high in the Alps and sold to neighboring nations.

No, if all but the most solvent watch factories were to go bankrupt, Switzerland would still stand, Walter thought, but the morale problem would be utterly without precedent, totally beyond the power of the average Swiss to comprehend and cope with.

Swiss out of work? But this was the same as saying that God had removed His personal protection from His personal mountain republic. Of what use is it to serve God as He would want to be served if the result was unemployment? Clearly no true Swiss would be able to handle the angst involved in the wholesale collapse of the watch industry. Only The White Fox stood between his fellow Swiss and emotional chaos.

The Mercedes slowed as it passed through the lake town of St. Blaise. To the left, the morning mists over the water were lifting almost visibly under the pounding energy of the August sun. To further humidify the air, Walter added unhappily. Low humidity was essential to any precision-machine production, but especially so with these circuits arriving by the thousands from Japan.

They came, as Walter had ordered, in big wooden crates stenciled in German and French with such labels as "Auto Parts" and the names of a few of the more common chemical reagents. But when they were opened in the sealed-off shipping and storage areas of the converted watch factory near Valangin, they all contained the same thing, hundreds of neatly wrapped calculator circuits, each with its black plastic case already marked "Made in Switzerland."

The wooden crates were filled with peculiarly twisted bits of foamed plastic, which resembled immense unshelled peanuts and helped cushion the calculator circuits from handling shocks. Small bags of silica gel were interspersed in the plastic foam to absorb excess humidity. Too much moisture, at this point in their lives, could short out the tiny subminiature circuits. And too much humidity at Valangin could do the same, Walter worried.

The first run of the calculators had already been assembled, tested and shipped in cleverly designed cartons, each with its "Staelicomp" name and logotype artistically displayed. Walter had had the packaging designed in two different places, neither one in Switzerland.

A studio in Milan had created the overall artistic concept and a print shop in Munich had handled the typography. The printing itself had been done by one of Basel's many excellent printer-binders, one who was collaterally related to the Staeli clan and heavily in debt to Staeli Internationale, GmbH. Walter felt that such a printer's discretion could be relied upon, if only because of routine family blackmail.

Within a day or two at the most, assuming the quality-control section passed them, the second shipment of calculators would be on its way to such widely separated locales as London, Paris, New York, Brussels, Milan, Frankfort and other financial capitals. Once again, what had begun as a dream in the mind of The White Fox was now a stunning reality.

Already full-page advertisements were scheduled to appear in the leading financial reviews and periodicals of Western Europe and the U.S. The focus of the advertising was highly selective, being beamed almost entirely at banks, brokerage houses and other financial institutions. With the Staeli name, and the special fiscal functions programed into the calculator, as well as the giveaway price, Walter felt certain that the second shipment would be snapped up as fast as the first one, sold without fanfare. Moreover, the advertising would carry testimonials from banks already using the Staelicomp. Oh, it had all been worked out with the precision of genius!

The Mercedes was skirting the outer edges of Neuchâtel now, moving further from the lake until the chauffeur found the northbound highway that led to the border at La Chaux-de-Fonds, another watchmaking town perhaps better known for being the birthplace of the architect called Le Corbusier. Valangin appeared in a matter of a kilometer or two, and a moment later the heavy car pulled to a halt outside town in the loading area of the small factory which, even now, still bore its original signs as a watch factory.

Walter allowed his driver to open the door for him. Normally, in Basel, he let himself out of the car. It marked him as egalitarian, modern and, besides, in the hurly-burly of Basel traffic, one had no time or room for such feudal charades.

But here, with all the life-and-death power of a seignorial lord, as in fact the benefactor who had single-handedly brought jobs and wages back to this benighted backwater, Walter Staeli allowed himself the full satisfaction and pomp to which he was entitled in a democracy. The chauffeur opened his door for him, a small thing, but vast in its implications for The White Fox.

As he stepped from the Mercedes a group of factory officials lined up to greet him on the immaculately raked gravel of the driveway. Preparing his words of greeting, Walter's mind suddenly had one of those peculiar flashes of insight that had nothing to do with matters of the moment.

White Fox? White was the color of purity, true. But also the color of cowardice, was it not so? The white flag? White-lipped with fear? *Und so weiter*.

Why not *Silver* Fox? Silver was the color of only one thing.

As he moved toward his welcoming committee, Walter smoothed down his straw-colored hair. It would not turn white for many years to come. But even now he had rechristened himself with a new name, better fitted to his accomplishments.

Or, more accurately, to his expectations.

CHAPTER 26

On his second week in Basel, Burris had called in carpenters to remove the wall that separated Shelter's office from the rest of the small UBCO branch. He had at the same time done away with Ingo Huffel's office. He sat him at an open desk near the other clerical employees. Then he fired Huffel. He was replaced by a young man named Mario from Lugano. Within a few more weeks Burris had replaced the three clerical people with new employees from other parts of Switzerland. None of them knew each other, or Basel.

On this morning in late August, as Burris sat at his desk and examined a thin packet of correspondence, he glanced up from time to time to see how Mario and the other newcomers were doing.

The fact that none of them spoke the Basler dialect was no loss, Burris thought now, since most of the customers coming in off the street were Americans wanting to cash personal checks from their UBCO branch in the States, or exchange dollars for Swiss francs. In point of fact, any bank that did nothing but this kind of business would have gone broke long ago. Until now the expense of the branch had to be written off against public relations, not profits, because until Burris' arrival, the only purpose of the branch had been as a convenience for visitors.

According to the way Palmer had planned it, however, the office's volume was supposed to show an increase over the summer, not too sharp to excite Basler bankers, but enough to justify having sent a full v.p. like Burris into action.

Burris had accomplished this mostly by having an attractive folder printed in English. It had been mailed to every U.S. citizen living within fifty miles of Basel. It was prominently displayed on the check-in desks of large and medium hotels in the area. Back in the States, it had gone to large travel agencies as well, just in time for the summer vacation rush. The folder posed a rather ingenuous headline question: "A full-service U.S. bank with full Swiss secrecy?"

Yes, the folder had assured its reader, and yes again. The basic mix had been patriotism and greed.

As a result, time-deposit accounts had jumped by 24 per cent. The number of personal loans had more than doubled. So had safe-deposit services. So had Eurobond investments, which were tax-free. So had certificates of deposit. The result was that, by midsummer, the UBCO branch had almost doubled its volume and all Basel knew it was showing a small, tidy profit. Burris could get on with the real job for which he'd been sent to Switzerland.

He watched the back of Mario's head now as the assistant manager finished a low-pitched interview with a horsey, elderly lady, the widow of a U. S. Air Force general. She was converting all her American securities into a single certificate of deposit, worth one hundred thousand dollars, which would pay a guaranteed 10 per cent in Swiss francs.

Chicken feed. Burris smiled lightly. There had been a time in his banking career when a deal of that size was large. But Palmer's dream for the Basel office was far grander. He had alerted UBCO branches in financial capitals outside Switzerland to begin developing heavy commercial interest in the Basel office.

Slowly, as multinational companies around Europe agreed to secure Swiss franc financing through the Basel branch of UBCO, this business would be placed on Burris' books. Some of it he would generate in trips around the continent. Some would be sent him from New York and other banking centers of the world, as leverage was placed on the multinationals to shift accounts into Swiss francs via UBCO-Basel.

This part of the plan went ahead without Burris needing to know the details. UBCO had men on the board of nearly every U.S.-based corporation of any size. The rest was easy, a combination of carrots on sticks, not the least attractive being that an American corporate executive whose company dealt with UBCO-Basel could be assured of expert handling of his own private funds, and of getting the highest possible tax-free return on them. In this and a dozen other ways, corporate business began to move into Burris' office.

And none of this was yet known to the Swiss banking community, not until Burris decided to reveal what was being done.

Obviously the cloak of secrecy covering this gradual buildup could not last forever. Even now, Burris suspected, some of his new employees might learn by accident about the large commercial accounts being placed on UBCO-Basel's books.

In essence, the strategy—Palmer's strategy—was a combination of feint and sneak-punch. By seeming to concentrate on raising volume through such open ploys as the flag-waving leaflet, UBCO was justifying the use of a slugger like Burris. But this was only the feint.

The slow accumulation of hundreds of millions of francs in commercial financing, all of it secret, was the sneak-punch. When he felt the Basel office was big enough to declare its hand, Palmer would let Burris announce to the world that the assets now stood at—? Who could foretell how high the figure would be? And the customer list, how vastly impressive?

Overnight, while Switzerland had been watching without seeing, UBCO-Basel's assets would reach that mysterious level of critical mass. Like plutonium, they would then erupt mightily into new, arcane, varied, sophisticated and always secret operations of sharply increased yield.

Through a German intermediary of the utmost discretion, Burris had already made a deposit against a seven-year lease on a large new building about a hundred yards down the Aeschenvorstadt. When the moment came, the intermediary would step aside and the new, powerful, globally connected UBCO-Basel office, replete with computer terminals at officers' desks, visual readouts included, would stun all Basel with its strength and ability.

Already, in a number of other banking capitals of Europe, young UBCO officers of the assistant-vice-president level who had recently applied for transfers were being told they were under consideration for a new post in a key banking city. They were to be ready to move on fourteen days' notice.

In time, these new men would be placed as directors of multinational corporations funded by UBCO-Basel. When critical mass had been reached, the explosive expansion of power and profit lay here, in the influence of UBCO on the boards of its customer corporations. There is no substitute for being an insider.

The records and correspondence covering this new business Burris was slowly accumulating went through no one's hands but his. A rather complicated security system made certain that no one in the Basel office saw the incoming correspondence, nor typed Burris' answers. It was typical of the rock-hard security Burris had established that although outgoing correspondence—letters, receipts, advices, statements and the like—bore a Basel postmark, none of it was actually processed in the city, nor even in Switzerland. No Swiss was involved in this secret side of his affairs at all, unless one counted Margit Staeli.

Watching Mario now as he took the American widow through the intricacies of her new investment, Burris found himself thinking back over the summer with Margit. Considering how much time they had lavished on each other, it was a little unbelievable that he'd gotten so much of his secret business done.

Margit had been a great help to him with this hidden side of UBCO's affairs. It didn't bother him that she bore the same last name as one of his chief competitors. She and he were both products of the same training, the same basic hypocrisy taught most students of business administration, the so-called "American position" in economics. It held that the open marketplace was the highest form of capitalism, that unbridled competition produced the greatest good for the greatest number and that there was more than enough profit for everybody, boys, so don't be hogs.

This official position contrasted so sharply with reality, Burris reflected now, that he was surprised it was still being taught. In real corporate life companies stole each other's secrets, formed illegal combinations to inflate prices or choke down supply, drove each other to the wall by proxy fights and merger takeovers and, if things went badly, begged tearfully for a government bail-out.

Yet Margit, who didn't yet operate in the arena of modern international business—but soon would when she took over control of her family interests—still believed what they'd taught her at Harvard.

Or maybe, Burris mused now, it was just that for a lover she trusted, Margit Staeli would do almost anything.

It was an odd affair, but the best summer he'd ever spent. They were good for each other. It was working better than either of them expected. But, over the summer, Burris had come to depend on Margit for many things, and this part of the relationship bothered him.

He didn't like to be beholden to anybody, especially anyone as powerful as Margit. It wasn't just that he didn't want her money. It was that he didn't like depending on her knowhow. The intricate security arrangements for the new, secret UBCO business, for example. She'd been the one to invent the procedures necessary to keep it all secret. Palmer would have been very upset to learn this.

Burris trusted her, but he didn't like owing that much to anybody. It was this same itchy feeling, he knew, that made his relationship with Palmer so odd.

Aside from half a dozen telephone calls he hadn't even met the man, yet he'd had a drink once, in July, with Curtis, who filled him in on the whole Shelter story. Otherwise, he'd been in no rush to cement closer relations with Palmer, the man to whom he owed his career at UBCO. Many a weekend he had spent with Margit in some hideaway they'd found, Burris could well have used to fly down to Lugano and make the pilgrimage up the mountain to Palmer's lofty retreat. But he hadn't. He didn't want to be *that* close to someone he owed so much.

Yet, here he was, *that* close, to one he owed even more: Margit.

Burris smiled sourly as he sat at his desk. In front of him, Mario was winding up the amenities with the tall, gaunt, gray-haired widow. Burris waved to her as she signed several forms. Mario brought her to Burris' desk to have her signature witnessed, a totally unnecessary procedure. But, although Burris had made himself somewhat unavailable to the American colony around Basel, he did not wish to appear unfriendly to a customer.

He got to his feet. "Mrs. Hagen," he said. "Delighted to see you. Is everything to your liking?"

"Well." She pursed her furrowed lips for a moment. "The 10 per cent is." She laughed like a horse, neighing and showing all her gums.

"I should say so." He scribbled his signature on two documents and returned them to Mario. "Mr. Fontela, you want to keep taking very good care of Mrs. Hagen. She's our kind of customer."

Burris watched the two of them return to Mario's desk. Well, perhaps in a way this haggard old lady was his kind of customer. When he'd lived, her husband had been on the board of several multinational conglomerates, another of the ghosts in olive drab that haunted the back passages of the business world. He'd been a brigadier but, on his pay alone, he couldn't have accumulated the hundred thousand his widow was now socking away in a CD. And it was far from being her last hundred thousand.

Playing with the pen he had used to witness her signature, Burris fell to thinking about his own old age. How much would he accumulate for his retirement years? His deal with Palmer produced a 1 per cent override on all new business over a certain level. It was an unusual arrangement for a bank, but Palmer had insisted on it as "combat pay."

Fine, Burris thought, but I don't plan to spend the rest of my life in the combat zone of Basel, do I?

Then where? Doing what? The trouble with aiming so single-mindedly at a single thing—as Burris had been trained to do—was that there was no other side to him. Most of the people he knew were that way. They might play golf or something, but there was really nothing for them once they retired except to sit there and watch the wrinkles form.

Palmer, at least, kept his mind active by spinning immense webs of intrigue. Burris had been talking about this with Margit only the previous weekend in Copenhagen. Unlike some of their other trips this summer, this one had been purely sightseeing, no business. Margit had pulled him around town like a tour leader, showing him everything the Tourist Board wants visitors to see, even down to the Little Mermaid statue in the harbor.

"If one's only been trained for business, as you and I have, then it's important to cultivate a taste for travel and sightseeing."

Burris understood why, of course. But he also knew that Margit was being polite. She had a deep interest in music and art, which were subjects Burris had never studied. It was typical of the rich that they gave their children this background, typical and clever. Later on, in her old age, Margit would be a patron of the arts, much respected, adding luster to the Staeli name and, incidentally, keeping herself from going mad with boredom. Clever.

Watching Mario escort Mrs. Hagen to the front entrance of the bank, Burris found himself wondering what his old age would be like. And with whom he'd be spending it.

In the doorway, the August sun silhouetting her thin figure against the Aeschenvorstadt outside, the widow of the Air Force general whinnied loudly at Mario and showed her gums again.

CHAPTER 27

Late in the morning, on her way into Basel, Margit parked the borrowed sports car by the bank of the Rhine in a tiny bit of grass well off the road. She had finished the busywork at her office in Schloss Staeli and it was hours before she would be driving out of town, well after sundown in fact.

This had been a strange summer. She had plunged into more activity than she could ever remember in her life. It seemed to her that she was either driving somewhere in Erich's little vintage car, or coming back from there, or meeting Matt, or saying good-by, or making long-distance calls from telephone booths and—

She lifted the golden leather flight bag from the car and walked to the very edge of the riverbank.

Below her a log had caught temporarily against the shrubbery and the swift pressure of the river was churning up a small circle of foam. It grew fluffier, more bubbly, from the impurities of the water.

Factories poured their industrial waste into the Rhine over most of its length. At this point, so close to its sources in Switzerland, the water should have been cleaner, but it wasn't. It always offended Erich that by the time it reached Basel—and partly because of Basel's own drug factories—the majestic Rhine was already unfit to drink. Swimmers occasionally swallowed a mouthful, but tried not to.

She missed Erich.

She hadn't seen him or talked to him for months, and it was not entirely the fault of her intense concentration on Matt. Several times she had called Erich, only to get Bunter, who, always very correct, had nevertheless exuded an aroma of guilt-by-proximity that could be smelled over the telephone wire. Obviously Erich had something of his own on the fire and it embarrassed Bunter to be making excuses to the official fiancée and future Madame Lorn.

She had no one but Matt to talk to. And with Matt, talking was an entirely different experience. They had a lot to tell each other about themselves, decades of their youth to share. What one confided to one's lover was not at all what one wanted to talk about with a confidant.

She opened the leather bag and groped inside it for the composition book she carried as a sort of journal. She had made very few entries in it since England. She paged slowly through the book, rereading the questions about famine that the British fellow had asked, and then a series of cryptic entries noting her weekends with Matt, one in Rome, one in Madrid, one in Nice, their most recent weekend in Copenhagen and others.

The entries were really nothing more than the name of a city and the date. During that time she had left several messages with

Bunter. Erich had never called back or, if he had, had left no message.

They'd both been out of contact, each absorbed in an affair. Was it terribly corrupt of her to want to spend all her time with her lover but occasionally talk to her fiancé? Matt would call it "European." She began to write in the journal suddenly, on impulse.

"Matt doesn't realize when he's insulting. Subtlety isn't his strength. Things I would discuss with Erich and not Matt."

Such as love, she thought. Erich is the expert. She began writing again. "Growing up together in Basel. Two little jailbirds. Prisoners raise baby birds in their cells. The birds become prisoners, too."

A great deal of money, she mused, had been spent by her family and Erich's in decorating the cells of the prison in which they had grown up. "Erich and I," she wrote, "grew up thinking we were free."

She stared down at the journal. Ugly truths never grow beautiful by being put down on paper. Ugly journal.

She closed it with a sharp noise like a clap. The foam around the base of the log had become rather extensive now, like the head on a stein of well-brewed beer. If one dipped a glass in the Rhine and held it to the light, what would it look like? Brown? Straw-yellow?

Everything seemed to have changed this summer, with Matt and without Erich. With Matt, the summer had been hyperactive. But she remembered the long, lazy summers of past years, Erich and she and a few of their friends lying by the river, sipping long drinks, gossiping in faint voices, soft malice, unreal half-thoughts.

In Matt Burris' world there were no long, lazy summers. If one took it, vacation would be two weeks, or three. Then it was back to making a living. But it had never been so for her, nor for Erich. They shared something that she and Matt would never have, endless stretches of leisure.

Perhaps she should drive to his house and leave another message for Erich? But where could he call her? She was as elusive this summer has he. That was only what one might expect when one released the little bird from its jail. But still, she missed him.

She would visit his house, if only to salute Bunter and leave yet another message.

* * *

A sense of duty, not family loyalty, made Margit walk to Number 17 Aeschenvorstadt. After talking briefly to Bunter, she had left the L2 Magna parked in front of Erich's house and walked over the bridge to Grossbasel. Climbing the steep hill up along the Rhine from the ship landing, she strolled past sixteenth-century houses in which the university now held classes.

A few students—of art or architecture, perhaps—sat on curbs and sketched façades of buildings, the way dormers fitted into roof lines, the design of a window or a doorway. Margit felt a sudden pang of deprivation.

Why hadn't she elected to study the arts? An occasional course in music or art wasn't enough. These young people were preparing for an entire life in art. Margit felt left out of something, a feeling she often had in museums or at concerts. Something vital to life was going on, and she had been trained for another matter, utterly different.

She was walking past the courtyard of the Kunstmuseum now. She stopped for a moment to stare through the iron gate into the open courtyard where the Rodin group of Calais burghers stood. Far beyond, in a corner of the Roman-style courtyard, stood a separate sculpture group, more modern, of three young children reaching up as if to the sun. Jailbirds reaching for freedom?

Margit's eyes narrowed. She turned suddenly and dashed along St. Alban Graben to the corner of the Aeschenvorstadt, turned left and continued striding on her long legs until she reached Number 17. So caught up was she in an unhappy private vision of her life that she forgot to glance across the street at Matt's office.

She stopped just inside the entrance of Staeli Internationale, GmbH. Like everything Swiss and powerful, it was dully understated. The lobby area was narrow. Several dusty potted palms stood about in ugly majolica jars too small for them. At a plain oak desk a bald little man in his sixties was making entries in a ledger with a pen he occasionally dipped in an inkwell. The smell of dust and age filled Margit's nostrils.

The little man paused in his penmanship and looked up. "Yes?"

Suddenly, behind his gold-rimmed spectacles, his eyes widened alarmingly. "Fräulein Staeli!" he barked, rising to his feet so quickly that he rapped one knee sharply against the underside of the desk. He winced with pain. His mouth trembled as he limped around the desk and held open the heavy swinging doors to the inner offices.

Normally, Margit would have inquired solicitously about his health, or at the very least the present state of his kneecap. Instead she let the doors swing shut behind her as she surveyed that which would one soon be hers to command.

The ground floor, being the public area, was a further study in plainness. Along one banking wall tellers stood behind glass-enclosed wickets, but this was merely a convenience for a few older customers. The main Staeli banking facilities were elsewhere in Basel.

Along the wall opposite the wickets a series of cubicles lifted opal glass partitions to the high ceiling. Outside each cubicle a male secretary sat at a desk. The cubicles were used by customers for various purposes, clipping coupons, discussing estates, checking the contents of safe-deposit boxes and occasionally dozing.

Staeli had enough good customers past a certain age who simply refused to do business at one of the sleek, modern glass-and-chrome offices the bank maintained elsewhere in the city. It was for these diehards, including the grandmothers and ancient maiden aunts of all Basel's oldest families, that the ground floor at Number 17 was kept in such a backward and nostalgic state.

Beyond, in the far wall opposite the entrance, two elevator doors stood side by side framed in mahogany. One went up to others of the five floors at Number 17. The other elevator went only down. There were, under the earth of Number 17, at least four levels of vaults and other storage facilities. It was not the largest subterranean keep in Basel, but it wasn't far from it.

Margit moved quickly through the center aisle, her long legs covering the distance in great strides to avoid any of the usual smiling greetings from employees who had known her since she was barely old enough to walk. She did not want smiling greetings this morning. As she stood at the elevator doors and nodded curtly to the uniformed attendant, she found herself wondering whether this foul mood had begun when she decided to visit

Number 17, or if the mood had come first and she was doing the visit as a penance.

Which elevator? Both had been summoned and both now stood open before her. Down into the depths, where the gold ingots lay neatly stacked? Where the diamonds lost their glitter in the semi-darkness? Or up? Up to see the startled faces of treacherous relatives like Cousin Walter and Uncle Dieter, startled because she so rarely visited Number 17.

In her tan flight bag she was carrying a sheaf of correspondence, the replies to which had to be typed and mailed. Two secretaries on the fourth floor were assigned to Margit. One of them usually picked up work at the schloss and brought it back. Or Bodo brought the correspondence to Number 17. It was rare for Margit to set foot in this place, because she felt uncomfortable here, unwelcome, a stranger.

She entered the "Up" elevator and held her hand palm out to stop the attendant from entering with her for the sole purpose of pressing the button marked "4."

This complex job Margit handled entirely on her own. At the fourth floor she caused a more than minor sensation by appearing in the large office her secretaries shared with the rest of the female secretaries at Number 17. Strictly speaking, Staeli employed no women secretaries. They were, in fact, file clerks, stenographers and typists. The title of secretary was reserved for the young men on the ground floor.

When they saw her, both the women assigned to Margit jumped to their feet with the same alacrity as the elderly receptionist on the main floor, but managed to avoid savaging their kneecaps in the process. Margit nodded and kept on walking to the conference room at the front of the building, which looked down on the Aeschenvorstadt. It was reserved for visiting officers of Staeli Internationale, GmbH., like herself, had dropped in to get some work done. Usually they arrived from farther away, Hong Kong or New York.

Margit stopped in the doorway of the room. "Give me five minutes," she told the older of the two secretaries, a woman her age named Aneke. "Then you can both come in."

She tried to produce a smile but her face muscles seemed locked. She shut herself in the conference room and, moving

179

briskly, proceeded to disconnect the microphone hidden under the long table as well as the one in the cupboard against the wall where the coffee-making things were kept. She checked behind framed photos on the walls, under chairs and in the newly installed air conditioner. It wasn't possible to keep up with the cretins who had this place under surveillance and, in fact, there was nothing she would give her secretaries today that was confidential. But there was a principle here and Margit was making her statement about it in this entirely silent fashion.

She stared through the window at the street outside. From this height the glass façade of the UBCO branch lay in a distorted perspective that gave her no glimpse of the inside. She glanced at her watch and saw that it would be lunchtime for her secretaries in a few minutes. She opened the door to the room and beckoned them in.

Instead of thinking ahead to what work she would be giving them, Margit found herself wondering what Matt was doing across the street. He would probably have lunch on the terrace of the Drei Könige today. He had fallen into a habitual routine, like most Basler bankers. And, like most respectable Baslers, he reserved most of his love life for the weekends. Margit smiled slightly. The two secretaries, seeing this, returned the smile in a tentative way.

"Aneke, I'll give you the banking correspondence," Margit began quickly. "Sit down, please. Lisl gets the rest, yes?"

Both women nodded. They seated themselves at the long table and were now arranging their pencils, pens and notepads in a businesslike array.

Margit sat against the edge of the window frame and crossed one leg over the other. She handed the entire pile of correspondence to Aneke. It was an awkward moment for all of them, Margit knew, because they so rarely had any personal contact with each other. Aneke was married and had a child with an asthma condition. And Lisl was . . . single?

Margit supposed this routine work must bore the two women as much as it bored her. When they weren't doing her work, they were part of the regular typing pool, handling other routine work. Nothing in the spectrum of Staeli's holdings was really exciting, but the work relegated to Margit was possibly the dullest of the lot. Perhaps a man who did this for a living, but who had a wife and children to support, would somehow kid himself into getting a dramatic thrill from some of this drudgery. Not Margit.

She indicated Aneke's notebook. "First, the letters from France. They pertain to a request for revolving credit funding on a twenty-year basis by a perfume company. Type the two letters of response I've drawn by hand. Sign and mail them. Then forward the following memorandum to Alois Hü in Corporate Finance: Regarding the perfumery matter, suggest ten-year limit on funding program. Do not under any circumstances extend beyond this limit without thorough review. This is a volatile business and the company does not show a great deal of forward imagination."

Aneke looked up as she paused: "A second memorandum to Herr Kwarl in Staelichem. Regarding the perfumery matter, suggest the French consider buying attar and jasmine base from the Staelibel division. Please co-ordinate with Hü. Our funding of the French is not contingent on their placing large orders with you, but they should also listen favorably to your sales approach concerning Staelichem industrial reagents, particularly alcohol, and the new synthetic substitutes for ambergris fixative."

Margit stared at the top of the pile of correspondence she had given Aneke. The contents of the sheaf of papers bored her, but she could nevertheless remember each numbing piece of paper there.

"Next, on the consumer credit matter, there are three letters of response to be typed, signed and mailed. Then a memorandum to Dieter Staeli as follows: Regarding extension of Staelifranc credit-card privileges, our research people have highly favorable projections for consumer categories for which we are considering this convenience. To wit: career women earning twenty-five thousand francs per year or more; wives of executives earning thirty-five thousand francs per year or more; widows of such executives; daughters over age twenty-one of such executives. Note basic contract is not cosignatory note with the husband or father assuming financial responsibility. This would hardly be a convenience or even a new service. On the contrary, these are to be individual accounts, managed by each card holder as she sees fit, with normal service and debt-maintenance charges."

Margit paused for breath and, in taking one, heard it come out very like a sigh. Dieter had already, in advance, vetoed this particular project, although not officially. It was up to her to keep pushing it. She had few illusions it would happen, but she did not want her own sense of futility to be the determinant.

"Next," she told Aneke, "you'll find a long presentation on a new chain of boutiques in the ski resort towns, by a consortium from Milan and Paris. Prepare and mail the various letters I've written and take this memorandum to Herr Littke in Retail Financing: This is a high-markup situation of strong leverage based on short-term factoring of accounts receivable. There is little for us in the proposition unless we take a capital position in the parent consortium. Suggest we ask ten per cent participation and settle after negotiation for five. This will give us a continuing profit base through off-season periods when retail income is minimal."

She watched Aneke scribble this down in shorthand. Then: "That's the end of the banking correspondence. Lisl, you'll find a series of short letters of acknowledgment to various charitable and medical research foundations who have thanked us for contributions. There are about a dozen of them. Underneath are two proposals to be forwarded to Herr Slück in Staelichem Philanthropic. Put them in the same envelope with the following memorandum: Regarding proposal for founding a university chair of paraplegic rehabilitation, specifically concerned with research involving victims of massive burns from chemical weapons of the napalm type, I suggest this is simply too ironic to bring us anything but a bad press. I have asked the university about the possibility of establishing, instead, a research program into high-yield synthetic fertilizers not derived from petrochemical sources. This is a positive program and, if successful, will produce a good press for Staelichem.

"As to the second proposal for a traveling bus-theater company that tours the smaller towns with a repertory of classics like Shakespeare, Goethe and Schiller, I have responded affirmatively and you will be hearing from the organizers. They have been cautioned to limit their repertory to those plays studied in elementary and secondary Swiss schools."

A faintly mocking smile twisted one corner of Margit's mouth as she finished and watched the younger woman transcribe her words. Then: "Have a check for five thousand francs drawn to the order of the Opera Company as a separate contribution from

182

Staelifer for the production of the new *Dreigroschenoper*. You'll find a covering letter at the bottom of the pile. That's all."

She smiled a bit more genuinely now as she watched the women pack up their pencils and papers. "How's your little boy, Aneke?"

Aneke's eyes flew wide open with surprise. Since Margit's back was to the sun-filled window, Aneke's bright-blue irises seemed to blaze with light. "He's . . . he's fine," she stammered. "The new medicine is working."

Margit nodded. "And Lisl, have you set the date yet?"

The younger woman blushed. "Next June, Fräulein Staeli."

"So long a wait?"

Lisl shrugged philosophically. "He doesn't graduate till then."

The interchange had given Aneke a chance to pull herself together. "I don't know how you do it, Fräulein," she said then in an admiring tone. "You keep all that"—she indicated the pile of correspondence—"in your head, every little twist of it. And also you remember about people."

"Believe me, people are much more interesting than . . . that."

All three women smiled then. "For us," Aneke said in a slightly conspiratorial tone, "the most interesting is to know when . . ." She stopped, considering her about-to-be-committed indiscretion. But she went on anyway. ". . . to know when you will be, ah, working here at Number 17 all the time."

She stressed the "all" in a way that made her real meaning clear. Her question, Margit reflected, was really just another version of the question to Lisl about naming a wedding day.

Margit stood up from the window ledge and took a pace or two to stretch her legs. She turned to glance down at the Aeschenvorstadt, filled now with people on their way to lunch. Wouldn't it be lucky if she suddenly caught sight of Matt? She waited a moment, but no one came or left the UBCO office across the street.

She turned back to Aneke and Lisl. "Not long," she said then. "Sooner than I would like. The way it is now, I have so much freedom. Later on, there'll be very little." Aneke nodded thoughtfully, her blue eyes bright in the sunlight. "For us, it can't come soon enough, Fräulein."

The room lay in silence for a long moment. Margit found herself hoping she had found and disabled all the microphones. The room seemed to have fallen under a spell. No one moved or spoke. The two women were watching her with rapt attention.

Margit realized for the first time what it would mean for other people if she took control of the family holding company headquartered here. She had only seen it, until now, in terms of her own assumption of power. When she thought about it, this was more or less in negative terms. She knew the things she wouldn't do, the mistakes she wouldn't repeat, the Walter-type thinking she would refuse to let pass, the Dieter-like arrogance that would no longer be countenanced.

But it wasn't until just now, seeing her future triumph reflected in Aneke's eyes, that she began to realize how much her plans meant to others. This rare encounter with her secretaries also showed her what life would be like when she had to come here every morning of every day. She had been living a permanent holiday until now.

"It's lunchtime," she said then, breaking the spell. "Don't let me keep you."

She watched them leave, wanting instead to invite them to lunch with her, but knowing it was too soon for that. One day she would take them to the terrace of the Drei Könige and treat them to something special.

Perhaps, from his table across the terrace, the handsome Herr Burris would be watching. They might exchange a secret smile.

Margit turned back to the window to gaze down through the August sunlight to the entrance of the UBCO office. She had been in a bad mood this morning and now she felt better. Perhaps work agreed with her. Or perhaps what pleased her was getting work out of the way. Or was it that she had already planned a three-day weekend with the attractive American who worked across the Aeschenvorstadt?

Summer was ending in a blaze of warmth and good feeling. Perhaps it was a turning point. An omen. As if to confirm this, she saw Matt Burris leave his office, squinting against the sun, and head in the direction of the hotel, moving briskly along like a born Basler.

Margit nodded. A portent, certainly. Only good things would happen from now on.

CHAPTER 28

Elfi wandered slowly through her mistress's deserted study, the long room of windows looking down across wooded lawns to the Rhine. Aside from an hour this morning, Margit Staeli had not been here for some time now, off on another of her private trips, and the room needed no attention, not even dusting, which, of course, Elfi did not do. A maid dusted.

Elfi was Miss Margit's personal maid and, aside from sending a few things to be cleaned, she had had nothing to do for most of the summer. Her mistress had been absent most of the time, returning only for a few days, just long enough to deal with her accumulated letters, pack her flight bag with fresh clothing, and take off again. It was unusual.

She had borrowed—permanently, it seemed—Herr Erich's cute little orange-colored sports car, the one that made such funny noises going up the driveway to Schloss Staeli. Of Herr Erich, the official fiancé, nothing had been seen at the Schloss for several months now. There were, of course, rumors.

Like any city based on a foundation of official secrets, Basel was a great rumor-factory. Even at her rather low level of society, Elfi heard all sorts of stories. There were secret hints of a disaster at one of the chemical plants that ringed the city, hushed up by the tremendous financial power of the drug companies. She had heard delightfully shocking tales of deposed South American or Arab potentates, reveling with their women as they visited their hoards of gold beneath the streets of Basel. The sacking of some major bank official for poor judgment had also been kept from the newspapers by the even more awesome power of the banks. And the perennial rumors about Erich Lorn this time centered on the notorious Madame Michele and her youth factories. Oddly, there had been no rumors at all about Miss Margit.

Elfi wondered idly what her mistress was really up to this summer. Whatever it was, it probably had to do with the Staeli businesses. She could be extremely secretive about her business plans when she wanted to, Elfi recalled. Well, then, more power to her.

Elfi glanced at her watch. The boat for Basel would reach the Staeli landing in fifteen minutes. She had a ten-minute walk through the grounds to the river and nothing here to keep her from leaving now. She gathered up her bag and a floppy broad-brimmed straw hat her mistress had given her against the August sun.

The stroll through the grounds of Schloss Staeli was, as always for Elfi, a lovely walk under spreading trees past carefully tended beds of flowers over which the gardeners worked unceasingly. For whom to see and enjoy? Not Miss Margit. None of the household staff bothered to stroll about the place. For Elfi, then, and no one else.

She swung her hat in her hand as she strolled along, feeling as if she and not her mistress were the real owner of Schloss Staeli.

Without such fantasies life would be dull indeed. The work this summer had been almost too light to be called a real job, except that her wages were paid regularly. Today was Thursday, Elfi's half-day off, and she was taking the noon boat back to Basel, rather than getting Bodo to drive her, because she had all the time in the world and no responsibilities.

Her half-day of leisure would begin with the ride along the Rhine. She had promised to meet her roommate for lunch at one of the small riverside hotels in Kleinbasel, across the river from the main part of town, a pleasant, relaxing lunch with some man from Christa's office paying for all of them. Pleasant. Christa was no great bargain as a luncheon companion. She had become a great questioner, always eager for information about the private affairs of Schloss Staeli. But perhaps the fellow, who was single and not dating Christa, would be a pleasant distraction.

There had been so few in these summer months. Elfi missed the foreign cities and the foreign men. She missed the excitement of luxury hotels and the occasional theater ticket her mistress had bought but couldn't use.

As she stood at the ship landing and gazed across the fast-moving water toward the German shore, Elfi realized she had been spoiled by her job and her undemanding mistress. The work had grown dull without the trips abroad, without the decisive, quick conversation of Miss Margit, her sudden questions, her abrupt comings and goings, her batches of mail to be posted, her telephone calls to be answered and messages carefully taken.

Elfi missed the activity. She found herself wondering how her mistress was filling the long summer days away from Basel and Schloss Staeli.

At that moment, the small *Personenschiff* pulled in with a churning of water. A deckhand lassoed the piling with one deft loop of the hawser. Elfi nodded as he blew her a kiss. She boarded the boat and a moment later it moved quickly off toward its next landing. Depending on the weather and the time of day, the boat ride to Basel was often faster than either car or train and, of course, much more pleasant.

Elfi decided not to sit inside the cabin like the handful of passengers already aboard. She moved forward, holding to the rail, until she was almost at the prow. The ship sliced through the water with a faint hissing sound. Elfi found herself mesmerized by the river's flow, her mind wandering as her glance locked on the shifting swirl of water.

She still held the broad-brimmed hat at her side, the straw flapping in the breeze. It was a hat in which her mistress looked gorgeous but which seemed pretentious on Elfi. She had tried wearing it many times in front of mirrors without once having the nerve to wear it in public.

Its thinness, its butterfly lightness, its shimmering white glare, all of this belonged to a rich milieu and not to the scenes in which someone like Elfi would wear the hat. It bothered her that, even though she was as slender and tall as Miss Margit, she didn't seem able to carry off wearing such a hat.

Elfi knew the trouble was all in her mind. She knew she looked good in the privacy of a mirror. She also knew that something inside her cringed when she pictured herself wearing the hat on the riverboat, or coming into her apartment house, or meeting Christa for lunch.

By half-past twelve the boat had tied up at the *Schifflande* at the foot of the main bridge that connected the two Basels. Elfi got off and stared up at the outdoor terrace of the Drei Könige. From this angle she couldn't see who was seated at the tables overlooking the river, but occasionally the sleek head of a waiter could be seen moving briskly to and fro or ducking out of sight with a deferential air.

Elfi walked across the bridge to the outdoor café of the Krafft Hotel, a small place popular with younger tourists because of its prices and its view of the old city.

It was true enough, Elfi thought as she walked, that one's best view of Grossbasel, with the cathedral and all the rest, was not from the town itself but from the opposite shore of the Rhine where flat, lower-middle-class Kleinbasel spread out in all directions until it ended in a wall of mighty chemical factories, Autobahn-approach cloverleafs and the like.

It was on this side of the river, Elfi knew, that Herr Erich Lorn kept his bachelor house. She even knew which one it was because Bodo had pointed it out to her once. As she strolled across the bridge she eyed the house and felt a little shock of recognition. The sports car sat there. Was her mistress in town again? Was she needed at Schloss Staeli this afternoon? But today was Elfi's half-day. No sense worrying. If she missed this flying visit of Miss Margit, she missed it.

Christa was already at the outdoor café, seated in a small corner table under a broad cloth umbrella advertising an apéritif. The good-looking young man with her was certainly not as young as Christa, who was in her mid-twenties, and possibly a year or two older even than Elfi, who was almost thirty. He looked short, seated beside Christa, and when he jumped to his feet at Elfi's approach, he was able to stand under the umbrella without ducking his head. Elfi's own height made her less interested in short men.

". . . Paul Iselin," Christa was saying as she introduced the young man to Elfi.

The personal maid of Margit Staeli sat down slowly, thoughtfully, mouthing the usual amenities, but thinking about the Iselin name. Basel was an old town, pre-Roman to tell the truth, and filled with old families. Iselin was almost a more ancient name than Staeli. It ranked with the great families of Basel, the Sarasins, the Merians, the Burckhardts and even the Vischers themselves.

It was common enough, of course, that poor, even disgraced branches of these great families existed. Paul Iselin could be a poor Iselin without powerful connections, just as there were countless Fischers who claimed lineage from the true Vischer line. This was why, among Baslers, it had become a test of origin to check the spelling of the last name. One only accepted, for example, *"Vischer mit der Vogeli Vau,"* meaning with a V as in Vogel. And no Burkhart was ever allowed to claim descent from a true Burckhardt.

"Paul is a coworker," Christa Ruc was saying in her school-teacherish way. "We have adjoining cubicles in Gold Deposits." Since she had never mentioned him before, Elfi assumed this was just a white lie.

"It's quite a golden relationship," Paul added, turning his handsome, narrow face so that only Elfi, and not Christa, could see the wink that accompanied this attempt at humor.

Elfi smiled to show that even a labored witticism was better than none. She missed Bodo, with his rough-and-tumble sexual joking. But it was too soon to write off an Iselin just because he was short and unfunny. "I can picture the two of you in your little caves," she said, smiling, "counting up your bricks of gold all day long. Tell me, that deep under Basel, are there trolls?"

"Natürlich," Paul responded. "I myself am half troll."

And half what, Elfi asked silently. She turned to smile at Christa. "What will you drink?"

"Weissweinschpritze," the girl said in a tone that made Elfi realize this was a daring drink for Christa to order during the working day. The slight amount of white wine, diluted with sparkling water, was a real escapade for anyone who worked in Gold Deposits.

"And for you, young lady?" Paul was asking.

Elfi toyed with the idea of a stronger drink, a modern drink, one with a foreign flavor like scotch and soda or a very dry martini. It would cost three times as much as the wine spritzer and Herr Iselin was paying, but one didn't meet a new man for the first time and instantly impress him with one's expensive tastes, not if one is Swiss.

"The same for me."

Iselin attracted the waiter's attention and ordered three spritzers, *mit Eis.* Even under the umbrella, the day was unseasonably hot. The three young people glanced about them.

Watching them and herself at the same time, Elfi felt quite

smug. They were young, reasonably attractive—with the possible exception of Christa—and able to afford the modest outdoor lunch at the Krafft. To be all these things in Basel was to have risen as far as Elfi had ever dreamed of rising.

The only place she might feel more exalted would be in a foreign city, wielding the surrogate power of the Staeli name as she ordered around bellmen, waiters and valets. But those trips with her mistress were a fantasy life. Elfi was realist enough to understand this. In the real world of Basel, here and now, this lunch on the sunny bank of the Rhine, with a lovely view of the city and a new man with the suggestive name of Iselin . . . this was as high as Elfi knew she would reach.

She glanced at Paul Iselin. He was much too thin, in the modern French style, caved-in chest, tight-cut shirt of some almost see-through fabric, and a rather flared-out light-colored jacket, perhaps too modern for a hard-working troll in Gold Deposits. But of course that had been a lie. He was no banker, that was obvious. He sensed her examination. His eyes shifted slightly to watch her more directly. If they had been alone, perhaps he might have . . .

"And your mistress," Christa Ruc cut in suddenly in her small, worrying voice, "she is well?"

Elfi shrugged, but was spared from answering by the arrival of the waiter. The three young people lifted their glasses silently to each other and took a small sip of their white wine and soda. Elfi noticed that none of them gulped. The first sip was a ceremonial one, no matter how hot or thirsty they might be. Iselin was, if nothing else, well-bred. Bodo would have slugged down half the glass and gasped with gross animal pleasure.

"You . . . ah . . ." Iselin stopped for a moment, as if unable to recall what he was about to say. "You work for the . . . ah, the Staelis, yes?"

"For Fräulein Margit."

He nodded vigorously. "Quite an opportunity."

Elfi eyed him. Opportunity for what, she wondered. There was a knowing undertone to his remark. "For travel, yes," she admitted cautiously.

"Surely not these past few months," Christa suggested in her thin, nagging tone, a star pupil reciting in class. "She's been out of town most of the summer, hasn't she?"

Elfi nodded and sipped her drink. Christa for some time had been terribly interested in the comings and goings of Miss Margit. At first, just before summer, when the girl had begun asking these questions, Elfi had responded fully, but the sheer volume of the inquiries had finally suggested that Elfi be more discreet in her answers. Christa seemed to have an obsession about Margit Staeli. It might have been heroine-worship or only idle curiosity, but she clearly needed to know more about Elfi's employer than Elfi thought she should know.

A few weeks before, in reply to another in the endless round of questions, Elfi had finally sounded off, telling Christa in such forceful terms that Miss Margit's affairs were no business of hers that the girl had broken into tears. The questions had stopped.

"A woman like that," Iselin said then in his knowing tone, "has many affairs to attend to, no doubt, all over Europe, wouldn't you say?"

Elfi let her eyebrows rise. "I imagine so," she said after a pause.

"I use the term 'affairs,'" the young man added with a confidential lowering of his voice, "in both its meanings."

Elfi continued sipping her drink. As long as she did so, she was under no immediate pressure to reply to this double suggestion. She had never paid that much attention to any affairs her mistress had had with men, assuming that, like any Swiss woman of even moderate intelligence, these would be conducted so circumspectly —and so far from Switzerland—that one's fiancé never heard even a whisper of them. Elfi was sure, for instance, that without her own presence in London last spring, several of the younger milords would have wanted entrance to Miss Margit's hotel suite.

Elfi took a rather relaxed view of the whole thing. She appreciated the fact that her mistress never asked any of those insulting intimate questions the rich often threw at their employees. She had never once wanted to know about Elfi's men, and Elfi, in turn, had been only minimally interested in Miss Margit's love life. Herr Erich, of course, was another matter. One day Elfi would have to live in the same house with the celebrated seducer when he married Miss Margit. Until then, though, this was a problem that did not really press for instant attention.

"Are you suggesting," she asked then in a deliberately cold tone, "that Fräulein Staeli is a loose woman?"

Even in the full flush of the midday sun, Iselin's face went chalky. His hands began moving negatively in front of him even before he found his voice. "Nothing of the sort, my dear young lady," he burst out. "Such a thought would be grotesque, impossible, beyond the pale."

"Then what was all that about affairs?"

"A bad attempt at humor, only that."

And you, she added to herself, are a noted expert at bad jokes. But she couldn't let him off that easily. "I can imagine," she said, "what sort of rumors collect about well-known people in this town. It's vulgar. And it's depressing." She turned on Christa, determined to include her. "Isn't it, Christa?"

"Yes, of course," her roommate agreed. "Paul was only—"

"I'm not very good at witticisms," Iselin admitted then in such a shamefaced way that Elfi was forced to smile. He might be short and maladroit, but he was . . . cute.

The three of them sipped in silence. A powerful speedboat roared upriver with a water skier in tow, a man in a bikini brief who seemed able to jump at will over the spreading wake of the boat, turn backwards and forwards, and all on one ski.

A few of the diners went to the railing to watch him. That was Basel, Elfi thought privately, exciting, cosmopolitan Basel, where the biggest thing in everyone's life today would be the fact that someone was water-skiing on the Rhine in midweek. Weekends the river was filled with skiers, but a midweek appearance was enough to excite everyone's attention. Lunches grew cold as people pressed against the rail, trying to guess which fool was out there on his lunch hour water-skiing.

Christa was among the gawkers, but Elfi noted approvingly that Iselin was not. He sat there, slowly turning his drink in a small ring of water that had gathered on the table. He seemed to sense Elfi's glance because he looked up directly into her eyes at that moment.

"You must excuse my remark about your employer," he said in a tone that was subtly different. It had a strange tone to it, a feeling that disturbed Elfi. "Everyone is, of course, very curious about celebrities like Fräulein Staeli, especially those like myself who work in her family's interests."

Elfi nodded, but felt suddenly out of her depth, as if being reintroduced to Iselin and finding him a different person. Their glances had locked by now as if they already shared some strange secret.

"There are even people," Iselin was saying in a soft, smooth voice, "who would pay a great deal of money for confidential information about your employer." He paused and smiled very faintly. "Does that shock you?"

A shower of laughter greeted some antic of the water skier. Elfi found herself unable to glance around at the river and see what had happened. She seemed not only locked in a secret understanding with this man whom she had just met, but more than that, a guilty understanding.

Past Iselin's face, by an odd trick of perspective, she could see the little sports car parked in front of Herr Erich's house. The sun was hot on her head, hammering down with unusual fierceness. In this strangely languorous moment, all Basel was spread before her, an entire Thursday afternoon of sheer idleness to be wasted frivolously, if she wished, like a lady of leisure.

"Do you see that car," she said abruptly.

Iselin turned. "Erich Lorn's, isn't it?"

"Oh." Elfi tried to keep the disappointment out of her voice. She had wanted to score over the superior Iselin by identifying the car for him.

"He's had it forever," he went on. "Even at college, I think."

"You went to school with him?"

"For as much as Erich could take," Iselin said. "He had a habit of getting himself expelled."

Elfi nodded sagely. So this *was* an Iselin Iselin. And he seemed quite interested in her. Not in Christa, in her. What was one to think of such interest? The usual? But a Paul Iselin is not a Bodo. Perhaps, after all, there were men who could be interested in her without wanting to instantly throw her down on a bed. But he was too short for her.

". . . over there, the oyster-tan one," Iselin was saying.

"I beg your pardon."

He smiled softly at her and laid his hand over hers. "You haven't heard a word I said. And here I imagined I was making an impression on you."

"Is that your car?" Elfi asked, peering in the direction Iselin had pointed. The car was longer, even lower-slung and more modern-looking than Herr Erich's car.

"It's a Jag," Iselin said in a careless tone. "E-type Jag. It does two hundred in third gear forward." He squeezed her hand. "Now, are you impressed with me?"

"No. But with your car, yes."

Iselin laughed appreciatively. Elfi found herself wondering why it had taken this long for her to find a man who appreciated sophisticated talk, And he was serious about her. No man of his class held one's hand without being serious, not in public, anyway. Gently, Elfi disengaged her hand from Iselin's.

Their glances met, curiously hot under the cool shadow of the umbrella. Elfi was determined not to be the first to look away. If it was burning glances he was offering, she had a few of her own in reserve. Underneath all this, she was congratulating herself on the whole lucky encounter. It would have been just like Christa to bring some utter nonentity along. But this man was an entirely different matter and possibly just the one she had been looking for without hope, the man who would rescue her from all the Bodos of her class.

"Yes," he was saying, his voice light, but his glance pressing even harder, "it's clearly a case of the employee being even more mysterious and charming than the employer."

Elfi's eyelids lowered slightly. "How well do you know Fräulein Margit?"

"It's not Fräulein Margit I want to know well. It's you."

"I seem to remember something about . . . people paying a great deal of money to know more about her."

Iselin's small white teeth showed in a faint smile. "What a memory behind that lovely face. Did I say that?"

Elfi nodded. "And you asked if it shocked me."

Slowly, smoothly, as if she had been born to the gesture, Elfi placed the lavish straw hat on her head at just the right angle. Let Iselin understand that she had that much breeding at least. She spoke to him now from her own shadows, a sibyl in a cave of female mystery.

"Should it?" she asked provocatively.

194

CHAPTER 29

By one o'clock, the terrace dining room of the Drei Könige was fairly crowded for a Thursday, perhaps half with those tourists who could afford the prices and half with local business types.

Yet in the far corner there sat a large round table for four somewhat removed from the rest, a kind of clearing of extra space around it. No matter how many well-heeled customers with or without reservations pressed the maître d' for a table, this round, isolated one remained empty, its white damask cloth almost blinding in the hot sunlight, its silver sparkling, glasses shooting out piercing slivers of light.

Precisely at one-fifteen, two men approached the maître d' from slightly different angles. They seemed to have little in common, physically. One was tall and in his thirties, the other short and in his sixties. But there was a broadness of jaw in both men that suggested, if nothing else, a large element of doggedness.

Dieter Staeli reached the maître d' a moment before Matthew Burris. The maître, seeing Staeli, seemed to melt before everyone's eyes from a starchy and unapproachable figure to a groveling mass of jelly. With infinite duckings of the head and archings of the spine, he ushered Staeli to the lone corner table, scattering invisible rose petals before him as he led the one-man parade to its destination.

Seeing the farce in progress and recognizing Staeli from his photographs, Burris simply followed in the older man's wake, like a ball-carrier behind his interference.

All three men touched down at the goal line simultaneously, the maître d' turning in horror to see Burris behind him while, at the same time, Dieter Staeli produced suitable grunts of welcome and delight, thus preventing the maître d' from bodily throwing—or perhaps only trying to throw—Burris over the railing and into the Rhine.

Both men seated themselves, Staeli taking care to keep the sun behind him and, thus, glaring in Burris' eyes. Staeli realized that in a little while the sun would shift and a shadow would spoil his game, but it was worth playing for the moment.

He had deliberately taken the bull by the horns this way and called Burris to invite him to lunch because Staeli's own intelligence network was producing nothing useful about the American. Staeli's various agents, both his professionals and amateurs like Christa Ruc, were filing their usual voluminous reports of comings and goings and tapped telephone conversations, but Dieter Staeli could recognize padding when he saw it.

Since he was paying for it, he hated the idea that he was getting so little for his money. There is a point in all spy work where the spy begins to stuff his reports with padding because he has either lost his touch as a spy or his quarry has begun to behave too cautiously. At that point money spent on spy work is wasted money. Staeli had reached that point.

His offices in Frankfurt, Brussels and London had continued a flow of negative information. Nothing unusual was happening elsewhere in the financial world to affect UBCO-Basel. True, the branch was doing well on its promotion of special service to Americans. But this was a limited market. It made sense, but it didn't make *enough* sense.

In short, Dieter Staeli reminded himself now as he beamed in grandfatherly fashion at Burris, there is something more to the *verflüchte* Palmer's master plan than simply increasing UBCO business in Basel. There is something hidden in the plan, hidden so deeply that perhaps even this chunk of steer meat sitting in front of me doesn't know what it is.

It was typical of Palmer's devious mind, Staeli recalled, that his schemes could be spun as elegantly as a spider's web, with hidden strands of which only he knew the existence. But what Palmer could create, Staeli would soon uncover.

"Terribly warm, is it not, for August," Staeli was telling the younger man in his correct but poorly pronounced English.

"Downright hot," Burris agreed. He was squinting into the sun and not enjoying it. But he, too, had seen that the shadow's movement would soon bring some relief. He glanced across the river, where at several hotels on the water, people were seated at outdoor tables under parasols. "They seem to be having fun," he said, indicating the diners across the water. "It's very colorful, isn't it."

Staeli nodded cautiously. He knew, because he had ordered it, that at the Hotel Krafft's outdoor café, at this very moment, sat the Ruc girl, his man Iselin and Margit Staeli's personal maid. He squinted but failed to make out anything at this distance that would suggest three young people around a table.

Turning slightly and still squinting to improve his focus, he noticed the stupid orange sports car of his soon-to-be nephew-in-law, Lorn. He supposed it was parked in front of Erich's house. An idea took shape in his mind and he began speaking almost before he'd worked out the whole thing.

"You see that orange car across the river?"

"Yes."

"It belongs to Erich Lorn. Have you met him yet, Herr Burris?"

"Lorn? I don't recall the name."

"He's the fiancé of my niece. You have met my niece, Margit."

Dieter Staeli managed to give the sentence a downturn that changed it from a question to a statement without letting Burris know whether it was one or the other. Staeli had mastered this technique in several languages but was a bit rusty with it in English. The idea was to suggest definite information without confirming it, thus giving the victim a chance to impale himself on a downright lie.

"Yes, of course," Burris said then. "Right here in the hotel dining room. She was to have lunch with her fiancé, who didn't show up."

"That is Erich," Staeli agreed, chuckling. "He's a very adventurous young fellow and full of courage, but quite undependable for punctuality. This was surely not the first time you had met Margit?"

Again the emphasis fell between a question and a statement. Staeli kept poking into the relationship, hoping to cause Burris to produce a lie. In these matters a lie tells the questioner much more than a mere recital of truths.

"At Harvard," Burris agreed, "but this was years ago."

"Yes, Harvard." Staeli tried to keep from looking grumpy at the truthful answer. If only Burris had lied, this would suggest a current liaison between him and Margit that had to be concealed. "I think all our problems stem from your Harvard college, Herr Burris."

"University," the American corrected. "We attended the Graduate School of Business Administration."

"Yes, quite." Staeli could hear the note of annoyance in his voice. He took a slow, steady breath and calmed himself thoroughly. "But, correct me if I am wrong. Is it not in the American universities that these new ideas of women's liberation have been, so to speak, created?"

Burris sipped his ice water and watched the maître d' present a menu first to his host and then to him. They ordered. "But, while we sympathize with you," Staeli rumbled on, "we forbid you to import these problems into Switzerland." He let his eyes crinkle as he produced a jolly expression to show that, while he was joking, he was not joking.

The younger man didn't seem to understand. "The problem," he was explaining in a somewhat dogged fashion, as if to himself as much as to Staeli, "is that even most women don't understand the problem, let alone the men. So, if it's a problem, it's a universal one. The women suffer from being held down so long, and the men suffer from having become your typical muscle-bound dummy who has to keep up a big front because he already feels guilty."

Dieter Staeli let this confusing statement waft away in the slight breeze. "My English friends who like to be birched by young girls," he said then, "tell me this masochist tendency is very common among their men. Is it common among yours? The secret fantasy of being enslaved and punished by women?"

Burris looked even more confused. He closed the menu and put it to one side. "Now and then you read about the cops raiding places like that. Why?"

"Simply that it reflects this guilt of which you speak. If men have made slaves of women for so long, naturally their guilts will produce this perverse desire to be humiliated and mastered by women. We Swiss," he went on quickly, "do not suffer from such fantasies of weakness and doubt. We have kept our women in their place because that is where they belong, not through our own choice but through divine preordination." He frowned. "Is that the correct word? God ordains that women bear children. He limits their lives to that function and the others that surround it. Preordination, yes?"

"In Switzerland," Burris added.

"I beg your pardon?"

"In Switzerland you're letting it all become a major confrontation. It would surely be a problem of sorts in France or Germany or the U.S., but somehow the woman would get recognition, even if it took a stiff fight. But Swiss men only play the game one way: no-lose."

"What is this?"

"No-lose. I used to play football, uh, rugby to you. We once had a no-lose coach. There was nothing in his head, no tiny corner of his mind where he would ever allow anything to suggest the possibility that his team might lose a game. Most coaches like to seem that way, but you know they're human and the thought of losing doesn't throw them into cardiac arrest. You lose some and you win some is their motto. They try to win more often than they lose. That's a human attitude. But total no-lose, that's the concept of a machine. The big trouble with no-lose is that when the time comes—and it has to—that you *do* lose, it throws you for a complete loop. The machine isn't flexible enough to survive. It hits head on and smashes itself to pieces."

Dieter Staeli sat back in his chair and surveyed his luncheon companion. He had been prepared for a rather inhuman person, like most bankers, someone who could handle figures and sniff out profits and maximize them as fully as possible. But none of this manipulation called for any thinking about human nature beyond a thorough understanding of greed.

"Herr Burris," he said as the smoked salmon arrived, "I think I am going to take you into my confidence. You are a man of some feeling. I am heartily sick of all the soul-less bankers with whom I deal every day of the week. You understand the human heart. To you I can unburden myself, I think."

"About what?"

"About my sweet, lovely niece."

Nothing about the way Burris cut off a bit of salmon and conveyed it to his mouth indicated that he was either interested or bored by the topic. Staeli for the first time began to wish the hulk-

199

ing bastard was on the Staeli side, not that of Palmer and his hated UBCO. Perhaps there was a way . . . ?

"Tell me, dear Burris, has anyone in Basel explained to you yet the *Abschaffnung des Patriarchats?*"

The younger man frowned and shook his head. "Can you translate that?"

"It is simpler to explain than to translate," Staeli assured him. "There is a law that has governed us for hundreds of years. Even before written laws, I am sure, this same law had force back to the very beginnings of Switzerland in the thirteenth century, when we formed our first defense confederation. The law is very simple: within any family, the last word belongs to the husband."

"The last word? I don't und—"

"The problem is not the law," Staeli went on brusquely. "The problem is a definite movement now under way to remove the law from the books. If this happens, in every family the husband will have one vote, the wife will have one vote and each mature child will have one vote. Have you ever heard of such nonsense?"

"Yes."

"And what is even more ludicrous," the older man continued, "is that the government is actually prepared, once the law goes into effect, to establish a . . . a . . . an apparatus," he sputtered, "to help these children cast their family votes. A counseling bureau," he added in a jeering tone, "guidance, all the idiocies of modern sociological cant. Can you picture such lunacy?"

"Yes."

"So." Dieter Staeli addressed himself to his smoked salmon and demolished it in short order.

He was both pleased and disturbed by this encounter which he had taken some pains to arrange. It was a major risk in intelligence work to fraternize with the enemy. This could only be done at the highest levels, the way presidents and premiers consorted at summit conferences. Well, in a way, this was a kind of summit conference, although Palmer should be across the table now, not his underling.

Perhaps he would not be able to control himself this well with Palmer. The temptation to poison his smoked salmon would be too powerful to resist. But this clod here was manageable, this rugby player, this hulk, his brain thoroughly scrubbed, rinsed and hosed out by women. He had heard the Americans were all under the thumbs of their women, but he had never seen the idea in action before. His diatribe against no-lose thinking! As if the women in his life had not already implanted him with a no-win philosophy.

"So you would let our women—what is the new phrase?—do their thing?" he asked then as the salmon plates were cleared away.

Burris leaned back and sipped his wine spritzer. "Mr. Staeli," he said then, "do you have any other choice?"

CHAPTER 30

Linate is by far the busier of Milan's two airports. It handles both domestic flights within Italy and those to other countries around Europe, while Malpensa Airport is concerned mostly with the heavy jumbo jets that trundle off across the Atlantic.

Arriving from another country at Linate, one passes from the international to the national side of the terminal almost without realizing that one has actually passed through customs. The average tourist will then head for the city itself, nearly two million harassed northern Italians trying to live amid the noise, congestion and pollution of their nation's business and financial capital.

This particular tourist, a thin man of average height carrying his blue-and-white seersucker jacket in the August heat, ignored both the turmoil of Milan and its cultural treasures. He headed, instead, for the island in the middle of the upper-terminal lobby where all the car-rental concerns have their counters, picked up the keys to a vehicle reserved in the name of Curtis and walked out of the warm, humid terminal into the hot, humid open air.

The Fiat 128-Sport was a light blue of almost the same color as Curtis' seersucker jacket. The white roof was dirtier than the white denim jeans he wore, but it would serve in this weather to help keep the car's interior cool.

At border control into Switzerland the lines of cars and trucks moved slowly, despite the fact that there were four inspection gates and none of the lines were long. There was no other car, in fact, behind the blue-and-white Fiat. At the Italian customs barrier, Curtis surrendered his passport.

The uniformed guard squinted mightily at it. He walked in front to examine the license plate, as if this were somehow mysteriously connected with the driver's passport. He frowned at some length, comparing the face of the driver with his picture. It was a green passport of the normal kind issued by the United States, but the border guard's frown deepened as he stepped close to Curtis.

"*Americano?*" he demanded suspiciously.

"*Sì, claro.*"

The delay continued without in any way making Curtis anxious. He had been through enough border controls in Europe to understand the routine. A guard could never be caught short with *only one car* in his lane. Although there was nothing wrong with this car or passport, the guard was honor-bound to delay its passage out of Italy until *another car arrived* in his lane. That way he would seem to be as busy as the other guards, all of them playing the same game.

Thankfully, Curtis saw in his rear-view mirror that a yellow Volkswagen had pulled behind him. The passport inspection stopped at once. The guard almost flung the passport back at the driver in his haste to move him along.

When Curtis reached the long sweep of corniche road that fronts the Lake of Lugano, he slowed for a moment until he reached the Splendide Royale Hotel. He parked beside its square, boxy, old-fashioned bulk rising high over the corniche for a view across the lake.

The room clerk pushed a register card across to Curtis, then began searching through a pile of envelopes. "Here you are, sir." He handed Curtis a hotel envelope, took back the filled-in register card and snapped his fingers for a bellman. "We have you in a back room, sir, as you requested. It's much quieter."

Curtis nodded as he tore open the envelope. The message had been written in a typical European hand. "Sonny Boy. Call after 5 P.M. Dad." Only two people ever sent Curtis messages addressed to Sonny Boy and signed Dad. One was his immediate boss in the New York world headquarters of the UBCO bank. The second was UBCO's honorary vice chairman, the semiretired and almost legendary Woods Palmer, Jr., who lived not far from Lugano.

In his room he tipped the bellman. *"Acqua minerale, per piacere,"* he told the man, *"con ghiacchio."*

"Very good, sir, and may I bring some whisky with it?"

Curtis eyed the linguist sourly. "No, I brung me own hooch."

Several emotions crossed the bellman's face before it lapsed into utter docility. "As you say, sir." He was back with the soda and ice in a minute or less and had the good sense not to linger for a second tip.

Curtis glanced at his watch. Four P.M. He made himself a scotch and soda, lay back on the bed and sipped his drink slowly but steadily, as if determined to keep a very thin, regular flow of the amber liquid coursing down his throat at all times and without a break. He managed to do this twice more in the next hour before it was time to call Palmer.

"Sonny?" Palmer asked, "is it you, Sonny?"

"Yes, Dad," Curtis responded in a disgusted voice. "Where and when?"

"Come out here for dinner. How soon can you leave?"

"Give me an hour's nap. I'll leave here about six or six-thirty."

"Fine. You know the road. And you'll be staying the night here."

"But, I—" The line was dead. Curtis stopped talking. It wasn't that Palmer was rude or arrogant—although Curtis had never met a banker who wasn't both, no matter how hard he tried to seem normal—but only that there was no point, in Curtis' business, tying up an open telephone line that ran through a hotel switchboard. It could be tapped at any point along the way by people listening for any crumb of information a careless talker might let slip. After a nap, he paid a day's rent for the brief privilege and checked out of the Splendide Royal.

The Lago di Lugano, one of the celebrated pre-Alpine lakes of Italy and Switzerland that also includes Como and Maggiore, is shaped something like a checkmark, a V with one arm elongated. The peninsula that drops down into this checkmark begins with Lugano but comes to a point at its southernmost tip in the scenic town of Morcote, which looks across the narrow lake both at Italy and a tiny extra piece of Switzerland.

At six-fifteen, Curtis steered the blue-and-white Fiat down the peninsula toward Morcote. A small ship traversed the lake, bringing travelers to various ports of call and ferrying gamblers across to a tiny sealed-off enclave of Italy called Campione, where the only industry in the tiny postage stamp of land was its casino.

One could gamble in Lugano, Curtis recalled from a previous visit, but only in a way that was typically Swiss, with a five-franc limit per bet. Real death-wish gamblers could bankrupt themselves infinitely faster at Campione, and did.

Curtis was not a gambler, nor was he an alcoholic, at least not quite yet. The slight, blond, nondescript man led a life so peripatetic that he literally could call no city home. He went where he had to go and spent what free time he had enjoying the visit, but, aside from a complete lack of any desire to return to the States, Curtis could not be said to favor any one place over another. He had things to do everywhere.

Like all giant institutions, UBCO had its own intelligence section. Curtis was assigned the European work, usually such routine things as tracking down a defalcating vice president in menopause, or a customer who had gone bad on a large loan.

In the distance two gaff-rigged sloops chased each other gracefully back and forth over the lake. The architecture of the houses was Alpine, with sloping roofs and brown-stained half-timbering. Many of them looked brand-new, someone's vacation retreat designed to exude a powerful bucolic aura. To Curtis' right, the mountain rose steeply over the road. Often there was only enough room at lake level for two cars to pass rather carefully.

Before he actually reached the tip at Morcote, Curtis swung the Fiat off the main road and up a steep series of switchbacks, climbing constantly for fifteen minutes until he had gained the top of the crag that formed the tip of the peninsula.

He found the narrow gravel road that seemed to lead, if it were possible, even higher up the mountain, the absolute peak of the wooded terrain. At a certain point the road squeezed down to the width of one car. Palmer country.

The smell of pine was sharp in the cool evening air. At one turning, Curtis paused to look down on the lake far below. He was so high that the lake seemed to have been sketched there, as if on a map.

Two turns later the road became concrete at a gatehouse. Curtis got out and picked up the telephone. "Hello? It's Curtis here."

"Right," Palmer's voice said. The gate buzzed open. He drove between rows of cedars and yews around the last rise of the entire peak to a house he could already glimpse.

Curtis decided it was simply not big enough for a man with Palmer's money. Made of fieldstone to the window line, then rough-hewn cedar board-and-battens to the roof, the house looked like the hideout of a hermit, a well-to-do hermit, but certainly not the internationally known Palmer.

From his last visit, Curtis remembered that the house contained three bedrooms, the rest of it being taken up by an immense living room designed around a walk-in fireplace and kitchen-bar counter. Expensive paintings hung here and there. One wall of the house was glass and led onto a terrace from which Palmer waved lazily to him.

"Good to see you, Sonny Boy."

"Can we dispense with that now?"

Palmer's laugh, even at a distance was a tight sound, not stingy exactly, but cautious. He stood up as Curtis arrived on the flagstone terrace. "Welcome."

They shook hands. Curtis decided Palmer looked older than he had the year before. Always a thin, tall man well over six feet, Palmer had a narrow face that was beginning to show its underlying skull when he lost even a few pounds. His high forehead looked tan. His dark-gray eyes squinted slightly as he grinned at Curtis. "You're looking fit," Palmer said.

"You, too. Play much tennis?"

"A little. My partner isn't here this week. You remember her?"

"Miss, ah, I don't recall her name."

"Good," Palmer said, still grinning. "You're not only a liar, you're a discreet liar. Anyway, she usually runs me ragged on the court out behind the house but she's away for a while. I've got both my sons here, you know, but I can't get either of the lazy bastards on the court. How about you?"

Curtis frowned. "Will we be able to talk with your boys around?"

"Oh, they're not here tonight," Palmer explained. "As a matter of fact, they're down in Lugano this evening looking for girls.

They've got till the end of August and then they go back to school. Their sister might be here tomorrow. No way of knowing nowadays. Children don't really spend much time keeping parents informed of their whereabouts, especially Gerri. She's my brainy one."

"But we're alone this evening?"

"Except for the cook and the housekeeper. But they live in their own place behind the tennis court. It's quite a Palmer compound."

"You own the top of the mountain, don't you?"

"About four hundred acres."

"How the hell did you get the Swiss to let that happen?"

"Bought it through a Swiss intermediary," Palmer said. "Scotch, isn't it? With soda?"

Curtis nodded. He followed Palmer into the gigantic living room and watched him make two scotch-and-sodas. "Are you a legal resident now?"

"I got my permit a year ago. It wasn't easy because they were still touchy about the way I bought the top of their blessed mountain. But I transferred everything I had into Lugano banks and their hearts softened and lo, they conferred residency upon me. Today it would be a lot harder to swing."

"So you're taxed at the local rate?" Curtis asked.

"Yes. Are you compiling a dossier or what?"

Curtis made a Christ-I-put-my-foot-in-it face and accepted his drink. "Just naturally nosey, is all."

"Your nosiness, my boy, is legendary." Instead of leading the way out to the terrace again, Palmer sat down in one of a long row of Mies Van der Rohe "Barcelona" chairs, all stainless steel and soft brown leather. He waved to a more upholstered chair that sat on the other side of a large, low coffee table.

Curtis sank into the chair and immediately began worrying about staying awake. Palmer had that effect on him. His manner was easy and the chair was soft and this would be his fourth drink and he'd been on the go all day, trains, planes, cars, London, Paris, Milan. Curtis made his eyes go abnormally wide. He decided not to try any tricks with Palmer, who had a reputation for being able to outthink the brightest spy.

On the wall over Palmer's head hung four oil paintings in rather plain strip frames. One he recognized as a small Pollock of the pre-drip school. Two were Picassos. The fourth Curtis couldn't place. He stared at it until his eyes began to glaze.

"Would it be a lot of trouble if I asked for coffee? Black, no cream or sugar."

"Espresso okay?"

"Perfect." He watched his superior officer in UBCO get up and start working a large restaurant-sized espresso *macchina* in the kitchen area. Palmer tapped the steel cup clean, filled it with black ground coffee, tamped it down, swung it into place on the machine and pulled the lever to shoot live steam through the mechanism. He put two tiny cups under the twin faucet in time to catch the first drops of pure caffeine. A moment later he was carrying the cups back to the living room and handing one to Curtis.

"That's my life's ambition," Curtis murmured, sipping the acrid black brew. "To own a real espresso machine."

Palmer watched him drain his cup, then handed him the second one. "Been on the go?"

"I'd like to stop trying to keep tabs on Matt Burris. Nobody is dogging his trail any more. That business with Shelter was a one-time fluke."

Palmer smiled coldly. "And a convenient heart attack swept the slate clean? You people are all the same."

"Me people?"

"People in intelligence work. You like neat packages you can file and forget."

Curtis started to give him an argument, then lapsed back in the chair. He stared at one of the modern paintings for a long moment. Then: "I think someone on Staeli's payroll took out Shelter. Did it like a pro. The inquest called it cardiac failure. Well, hell, we all die of cardiac failure, don't we?" His glance shifted to Palmer's bony face. "The only thing we have to wrap up in a neat package is why the Staelis had Shelter hit."

"All right." Palmer's wide mouth thinned into a straight line. "What's your thought?"

Curtis shrugged. "Shelter may have held them up for a lot of loot and then couldn't deliver because he didn't know enough. Maybe he went up against Burris with a gun to scare some more information loose."

"That's a scene I would have enjoyed watching," Palmer said. "Burris doesn't take to that kind of treatment."

Curtis had a quick picture in his mind of Shelter breaking in on Burris and Margit Staeli. In his report on the incident, he'd left the woman out of the story. "Those long-barrel Staelifer .38s are a powerful inducement to co-operation." Curtis rubbed his left arm.

"I know, I know," Palmer said quickly, in a tone as close to apology as a banker ever got. "But it's healed well, hasn't it?"

Curtis nodded. "And that's all that counts," he added with barely conscious irony.

Neither spoke for a while. Curtis had been waiting for the first question about Margit Staeli. He hadn't made up his mind yet whether it was any of Palmer's business. True, UBCO paid him to get whatever information it felt like knowing. But the Margit Staeli thing was, at least for now, a personal matter. Having to talk about it somehow reduced Curtis in his own eyes to keyhole peeper. Not that he knew all that much to report.

"The Basel police," Palmer asked then, "have closed the case?"

"Finished."

"And nobody new is on Burris' tail?"

Curtis paused for a long moment. "I think he's spotted me a few times. He's almost impossible to tail. But nobody else is doing any better. Or even trying. So I think we can let me get back to other things."

"What other things?"

"I have things under way in Paris and in Luxembourg."

"Nothing you have is more important than making sure the Basel project moves ahead unhampered."

"Nobody's hampering it now."

Palmer failed to respond for a while. Then: "How much briefing have you had on this whole project? I mean from the beginning."

"Not all that much."

Palmer nodded. "You can start on that scotch now. I promise not to put you to sleep."

Curtis tried a slight smile. It was disconcerting to have anybody read his thoughts, much less the man he was working for. He picked up the drink but delayed sipping it for a moment.

"You know, for years," Palmer began then, "the Swiss banks

have been the envy of the world. Their secrecy, the stability of the Swiss franc, the banks' freedom to invest in just about anything they like, and the fact that their government can't really pry into what they do. It's a textbook example of real nineteenth-century capitalism in action."

"Compared to our banks?" Curtis asked.

"Especially compared to U.S. banks. We're so heavily regulated we can't turn around and scratch our neck without getting an enabling law from some legislature or another."

"From your tone, I gather something's changing here in Switzerland."

"Not really," Palmer explained. "The banks still have all their freedom here. But banking's no longer a big growth business in Switzerland. Money's still coming in, but there are more attractive places to invest these days at a higher return. Running the Swiss banks is getting to be a problem. Help is hard to get. They have to be Swiss and they have to be highly trained. You can't just import a boatload of workers from Sicily or Turkey."

"The Swiss don't trust them to work in the banks?"

"No way," Palmer said. "Then there's inflation. The Swiss have it as bad as we do. Their way of curbing it is to limit foreign investments and offer a ridiculously low rate of interest, around four per cent. Hell, right this minute you can get twelve in London. Of course, that's in sterling."

"Not as good as Swiss francs."

"By no means. But there are other dark spots to the bank business here. Look at Switzerland itself as a market. There are over seven million local accounts for a population of, say, five million, including infants. You could say the place was vastly overbanked. And the Swiss are making it harder than ever for foreigners to invest in local real estate, the way I did. So, you see, the Swiss banks are having their problems these days."

Curtis finally sipped his drink. "Then why," he asked after a while, "do we want to cut ourselves in on the Swiss banking business?"

Palmer's tight mouth relaxed in another of his grins. He stood up and his long legs carried him over to the fireplace for a moment, where he picked up a cigar humidor and brought it back. "Smoke?"

"No, thanks."

"Upmanns from Havana."

"Wasted on me."

Palmer started to open the humidor, then seemed to think better of it. He put it aside for a moment. "It's precisely right now, when the Swiss are worried about their profits and the expansion of banking that we want to leap in and grab up a chunk. They're wobbling a little. It's like a boxer who's taken a hard punch. While he's still a little groggy, we want to sneak in under his guard and wham him a good one."

"Why does UBCO want in on a failing business?"

"Not failing. It's rate of expansion is slowing. That's hardly the same as failing."

"Okay," Curtis agreed, "why do we want a piece of a slowing-down business."

"Because whatever shape it's in, the Swiss banking system is a license to steal."

Palmer's cold gray eyes seemed to light up. "Sure, we can get the same freedom in places like Panama and Lebanon. And we're there, too, you can be sure. But doing business in those currencies is just not the same as doing business in Swiss francs. Each franc is covered by gold. Not just a percentage of each franc. There's enough gold reserve in Switzerland to cover every franc by more than a hundred per cent."

"But we've taken the dollar off gold permanently."

Palmer shook his head. "Get used to not thinking in dollars. We're doing business in sixty countries around the world. The U.S. is only one of them and it happens to be our home, but we're not married to the dollar. We're married only to profits. And when you deal in a currency as stable as the Swiss franc, your profits don't melt away through devaluation."

"All of this would make more sense," Curtis suggested, "if the economists were predicting a rosy future, worldwide. Any amount of skullduggery would be worth it to get a solid Swiss base for UBCO."

Palmer nodded thoughtfully. "You have to know how to decode what the economists say," he told him. "A good half of the world is in for big trouble. But we're not part of that half."

"That's good. Who gets the ax?"

"Marginal people." Palmer made a face. "I didn't make up that term, someone else did. Marginal people are superfluous. It's not that they're unemployed. Hell, that can happen to anybody. It's that they can't *do* anything that'll earn them a living."

"Dig ditches?"

"No good. Backhoes do it a hundred times as fast."

"Plant food, cotton?"

"Them that plants it is soon forgotten," Palmer quoted with a wry smile. "It's all machinery now. Agribusiness. It used to be that a peasant in the back reaches of Africa or Vietnam could grow millet or rice or something that would keep him alive as a food and give him a bit more to sell for other commodities he needed. But drought is taking care of him one way, and the lower cost of machine-produced grain is pricing him out another way. He's finished. He's dying. It's already happening. And the only thing you can say for certain about it is that the famine will keep growing."

"But we can ship them what they need."

"As charity?"

"Why not?" Curtis insisted. "We've been doing it for generations for our own marginal people in the States."

Palmer shook his head. "Not much sentiment in affluent lands for do-goodery. Too much inflation chopping holes in too many pockets. No politician could last if he started shipping food to the starving peoples of the earth."

"So they just die?"

Palmer was silent, staring at the palm of his hand, fingers outstretched. "They just die."

Curtis got to his feet and strode to the window wall. "And that leaves the rest of us King of the Hill, is that it?"

"Fat cats," Palmer agreed. "We've done something damaging to our ecology. But that can often be repaired if we have the will to turn it around. The trouble is, nobody's interested in repairing it. Because we've done something even worse to our system of distribution. It's irreparable. There is no cure. So these people will die to keep us sleek and slightly overfed."

"And busy making money."

Palmer looked up to see Curtis return to his seat. "That goes," he said somberly, "without saying."

Neither man spoke for a long moment. Curtis had no idea what Palmer was thinking about. Who did? But whatever it was, he saw now that the man hadn't really wanted to brief him as much as he wanted to express ideas to someone he could trust. It got lonely up in this eagle's nest with just a tennis playmate for company and horror to think about. No wonder Palmer spent his time dreaming up elegant schemes more complex than the war plans of a major world power.

"I see now," Curtis began then, "why a banker would love to become a Swiss banker. I understand the incentive. But, groggy or not, the Swiss have an even stronger incentive for keeping you in your place as an outsider."

"Well, not exactly."

Palmer opened the humidor and removed a long, thin panatela cigar with a faintly greenish wrapper. He stared at it for a moment, then put it back and screwed the humidor shut.

"You have to understand," he went on then, "that we already do a lot of business in Switzerland with Swiss banks, as we do with the banks of other countries. It's small potatoes, but it's profitable. The only trouble is that no Swiss bank will deal with us openly, as a partner. They don't even deal with each other that way. It's the national mania for privacy. And the big Swiss manufacturers won't bank with us. If we could start financing them, we'd be home free. My original idea was to start doing business in Switzerland as a Swiss bank, through a newly organized subsidiary here, and tell the Swiss to go chase themselves. We can be just as secretive as they are, once we're protected by Swiss law. My idea was to pull together as much business from other countries as possible, even at a discount, and handle it through our Swiss bank, building volume by leverage until we'd achieved the same level of assets as our Swiss brethren, protected by the same secrecy laws."

"That was your original idea," Curtis said, letting the words hang for a moment in the air as if, perhaps, a newer idea was to come.

"My original idea is still the core of the operation," Palmer replied. "I'm still working with Burris to funnel a lot of new foreign business through Basel. Burris is geared to handle it and he already is, to some extent."

He opened the humidor again and this time he sniffed the aroma rising from it. "To grow this sort of luxury, there is all the money in the world for fertilizer, labor, bug killers, packaging, distribution, everything. This cigar is proof that politics has nothing to do with what's happening in the world. Ninety miles off the coast of Florida, on a communist island, they have already figured out the priorities as ruthlessly as we have."

He lifted out a cigar in the air. "Nothing less than who shall live and who shall die. There is just so much money and resources in the world. The decision not to irrigate the areas surrounding the Sahara was a simple one to make. As simple as automating the cotton harvest or the California vineyards. You minimize costs to maximize profits. It's right out of any elementary textbook in business administration."

He replaced the cigar in the humidor and shut it. Then he pushed the humidor as far away from him as possible. "You wanted to ship food to starving people. I tell you there is no one who will ship them even money any more. Or seed. Or fertilizer. They're a write-off. The best thing they can do is go away and stop reminding us they're there."

He nodded twice, as if reaffirming this vision. Then, savagely: "Let them die quietly. This is our prayer. Die quietly and leave us alone to maximize our profits. That's life. Someone loses, someone wins. And if you apply it to Swiss banking, you see that it's time for us to win, finally. It's a slow process, this Basel operation, but there are some shortcuts, don't you think?"

Curtis said nothing. He'd known from the beginning that he'd been invited here—or was it ordered? When someone was as shrewd in handling people as Palmer, it was hard to tell—to debrief himself of every shred of material he'd picked up in Basel. He'd also known there wasn't that much. Palmer would be unhappy with how little there was. And at the core of it lay the nasty part.

Palmer hunched forward in the Barcelona chair, his face drawn with intensity of thought. Curtis reminded himself that his employer wasn't that old . . . fifty or fifty-five? He had no right to look that skull-like.

He'd taken early retirement, if that was what one called what he did now. Was it the intensity of his commitment to this Basel thing that made him stare so fiercely? Curtis liked to hang loose. This much intensity worried him.

"Now," Palmer said, "about Miss Staeli."

CHAPTER 31

If, on leaving the calculator plant near Neuchâtel, Walter Staeli had directed his chauffeur to drive back to Basel by a more easterly route, he would have passed quite close to Michelebad. But the Jura range of mountains made it sensible to return by the same low-level route he had used in coming, thus duplicating the scenery. The Silver Fox was nothing if not sensible, which is why he came no closer than fifty kilometers to the celebrated youth clinic and spa.

However, visiting Michelebad would have done Walter little good today. On the first Thursday of every month the gates were closed to casual visitors. Only incoming patients or the families of patients were allowed entrance this Thursday, because it was on the first Thursday of every month that the board of directors of Euromichele, GmbH. met.

At the same time, the almost identical boards of several subsidiaries of Euromichele also met at Michelebad, including the directors of Technicon, Pty. Ltd. and Omnitrans, S.A.

It had been in mid-July, hardly more than a few weeks before, that Erich Lorn had been elected unanimously to the boards of all three companies. Attending these monthly meetings took most of the day, Erich saw, as this particular Thursday wore on. These were his first meetings and he was impressed by the staff preparation that made them run so smoothly. He was also—because Erich's hypocrisy detector could never be entirely switched off— somewhat amused at the grandiose names devised for Michele's empire of youth.

He sat now, at three in the afternoon, at the final session of the day, the Omnitrans meeting, and looked around the long table at the faces of his fellow directors. He had seen them all today at other meetings, including Michele herself, who always took a seat just anywhere, declining the head of the table. While this might be an affectation, Erich decided, it helped loosen everyone up a bit and keep the thing from looking like a formal Christmas dinner with Grandmother serving.

No, the meetings were all right. It was the corporate nomenclature that Erich found laughable. He loathed the rash of telescoped one-word, omnibus, multilingual corporate names that had sprouted all over Europe these days. Everywhere he went, and especially in Basel where all of them seemed to have offices, he was surrounded by Uniplans and Omniprojekts and Instabanks and Intertechs and Chemitechs and Eurotechs and Techomechs and Mechotechs.

Was there room in the world of business any more for a firm called something like Schultz's Pickle Company?

Looking around the room at his fellow directors of Euroyouth or Youthotech or whatever this subsidiary was called, Erich wondered why Michele had surrounded herself with such intense nonentities. He had attended many corporate meetings, unwillingly it was true, as a representative of his family bank, Lorn et Cie. (*There* was a name!) But he had rarely seen people with so few ideas and so much verve and style in presenting them.

Basically, he guessed, they came from the field of marketing, a new mystery with its own high priests and acolytes, its own language and ritual. One of them was talking at the moment about a plan to franchise Michele clinics all over France.

"If we consider only the incredible numbers," he was saying with a tremendous intensity and severe exophthalmia, "to maximize potentiality in a nonlinear manner, we simply cannot overlook the incredible French Riviera as our launching pad. The synergies there are incredible. The synaptic shortcuts work in our favor, and within an incredibly short time we target out at full increment."

When he stopped talking the air seemed to vibrate for a long time with the strange syllables and the pounding surge of "incredibles." Erich looked around him.

The rest of the dozen or so people were nodding with the same popeyed intensity, as listeners to this drivel, as the driveler himself. All except Michele, who continued to make what seemed to

215

be one-word notes on a pad. She remained grave and still, one hand in her lap, as did a man named Gloggner, who seemed to be Michele's chief financial officer. He had stopped taking notes long ago and merely sat still, eyes glazed, staring out the windows at the Juras in the distance.

"In other words," Erich said then, more to fill the silence with something sensible than for any other reason, "you're suggesting we start franchising on the Riviera because it's a resort area filled with well-to-do people."

"That's precisely it!" the man responded so fiercely that for a moment Erich thought he was being attacked. "You've got it!" the man almost shouted, eyes bugging again, as if understanding him was possibly the most difficult of human tasks and success was vouchsafed to but a few.

Michele's big eyes lifted slowly from her notepad to stare across the table at Erich. A faint smile touched her lovely lips. Her broad face remained placid. She said nothing. In fact, Erich realized now, aside from opening and closing each meeting, she had not really said anything all day.

He watched her as she resumed her note-taking. A few sharply intense reactions were batted back and forth across the table by other directors. Increditech. Interincreditron. Incredorama.

Erich had never spent this much time with a mistress before. It was now—what?—more than three months, four perhaps, since that first morning in her rosy bedroom, that first broken luncheon appointment with Margit.

Since then he had been with Michele every night and perhaps half of his days. They had gone to Cap Ferrat in June, before the heavy crowds, then to a little cottage she kept on the island of Malmö off the Stockholm shore. In early July they had flown for a quick visit to Scotland and another cottage of Michele's on one of the Hebrides.

She had a thing about island real estate, owning perhaps ten or twelve vacation homes on such islands as Kos, Sark, Aran, one of the Scillies off England, the smallest of the Maltese islands, called Comino, one of the Aeolians above Sicily, Djerba off the Tunisian Coast, and an unnamed islet just above Sardinia.

At first, in the early stages of his affair with Michele, Erich had thought this was a sort of peasant shrewdness on her part, this obsessive investment in real estate. But after a while he realized that these isolated island hideaways were meant only for that, as self-sufficient retreats independent of servants or other outside distraction.

They were, and Erich hated to use the term, love-nests. She had diverted the normal nest-building trait to one specific kind. Erich had no idea how many men had shared these hideaways with her over the years, but he had the notion she rotated her use of the cottages with quite a delicacy of understanding. There were enough of them that she might not use a particular island for, perhaps, two years. That was surely long enough for the place to have lost the aura of its previous male occupant.

She was a clever woman, in love as in everything else. Each cottage, each island, came freshly to her, without memories. Erich found himself wondering how long it would take for the memory of him to die out of these places.

To think that he, of all people, would already be wondering about the end of the affair. It was always he who named the termination day, not the woman. But with Michele he seemed unwilling to bring it to a close. He found that he was content to let it drift along. Very un-Erich.

He had the idea, as he sat there now watching Michele, that her chief attraction for him, and the reason he was so reluctant to bring the affair to a close, was that he still didn't know her. After all this time she was almost the same mystery she had been at the beginning. Oh, some things he knew. Her sexual repertoire was by now predictable, although highly varied. There were, after all, not that many roads to satisfaction. He also knew, or thought he knew, why she had placed him on her boards of directors.

One had only to attend one's first meetings, as he had today, to realize that, with the possible exception of the silent Gloggner, the board was made up of poseurs, lightweights and fakers of great artifice but small use. They performed a function only because of the quasi-fake, entirely lightweight nature of the business they were in. In any other business they would have been sacked almost at once.

So it made sense for Michele to add a banker to her board, although in Erich she had chosen about as unbankerly a banker as she could have found. Her next step, or so Erich felt, would be to look to Lorn et Cie. for the financing of her big marketing plans.

And they were big. France was only a beginning. Germany and Italy were other targets, but the country in which the most money was to be made was the country that required the greatest capital investment, the United States. Here the medical associations and the government food and drug agencies would be watching over Euromichele's corporate shoulder for one false move, one fake claim, one unorthodox ingredient.

It would take perhaps a million Swiss francs to buy Michele's way into the American market. But, once established, every centime of the cost would be worth it. Properly worked, the States would produce billions in profits over the years. It was all a matter of paying off the right people first, and of buying the best advice. The rest was dreams, the marketing of fantasies, at which Michele had already proven her expertise.

More than that, Erich realized now, she had placed herself far above her major competitors. The Aslan method, for example, depended on one's going to Rumania for procaine injections, or on capsules of dubious freshness sold in only a few countries. There were Swiss clinics that specialized only in gland-extract injections and one in London that introduced similar substances by suppository.

All of these processes hung their success on a single idea, what the Americans called a gimmick. It was always possible to overthrow a system based on so narrow a pedestal. But Michele's was an Omnipantechnicon of treatments, everything from negative-ion therapy to acrobatics, from diet to hypnosis, from whirlpool baths to lithium injections. In this shotgun blast of treatments something *had* to work, even if only temporarily.

He had never stopped watching the creator of all this. His open, unblinking stare had been focused on Michele throughout the sprightly debate, heavily peppered with "incredibles" that was going on around them. Finally the weight of his gaze cut through her self-absorption. She looked up at him for a moment, almost startled, as if he had somehow rapped on her forehead.

"Yes?" she asked him, as if he had spoken.

The room went silent in a second. "I didn't say anything," Erich told her.

218

She glanced around the room and favored all of them, the men and the two women directors as well, with a soft, enticing smile, a kiss-me smile, welcoming and almost hot to the touch. "I think that was the last item on our agenda, was it not?"

A chorus assured her that this was true, ignoring the question of whether or not the item had been fully decided.

"Then, unless there is any other matter," she said in a slow drawl, her glance on Erich again, "I will entertain a motion for adjournment."

"So move," Erich said.

"Second," said the man who wanted to target out at full increment.

"We stand adjourned," Michele said, getting to her feet. "There will be cocktails in the lounge on the ground floor in half an hour. I hope to see you then." She turned and led the way out of the board room. Somehow she had taken Erich's arm and contrived to make it seem as if he were leading her along the second floor to the tall doors at the far end.

By the time they reached her bedroom, the other directors had gone. Michele lay back on the bed, slowly rubbing herself. "You cannot imagine," she said in a low, sleepy voice, "how I have been amusing myself during this ungodly meeting."

Erich stood before her. "Thinking unpure thoughts?"

"Playing with myself."

"Like a novice in a convent?"

She laughed softly. "Hardly a novice. Pull those blinds, will you, darling? And then help me get on with what I was doing. We only have half an hour."

CHAPTER 32

By five o'clock on the Aeschenvorstadt the long, narrow, green streetcars, linked together in pairs as a kind of minitrain, were already filled to capacity with people returning home from work.

Watching them from inside his office, Matthew Burris promised himself that one of these days he would have to learn the Basel streetcar and bus system. It didn't look all that complicated. At every stop there were lighted machines that not only showed you the routes but also how much a trip would cost. The amount of centimes lit up in a window, and one fed coins into the machine until it produced a small paper ticket, which then had to be put into a date-stamping slot in order to be valid.

In his months of walking or taking cabs around Basel, Burris had noticed that many people carried one-week tickets for the streetcars. In any event, most of the cars carried only a motorman. Riders were on their honor. If an occasional inspector boarded the car to ask to see tickets, Burris felt sure the only people he might catch would be tourists. The Baslers didn't cheat, not even the presumably impoverished students at the university or the hordes of teen-agers wandering about the city during summer vacation.

Burris yawned and stretched. He was the only UBCO employee left. Like all Basel banks, the branch opened at eight-thirty and closed at four. After that, Burris did most of the secret work for which he'd been sent to Basel originally.

He had developed a fairly foolproof routine. He would dictate correspondence into a miniature tape recorder, lock it in an attaché case with a supply of bank stationery and leave the case at the Drei Könige for a courier to pick up each evening at seven.

The attaché case went up the E-4 Autobahn to Strasbourg, in France, where a secretary typed the letters, signed them for Burris, sealed them in Swiss-stamped envelopes and put them back in the attaché case. The courier returned the letters to Basel by midnight, posted them and left the empty case at Burris' hotel.

Incoming mail from customers, corporations and other UBCO offices went to a box number in Basel to which Burris himself, and no one else, had the key. So the system, while awkward, functioned fairly smoothly. Letters he would pick up each morning from the box were answered and posted by midnight. No one but Burris, the courier, the French secretary in Strasbourg and Palmer knew that the correspondence wasn't actually handled by the Aeschenvorstadt office.

In this way, and by being very careful each time he went to the post-office box, Burris managed to keep almost all secrets secret. Palmer had been very pleased with the plan and had commended Burris highly.

"You're beginning to think like a real Swiss, Matty."

Burris smiled at the thought. The scheme had actually been devised by Margit, who spun it out of her head in about five minutes one night.

Five-fifteen, Thursday evening. Burris finished off the last of his dictated letters, made notes in the private ledger he kept of these clandestine transactions, and snapped the attaché case shut. He sat for a moment, not wanting to buck the homebound rush hour.

He had nothing special to do this evening. Thursdays were Elfi's half-day off, which meant that Margit would spend the afternoon and evening cleaning up her own work without having to worry about interruptions. In this way she served both her own interests and the greater good of Staeli Internationale, GmbH.

All during lunch with the devious old bastard today, Burris had found himself near hysterical laughter at the thought that Dieter Staeli had reached such a dead end that he actually had to make contact. His next move, probably would be to dangle some sort of bribe before him. What might make a good carrot for the young Yankee donkey? A piece of the Staeli business, perhaps? He might let UBCO finance some small undertaking of Staelichem or Staelifer, a perfectly normal piece of business but one calculated to make Burris a loyal ally and, later, a dupe.

God, what a city! What a business! Burris got up and hitched his pants higher, tucking in his shirt as he did so. If it hadn't been for Margit, these past months would have been the undoing of him. He'd had given up long ago and Palmer would probably have sent him to manage a side-street office in Brooklyn.

At six o'clock the streets had emptied. Burris let himself out of the bank, locking the door behind him. He glanced across the street, almost without thinking, at the gray stone pile of Number 17 Aeschenvorstadt. Surely no one was at work behind those curtains any more. Dieter had probably gone home. But no. Someone stood there at a second-floor window watching. A youngish fellow with thin sandy hair and a pale face. Burris wondered if this were the son, Walter, known as The White Rat.

Burris resisted the impulse to wave to Walter Staeli, or blow him a kiss. Instead, he moved at a leisurely pace to the corner of St. Alban-Graben where two of the largest banks in Switzerland had office buildings, the Swiss Bank Corporation and the Swiss

Credit Bank. The buildings contrasted neatly with each other, one being traditionally and properly gray with massive stonework and an immense brass-and-glass corner entrance up a broad flight of stairs worthy of a cathedral. The other was aluminum and glass, indistinguishable from any office building built anywhere in the past ten years.

He had time before the courier arrived. He strode into the Freiestrasse, where every kind of shop and department store could be found. At this hour, on a week night, not many were open. After a few blocks the street widened dramatically into the Marktplatz, the city's original marketplace dating possibly from the eleventh century.

Burris paused for a moment. He had grown to love this walk, which he took almost every evening. He had grown to love Basel, with its medieval heart still intact and beating. He liked the fact that it had always been a business town, even when ruled by archbishops, that in this square, for the past nine centuries, merchants and craftsmen had set up their booths to sell.

It was impressive to him that from this had sprung the guilds which had overthrown the church's power and won from the Pope the right to a university that was still in existence four centuries later and an annual trade fair that had been held every autumn for nearly five hundred years.

The booths of the people who sold vegetables, fruit and flowers in the Marktplatz every morning were now folded and taken down. The ancient square was given over to car parking until tomorrow morning. Burris walked past the ocher-red façade of the old Rathaus, the town hall, with its gilded towers.

He walked into the quiet courtyard, its walls distempered in dark red with allegorical nudes in a dull yellow. He sat down on a long bench near the bicycle rack and stared up at a garland painted on the far wall with three Cupids holding it aloft. Three mottoes in German had been painted into the garland. By now, Burris knew enough of the language to decipher only one of the sayings.

"Freiheit ist über Silber und Gold."

He smiled lopsidedly at the motto, not because it took very little knowledge of German to translate it, but because it was such blatant Swiss hypocrisy.

He leaned back on the bench for a moment, trying to puzzle out the other mottoes, then decided he'd copy them down sometime and show them to Margit. It would have been much simpler, of course, to walk her past the Rathaus some fine morning and have her translate the sayings on sight. But, except for that first afternoon and evening when they'd met, he and Margit had never been seen together in Basel during the entire summer.

Burris roused himself finally and strolled around the curving street to the Mittlererhein Bridge. Down below, on the ship landing, a light had been switched on even though the evening sky was still very light. The river moved swiftly past, creaming slightly against the heavy masonry pedestals of the bridge.

The light had been turned on because there were still a few boats expected from various places along the Rhine. Burris descended the stairs and stood beside the light for a moment, checking the schedules on the bulletin board next to the ticket window.

"Personenschiffahrt Fahrplan," the schedule read. It gave Burris the times for every kind of Rhine trip, including excursions with and without *"Musik und Tanz."* Burris glanced at his watch. Six-thirty. Swinging the attaché case, he mounted the stairs and turned up the street to his hotel, got his key and went upstairs.

For no reason, other than sentimental, he was still in the same suite overlooking the river, which still cost the bank a tidy sum, even though he was now on a monthly rate rather than a daily one. Burris took off his light-tan summer suit, a veteran Palm Beach number he'd bought five years ago, and removed his white shirt and tie.

He pulled on a dark-green sweatshirt Margit had bought for him, and stepped into a pair of nondescript jeans of the ordinary, nonpatched, nonbleached, straight-off-the-farm variety, also five years old and bought in a J. C. Penney store for two dollars and seventy-nine cents. At a few minutes to seven, he went downstairs with the attaché case and found that the courier, too, had arrived a bit early. He gave him the case and sent him on his way in a dark-brown Opel.

Margit had told him of an eating place, saying that it was too rough and tumble for tourists, but that students loved it, a place called Hasenburg, quite close to the hotel, on the street of tailors, Schneidergasse.

There had been a time, several months before, when Burris had been able to get lost almost without effort, primarily because the names of the streets bemused him. He pondered over a *Bernoulli-strasse,* named after the great physicist, or *Holbeinplatz,* or the nearby *Totentanz,* which had lost its power to worry him. But after a few weeks with a small map he knew the old city quite well, and almost never went anywhere else.

The Hasenburg, or Rabbit's Castle, turned out to be a noisy street-front *Bierstube* featuring long tables at which you simply sat down if there were an empty seat, first asking if it were, indeed, empty, then either joining in with the shouts of neighboring strangers, or keeping to oneself. Inability to say too much in German kept Burris to himself at one end of a long table, but it was doubtful if anyone noticed his silence.

A group of young men who seemed to be off-duty bank clerks were raucously arguing a fine point in soccer, or so it seemed, while across from them, but apparently under the illusion that she was part of their conversation, an elderly, raddled lady was alternately sipping her beer and shouting abuse at the young men. It wasn't until one of them ordered her a fresh beer that Burris began to suspect she actually was a member of their party, or had at least been granted abusing rights.

At the far end of his own table, a very old woman with one eye smiled sweetly at Burris and lifted her glass of white wine to greet him. He lifted his beer in return. A man of her age, with a cap pulled over his forehead lopsidedly, sat across from the old woman and stared into his red wine, the short butt of a dead cigar in the corner of his mouth. They had either been hired to lend atmosphere, Burris told himself, or else this place was the genuine article.

He ordered a plate of goulash with *Röstli,* the julienned potatoes and onions that are pan-fried into a kind of lighter-than-air pancake of great diameter. With them came a plate of bread and butter. Burris had been trying to bring down his weight, an almost impossible task. He wondered how he might contrive to move his bread and butter toward the ancient couple at the far end.

He found it hard to think, the air was so shaken by noise. People were laughing uproariously. Somewhere a jukebox was adding to the din, and across the room students were playing a slapping game that produced yelps of pain and loud thumpings on the table.

Burris caught the old man's half-open glance. He stared into its depths and began to feel terribly depressed. He switched his glance to the old woman, whose one eye was jollier. He pointed to his bread and then to her, making a "want-it?" gesture. She laughed pleasantly, displaying three teeth.

Burris had about given up the whole idea of communicating when the old man rose slowly, solemnly, and reached across the table. Delicately, he slid the plate toward the old woman, who picked up the bread and dropped it into a tattered paper shopping bag so quickly that Burris almost missed the movement. He winked at the old man, who winked back at him with his least disillusioned eye.

Burris asked the waitress for another beer and more bread. After a few more minutes of this, someone else at the table got the idea and soon bread was flowing into the paper shopping bag at a brisk rate.

By the time he got back to his suite at the Drei Könige, Burris had several more beers and was feeling quite cheerful. He stood at the window overlooking the river and tried to see if the L-2 Magna was still parked across the way. It was gone. He checked his watch and saw that it was now after ten o'clock. She was right on schedule.

Burris set his travel alarm for 7:30 A.M., undressed and got into bed. He switched on television and sat through about an hour of *Sunset Boulevard,* listening to Gloria Swanson and William Holden talk effortlessly in German. About the time Holden settled in as Gloria's lover-in-residence, Burris switched off the set and room light.

In Strasbourg, the secretary would have signed and sealed the letters. The courier was on the E-4 now and would reach a Basel mailbox within less than half an hour. Was this any way to run a bank?

Burris sighed and settled in under the single sheet he used in summer. He thought for a moment about Margit in the little sports car, driving through the night. Then he thought about tomorrow, Friday, which he was taking off. Then he thought about the long weekend. Then he slept.

CHAPTER 33

The dark-brown building on the Freiestrasse is very old. The fret-worked stone façade, several stories high, dates from the seventeenth century, perhaps. The intricate ironwork of the gates and windows is of later date, but the entire antique effect is quite impressive. It was meant to be. When the locksmiths' guild was active and powerful nothing less impressive than this would do.

The Schlüsselzunft is now primarily an eating place. It is not the most elegant of Basel's restaurants. It has no view, but the cuisine and the ambience are *echt Basler*. It is still quite an impressive place, especially for a local girl, let us say, of modest origins.

It was to the Schlüsselzunft that Iselin took Elfi the night of the same day on which they met. The assignation had been made out of Christa Ruc's hearing.

Although she suspected Iselin was not at all worried that their fast-blooming liaison might be known to Christa, Elfi had agreed to meet him downstairs from her apartment house. He seemed a strange person, the more one got to know him, secretive in a special way, open to her but closed to Christa, with whom he still pretended to work in the Staeli vaults. Strange or not, however, he was an Iselin.

Elfi would have liked to invite him upstairs to the apartment she shared with Christa and make drinks for them. She was not lacking in social graces and wanted to make sure Iselin knew this. But she allowed him, instead, to keep pretending their relationship had to remain clandestine.

"The Staeli spy network is everywhere," Iselin had whispered that day at lunch by the river.

"Surely it doesn't include Christa Ruc?"

"One never knows."

His small, light-colored eyes had hooded mysteriously. This pinched, faintly arrogant look, as of a near-sighted bird of prey, together with an upper-class accent when he felt like using it, gave an exotic tone to Iselin that more than made up, in Elfi's eyes, for the fact that he was almost exactly her height, if he wore his normal boots with two-inch heels and she stood in her stockinged feet.

Nevertheless, and in flat shoes, she now walked easily beside him as they left his light-colored Jaguar, parked in the Marktplatz, and strolled along the Freiestrasse, through the ironwork gates and into the dark entry hall of the Schlüsselzunft.

As they mounted the wide oak stairs to the second-floor dining rooms, Iselin applied a very light but insinuating pressure to Elfi's elbow, ostensibly steadying her. The scene, the setting, this kind of man, even his sly touch on her arm, was exactly what Elfi would have chosen for herself if some good witch had granted her the power. She moved up the steps without weight, floating in joy.

Everything now proceeded as she would have wished. A captain, or whatever he was, bowed and broke into obsequious smiles. "Herr Iselin, a pleasure, sir." And, to Elfi, with a deeper bow: *"Mademoiselle, très charmant."*

Still inclining halfway from the waist, as if attacked by an agonizing muscle spasm in the lumbar region, the captain led them to what Elfi felt was the best table in the room. But Iselin rejected it with a double sideways wag of his index finger. Elfi felt a thrill of pride. No emotion had crossed his face, nor had he yet spoken.

When, at last, they were seated at the proper table for Iselin's taste, the meal progressed in dreamlike stages, stately pantomimes of gluttony, from cocktails through several courses, each with its own wine, to a rich chocolate torte.

Elfi could never remember spending this much time in a restaurant, at least not at one meal, but everything moved smoothly, the way it sometimes does in very good, very rewarding dreams. When they finally rose to leave and made their way slowly down the stairs to the street, the night was still young.

"And the moon is out," Iselin observed as he took her hand.

They walked back to the Marktplatz. Having had quite a bit to drink, Elfi realized, she needed some steadying. Apparently they had progressed to the point where hand-holding was in order.

She had not noticed their relationship moving forward this one important notch, since what Iselin talked of throughout the meal had been the meal itself. His behavior had been everything Elfi

227

would have chosen in an upper-class gentleman of definite opinion and the habit of expressing himself.

He had quarreled in his superior way with every dish brought to the table, sent two back, pronounced one decent enough, the rest merely edible, castigated *in absentia* the dolt of a vintner who had clearly mislabeled one of the white wines, commiserated with the captain on the shortage of good help after a waitress had accidentally spilled a drop of red while pouring it, glanced impatiently at the bill and scrawled a big signature across it without pausing to add it up.

The wine, Elfi thought. Because of the wine she let him hold her hand, the wine and the fact that, although he hadn't added the bill, she had. It was half her weekly salary . . . and she was well paid.

Her proximity to the Staelis should have accustomed her over the years to the spending of large sums, but Elfi had never before had that much spent *on her*. She felt drawn even more strongly to this slim, arrogant man who was obviously drawn to her. She had always hoped that someday such a man would notice her. It had never been beyond the realm of possibility, had it? Well, then.

The whole encounter, Elfi knew, had an air of the miraculous about it. But that is only what one might expect when a wish comes true.

Iselin got behind the steering wheel, then pulled her toward him until their lips met. It was a short kiss, but he held her for a much longer moment. Then he started the car and drove slowly through the old part of town. The Jaguar's tires danced in and out of streetcar tracks with a stuttering noise.

Driving past Number 17 Aeschenvorstadt, its gray façade black in the moonlight, Elfi broke the long silence. "This is where you and your trolls labor?"

"Here, there, everywhere."

"You don't really work here."

"Why do you ask?"

"You don't look like a banker."

"*Natürlich*. A troll is a supernatural creature."

"That's right," she agreed. "A supernatural creature. Something secret, too."

"And sinister?"

"I would hate to meet you late at night in some deserted place."

"How about the interior of a Jaguar XK-E?"

She laughed. "Exactly." Then she paused for a moment as the idea took clearer shape in her mind. "You're much different now, at night, than you were at lunch today in the broad sunlight. More assured, almost another person. You change at night, yes?"

"A vampire, perhaps?"

Elfi considered this. "You're too thin for that. All the rich blood would have bloated you by now."

"You are utterly flattering, dear girl."

She grinned, a bit recklessly. "But you do operate much better at night, isn't that so? It's your best time." She considered this as they drove along. "It's what you do. You are *of* the night. What you do is done at night. Just tell me if I'm right, and no vampire jokes."

"Right about what I do?"

"About what you really do."

"My lips are sealed."

At the complicated Aeschegraben corner, with its turning streetcar tracks and streets leading in several directions, he turned toward the river along the shrubbery of a mall that ran down the center of the street. When they reached the tiny St. Alban Tor park he pulled the Jaguar to the curb, its close-together headlights glaring down the long stretch of the Gellertstrasse.

Finally, Iselin glanced at his watch. "I may be a night person, as you seem to believe, but it's still terribly early. You have time for a last drink?"

"Of course."

"At my place, then." He put the car in gear and drove off along the Gellertstrasse. "You must excuse its appearance. I've sent everyone on summer holiday. I'm totally alone, but you'll be safe."

"With a notorious vampire?"

His small teeth shone in the oncoming headlights of another auto. "As safe as a lovely young girl would wish."

Elfi watched the dark masses of trees that lined the thoroughfare. Here, along the Gellertstrasse, most of the older families hid their mansions in private parks, safe from view. Naturally Iselin would live in such a place. Naturally he was taking her there. Why not? When a dream comes true, all of it falls into one's lap in a single gorgeous chunk.

"Is it nice, living here?" She was experimenting with his who-cares tone, trying for the casual sound of his class.

"Dull. Dull."

"*Schade.* Poor little vampire."

They both laughed, although not at the same time or at the same thing. He steered the Jaguar left across the thoroughfare and into a tree-lined private road that led deep into the parkland.

"Hansel and Gretel," Elfi said.

He steered around a tight turn. There stood the house, old, square, three stories high and totally dark. He avoided the front porte-cochere and drove on crisp gravel to the rear of the building. He switched off the engine. The silence was empty of traffic noises.

"But this house isn't gingerbread," Elfi pointed out.

"The time has come to tell you. I'm not a troll or a vampire, but the wicked witch."

He got out of the car and came around to open her door. The last time, on the Marktplatz, being unused to this treatment, Elfi had started out of the car before he reached her. But she learned fast. She waited to be helped into the car and led by the rear door into the darkened house.

The place smelled peculiarly of dust and lemon oil. Furniture loomed whitely in the darkness, swathed in muslin. Somewhere deep in the bowls of the place a clock chimed.

"Is it haunted?" she whispered.

"I promise we're alone. No ghosts. But, as you can see, we're shrouded for the summer. You wouldn't like a tour?"

"But I would."

He took her hand and led her through the rooms, flicking lights on and off, setting chandeliers aflame in a dazzle of leaded cut-glass pendants as they moved past immense, mummified sofas, chairs, ottomans, bureaus, a grand piano of concert length, long inlaid tables, towering highboys and pictures filling the high walls almost to the ceiling far over Elfi's head.

She had been used to the understated grandeur of that part of Schloss Staeli still kept open. This was a smaller house but it had been spared nothing. Even the walls bore intricate curlicues of plaster bas-relief decoration. Elfi caught sight of her reflection in a

230

mirror taller than she was, with Iselin beside her. They paused to watch themselves in the glass, framed by a rim of thick gold-leafed carving.

"There," he said. "One cannot see a vampire's reflection. Don't you feel reassured?"

"Not at all."

"You look very much at home." Iselin's arm was around her waist. "It's too bad I've shut up the place for the summer. Wouldn't you love the idea of being my hostess for a really big party? All of Basel society would be introduced to you."

"They are not even aware I'm alive."

"They *will* be."

Elfi's heart knocked sharply against her ribs. "I'm nobody."

"You . . ." He pursed his lips, examining her in the mirror. "You are a lady. Or will be, once I finish with you."

He swung her toward him and they kissed, much longer this time. His tongue began to force her lips apart. The smell of dust and lemon oil was mixed now in her nostrils with his cologne, musky and intimate. She returned his embrace. Her lips parted.

They were falling backward onto a couch, its contours half hidden under a great dusty muslin cloth. For a moment she was on top of him, their mouths locked together. Then he was on top of her, straddling her as if he were a jockey, his hand up the inside of her leg. He pulled off her panties and held them at arm's length admiringly.

The chandelier overhead dazzled her as she stared up into it, smiling foolishly. He buried his face in the panties and inhaled deeply. "Lovely." He pulled up her skirt and gazed at her. "Now," he said, pressing her legs apart with his knees, "your lessons begin."

The chandelier was blinding. Dust choked her. He was riding as hard as he could, as if to force a cry or whimper from her. In the glitter of the overhead lights she couldn't see his face, just an eye or bared teeth, all mixed with the spinning fire of the chandelier.

She caught his rhythm and her body surged up so violently that he almost fell off. "Easy!" he shouted in a hoarse tone that would have done as well for "whoa!"

Neither of them held the other. Their only contact was between her legs where his knees had spreadeagled her. She began to enjoy

231

the sensation. Like a jockey, he was light enough to get away with it. Once again he nearly toppled off.

"Try that again," he grunted, "and I take the whip to you."

"You want me to cry, you vampire?"

He bit down on his lower lip and rammed into her with all his weight. They rocked this way for a moment and then, grinning up impudently, she asked: "Do you make your high-born ladies cry?"

The slap caught her off-guard, raking across her left cheek. "Lie still," he hissed. "When I want you to move, I'll give the order."

Elfi was shocked. Not that the slap hurt. But this cute little fellow? Who held open doors? Was it possible? He looked so dear, the tiny jockey riding his mare for the finish line.

Iselin climaxed suddenly, long before Elfi had begun to get much from the encounter. The room was hot, choking with dust. Streams of perspiration ran down his face and mixed with the smell of his cologne. She flexed her thigh muscles easily and forced his knees out of her way.

Then, crossing her legs behind him, she pulled him down against her breasts and tightened her body around him. A long, shuddering sigh escaped him as he felt her arms and legs lock over him, enfolding him into her.

The chandelier hurt to look at. Elfi closed her eyes and watched the red after-image whirl dizzily on her retinas. Slowly she rocked him to and fro in the darkness of what would be a long night. He grunted, then pulled his arm free to glance at his watch. He frowned, broke her hold and jumped up, zipping his fly closed. "Time to take you home."

Elfi blinked lazily. "What?"

"Dear girl, it was you who said it." He smiled maliciously. "It's night . . . and I have work to do."

CHAPTER 34

Behind Madame Michele's huge bedroom, facing to the rear of the main building at Michelebad, a second-story balcony jutted out. This rather large area was where as many as eight or ten guests could be entertained in the open air during a soft summer night like this one, with the mist settling in curves of the landscape as the sun died slowly in the sky.

This night, one guest had the balcony to himself. He lay naked on a low chaise longue and contemplated the bubbles in his glass.

The balcony faced west and north. In one corner stood a table whose top was an expensively prepared reproduction of a Pompeian wall mosaic, the one in the fifth house that depicts the heroic efforts of two nymphs to arouse an aging satyr.

Tonight the scene, in all its bright-eyed fierceness, nymphs trying everything, satyr straining mightily, was obscured by a champagne bucket and plates of smoked salmon and sliced prosciutto of an almost intimidating darkness, hinting at years of curing. It was a light repast for two and only two.

Glancing at the table as he lay back on the chaise, Erich found himself wondering how long in their already lengthy affair would Michele keep trying to slim him with Spartan samplings of bird food.

Not that the salmon wasn't of immense perfection, pink and only faintly oily, flown in twice a week from Jackson's in Piccadilly, nor the prosciutto particularly crisp and nutty. Nor was it that Erich's metabolism could readily withstand typical Swiss cooking, with its thickened sauces. Like most people in this corner of European cuisine, inundated by a flood of starch, he had to watch his intake.

No, he reflected now as he watched the bubbles again, what bothered him about the steady diet of lean protein his inamorata provided was the fact of it alone: that in the midst of their affair, flaming now or otherwise glowing with heat, some corner of her was still busy calculating calories.

He glanced down at his naked belly and probed it for a moment, feeling for fat. There was none, he convinced himself, or, at any rate, nothing new. He made a face. During the course of any other affair, if the woman had caused him even this minor attack of uncertainty, Erich would have dressed and walked out. For good. But not with Michele, he noticed. His face grew somber.

None of this prevented him from reaching over now and picking up a rolled slice of prosciutto which he munched—thoughtfully— with his fourth tulip glass of Taittinger *brut*. He was alone on the balcony, which could not be overlooked from any other window, while Michele tied up loose ends of the various meetings that had been held today.

There had been only one surprise in the otherwise dull routine, and it had come after the meetings were adjourned, at the cocktail party where everyone got more than slightly drunk in self-congratulation over a day of what, in any other setting, would have been considered idle chitchat. Gloggner, the other financial man on the board, had cornered Erich at one point to ask if there was a way to solve all the refinancing by one major line of credit from Staeli Internationale.

"Your fiancée," Gloggner had suggested, lowering his voice, "would be the ideal person to handle the matter, yes?"

"Yes, ideal," Michele had added, popping up suddenly at his elbow. Her smile was only faintly ironic as she watched the effect of the idea on Erich.

Lounging now on the balcony as he recalled the scene, Erich assured himself that the sudden suggestion had been worked out well in advance. And only Michele could have created the scenario. It was more or less an Erich Lorn thing to do, of course. Perhaps she'd counted on his seeing it that way. Have the fiancée finance the mistress. The talk of Basel. That Erich!

When Michele arrived on the balcony she had changed into a filmy peignoir more orange than rose through which her breasts resembled ample portions of some terribly rich cream dessert. It was obvious, despite the costume, that she had only shed the clothing of business, not the cares.

"Gloggner is impossible." She accepted a freshly poured glass of Taittinger from Erich. "Put on your briefs, darling."

"It is the function of all Gloggners to be impossible."

"Mm." She pushed a roll of ham in her mouth and gazed down at his body for a moment. "He wants to begin the refinancing by the end of the year."

Erich sipped his wine and studied her as she moved abruptly from the Pompeian table to the railing of the balcony, carefully positioning her face to the faint glow that remained in the west. "I'll go to Basel in the morning, then."

He had put the promise in its weakest form. What he should have said, if he were truly and firmly her slave, was: "I will present Gloggner's draft agreement to my fiancée in the morning and she will dutifully shepherd it through the maze of Staeli machinery so that we get quite the most favorable terms possible on the new funding." But he did not intend to place the matter before Margit. He doubted she would appreciate this typically Erich Lorn thing. He doubted that channeling the request through Margit was the best route, since the male Staelis were girding to do her in.

If pressed, however, the reason he would give Michele was a much more obvious one: he'd been out of touch with Margit all summer, for an obvious reason. He had little idea where to reach her except by leaving a message at the schloss.

"No," Michele said at last, when it became obvious that Erich had nothing more to promise her, "both of us will drive to Basel tonight, to my little villa outside town, yes?"

She produced a formidable smile, bright and determined. "I have a technical demonstration there tomorrow morning anyway. And these things bore you, darling, so you can enter the secret Basler vaults and bring back gold ingots, or something equally heroic."

"A commando raid?"

"But with your clothes on."

"Concealed weapon, eh?"

She failed to respond and, when she did, her tone and content made it clear that she had stopped making even small jokes. "You know," she told him, "perhaps the Basler mystique impresses another Basler, or the entire Swiss nation. Everyone stands in awe. But, not being Swiss, I am unimpressed."

Erich laughed abruptly. "The Basler banker is content to let the world think his city is where chemical companies have factories. If someone with sharp eyes points out that every major conference of world bankers takes place in Basel, and always has, the Basler shrugs as if to complain that there is no accounting for tastes."

Michele shook her head. "No, I am unimpressed by their performance as bankers. Hardly a week passes without a communication to Gloggner from an international bank. The Americans constantly solicit our business. But never once a Swiss bank. Never once."

Erich refilled their glasses. "It's the Swiss way. Business comes to us. Of course," he added, taking another roll of prosciutto, "if things continue as they have, we may be forced to solicit business . . . someday."

"Amazing."

"We're relative newcomers, *chérie*. There are French and English and even American banks twice our age."

"Then, how have you grown so powerful?"

"Necessity. We were locked in a ring of mountains. Originally, we set up banks to finance the digging of railroad tunnels. But then we were lucky enough to enter an era of disasters. Wars, revolutions, chaos everywhere but in Switzerland. God, how we thrived."

"The political neutrality thing."

"More than that. In the chaos, families of great wealth learned that a government can raid anyone's bank balance. Oh, cruel truth: total war demands total financial commitment. It's a hateful thought to any private dynasty. And, nowadays, to any international corporation."

"So you became the safe-deposit box of the entire world."

"Safe," he nodded, "secret, prudent, anonymous, all the qualities the owners of great wealth required. And everything based on a currency of the utmost stability, our most redeeming feature."

"Your most golden feature." She smiled at him.

"The magic metal. More of it is hidden away, propping up our franc, than the face value of the currency we've printed. Now, *that's* prudence."

He helped himself to more champagne, his face a series of smiling V's. "And that's why we attract such filth as customers."

She blinked. "What?"

His smile cut deeper in his face. "International gangsters. Promoters. Financial raiders and bandits. Corrupt politicians. Terrorist groups. Lawyers and sheiks and brokers and presidents. All seeking anonymity with security. All evading taxes in their own countries. And, dear God, what don't we do to attract such filth? Will you believe that we even have ways for them to avoid paying Swiss taxes?"

"And you know all the ways," she said. "I knew there was a reason for making you one of my directors. Some salmon, *chéri?*"

Without waiting, she covered a thin slice of brown bread with a

236

thick folded slice of smoked salmon. She moved toward him, aiming the tidbit at his mouth.

"You're amazingly consistent," Erich said.

"I beg your pardon?"

He dodged his head sideways to avoid the oncoming morsel. "It doesn't matter whether we're talking of gold or sex or crime or pleasure, you still count calories. That sandwich."

She drew it back from his mouth and frowned at it. "Yes?"

"It has a guaranteed protein-to-carbohydrate ratio of what? Three-to-one?"

"Pf."

As he pulled her down into his lap she tucked the salmon in his mouth and rested her head against his bare chest. "And now," she said, "for dessert."

CHAPTER 35

The dark-brown Opel had left Strasbourg about ten o'clock on its return run to Basel. The volume of correspondence had not been that heavy and the French girl—a regular employee of UBCO moonlighting for double pay—had rattled off the letters quickly. The courier had crossed the French-German border and was now driving rapidly down the E-4 Autobahn, congratulating himself that, with any luck, he might be in the northern suburbs of Basel by eleven o'clock and post the letters there.

To tell the truth, like the secretary in Strasbourg, he was fed up with the job, which monopolized their evenings and for what? Double pay? Big deal. He himself hadn't had a girl in over a month. When could he take a girl out if he had to be on the go from seven in the evening to damned near midnight, with a big yawning wait in Strasbourg while the girl typed her letters.

She was an attractive little French number, the courier thought as he steered the Opel down the Autobahn, holding its speed to a steady 110 kilometers per hour. But the trouble was, she couldn't fuck and type at the same time, could she? So did she have a roommate, perhaps? A girlfriend, a sister, a cousin . . . an *aunt*.

Two hours to kill every night and nothing to do but lounge around Strasbourg.

Like all cathedral towns, it was dead at night. There was something about having a famous cathedral that stifled night life. And after one had sampled the local *choucroute garnie*, which they did much better in Vienna, let me tell you, what was left of the famous Alsatian cooking, I ask you, eh?

Damned monk's life he was leading, with this nightly excursion, rain or shine. True, he had his weekends free, but by then he was so tired and so out of touch with the girls he usually saw that all he could do was sleep.

A monk's life? A dog's life. And all because the Americans were insane about spying. What made them so sure they could trust him? Or the typist in Strasbourg? Yes, neither of them was Swiss, that was true. But one didn't have to be Swiss to be shifty, eh?

The courier glanced in his rear-view mirror and saw two headlights set very close together on each side of the grille, and very high. A funny layout for headlights, wasn't it? Where had he seen such an arrangement before? Yes, tonight. Certainly. The cream-colored Jaguar E-type parked down the street from the UBCO office in Strasbourg.

The courier liked fast cars. Being patriotically German, he had never yearned for anything speedier than a Mercedes 200SL and was, in fact, saving his money for a Karmann-Ghia with a cloth top and the newer, more powerful Volks power plant. But he couldn't help having admired the creamy Jag. Surely this couldn't be it, behind him?

He let the black Opel slow down by taking his toe off the gas pedal. In a few moments its speed was down to 80, then 70, much too slow for the Autobahn. But the headlights kept their distance. The Jag, which could easily have passed the Opel even at 110, was holding back.

The hairs at the back of the courier's neck stood up slightly. It felt as if each one were ringed by ice. When he'd signed on for this spy stuff, he hadn't been serious about anything but the money. At the rate Herr Burris was paying him, he'd have his Kharmann-Ghia in a few more months. But he hadn't signed on for being followed at night.

He accelerated the Opel to 100 and was unhappy to see that the

238

Jag increased its speed to keep pace. All right. Test Number Three. He jammed down the gas and watched the speedometer needle crawl slowly, painfully up to 120. The Opel wasn't really meant for much more. 130 . . . 140. And still the Jaguar held its distance.

Roadside posts and fences flashed by in his headlights' glare like the images one sees in a fever, there, not there, here, gone. He let the Opel slow down to 110 again. And again the Jaguar kept its position. He had already flashed through the cloverleaf turnoffs to Freiburg. He'd passed the halfway point. No sense killing himself. There could be all kinds of reasons for the Jaguar holding its distance. It might not even be a Jaguar at all. He was getting much too jumpy with all this night work.

The E-4 Autobahn led out of the forests and down along the Rhine, running beside it on the smooth floor of the river's broad valley. The Opel raced through the night. The headlights behind the courier stayed the same size and the same distance apart. Nothing changed for kilometer after kilometer.

But, damn! Maybe it wasn't the cream-colored Jag. But any car that could do 140 had no business tagging behind him. The unwritten law of all Autobahns, at least to a German, was that powerful cars *always* overtook slower ones. The Mercedes always passed the Volkswagen. This was the immutable pecking order of nature. And yet the Jag, or whatever it was, seemed content to keep its distance from him. Odd. Strange. *Sehr komisch.*

There was no break now in the Autobahn for many kilometers to come. This was the section between Biengen and Neuenberg. There were no cloverleafs, no turnoffs and very little dividing grassy mall between the northbound and southbound lanes of the highway.

The courier knew, from making this run in daylight so often, that here the Autobahn, the Rhine and the Grand Canal d'Alsace all flowed along in parallel, almost to Basel itself. If one ran out of benzine here, it was one hell of a walk, and if one's car broke down, one simply had to pull off and wait for the *Bahnpolizie* to show up, in their own good time.

Perhaps because he was thinking too much, he'd let the Opel slow down to about 90. That was why, as he rounded a curve and his headlights raked over the grass divider to the northbound lanes, he got a clear glimpse of a little orange MG. At least it looked like an old MG, or a sports car like it, but there was no mistaking the orange color or the fact that a slim girl was driving it.

Mystery. Adventure. Jaguars and MG's tearing through the night. The courier smiled cynically at his fantasies. At that moment, glancing in the rear-view mirror, he saw something his German eyes had never before beheld.

The Jaguar was *turning off the Autobahn*. This was impossible. There was no turnoff. Worse, the car was jumping over the grass divider. This was *streng verboten*. Never in his life had the courier seen a car do this. It was as if the Jag had deliberately been put into an illegal U-turn and was now heading north on the E-4, hot on the trail of the girl in the orange MG.

Sehr komisch. But, at least, the courier reminded himself, he didn't have to worry about being followed any more.

CHAPTER 36

By eleven or twelve o'clock at night, the fifteenth-century heart of Colmar is a city of ghosts. The signs are in French, but the names on the shops are all German. This is Alsace, a land that has been disputed more than once.

The cream-colored Jaguar moved slowly along the narrow streets. The driver wasn't sure, at this point, if he'd made a mistake. It would have been easy enough, considering the route he'd followed.

After deciding, on the spur of the moment, to abandon surveillance of the UBCO courier's brown Opel, he'd managed to get the Jaguar on the northbound lanes of E-4 and follow the Autobahn back to Bienen. The orange sports car seemed to get off there and head toward the town of Breisach am Rhein. But, before reaching it, the car swerved onto the bridge over the river into France. It then led the Jaguar along N 415 into Colmar.

Once past the outer ring of the city with its modern high-rise buildings, extensive factories and the warehouses through which most of the wine of Alsace was shipped, the trail had gone cold. The driver of the Jaguar had missed a turn and, while he knew the orange car was headed into the small medieval center of the city, he knew little more.

He was beginning to think he had made a bad choice in giving up the brown Opel for the orange sports car. He'd suspected for some time that Burris was using a secret message transfer and, although following the Opel to Basel would have clinched the point conclusively, it really was fairly obvious to him how the pickup and delivery was worked.

But the orange sports car was another matter. He'd been right to follow it into Colmar, a lucky break even seeing it at night on the Autobahn. And the girl driving it hadn't remotely suspected she was being followed, unlike the courier in the Opel, who'd started playing tricks with his speed. But it had been a bad break losing the car in this maze of ghost-haunted alleyways, running between the narrow, half-timbered houses.

No one walked these streets this late. There was no one to question. Shops were shut up tight. He steered the Jaguar into an open square where cars were parked, headed into a space and shut off the engine and lights. A small neighborhood café was almost deserted but not yet closed. Chairs and tables stood on the sidewalk, but no one was seated at them.

Across the square stood the ancient customs house. He'd seen enough pictures of it to recognize it at once from its huge, broad arches, leading into the shadowed arcade where, in the fourteenth and fifteenth centuries, perhaps, people laid out their bags and trunks for inspection. More ghosts.

He glanced around at the street signs and saw that this was called the *Quartier des Tanneurs*. Like the same quarter in Strasbourg, this one had been preserved by the process of selling crumbling buildings to people who agreed to renovate them in strict accord with the old plans and designs.

This sort of project usually appealed to artisans and artists of one kind or another. As the driver sat quietly in the Jaguar, he saw that there were already several signs of cultural beachheads here, including a potter's atelier, an art gallery and, through a large arched entry into a medieval courtyard, a shop selling ceram-

241

ics, sculptures and other works of art, as well as the ubiquitous organic-food shop.

The arch was more than a decoration. It supported an apartment that seemed to run between the two buildings that formed sides of the inner courtyard. The driver got out of his car, a slight man under average height. He walked over to the café, sat down outside and ordered a beer.

Waiting for it to be brought, he gazed about him with some satisfaction. He was not insensitive to the resonances of places. He could almost see the ghosts, some of them more modern than travelers of the fourteenth century. He was not, of course, old enough to have lived through it, not quite, but here one also felt the ghosts of the Wehrmacht and of the American GI's from tank battalions that had died here in that last-minute carnage called the Colmar Pocket.

"Tell me," he asked the young waiter who brought the beer, detaining him for a moment, "I'm a sports-car fan, as you can see." He indicated the Jaguar. "I'm looking for a friend who lives not far away. She owns an orange car that looks something like an MG."

The waiter nodded. "That's five francs, *m'sieur*."

"Have you seen such a car in the quarter?"

The waiter took the coins. Then he indicated the square with its dozens of parked cars. "Orange, gray, red, white and blue." He laughed apologetically. "They don't stay long enough for me to notice."

"Maybe in a garage?"

The waiter's eyebrows went up. "One would have to be rich to use a garage. There are a few of them back there." He indicated the courtyard with a tilt of his head. "When they rebuilt the place, they put in the only garages in the whole quarter."

"And you haven't . . . ?" The driver let his question die away because the waiter's head was already moving from side to side.

Silly to think, because he'd been very lucky once tonight, that his luck would still hold. He sipped the beer and stared at the half-shadowed customs house across the square. This was a lovely old quarter. He himself wouldn't mind living here, if he weren't so tied to Basel.

Very few corners of Basel were as charmingly kept up as this.

They were clean, to be sure. What part of Basel wasn't? But they were dull. Basel had no ghosts. It had famous residents like Erasmus and Holbein and celebrated native sons like Euler and Bernoulli. And, of course, it was the wealthiest city in all of Europe, with an income far above any town in Switzerland, or any other country for that matter. But it was dull. There was no resonance. One failed to hear the tread of ghosts.

At the thought of Basel being the richest city in Europe, the driver smiled bitterly. Here he sat, one of those "rich" Baslers, and if he didn't make another payment on the Jaguar by the week after next, back it went to the dealer. As for the mortgage on his house . . . foreclosure was only a matter of a few months. Rich!

He finished his beer and got up for a stroll, glancing at his watch. Midnight. Time to take the E-4 back to Basel, a short enough trip. At this time of night, under half an hour. But, first . . .

He was not new to this sort of work. He'd done a lot of it during his military service. They'd made him an officer and, once a year, he gave Army Intelligence a month as part of his duties in the reserve. But he wasn't really a true professional, only someone who occasionally had luck. Nevertheless, it was worth taking a look at those garages.

He walked under the arched apartment and into the courtyard, where he stood for a moment in the half-dark and stared into the window of a shop called Atelier de l'Ern, its windows filled with an intriguing combination of traditional carved-wood figures and extremely modern ceramics.

The bells of a nearby church began to toll twelve times. The driver of the Jaguar hurried on until he found the garages. There were only three and they were almost hidden around a turn of the wall. None of them were locked. In the left-hand one the orange car had been neatly tucked away. Its radiator was still hot to the touch. He admired its vintage lines at close range, the grandfather prototype of the MG.

He carefully closed the garage door and checked any windows that looked down into the courtyard. No one was awake at this hour. No one had seen him. There was no one to congratulate him on the fact that tonight he had twice been very lucky.

He walked back to the café as it was being locked up and got from the waiter the name of a small nearby hotel. It, too, was shut for the night when he arrived, but by ringing the bell he roused a sleepy desk clerk who padded to the door in stocking feet and let him in.

The driver filled out the identity card and shoved it back across to the clerk, who seemed still half-asleep. "Please wake me at six-thirty," the driver said. "Do you need my passport?"

"No, that won't be necessary, Mr.—" The clerk squinted at the identity card, "Mr. Iselin."

PART FOUR

Perpetual neutrality; prosperity; yodeling; chaste and simple morals; hospitality to the persecuted . . . But the road to such [Swiss] exemplariness was not easy . . . From 1291 to 1848 the history of Switzerland was one of foreign and domestic warfare.

—J. Christopher Herold

CHAPTER 37

Awakened at seven-thirty by his travel clock, Matthew Burris rolled over and stared for a moment, blind-eyed, at the windows of his hotel bedroom. He had pulled the curtains last night before going to sleep, but enough light came through at either end of the window to give him a clue as to the weather.

He'd lived in Basel long enough now to be able to judge if the sun was out or not. The quality of the light that leaked in past the curtains gave him the idea that today was sunny. Yes!

He rolled out of bed and padded to the window, pulled the curtains open and confirmed his guess. Already busy, busy Basel was stirring. Another working day had dawned, for them, not him. Pedestrians strode purposefully across the bridge from Kleinbasel on the other side of the river. The long, green streetcars were already at work shuttling people from one Basel to the other.

Until he'd asked, it had seemed odd to him that where he was, the older part of the city, but the smaller part, went by the name of Grossbasel, while the newer, more spread-out part was called the smaller portion. It was explained, at last, that in the old days, when this particular bridge had been the only crossing of the Rhine in all of the lands watered by the river, the landing across the way had been walled to defend it against invaders. It had been quite small, hardly more than a stockade. Thus, Kleinbasel. Who had explained it? Margit, no doubt. She had explained so many things to him this summer.

By eight-thirty, Burris had made his way rather circuitously to the ship landing at the base of the bridge. There was a quick, easy way to descend to the terminus, but it gave him no time to see if he was being followed. Instead, he backtracked through the Totentanz district almost to the Johanniter Bridge further up the river, then made his way along the pedestrian walk that edged the river. It was impossible to follow someone on the narrow path without being discovered.

Burris timed himself so that he got on the little steamer just as the long landing planks were about to be pulled in. The deckhands slammed the railing gates shut and cast off the hawsers. An instant later the steamer began nosing downriver, moving much faster than it should have because of the force of the current running with it.

Even more than the city itself, Burris loved these little Rhine steamers, the *Personenschiffe* that chugged out in several directions to nearby ports, some of them commuter specials, some day-excursion boats with snack bars, restaurants and bars, some with music, some even with a dance floor.

The early sun slanted sideways against the flow of the river. The ship was clipping right along, to judge by the rapid flow past of buildings on either side. But when Burris looked down at the water, the ship seemed to be standing still, the fast-running waves motionless.

Burris glanced at the sky and saw that there were only a few clouds, tiny ones, puffballs of vapor wafted in from France over the Vosges range.

He had never paid that much attention to weather before. Living in big American cities, or the imitation New York called Tokyo, he had seldom glanced at the sky. His weather was always interior weather, conditioned by machines, dehumidifiers, coolers or heaters.

It had been twenty years or more since weather had meant much to him. As a boy in southern Illinois, living back of the tracks in the Polacktown slum of Carbondale, even a day as cheerful as this one couldn't make that much of a dent in the pervasive, coal-dusted gloom. The depressing effect of the place had less to do with how it looked, Burris recalled, than the internal depression of being poor and as ignorant as dirt, and knowing it.

He understood from gossip that the town had vastly improved, perked up by a rather prestigious university with a resident global genius, Buckminster Fuller. But Burris had never returned to Carbondale and never would. Never.

He produced a grimace now as he stared at the sky, a look half grin and half pain. Why say never? On a day like this, he told himself, why close off your options? On a sunny day, every option is wide open.

This was Margit's doing, of course. For decades he'd paid less attention to the weather than to the price of sow-belly futures on the Chicago Exchange. But Margit was what she called a *Sonnevogel,* a sunbird. Over these past months, Burris recalled, she had also proved to be a temperature-bird, a humidity-bird and a barometric-pressure-bird.

He had never met anyone so sensitive to weather. She felt it all, and especially the state of pollution in the air. Basel's drug factories—religiously referred to by Baslers as "chemical plants," as if it wasn't known throughout the world that the chemicals they produced were mostly drugs—ring the city. On a particularly bad day, "bad" by the state of Margit's reactions, a combination of thermal inversion and high humidity seemed to trap the byproduct gases released into the air from the manufacture of drugs. The effect was choking to Margit and probably most Baslers, weatherbirds or not.

Burris wanted the weekend to be particularly fine. They had an excursion planned in the little Magna, and with any luck they could keep the top down. It wasn't that Margit was hard to take during bad weather. She had the flexibility to rise above the depression it caused and produce a fair imitation of well-being. But by now Burris knew her moods. He knew her acts, her real states of mind and the false ones she used as shields.

As the ship moved up the Rhine now, passing out of the commercial zones and into greenery, Burris wondered just how delicate a mechanism he had fallen in love with.

He hadn't lied to her. Six years before at Harvard she'd been a big, strapping farm-girl type. Now there was a lot less of her and the process of refining her body seemed to have produced a strange added emphasis on its interior electrical connections. She seemed to have done something to the synapses of her nervous system, honed them, buffed them to a brilliance.

Her reactions were faster. Her mind never idled. It seemed permanently meshed in gear and ready to drive. Being considered by such a woman, as he had been all this summer, was something like becoming the subject of a study by a committee, using the latest instruments of examination and detection.

Nobody had ever paid this kind of attention to Burris in his whole life, not even his locker-room trainer at college, who was constantly fussing over bruises and strains. No woman had ever lavished this kind of bone-deep scrutiny on him. He didn't know whether to feel pleased or angry at being the object of so much concern. On the whole—and today being such a great day—he felt pleased. But not always.

This was only the second time he'd used the riverboat approach to Colmar. It had been agreed that he would try different ways of getting there so as to avoid setting a pattern that could be detected. He'd taken buses on occasion, hired a car twice, even flown Air Alsace to the field south of Colmar. Once he'd taken the train, another time he'd stayed on it to Strasbourg, then doubled back. Getting there was the point and neither of them was that young that they begrudged an hour or two of delay in order to keep their secret safe.

And, of course, it had to remain a secret. They couldn't help the fact that they'd met under such public circumstances, but they could then exert as much intelligence as possible to keep their later meetings unknown to Uncle Dieter.

"Christ," Burris had pointed out, "isn't it Erich you should worry about? He's the fiancé, not Uncle Dieter."

"Erich?" Margit had laughed quietly, as if at the antics of a pet sheepdog. "He's wrapped up in his goddess of eternal youth. Have you met Madame Michele?"

"Just heard of her."

"I must make certain you never do. This is the original Lilith." Margit's hazel eyes darkened slightly. "She is old enough to be Erich's mother, of that I am certain. I find the whole thing so . . . so . . . ," she began to break into giggles, "so Oedipal."

Another time, late at night, in the immense king-sized bed she had bought for the tiny Colmar apartment, the telephone had rung and they lay there, galvanized, letting it ring itself out. Whoever was calling—and it could easily have been a wrong number because the phone was listed in the name of the apartment's owner —the ringing persisted for what seemed like hours. Twenty rings? Thirty?

"Erich?" Burris asked after the ringing stopped.

"Darling, you have this ridiculous Victorian ethic about Erich. He is a boy I went to dancing school with. We are betrothed by our families. This is a completely different thing from being in love. We like each other, that's all."

"Then, who's calling?"

"More likely one of Dieter's people, or dear Cousin Walter. If we have been traced here, I'll kill myself, Matt, I swear I will. They are not going to be allowed to spoil what we have."

"Why would Dieter want to spoil it? Victorian ethics?"

She had fallen silent for a moment. "Dieter is still an unknown quantity to you. Let me explain him. His motivation is always business. So is his son's. Between them there isn't this much feeling for human values." She showed him the long, narrow nail of her little finger. "They are such typical Baslers that it depresses me even to think about it."

"But what's a business reason for lousing us up?"

"I'd rather not think about it."

"Just give me a clue," Burris suggested with sarcasm. "Maybe I'll be bright enough to work out the rest."

"A clue? What would you like?" she demanded angrily. "The fact that if someone can be proved of low moral character, her inheritance can be thrown into question? Is that enough of a clue?"

Standing on the foredeck of the Rhine steamer, Burris grimaced again at the sky, half grin, half pain. These Swiss played for keeps. They looked mild on the outside, easygoing, long-fused, but it was an act. Funny how they resembled the Japanese in that respect. Both peoples cultivated this deceptive calm, this utterly correct blandness. And underneath . . .

Of course, it all came back to that thing his first college coach had talked about, the same thing he'd started to mention yesterday to old Dieter himself. The coach had called it the killer instinct, which was something Burris was not about to uncork for Dieter's ears.

"You hear a lot about winning being the only thing," the coach had told Burris once. "The only player who always wins is your true killer. I mean he will kill to win. Every team could use a few of them. Personally, they make me uncomfortable. The first time I met you, Bryszk, I said, 'uh-oh, a real Polack assassin.' But you

251

turned out to have some feeling. That's why I'm telling you. When you graduate, they'll be ready with the pro contracts. Walk the fuck away from them, you hear me? Stay out of the pro game. You got a brain, baby, and feelings. I want you to live off them, not your muscles. Okay?"

The man had been his first coach, but not his last. Predictably, the college had let him go when Burris was a junior, hiring a go-go, no-lose killer to ram the team into more victories. The trustees had fired the first coach before he had tenure, citing some small print in his contract. But the basic reason was to be found on the Sunday afternoon scoreboards.

So old Dieter played for keeps, Burris thought now, and Margit was taking a hell of a chance with this affair. She was exposing herself in a way that would have been dangerous enough for any respectable middle-class woman slated to marry someone else. But it was particularly bad if it also endangered her hold on the entire incalculable amount of money—that made everything it touched infinitely more serious.

Burris found himself wondering how it would feel to grow up with a billion-dollar albatross around your neck. He decided he'd never know, a poor boy who'd got lucky because Woods Palmer liked his style. Now there was another killer, Palmer, a real match for Dieter Staeli. Never mind your Polack assassins, for the real cold-blooded killer you had to have one of those skinny Wasp types with the ice-gray eyes and the Goebbels cheekbones.

Burris shook his head. It was too nice a day to be carrying all this mental freight to Colmar. Palmer was the man who had made it possible for him to be in here, and to have Margit come back into his life. What kind of ingrate would bad-name such a man?

To the west, across a broad swath of French forest, Burris could see the high-rise buildings and factory smokestacks of Mulhouse. The steamer was making good time but, being a Swiss steamer, it would not dock in Breisach am Rhein one minute before or after its advertised arrival time.

Margit would be waiting for him with the little orange car. Instead of rushing back to the apartment, they had planned to have lunch at the only three-star restaurant in the area and enjoy "the real Alsatian cuisine," Margit had promised, "not all this sauer-kraut and sausage stuff."

Burris found himself wondering whether they were settling into a new phase of the affair. Most of the summer they had spent in bed, the apartment over the arch in Colmar being a perfect place from which to watch the passing scene without taking part in it.

Naked, they had peered through the marquisette curtains at the comings and goings of tourists visiting the Old Custom House, or one of the local ateliers. In the evening they had watched the neighborhood people at their ease outside the café at the corner. By now they knew many of them, not to talk to, because that was too dangerous, but by nicknames the two of them had created in their curtained-off private place.

And always, before and after and during, the love-making. Burris had been cautious with Margit at first. She had become too finely drawn to handle in the rough-and-tumble way they'd enjoyed six years before. But under the newly taut skin she was still the same Margit and, like a cat, she enjoyed hard stroking.

Yet this weekend was to be different. They would come into Colmar each night to sleep, of course, and make love, of course. But the weekend was to be spent sightseeing, quite like a married tourist couple with guidebooks and maps and must-see itineraries. Burris found himself wondering how it would all go and, perhaps more important, how they had reached this stage.

Ordinary criteria didn't really apply to them. Not that he was something special, but Margit certainly was. The money alone made that inescapable. When you added everything else up, her mind, her good looks, you could still fit her into a known category where certain general rules applied. But when you added all that money, nothing applied. There were no rules and there never would be.

The oddest thing of all, as he thought about it now, was that Margit didn't see this about herself. She had not been brought up in the super-rich-bitch pattern. Perhaps it had to do with not having a mother, a model for behavior and for creating attitudes toward the world. Whatever it was, Burris knew, she clearly didn't see herself as one of the wealthiest women in the world. The money was far less to her than the power.

Nights in bed in the tiny apartment over the arch, she had mused about the power that came with full control of the entire gamut of Staeli interests. "Even if it were just the banking," she

253

thought aloud to him. "Just having that immense leverage for good or evil. But it's so much more. I can understand why Uncle Dieter is so determined to keep it for the males in the family. Anything else is far too frightening for him even to think about."

"The immense power of the Staelis," Burris had told her, "is a secret power. Like all Swiss, they keep a very low profile."

"And I wouldn't!" she half-shouted. "I would finance everything good. I would squander money. The dreamers would know where to come for funding. And they'd all get it."

"And you'd get the headlines."

"So what?"

"And tax inspectors arriving in droves. That's what Dieter likes to avoid, the appearance of great wealth. Wealth lures tax inspectors the way shit draws flies."

She had doubled over with giggles at this. It was hard to know whether she took any of it seriously: him, Erich, her family or the money. Only one thing was serious to her: power.

Burris found it disconcerting. And what Margit planned to do with the power was laughable. She had no plan. Her desire for power was instinctive, not thought out, tied to no political idea, just an unfocused yearning to redress everything, change the world by shifting its fulcrum, power.

She hadn't even thought it out that far, Burris reminded himself. On those rare occasions when he tried to pin her to something specific, she'd grown cranky, and that was really not the purpose of an affair, any affair.

Leaning back against the railing of the steamer and letting the breeze cool the hot August day, Burris realized that she might very well have figured out what to do with the power. Anyone with Margit's mind would easily be able to work out such a program. But why tell it to your lover? That, too, was not the purpose of an affair.

Nor was sightseeing among the sleepy wine villages of the Alsace, although it was not a bad idea, was it, to move slowly from town to town sampling the Sylvaner and the Gewürztraminer? There would be little inns where one sipped the open wine and went upstairs for a nap. When you looked at it that way, it suddenly did become the purpose of an affair.

CHAPTER 38

The meeting with the Hungarians began at 9 A.M. in the small country villa Michele kept southwest of the city, at the French border.

Erich found it an odd place for a business meeting, mostly because he and Michele used this little hidden-away place for love-making. Like all of her secluded love nests, it was tiny and needed little in the way of domestic help except for a cleaning woman now and then. The Hungarian doctor and technicians, all three of them, arrived in a light van and were very pleased to be served coffee and croissants from the hand of the celebrated Madame Michele herself.

There had been a few financial preliminaries before the technical discussion. The cost of the new ion generators was considerably more than the ones now in use at Euromichele spas around Europe, but Erich could see that the generators themselves were considerably larger and, according to the technicians, vastly more powerful.

"We are getting fantastically increased emission levels from this clinic model," the doctor explained. He was a serious young man with a small beard, carefully tended, and thick spectacles protected by heavy black frames.

Erich's mind wandered. He found it impossible to remain serious for long on any topic, much less these arcane pieces of machinery that Michele used in her youth treatments. The negative ion generators were not used to promote youth so much as to clear up certain physical conditions in each patient so that she would be in better shape to profit by the youth treatments that followed.

Erich understood the principle of negative ionization well enough. It had become popular in the larger European cities as a way of offsetting air pollution in offices and homes. By producing an overabundance of negative ions, these generators helped make the air purer.

Proponents of the system sketched a broad spectrum of ailments and dysfunctions that ion therapy helped overcome, including hypertension, upper respiratory problems, ulcers, colitis, skin eruptions and burns and a long list of psychological or psychosomatic conditions ranging from anxiety and depression to suicidal and antisocietal tendencies.

". . . but also in mental institutions in Dijon and Manchester," the doctor was saying.

"I really don't make those kind of claims," Michele murmured, more to Erich than the visiting Hungarian.

"Freedom from anxiety?" Erich asked. "It's a precondition to youth."

She smiled slightly because although she never made jokes about her business (profession? calling?) she didn't want to embarrass Erich in front of the Hungarians.

"And not only freedom from anxiety," the bearded doctor went on, taking Erich seriously, "but also in the treatment of insomnia, fatigue, migraine, impotence and frigidity."

In the slight pause that followed, Erich stood up. "We can't afford to be without one," he murmured to Michele.

He strolled to the front door and stared out at the sunny day, at the light blue van in which the Hungarians had arrived, at his own gray Bentley saloon in which he had driven himself and Michele here last night. He missed the little orange L-2 Magna.

Where would Margit be driving it on a sunny Friday like this? She so loved good weather and so detested cloudy days, rain, low pressure. She was a strange girl, no doubt about it. The gilded youth of the Basler bourgeoisie were all somewhat strange, himself included.

In so many ways he felt much closer to Margit than he ever would to this tough businesswoman behind him now in the cottage bargaining with the Hungarians for a better deal. ". . . slightly lower emission level in the same case," she was saying, "and let me have . . ."

Not that Margit couldn't handle herself in the business world, but not in her own right. Neither he nor Margit could conceive of a life in which they took on the world hand-to-hand, without first donning the magic gloves of their family name and fortune. It made such a difference. It made people like Michele, who had done battle barehanded all her life, a strange, exotic breed.

He wondered who Margit's lover was. He himself had been so out of things that he hadn't had any contact with Basler gossip. On the few occasions when he went home, Bunter seemed eager to talk, but of course one couldn't ask Bunter for intimate news of one's fiancée's affair. Erich hoped the man appreciated Margit.

But, really, did anyone appreciate Margit more than he? Erich smiled at the sunny morning.

". . . tropic dermatitis," the doctor droned on, "urticaria, psoriasis, eczema, Meniere's syndrome and vertigo. It is also proving useful in—"

"Please," Michele protested. "Erich, explain to the gentlemen." Her English accent had grown more Hungarian in the past few minutes and she had produced a word that sounded like "shentlemon."

"Yes, of course." He turned back into the room and was blind for a moment after the brilliant sunshine. "You see, gentlemen, Euromichele is not at all involved in medical—"

He could hear his own voice droning on. He found it hard to keep listening to himself and wondered if Michele's profession (business? art?) would always seem this boring to him.

CHAPTER 39

Curtis imagined that they made a rather odd picture, the four of them. The tennis area was directly behind Palmer's mountain aerie, two red clay courts surrounded by extremely high fencing. Curtis had the feeling that, perched on the highest part of this peak, anyone who hit a ball over the fence could kiss it good-bye forever.

Not that any of the players were that maladroit. Certainly not Palmer, in his white shorts, long, lean legs moving with great precision as he manned his part of the court. Nor his younger son, Tom, who seemed to be nearly eighteen, a boy of such skinniness that Curtis worried about his being hit by a ball and knocked over.

Yet Tom, for all his slight stature, was really the best of them, fast and devastatingly accurate. Curtis himself was not that bad, if he did say so himself, but between the two seniors, he and Palmer, the older man was clearly better.

The dub of the four, if he could be called that, was the older boy, Woody, or Woods Palmer The Three, as his brother had called him. At the age of twenty-one he could hardly be called a boy, but his reflexes were still unschooled, like an adolescent's, and his big, hefty frame simply couldn't get around the court as fast as the others. Watching him at first Curtis had had a puzzling sense of *déjà vu,* although he knew he'd never met the boy before.

Later, watching him argue mulishly over whether a ball had been outside or in, Curtis suddenly got it. The older boy resembled Matt Burris. He was as tall as Burris or his father, but he had Burris' heft, the same thick shoulders, the same broad jaw. Neither boy resembled his father that closely, but if Woody resembled anyone, it was Burris. Perhaps it was this physical resemblance that had led Palmer to favor young Burris' career at UBCO.

The story of the ex-footballer's rise within the bank was fairly well known, if only because of the spiteful gossip of those who had been passed over for promotion while Burris had steadily advanced. Yes, he was bright. Yes, he worked hard. But, Christ, he was nothing but an awkward Polack fullback who couldn't be trusted socially or in any delicate business or political manipulation that required tact, breeding, grace and family connections.

Most of the gossip had sounded to Curtis like sour grapes. The one time he'd been able to talk to Burris, for that little while at Orly this spring, he'd certainly found him stubborn, even hostile. But that didn't necessarily make a bad bank executive.

His covert surveillance of Burris in Basel had given him respect for the man's cunning. Burris had lost him a dozen times when it was important to Curtis that he follow the man. His only consolation was that if Burris could lose him, he could lose one of Staeli's agents, too.

"Game!" Palmer shouted exultantly. He pounded Tom on the back, nearly collapsing the boy's spine. "Good stuff, Tommy!" He frowned across the net at Curtis and Woody. "Woody, how the hell much do you weigh these days?"

"Two-ten."

"Christ, that's thirty pounds overweight. No wonder you cover your court like a Mack truck. I mean, Curtis has some excuse, he's an old man like me. But you?"

"Old?" Curtis yelped.

"What're you now, forty?" Palmer countered.

"Thirty-six, dammit."

In the moment of silence that followed, Curtis had the distinct but confusing feeling that to the boys he had confirmed the fact that he was, indeed, an old man while, to Palmer, he had undiplomatically stressed the difference in age between them, perhaps fifteen years? It didn't pay to get a sensitive prima donna like Palmer upset about something unimportant.

Palmer dabbed at his forehead with the sweatband around his right wrist. He glanced up at the early morning sky. Although it was just after nine o'clock, the August sun was already hot, even on this breezy mountain top. "Another game?" Palmer demanded.

"Da-ad," Woody whined, with the same multisyllabled emphasis on the word that a much younger boy might have given it, say a five-year-old.

"You're the only one who is bushed," his father pointed out.

"Come on, Woody," Tom urged.

Curtis turned away as a method of staying out of a family discussion. From this great height he could see most of Lake Lugano. He squinted suddenly. The same two gaff-rigged sloops he had seen yesterday were out there again this morning playing tag with each other. They were beamy craft, with long bowsprits that carried two foresails. The whole effect was of a squat boat with tremendous sail area but no real danger of foundering. Swiss to the core.

From this viewpoint he could also see the switchbacked road that climbed from the lake to this almost inaccessible pinnacle. A taxi was slowly negotiating the curves, sending up spurts of dust at every curve.

"Curtis?"

"What?"

"Another game?"

He turned back to find himself under the scrutiny of all three Palmers. "Whatever everybody wants."

"Woody, you partner me," Palmer said. "Maybe I can get you to move around."

Curtis smiled slightly as they took their new places. Palmer had just sealed his defeat. The secret of this doubles game was that whichever side Tom was on had to win, even with a killer like Palmer across the net.

It went that way the first set, but then Palmer began to bear down, especially when he played the net. He made it a point to smash everything he could lay a racket on, aiming it all directly at Curtis. He'd obviously decided that anything sent Tom's way would be returned ferociously. Using such tactics, Palmer won the second set almost singlehandedly. He seemed to have forgotten about getting his older son to "move around."

Curtis wasn't sure at what point in the game a young woman with a camera appeared behind the screen, but after a while he became aware that she was snapping pictures with what seemed to be a rather expensive Nikon. Although Tom and he fought everything to the last possible point, Palmer's strategy managed to prevail. They lost the game.

Curtis found himself having to re-evaluate his opinion of Palmer's killer instinct. It was developed more keenly than any semiretired man had a right to.

"Gerri!" Palmer was walking toward the young woman with the camera. "You look sensational."

The three male Palmers clustered around her. All three kissed her on the cheek but there had been no hugging. Was it always this way in moneyed families, Curtis wondered. She *was* the daughter, was she not? Or perhaps they'd recently seen her.

"Nice work," she was saying, patting her father's belly. "Flat as a pancake. I figured you'd have bloated up since Christmas with all that good cooking."

"I watch it."

"But Ellie really ladles out them Austro-Hungarian groceries." The girl's dark blond hair was long and ironed straight, in a style that might have been current when she was in elementary school. But she was now about twenty, Curtis calculated, the middle child between two brothers. "Where is she?" the girl asked.

"Ellie's on a trip," Palmer said. And that was all he said.

The girl turned to her older brother and rapped his belly softly. "There's the family breadbasket," she said. Then, to Tom:

"You're beginning to resemble one of the lesser drawings of Aubrey Beardsley."

"And you," he responded, "have got to stop playing Christina Rosetti. What's with that hair?"

"Pre-Raphaelite enough for you?" She turned slowly to display herself. "I don't hear any low whistles of wonderment. It's a long, long time from December to August and things have changed."

"Huh?" Woody asked.

"Nothing," Tom explained. "She's got tits, is all."

Palmer winced. "What the hell kind of thing is that to say?"

"Right," Tom agreed. "Any girl who waits this long to have tits is too retarded to make fun of." They all walked off the court.

"Well," she said, "that's what I get for coming home." She turned to Curtis. "None of these yoyos has any manners. I'm Geraldine Palmer. If you're Curtis, I have a message for you from Bill Elder in New York. Had lunch with him yesterday." They entered the house.

Curtis frowned. "A message?"

"Well, not a message, a present." She left him for a moment to root around in a large canvas bag with the initials G.P. stenciled on it in foot-high letters. "Here."

She laid the box in his lap. It was about the size of a loaf of bread and printed in bright, cheerful red and dazzling white, the colors of the Swiss flag. The word "Staelicomp" filled two of its four sides, the "t" in the word designed to resemble the white equilateral cross in the Swiss flag.

Curtis opened the box and slid out two halves of foamed plastic which came apart, like the bread around a sandwich. Inside, with its instructions folder and other accessories, sat a small black plastic hand calculator. A note on Elston's UBCO business card had been wedged into the box next to the calculator.

"We bought five already," the note read. *"Was gibt?"*

"Does anybody know how to work one of these things?" Curtis asked.

All four Palmers clustered around him, talking simultaneously, snatching at the calculator, taking it away from each other. For a family that didn't live together—except during school vacations—they had an easy familiarity, cool but close. It was the father, predictably, who won custody of the toy.

"Here," he said, opening the instructions. "Let's load the batteries. They're rechargeable."

"Or you can work the thing off regular house current."

"Regular which house current?" Tom asked. "U.S. or European?"

"Both," Palmer said. "There's a little 110-220 switch. These people have thought of everything. Look, the usual four arithmetical functions, plus all sorts of garbage for banks and brokerages. They haven't left out anything."

His eyes lifted from the tiny machine to Curtis's face. "How long has Staeli been in the computer business?"

"This miniature kind? Never, as far as I know." Curtis retrieved the instructions booklet and examined it. "It's a company with the same name as the machine, incorporated in Basel, a wholly owned subsidiary of S.I., GmbH. The whole thing is Swiss made. Get this." He started quoting from the booklet. "A true marriage of traditional Swiss deftness with high-precision miniaturized instruments, and space-age Swiss knowhow in microelectronics. The land that gave you the chronometer now gives you the ultimate in desk and pocket computers for all the normal needs of financial institutions."

Palmer's glance was still on him. Curtis looked up in time to see a peculiar brightness in the gray irises. "How in God's name," Palmer was asking, "do the Staelis think they can beat the Japanese at their own game?"

"The Staeli name?" Curtis hazarded. "It's got good marketing value among banks."

But Palmer had already lost interest in his own question as he started punching data into the tiny machine and getting answers. He drifted over to the long row of Barcelona chairs and sat down, abstractedly tapping the calculator's keys. Tom followed him. Woody left to take a shower.

Gerri stood next to Curtis, watching her father put the calculator through its paces. "Face is too thin," she muttered. "Too much tennis."

"He's in great shape."

"For tennis. Look at him." Her voice went lower. "Doesn't know how to relax. Even Ellie says so."

"Ellie?"

The girl gestured impatiently. "What do I call her, my future stepmother? She told me last year: A man who gets used to wielding power never gets used to being without it."

Curtis realized he'd barely had a glance at the instrument Elder had sent him. It probably had nothing to do with the UBCO-Basel project, but it had to be checked out. Somehow or other he'd have to get it away from Palmer. Not easy.

He watched Palmer punch up a new problem on the keyboard of his new toy, tap one more button and grin at the result flashed by the tiny red numbers. Feeling himself the object of scrutiny, Palmer glanced up at both of them with an arrogant "so-what" look, then continued playing with the calculator.

"Your future stepmother," Curtis murmured softly, "is one helluva judge of character."

CHAPTER 40

The Aeschenvorstadt was fairly empty at eleven o'clock in the morning. The doors of the squat gray building at Number 17 opened infrequently to let customers in or out.

Although this was the world headquarters of Staeli Internationale, GmbH., the ground-floor banking offices were not the company's principal location. A much more modern office, spacious and decorated with displays of gold coins, was located near the Marktplatz. Baslers who used the Staeli bank for their normal business usually went there, or to one of the smaller neighborhood branches. Corporate customers used the facilities at Number 17, representatives of companies seeking financial services.

On this particular morning, at eleven o'clock, the corporate official walking into the bank was a director of Euromichele, GmbH., and a recently appointed one at that. He drove up in a Bentley, rather than his L-2 Magna, because he didn't have the use of his sports car this Friday, or all this summer, for that matter.

This was not the only reason Erich Lorn was feeling somewhat out of sorts. The absence of the car was only a symbol of the problem he had. The absence of his fiancée, with or without car, was the core of the problem. It was irritating in the extreme to have to do what Erich was now doing. But, having promised to get the matter into motion after the meeting with the Hungarians, he had called Walter Staeli and made the appointment.

It was true that Margit had left messages for him this summer, but never a number at which she could be reached. And he'd never had any luck trying her at Schloss Staeli. Nor did he feel like giving her one of Michele's numbers at which to call him.

The White Rat kept him waiting the ritual five minutes, Erich noticed as he stood in the second-floor waiting room and glanced through several business magazines without reading them. It was always this way with Walter. He was forever concerned with outward appearances, like most hypocrites, and the idea that he should have his desk cleared and ready by eleven on the dot gave the appearance of having little on his desk.

"A great pleasure," Walter said when Erich had finally been ushered into his presence.

Was he wrong, Erich wondered, glancing about the big room, or had Walter caused another few meters of *cordon sanitaire* to be added to the area around his desk? Was he still playing the democratic role, or was he slowly isolating himself even further from the other desks in the room?

"Thank you, Walter." The two men shook hands ceremoniously, as if they were meeting for the first time. Actually they had grown up together, skied together and done all the things that the offspring of Basel's most powerful families always did in small, protective groups during their formative years.

It was not, Erich reflected as he sat down across the desk from Walter, that their parents wanted to keep them from mingling with children of the lower classes. It was simply, and sadly, that their parents could find no mechanism for procuring, in a natural way, the companionship of such children, except for pay.

"I haven't seen much of you lately," Walter began then, smoothing down his sand-colored hair with a gesture that looked smug, as if he were patting himself on the head for a job well done. He seemed strangely distracted, as if Erich's arrival really had interrupted something important.

264

Erich's smile was off center. "Are you the only one in Basel who doesn't listen to gossip?"

Walter put up one hand, palm up, as if testing for rain. "Would I believe scandal, even if I heard it?"

"Would you?" Erich's smile broadened. "But we can always come back to that later. I'm here on business."

"The business of Lorn et Cie.?"

"The business of the conglomerate known as Euromichele." Erich's eyes were fastened unblinkingly on his former schoolmate. "You are, of course, familiar with the company's holdings?"

Walter's pale face reddened slightly. "Erich, is this some sort of joke?"

"Oh, I forgot. Permit me to introduce myself." Erich picked a card from his wallet and handed it across the desk.

Walter's mouth went down at the corners as he read the card. "A managing director," he said. "I see. Nobody told me."

"Don't rub it too hard or the ink will smear. It's rather new." Erich waited a moment for Walter to produce the requisite smile. Then: "It's embarrassing in a way to be placing this matter before you, Walter, when I know it's not within your province here at Staeli."

As expected, this remark mobilized all of Walter's self-protective instincts. "Not my province? Erich, let me be the judge of that."

"It's a matter of financing, or refinancing, I should say, several new projects and subsidiaries of the parent company, Euromichele. And since the conglomerate and its subsidiaries are almost entirely in the field of service to women, I know this should be placed on Margit's desk, not yours."

They were silent for a while, and Erich noted that other bank officers working in the same room, but at distant desks, were also quite silent too. He doubted that they could hear what was being said, but none of them wanted to miss anything audible.

"As you know," Walter began slowly to signify that he was choosing his words with extreme care, "Margit does not, strictly speaking, have a desk here. She has always insisted on working from the Schloss, which is her privilege, of course. Have you taken this up with her?" He sounded offhand, as if his mind were on other things.

265

"No."

A faint smile tweaked one corner of Walter's usually frozen mouth. "For obvious reasons," he murmured in a conspiratorial tone.

"No."

"No?"

"I haven't taken it up with her, Walter, because she's out of town and I'm not sure when she'll be back." He watched the effect of his explanation, which happened to be the truth, and saw that Walter preferred to believe his own suggestion instead. Erich decided to let him. No one is ready to believe scandal more than your true, holier-than-thou hypocrite.

"Is that so?" Walter resumed patting himself on the head. "Then, of course, you have come to the right place." He nodded several times, in a distracted fashion. Erich saw that in Walter's subconscious there was a serious priority problem of whether to keep nodding or resume patting. He couldn't do both at once without a lot of rehearsal.

"What sort of range are we discussing?" Walter picked up then. "What sort of expansion is being planned?"

Erich put a plain large gray envelope on the desk. "It's detailed in this draft proposal. I can summarize it loosely as a plan for extending the franchising operation throughout Western Europe, a separate plan for the United States, the creation of a new subsidiary to market negative-ion generators—you've heard of them, I'm sure?—and a proposal for retailing certain nonmedical products produced under the Euromichele patent."

"And the amount?"

"In the eight-figure range," Erich said.

Walter's brow contracted into ridges whiter than normal. "Swiss francs?"

"*Certainement.*"

"Eight figures." Hiding the paper from Erich, Walter began to scribble with a pencil. Erich knew he was writing a row of zeros so as to reassure himself that the sum was actually somewhere between ten and ninety-nine million francs.

"A substantial sum," he said at last.

"Not all at once, of course, but on a timed payout over the years."

"Which end of the range, high or low?"

"Mid range. Say fifty million."

"Swiss francs?" Walter seemed unaware that he had already asked this question.

"It might prove possible to arrange financing nation by nation, if Staeli would prefer. We could take Deutschemarks for Germany, dollars for the U.S., and so on." Erich tried to keep his tone negligent.

"It's a sizable piece of business," Walter said in a tone that only an old schoolmate could have translated to mean: "so I'll have to bring it to my father for a decision." Neither man spoke for a moment. Then Walter broke the silence. "Have you taken it to Lorn et Cie.?"

"It's on my brother-in-law's desk right now," Erich lied. "But between you and me, Walter, this kind of multinational deal is not for my family's bank. They can handle the amount, of course," he added quickly, "but the currency exchange will be quite complex, a matter of arbitrage and forward buying or another kind of guarantee. You understand."

"Of course," Walter agreed. "It's the kind of arrangement that Staeli is particularly experienced with. But, as you know, Erich, when the range gets this high, we usually require representation on the board of directors."

When Erich failed to respond at once, Walter's head began to go up and down in further affirmation of his point. The condition was one Erich had already foreseen and warned Michele would be brought up. "That shouldn't be too hard," he told Walter. "Perhaps Margit would be interested in coming on the board. I can speak to her."

"Interesting," Walter said. A slight giggle escaped from his almost motionless lips. "I mean, Madame Michele and Margit Staeli on the same board. Quite, ah, racy?"

When for the second time Erich didn't answer at once, he began patting down his hair again with the preening motion a parrot will sometimes perform with its wing, or a cat with its paw. Erich watched it for a while and began to realize that Walter's mind wasn't really on the Euromichele proposal. He seemed to have something else he was dying to talk about.

"Let it sit the weekend, Walter. Read the proposal. Discuss it. I'll get back to you after Monday, *n'est-ce pas?*"

Walter took the gray envelope and placed it directly in front of him. Then he moved it sideways because it was covering a white folder encased in clear acetate. "Erich," he said then, "can you keep a secret?"

"You're getting married."

The look of incredulity on Walter's face was worth money. He picked up the acetate-bound folder. "I'm serious, Erich. This is so secret I haven't even told my father yet. It's imperative you treat it as confidential."

"You know me, Walter. I have trouble keeping my own secrets."

"I'm serious," Walter repeated. "You have no idea what this means to me . . . oh, and to Staeli, too, of course. Here." He handed the folder to Erich. "Sales report on a new subsidiary of mine. Sales of hand calculators to banks and brokerages. Read it."

"Um. Looks good."

"Good! We shipped a thousand ten days ago. Every one of them is sold. Our next shipment will triple that. And the third shipment will triple the second. And the fourth will—"

"Walter, you're shouting."

"Sorry." His voice dropped almost to a whisper. "This is the most exciting thing that has ever happened to me, Erich. It's all my own arrangement and it's working beyond my craziest dreams."

"How long have you known that it—"

"Just this hour. Just now. The first sales report just arrived by pouch from Brussels. Can you imagine how I feel?"

"Top of the world."

Walter nodded, but with a surprisingly grim expression, rather than a smile. "This is what I have always needed to show them, Erich. To show them that the logical successor to my father is me."

Erich nodded comfortingly. The Staeli clan were remarkably good at self-deception but he couldn't see them buying Walter as the heir apparent. Besides, hadn't Margit inherited a controlling share of the stock? "I wish you luck, Walter," he said. "Of course, there's Margit to contend with."

Walter blinked. "Margit?" His nostrils looked suddenly pinched. "But we count on you for that."

"On me?"

"As her husband, y—"

Erich nodded even more comfortably this time. No sense stirring up the poor, demented creature. You could tell plain truths to his father, but Walter never really had that firm a grasp on reality. "Yes, of course," he said soothingly. "And that will solve the problem of the loan to Euromichele, too. I'm already on the board. I can represent Staeli."

Walter's fingers groped for the white folder in Erich's hand. He took it and flipped it open at random. "You see? London, two hundred. Amsterdam, one hundred. Brussels, two hundred and ten. It's like reading a poem, Erich."

They sat for a moment, at ease with each other after all these years. Erich had never seen Walter in quite this state. He'd obviously come at just the wrong time to discuss the Euromichele deal. But perhaps it wasn't such a bad time. It would be mingled in Walter's addled brain with the happy news about his funny little machines.

They looked at each other, each of them smiling rather broadly, but for quite different reasons.

CHAPTER 41

The reservation had been made in the name of Hütsch, the same name in which the Colmar apartment had been rented. Seeing the restaurant first from the road, basking in the hot noon sun, the River Ill flowing slowly past its gardens, Burris thought he had never before seen such a peaceful place.

It was half-past twelve and a dozen cars were parked nearby, indicating that the good burghers of Alsace and eager tourists from across the river in Germany had already begun to descend in their hordes as they did every August. Most of the licenses outside indicated that a great many French had consummated their desire to eat in one of the *Guide Michelin*'s sixteen three-star establishments throughout all of France.

Margit turned toward the back of the car and rummaged through the small golden-tan leather flight bag she normally carried on a shoulder strap. It went everywhere with her, Burris had noticed, and it could expand from a very thin handbag to contain as much as she needed to take along on their weekend outing. At the moment, she needed only her compact from it. She stared gravely into the mirror as she quickly patted her hair more neatly into place.

"There. Let's go."

The main building was low, rambling and whitewashed. Broad overhanging eaves protected flowers and plants from the August sun. Burris and Margit strolled for a moment, walking slowly around the building toward a terraced garden that ended in a small clearing with a table or two at the water's edge.

"Can we eat out here?" Burris murmured.

Margit shook her head as she stared into the smoothly flowing river. "This river is so unlike the Rhine," she said, more to herself. "It tires me, watching that hurrying river. It tires Basel, I am sure."

"I don't suppose you get real three-star service this far from the kitchen," Burris said, answering his own question. He frequently found himself doing this. Margit had a way of replying to a question with an entirely different matter.

"Still," Burris went on, "we could ask. Yes, Matt," he said in a higher voice, "that's not a bad idea. Oh," he continued in a lower voice, "do you think so? He may find it gauche. We wouldn't want the son-of-a-bitch to think us Hütsches was gauche."

Margit's glance flickered up at him, then down. "They will do whatever we ask of them," she said then in an absent-minded way. "But you are right. The service is better inside."

"And it's air conditioned." Burris felt her hand, holding his, clench twice, languidly, as if the heat made it impossible to talk any more. "Something's bothering you."

"Yes. I'm never at ease as Berta Hütsch, but it's something else."

They sat down on a bench under a spreading willow, the sheaves of thin leaves dripping like green water. "What?"

"I don't know," she admitted. "I think the secrecy is getting to me. Do you realize that this is really our first full-fledged venture into the outside world."

"Do you think someone will recognize us?"

"That's not it," she said with a trace of irritation. "No one in Basel comes this far for a Friday luncheon. I can't explain it, Matt. You either have to get it intuitively or . . ." She sighed impatiently. "Perhaps this was a mistake. Perhaps our relationship is one of these hothouse plants. It can only thrive in a dark bedroom, watered with our body fluids."

Burris let the whole thing pass for a moment. The imagery was too upsetting. In the silence he could just hear the chuckling sound of the Ill against some post or tree root, a sound so fine-grained he almost had to convince himself it was actually a sound at all. No birds sang in the dense heat, but from somewhere nearby doves cooed softly. Across the clearing a butterfly of no particular importance rested for a moment on a long blade of grass like a child teetering on the upper end of a seesaw. Two ducks moved slowly through the water of the river, spreading ripples ahead of them.

"So when we venture out in the August heat," Margit went on then, "and expose our relationship to the scrutiny of a smart restaurant, the kind of place in which we would normally be dining several times a week, it suddenly looks furtive and faintly shabby. Which it is not," she added, her voice suddenly stronger. "I resent them doing this to us, Matt."

"Um."

"Say something, you banker. Commit yourself."

"I think the sun is frying your brain in its pan. I think we should have put up the top on the car. I think you need the interior of a cool restaurant and a long cold drink and a three-star meal."

She stretched out her long legs and wiggled her feet for a moment. "That's the kind of solid, sensible answer you bankers should give," she said in a mysteriously insinuating way.

"Don't you-banker me. You've got banking in your blood, in your genes."

"Oh." She laughed quietly, bitterly for a moment, then flexed her ankle this way and that, admiring what seemed to Burris to be the same pair of medium-heeled sandals she had been wearing most of the summer. "Perhaps you've turned doctor, Matt. You may have diagnosed me, at last. Isn't it possible for one's soul to be at war with one's blood? What if one doesn't accept one's genes? The transfer from one's parents didn't take, eh? What a predicament."

"Come on," he said, getting to his feet and lifting her long, slender arm. It felt cool beneath the very thin, flowered fabric of one of those see-through blouses that rode down over her hips and short skirt, cinched by a loose belt made of a number of fine-link gold chains.

They returned to the entrance and walked into the Auberge de L'Ill, finding the anterooms pleasingly low-key, filled with flowers and a few discreet certificates on the walls, framed and hung in out-of-the-way places. Attractive small oil paintings of flowers and modest landscapes occupied the center of each wall. Burris gave the Hütsch name to the maître d', pronouncing it badly, he felt sure.

Margit held onto his arm as they followed the man to a table by the window overlooking the river. As they sat down they could see the bench on which they had just been stting. Margit said something to the man in a language that was perhaps Schwytzer-tütsch.

"Is he Swiss, do you think?" Burris asked.

"I spoke the Alsatian dialect to him. It's very much like the Basler dialect. There is a string of these dialects along the Rhine, all variations of the old Burgundian language, all the way to the sea at Maastricht, in Holland. Basically, it's the same language and very old."

Burris nodded, seeing that of the perhaps thirty people in the dining room, no more than twenty-nine were staring at them. "Do you suppose someone hung a sign on my back?" Burris muttered.

"They are staring at this tall, handsome couple, obviously American, obviously rich like all Americans." Margit smiled crookedly. "How would I do as an American, Matt? Hair curlers, yes? Chewing gum? Motel adultery from five to seven every after-noon?"

"Christ, what a view of America."

"Tell me the truth about your country, then."

"How would I know the truth? I've been away more than four years."

"Does everything change that quickly?"

He frowned. "America changes everything all the time. We do a thing Monday that by Friday we pretend not to know about. We elect presidents we end up having to impeach. And the terrible thing is that when we choose a thief, we know in our hearts that he's the right thief for us. Only if the damned fool's caught do we have to repudiate him." He looked up gratefully as the maître d' brought menus. Any interruption was welcome.

"An imperfect society," Margit said after a while. "And Switzerland is the perfect one."

"Whatever you say, dear," Burris responded in a broad imitation of a husband. He looked at the menu. "This must be wrong," he said. "They don't have *choucroute garnie*. Are you sure we're in Alsace?"

"*Mein Gott,* never mention choucroute in this place, *Liebchen.* It's peasant food."

"How about this, uh, *truffe sur les cindres?*"

"It's unique here. They broil the truffles right on charcoal."

Their waiter loomed into view, small, mustached, cool to the point of gelidity. *"M'sieur-dame?"*

"I think we'll both begin with the truffles," Burris said. "And then?" He glanced at Margit.

"Something light. Perhaps the soufflé of fish?" She launched into an avalanche of Alsatian guttural, full of hiccups which the waiter, thawing visibly, responded to by launching a return flow of glottal stops. She looked up at Burris. "It's lobster today. He recommends it."

"You have that. And, for me, the breast of guinea hen. What local wine do you recommend?"

"We have a very good Sylvaner '74," he said in acceptable English.

"Very dry?" Burris asked.

"It is from Riquewihr, a nearby village. It is, ah, *herp.*" He almost smiled at Burris. "Do you know *herp?*" His eyes widened as if trying to implant the translation by mental telepathy.

"A faint taste of the fruit," Margit murmured. "Not fruity, but, ah, *herp.*"

"Let's have a bottle, then. But before everything, I think, and very cold. Bring it now."

"Ah, perfect," the waiter breathed, now definitely part of the Burris team. "At once, *m'sieur*."

Margit watched him leave. Then: "I'm sorry I butted in. I do that, even if the man and the waiter speak the same language. But he wanted to help you maintain your control of the situation, did you see?"

"We men stick together."

"Oh, really?" Her smile was crooked again. "I hadn't noticed."

Burris let the sarcasm dissipate for a moment. "I hope you don't mind that I didn't lay on a big banquet. Or do the whole sommelier bit. Local wine's fine, isn't it?"

"I know this Riquewihr '74. It's superb. And as for a large meal, I'm already faint with the heat, darling."

"That's not heat, it's lust."

"Another form of heat."

She watched the waiter produce a chilled bottle for Burris' inspection, then uncork it and pour the sample. Burris tasted it, paying a very brief tribute to oenology by pretending first to sniff the wine. "So that's *herp*," he said then. "Very fine."

The waiter poured their glasses, ceremoniously installed the long-necked bottle in a bucket of ice and bowed himself away. "To heat," Burris said, lifting the glass to Margit. They touched glasses and sipped.

"It's like being on the stage," Margit muttered, glancing around her. "They are all still watching us."

"No. I think we lost two."

"They know we're not married."

"Does that make us a curiosity?"

"Perhaps a scandal. Who knows unless one keeps staring? Did you see that, Hermann? They touched glasses. You never touch glasses with me any more, Hermann. You used to touch glasses, but not any more, Hermann."

Burris covered his laughter with the soft, thick damask napkin. "I suppose that's why the waiter was so solicitous. He wants to help me through this, uh, unusual relationship?"

"Partly. But partly you know how to get along with people."

"I do?" Burris asked, surprised.

"You've played on too many teams. You form a squad every time and you recruit players without even trying."

"Are you on my squad?"

"I?" Her hazel eyes went wide. "I captain the opposing team. A team of one."

"What's the score?"

She thought for a long moment. "It's seven to nothing, Matt. You've scored a touchdown and made the conversion and my team hasn't budged." A faint note sounded in her words, not bitterness or self-pity, but something Burris couldn't name at once. Resignation?

"Listen," he said then, "this is our first real outing."

"Yes, let's not louse it up," Margit responded in his own flat, Illinois accent. She reached across to pat his hand. "The Riquewihr is fine. I think perhaps, if we wait for the waiter to pour, I will die of thirst. Yes?"

Burris filled her glass again. "Another thing," he said then. "This weekend jaunt of ours. We will get back to Colmar every night?"

She sipped her wine. "If it goes this way, we'll be back there right after lunch. For a nap, at least."

He touched his glass to hers. "To naps."

"You're doing it again." She glanced out at the room. "He's my lover," she said in a voice that was possibly not as quiet as it should have been. "We sleep together. He's quite good in bed," she said, addressing a large woman across the room who was wearing, of all things, a hat with flowers. "And how about that man with you, madame? On a scale of ten, please rate his performance. No negative numbers permitted."

"I think she can hear you."

"Fine. Oh, not so fine." She glanced plaintively at him. "Am I making a spectacle of myself?"

"I just can't take you anywhere."

This had the effect of dissolving her in giggles. "So true," she said at last. "We have to go far from Basel even to meet secretly. And even farther to eat in public."

"That's what happens to residents of a perfect society like Switzerland."

"It would be the same in the States," she mused. "The problems are quite universal. The questions are always the same. Do I break up with Erich? Why? What happens to us? Do I marry you? Do

275

you even propose marriage? Why should you? Why do I have to be married? What happens to our affair? Does it stay the same? Get better? Deteriorate? Supposing we are caught? By whom? Can we set up housekeeping as an unmarried couple? Where? Who needs it? Or do we drift apart? Find other people? When does UBCO transfer you? Do I follow? Why? Shall you stay here? Why can't I keep you? It's terribly modern. Or can you and Erich and I work out a *ménage à trois?* I marry him and live with you. Is that acceptable? What does Basel think? Why do we care? Can we elope to an island in the South Seas? And what happens there? Do you and I slowly decay into middle age? Is it that far off? What then? Is there some dusky Polynesian girl you fancy? Do I catch the eye of a handsome young—"

"Enough," he said.

"I . . ." She faltered. "I really am lousing up the lunch."

"Is that the kind of stuff you think about all the time?"

"Only when I'm alone, or with someone, or late at night, or during the day. No other time."

The waiter arrived with the truffles and refilled their glasses. He beamed at both of them and backed away again. "We're a hit with the waiter, anyway," Burris said gloomily. "Are all you Swiss girls so moody?"

"A perfect society is a closed society. We have no room for change. Once moody, always moody." She tasted her truffles. "Eat these. They're already cheering me up."

After the soufflé and the second bottle of Sylvaner, both of them brightened considerably. More people had come to dine but the novelty of the couple by the window seemed to have worn off, Burris noticed, and everyone returned to whatever they had been looking at before the arrival of the tall Americans.

"What would you like for dessert?" Burris asked.

"This place is too good for these people," she said, producing another of her oblique nonanswers. "This wine is too good for human beings. Angels only."

"Dessert?"

"I do like this place, Matt. I am really, after all, very glad we came here. We should have gotten out of that apartment long before this."

"I agree. As to dessert . . ."

"The poached peaches, then, on their own pistachio ice cream."

"Sounds like a hot-nut, peach-split sundae, hold the syrup."

"It's actually *Pêche Haeberlin*. Ah," she said, turning her face away from the room. "I do see someone. Damn it." She stared blindly out the window. "Has he been there all along? The man eating by himself in the dark corner?"

"His back's to us. How do you know him?"

"He turned just now to tell the waiter something. I saw his profile. But seated as he is, perhaps he hasn't seen me."

"He'd know you on sight?"

"I have to assume that. No dessert, darling. Let's pay and go before he turns around, yes?"

Burris summoned the waiter and included a larger tip than he normally gave. He realized that bolstering the male ego at a restaurant table was quite a lucrative business for waiters astute enough to understand. They walked quickly, but not too quickly, into the brilliant August sunshine.

Squinting against the glare, Burris said: "He didn't turn around. You're safe. Who was he?"

They got into Erich's orange Magna, Burris taking the wheel. "A boy I vaguely used to see now and then at social gatherings."

"What would he be doing here alone?"

"I have no idea. He's a strange boy, really. Does nothing much. A bit like Erich."

"Name?"

"Iselin. Paul Iselin."

CHAPTER 42

As one drives along the Gellertstrasse on a sunny Saturday afternoon, one hardly realizes that what looks like a park on one side of this Basel thoroughfare is, in fact, a series of houses large and small, single and multiple, owned and rented.

Almost all are hidden from view. Some of them are impossible to see even when one intends to find them because they are surrounded by their own wooded grounds, reached by drives that are barred by gates, chains, "Private" signs and, in some cases, placards citing city ordinances and penalties for trespass, or the simpler and more direct admonition that uninvited guests will be arrested.

These houses are usually rather imposing, with architecture that sometimes goes back to the early years of the previous century. There are few names on gates or mailboxes. These families have spent a lot of time and thought on preserving their privacy. They all have the money to afford whatever thoughts they may have on guard dogs, special police, intruder alarm systems and the like, as well as the landscaping to hide even these safeguards from the eyes of invited guests.

It was well after five when the telephone rang in Dieter Staeli's private study.

This was a first-floor room roughly thirty feet square, paneled in rosewood of carefully matched grain. A glove-leather upholstered chair with matching ottoman sat by an immense desk, not cleared of clutter as was Dieter's desk at Number 17 Aeschenvorstadt, but with a lived-in look, torn envelopes, scribbled notes, old magazines, leather-bound folders, albums and scrapbooks piled haphazardly and dusted here and there with cigar ash.

The library, as it was called in honor of the single floor-to-ceiling wall of shelves that contained yards of finely bound books organized by the color of their leather, contained a large window that overlooked the rear garden of the Staeli enclave. Here Dieter's wife and several servants cultivated happy splashes of color, the bright red geraniums still aflame as the afternoon sun now hid from view.

It was here Dieter Staeli had sat every Saturday afternoon and most of every Sunday working over in his head the various coups and schemes that he would put into effect the following week. He would look out at what was now the garden, but was then a small, pleasant playground where Walter, as a boy, enjoyed swings and a badminton net.

In the years before Walter had been sent away to secondary school and then to colleges, he had played here with his carefully culled group of peer-children, the Vischers, the Lorns, the Burckhardts, the Iselins, and even a few of the scions of such old-line academic families as the Bachofers and Jasperses. In the early years there had been girls, too, including the skinny little Margit.

But by the time she and her girlfriends had started to grow tall and fill out, Dieter had enforced a males-only rule. High time. He had been negligent and permissive letting them mix together until the age of ten or so. Scientifically, they should have been segregated no later than age five.

Once this had happened, of course, and only boys were allowed to play with Walter, it seemed to Dieter that he had begun to see fewer and fewer children in his playground. They had discovered bicycles, of course. That must have been the reason they never came around.

None of these thoughts had been going through his mind when the telephone rang. Dieter had been asleep in the upholstered chair, short legs up on the ottoman, enjoying the thick, clotted sleep of one who has made his luncheon late, heavy and vinous. He grunted on the first ring, awoke fully on the second, and answered before the third. Even after a heavy lunch and a drugged nap, there was as yet nothing slow about old Dieter Staeli.

"Yes?"

"Guten Abend, mein Herr."

Staeli squinted thoughtfully. He wasn't sleepy enough to demand a name. This was the call he had been awaiting for for days now, from the young Iselin boy, the one who had been trained in Intelligence work as an officer in the Army.

He chuckled loudly. "A fine time to call. I expected to hear from you after yesterday's lunch."

"Something better. Something definite."

"What? No!"

"I have found where they go."

"Wunderbar!"

"There is an apartment in the Tanners' Quarter of Colmar."

"I'll be damned. Under another name, of course."

"Berta Hütsch."

"That bitch. I told you she was clever."

"And now?" Iselin asked. "Can I forget the maid, Elfi? I've done what I promised to do. It's yours from here on in, yes?"

"Just a second." Staeli's voice went hard in an instant. "Are you trying to back out?"

"All I promised to do was—"

"Your job has just begun, boy. You've only started to do what I asked."

There was a long pause at the other end of the line. Then: "I had thought I was finished. This is undoubtedly the most distasteful—"

"So sorry," Dieter sneered. "I think a young gentleman of such delicate breeding should perhaps think twice before letting the financing on his ancestral home lapse so far behind. And such an illustrious ancestry. Too bad the only help forthcoming was from Staeli. I had no idea you Iselins were so finely tuned. If you want the unsecured loan at evergreen terms, you finish the job, no matter how distasteful, my dear young gentleman."

"I didn't mean to sug—"

"It's not your role to suggest either. You simply give me what I want and I give you what you want. It's called enlightened self-interest. Now listen closely. I want dozens of pieces of paper. I want affidavits. I want transcripts, photographs. I want the sworn statement of the landlord, of the neighbors, of the gendarme on the corner. I want to *hear* what goes on in the apartment. Is my meaning clear? You have quite a bit more work to do."

"Weeks."

"Perhaps months," Dieter Staeli snapped. "I don't care. Now for the rest. All of this material is to be turned over to Walter, not to me. Do you understand? We have never talked. We are not talking now. From this point on, following your instructions, you will develop the material and deliver it to Walter. Are you planning to attend the Schützenhaus dinner tonight?"

"What?" Iselin sounded confused.

"The monthly dinner of the *Jungführerschaftverein*. Arnold Euler is giving a paper on the economic effects of the Arab oil position. You will attend."

"I? Oil?"

"Walter will be there. Make your contact discreetly. Report everything. Arrange for further contacts when you have material to turn over. Understood?"

"I'm not sure I—"

"You *are* a member of the *Jungführerschaftverein?*"

"I suppose I am."

"Of course you are. Your father enrolled you years ago. It doesn't matter if you haven't been attending. Do so tonight. Goodbye. We will not be meeting again for a long time, you and I."

As he hung up the telephone, Staeli could hear the young man's voice saying something, but it wasn't important. Nothing he complained of was important because Paul Iselin was in a squeeze. He would produce the incontrovertible proof Dieter needed of Margit Staeli's immoral, reckless, and dangerous behavior, which could not be tolerated in any executive at any level of Staeli management, let alone the highest.

Dieter's round face grew warm with approbation. He hadn't praised the young Iselin cub enough, but he would in time. He'd proved an extremely useful and efficient young man. Discreet, too, as the Shelter affair had proved, and amazingly resourceful as well. There were few limits to what Iselin knew how to do—or had been trained by the Army to do—and, considering the hold Dieter had on him, there were few of Iselin's accomplishments he couldn't call upon, when needed.

That he was a bit balky about the business with Margit only showed that he still retained a certain sense of class solidarity. It did the young pup proud. He'd had no such qualms about a piece of human flotsam like Shelter, had he?

Yes, Dieter told himself in his new, expansive mood, the boy had succeeded brilliantly in the Margit affair where everything else had failed. The rest was cut and dried. Even in the hands of Walter, the rest of the matter was a foregone conclusion.

CHAPTER 43

Erich awoke at five o'clock in the afternoon with a nagging sensation of having been under inspection. Was it something he had dreamed? He hated to be the object of scrutiny. It may be very Swiss to spy and pry, but it was even more Swiss to hate being spied upon. He opened his eyes.

The rosy darkness was comforting, the shades still drawn, only a pale-pink nightlight suffusing the room with its flesh tone. So many good things happened to him in her many bedrooms. He felt at home waking up in one, as he had so many times this summer.

Then he realized she was watching him. His eyes swung sideways to see her. Michele was sitting up in bed, propped on three or four pale-rose pillows, her hair fluffed out in billows of curls that the act of love had only barely disturbed. Her bright eyes were fixed on Erich.

"Spying on me?"

"I have every right," she said.

He thought he heard a distant note in her creamy voice, usually so rich with undertones of sexual tension. She sounded, in those few words, as if she were addressing him from the other end of a very long microscope and he was something pinned to a glass slide.

"Who gave you that right?" he asked idly, not wanting to come awake and face the world yet.

"I bought it with my body."

"Um. Then I owe you change."

"Yes." Her smile was faint, almost unwilling. "Yes, you do."

"Still angry about Walter?"

"Not angry. Surprised." She took a long breath that brought her full breasts up as erect as a young girl's, the areolas big and rose-brown in the half-light. "I had thought you would have easy access to the proper person."

Erich found himself laughing so hard he choked, coughed, cleared his throat, then struggled into a half-sitting position to stop feeling like a specimen under a magnifier. "If you mean my fiancée . . ."

"This proposal was to be taken directly to her. We discussed it, did we not?" Michele demanded.

Her voice was—not hard, Erich thought—quite different than it had been two hours before as they made love. She had been angry then, but she knew he was good for her. Like a cat, she could keep her mind on the main thing, food, while also enjoying caresses. And it was becoming obvious to Erich that the main thing right now was not what he did for her in bed but what he could do for her with Margit.

"We did discuss it," she said again, moderating her tone to a more friendly note. "It was your idea that this was particularly

282

something for Margit Staeli. That she would understand it and make it her own and shepherd it through the whole Staeli decision-making system to be certain it was approved. This you told me, my darling, not I you."

"Yes, I did mumble something to that effect."

"Mumble or not," Michele retorted, her voice sharpening, "this was the understanding we had, you and I. And then you take it to that prince of flunkies, Walter Staeli. *Schrechlich.*"

"I did explain it."

"Not really."

"I told you Margit's been out of town. And there is some reason for seeking a quick decision on the matter."

"You have no idea of your fiancée's whereabouts?"

"Nor she mine," Erich drawled. He was getting tired of the conversation. He had just given her his all, the full act of love, everything from caresses and small nibbles and tiny, licking kisses to the lengthy foreplay she loved so much. He put in a lot more time on each act of love with Michele than he had with any other woman. There were many reasons he did so and it was not a chore. He enjoyed every moment of it, but afterwards was supposed to remain a hazy, dusky rose. Reality was not supposed to return until he damned well had to leave.

He glanced at the small Florentine gold clock on the bedside table. Five-ten. He had a lot of time yet. They would pleasure each other at least once more before he left this little villa of hers on the outskirts of Basel near the French border.

"You can leave now if you're in a hurry," Michele said then.

Stung, Erich analyzed the voice. It was not petulant or muffled with anger. It was . . . businesslike. Was that the word? How treacherous. Come, friend, you have carefully, even skillfully brought me to my climax and I have arched my back like a cat and yowled with pleasure and I have let you nap a while and you can clear out now. The end.

"Michele," he said, "don't do this."

"Do what?"

He rolled over and put his head in her lap. Her thighs smelled of her perfume and his smell. He breathed in deeply. "Don't become someone else. Not because of some stupid business transaction. It's not you. Not you at all."

She was silent for a long while. "What is me?" She stroked his hair for an instant, then pulled her hand away. "You have known me a long time, almost four months. You know me inside and out like a gynecologist." She laughed for a moment. "I have given you everything I have to give. Is it so difficult to understand how I feel when I ask a little thing that is yours to give me and you don't do it? I assure you, Erich, that *is* me. The same me you have been enjoying so thoroughly. I would have thought you'd know how I taste by now. You've sampled enough of me."

"I know the taste. Apparently I don't know you."

"We are the same, my taste and I. I'm a very simple person. I am what I secrete."

He rolled over and kissed the downy-soft skin on the upper inside of her thighs. "Michele, this part here is lovely."

"I work hard on it. All the acrobatics. You have no idea what work that smooth skin costs me. If any of the women who come to me for eternal youth would be willing to work that hard, I could turn them back into adolescents." She laughed again and squirmed slightly under his nibbling. "When a lover glances at the clock, it means only one thing."

"No, I swear. I have nowhere to be for hours yet," he said.

"Ah. You do have an engagement. With her?"

"Margit? I told you, she's out of town."

"And you expect me to believe that you don't know where to reach her?"

"I don't know."

"Stop that. It tickles."

"Um, yes."

"Stop." She lifted herself gently away from him for a moment. "Are you seeing her tonight?"

"I have one of those stupid *Jungführerschaftverein* dinners. I never go to them, but Walter is sure to be there and I want to press him on your behalf. On *our* behalf."

"Touching solicitude. But Walter is not the one to make the decision."

"I'm afraid he'll have to be." Erich swung away from her. If she didn't want to be nibbled, to hell with her. "When one puts Walter on the spot in front of his peers, one can push him a lot farther than in the privacy of his office."

"How clever of you," Michele said in a softer tone. "But second best is still only that. Your fiancée will have to be brought into it."

"Perhaps next week."

"Definitely next week."

"She comes and goes. Michele, don't ask the impossible."

"Everything is possible." She bent over him and gently bit his left nipple. "Everything."

His arm went around her head, trying to trap her to him, but she ducked out of his embrace. "I'll be through with the dinner by eleven," Erich promised. "I'll be back here by midnight with a full report."

Taxiing home to his house on the Kleinbasel shore of the Rhine, Erich kept hearing his promise echo in his own head.

Why had he let her get away with it? Why had he let her make him feel guilty and apologetic? She'd asked a hell of a favor and he'd handled it as best as he could, under the circumstances. And then to send him home long before he had to go. And yet, somehow, to make him feel so much in the wrong that he was eagerly promising to crawl back with a report like a trained dog.

It really was too much, Erich decided as the cab cruised over the bridge and turned left onto the Unterer Rheinweg where his house stood. Even this damned dinner tonight.

He hated the boredom of these terrible gatherings of all the dullards with whom he'd grown up, all the pompous sons of pompous fathers, the so-called young leadership of Basel. He'd stayed away for years, except for some special event, and tonight was nothing special, just the chance to put Walter on the spot when he was busy preening himself and pretending to be exercising a hell of a lot more *Führerschaft* than he really had. And all to nail down Michele's proposal. Nothing more. An evening of crushing boredom for her own business interests.

He smiled lopsidedly at his fatuousness. Clever of her to make her business my business. She was infinitely more clever, and at the same time more direct and primitive, than he'd ever suspected. Had this been at the back of her mind all along? Had she cultivated him this long and shared the hot-rose pleasures of her bed with him for a simple business advantage?

It wasn't possible, Erich told himself as he paid off the cab and walked up the steps to his front door. He fished around for his keys and realized, abruptly, that he'd left them on the ring with the keys to the orange Magna. Margit had them somewhere, God knew where. When women like Margit planned an escapade, they went berserk. Unlike Michele.

He rang the bell and Bunter opened the door to usher him in. "Master Erich, so early? A pleasure."

Erich frowned at the elderly man. "No flattery, Bunter, not between the Swiss."

"As you say, sir."

"I'll have some whisky in the drawing room. Ice and soda. Then a quick shower and, let me see, what will it be tonight?"

"Black tie?" Bunter suggested.

"Oh, my God, surely not."

"There's to be a paper read, sir."

"A paper is it? God in heaven, how lucky I am."

"Yes, sir."

"Arny Euler talking about oil profits doesn't merit black tie. Let me have a light-gray summerweight with a dark-blue shirt."

"Foulard or tie?"

"Neither. That damned Schützenhaus isn't very air conditioned." He stared at Bunter's reproving face. "Christ, a tie, then. I can always loosen my collar discreetly after dinner."

"As you say, sir." Bunter opened the door to the drawing room and made sure Erich was seated with the evening paper before he left. He was back almost at once with a tall glass containing a large number of ice cubes. He poured the whisky slowly until Erich stopped him, then plied the seltzer stream over the ice to bring the level of the drink almost up to the top of the glass.

"Always refreshing on a hot August day, sir."

Erich took a long swallow and sighed. "Instead of a shower, a cool bath, perhaps. You can draw it now, Bunter, and lay out my clothes and take the evening off."

"Most grateful, sir." Bunter eyed him for a moment and seemed hesitant to leave the room.

"Yes, Bunter?"

"Nothing, sir. I was just wondering. You seem—" He cut himself off, sighed, then blundered on. "Have you lost something, Master Erich?"

Erich's glance lifted until he was watching Bunter head on. The damned old busybody knew something was afoot. He'd hardly have been able to ignore it. The Magna gone with Margit. He himself never sleeping home any more. And now this sudden return to attend, of all things, a dinner he religiously avoided under normal circumstances.

No wonder the circumstances didn't look quite normal to Bunter. But what a strange way to put it. "Have you lost something?" As if a person could have a look of having lost something. But, of course, one could.

"Not at all, Bunter. Thanks just the same."

"Alles ist in Ordnung?"

"Perfectly, Bunter."

"As the British would say, sir, all correct and ticketyboo?"

Under normal circumstances, Erich would have burst out laughing. But nothing was normal, was it? Instead, he only smiled and found himself wondering if it were a sad smile. "All correct, Bunter. Draw the bath."

"As you say, sir." He bowed himself out of the room in as erect and democratic a posture as any other God-fearing Swiss.

Erich sipped his chilled whisky. Peculiar of Bunter. Of course he had some right to ask. These elderly retainers always arrogated that right and Bunter was no exception. Probably looked on himself as a father figure to the neurotic, vacillating Erich Lorn, no ambition, no goal, no wife.

He got up and went to a small Urs Graf woodcut framed against the far wall of the study. The graceful Graf lines depicted two tough Swiss mercenaries of the Renaissance standing around a campfire, their pikes carelessly held in the crook of their elbows. Graf knew the look. He'd been one of the dreaded soldiers before turning artist.

Erich had bought the woodcut at auction for a lot of money some years ago. The print had tripled in value since. It had been framed to Margit's specifications in an intricate Renaissance frame of carved wood inset with smoky Venetian mirror all the way around as a kind of mat. It was into the mirror now that Erich stared.

He looked distant and hazy, as one always did in this ancient glass, but he did get a sense of what Bunter had been asking about. He did look a bit . . . what was the word? Shaken? The forlorn Herr Lorn?

As if he had lost something. Perhaps. His performance today with Michele—or rather her performance with him—had taken something away from him, the initiative. He'd somehow surrendered his initiative to her. She was in charge. It had been a very subtle thing between them for months, but they had been equals, equally free to choose, go deeper, stand back.

Now the initiative had become hers. It wasn't she who begged for a report late tonight. It was he who volunteered it out of some strange new lack of confidence. Why?

He moved slightly on the balls of his feet and watched the way the uneven smokiness of the glass made his face seem to contort into a grimace, a tic of tension or pain.

He was in love with her.

CHAPTER 44

At first when Burris awoke from the nap, it seemed to him that the whole bedroom was bathed in a golden light, as if they had been swimming in the shallows off a sandy shore.

He mumbled something and opened both eyes to find that he had, in his sleep, pushed his face up against Margit's golden-tan leather bag. Unzipped, it lay open on the bed spilling out a complete display of the woman to date: small red leather notebook on which she had penciled that first note in the dining room of the Drei Könige, small matching address book, compact, comb, lipstick, wallet, a battered exercise book she used as a journal, bundle of correspondence held together by an oversized paperclip, two clean beige bikini panties, a knit blouse neatly folded and now rumpled out of shape, an oddly old-fashioned cloisonné pillbox shaped like an egg, a ring of many keys, including those to the L-2 Magna sports car. The normal contents of any neat middle-class woman's overnight bag for a clandestine weekend. He muttered again and turned to see that she was still asleep.

Somehow their long legs had gotten tangled. They lay at right angles to each other and he realized, from the fact that they were still almost joined together, that they had both fallen asleep after their climaxes.

That Riquewihr Sylvaner. It turned the blood to a thick, viscous sludge. You felt it moving slowly through your veins as if you were being given a sensuous massage from inside your body, rubbed from within by your own blood.

They had barely made it back to Colmar and bed. This was going to be one of their better weekends.

"Mm?" she asked, eyes still closed.

"Nothing." He watched her come slowly awake, stretching her arms, finding out for herself that they were still tangled together, realizing on her own that they had fallen asleep almost at once.

"Look at this," she said then. "It's indecent." She rubbed herself against him for a moment. "My God, the best sleep of all, isn't it?" He nodded but she wasn't watching him.

"What time is it?" he asked.

"But this never happened with us at Cambridge," she responded in her usual oblique way. "We had to run off to classes or library or something drab."

"It's old age," he said. "In those days we were too young to need much sleep. Now . . ." He fondled the dark patch of her pubic hair. "Have you got your watch on?"

"Not there. You?"

"No."

"That settles it." She wriggled around until she was half under him, holding him over her. "Let your weight down."

"Squash you flat."

"No, I want you to. Stop supporting yourself."

"It's a habit of long standing."

"I want to feel all of your weight."

"Ready?" He relaxed the tension on his elbows and let his body settle down over hers.

"Yes," she murmured. "Yes, that's it. What did you used to be, a fullback?"

He immediately lifted his weight off her. "Bronco Burris," he said.

"Honestly?"

289

"Just a bit of humor there. You never heard of Bronco Nagurski, did you? Now, there was a real Polack fullback."

"Are you really a Pole?"

"Body and soul."

"And your pole is a Pole's pole?"

He let his weight down suddenly. "More?"

"Oof. I adore it. In small samples."

He rolled off her. "I've decided to let you live."

She breathed in deeply for a moment, her small breasts almost invisible as she lay on her back. "There is a lot of power in your body," she said then. "Not just mass. Power. But you have chosen a job that makes no use of it."

They lay silently beside each other for a while, watching the August sun, glinting off a passing car windshield, send a long flash of light across the ceiling. "They are taking a flash picture of us," Margit said then. "Smile."

"I'll take six glossies, eight by ten."

She turned so that her face was burrowed in under his arm. She continued to breathe deeply. "I love that," she said then. "Is this how the locker room smells after a game? I would go insane if they let me in."

"Not pro-team locker rooms. All those dudes endorse underarm deodorants for television. The place smells like a hairdresser's salon."

"I have never been part of a team."

"You didn't miss much."

"No," she said, "I missed quite a lot."

"Not even in school?"

She shrugged. "Basketball one year. We won a cup. But we were hardly a team, just the six tallest girls in the school."

He laughed, partly because her breath under his arm tickled. "Did they all turn out like you?"

"How do you mean? Wantons? Nymphomaniacs?"

"Yeah, sort of," he admitted.

"Don't you know that tall women have a much harder time achieving orgasm? The neural connections go on for miles. It's very difficult."

"I hadn't noticed."

"I am the exception that proves the rule." She bit him softly

290

under his arm. "You are very much a team player still," she said then. "You had that fish-faced waiter on your team after a few seconds. The one who was all set to do that crushing French thing waiters do to Americans."

"Only if you try to talk to them in French."

"Yes, that's true. You're very wise," she said. "From whom did you get all your wisdom?"

"Women."

"Nonsense. Didn't you tell me about that coach of yours?"

"The one who got fired for no-win? He didn't teach me about French waiters."

"And this, ah, mentor of yours at the bank. Potter?"

"Palmer."

"Another figure in your life like the coach, yes?"

"I suppose you could say that." Burris lay there thinking for a moment about something he'd never considered before. "And in high school I had a history teacher, an old guy who convinced me I wasn't the dumbest Polack in Carbondale, Illinois."

"That's all, only three wise old men?"

"Palmer isn't old," he corrected her. "He's in his early fifties."

"That's o-ol-d," she said, drawing out the word.

"He's a hotshot from a Chicago banking family who made it big in New York and somehow took a shine to me. Maybe because we're both from Illinois, but I doubt it."

"Why do you doubt it?"

"Baby," Burris said, "we come from such different worlds in Illinois that it's as if he's from Venus and I'm from Mars."

"You are not from Mars," she said after a moment. "You are not at all bellicose. Belligerent? Warlike."

"Not with you, anyway."

"I think," she went on in a faraway voice, "that this comes from being a team player and from being the confidant of wise old men." A pause. "It's a kind of passivity. You keep yourself in reserve. You have learned you may have to call on it for an extra effort, late in the game. You don't try any harder than you have to. And the wise old men have shown you how to judge exactly how hard to try."

"You're making me sound like a goof-off."

"I haven't expressed myself well. And this is after a whole summer of speaking English to you. It's depressing."

They lay silently for a while. "The Swiss, you know," she said then, "have a reputation for deceptively passive behavior." She snuggled up against him until he circled his arm around her shoulders. "We have produced some strange people in our time. Dreamers like Jean Jacques Rousseau. He ended up a paranoid. Did anyone ever tell you the story of General Jomini?"

"Never."

"But he is so Swiss it makes one's teeth ache."

"Tell me."

"Jomini had been sent to Paris as a clerk in a Swiss bank. This was, possibly, 1790? 1800?"

"I choose 1795."

"In his spare time he studied the campaigns of Frederick the Great. Do you get a picture of the bank clerk who becomes an authority on the Prussian Army? And word gets to Napoleon, of course. He makes a colonel out of a Swiss bank clerk and then bestows on him the title of Baron. Baron Jomini, *n'est-ce pas?*"

"So far so good."

"But this sudden promotion of a nobody angers Maréchal Ney," she went on. "He conceives an open distaste for the Baron Bank Clerk, even if he is the acknowledged expert on Prussian military tactics. Jomini feels he's being held back. He deserts to St. Petersburg in 1808 and the Tsar makes him a general. Are you still with me?"

"It's starting to sound unbelievable."

"No. The unbelievable is yet to come. Napoleon is very angry with Jomini. This one can believe, I assure you. What does he do? He invites his former colonel back to Paris. Jomini returns to certain death. Why? Only a Swiss can tell. Napoleon gives Jomini an ultimatum: become a French general or be shot as a deserter. Jomini chooses the general's baton."

"Believable."

"War breaks out between France and Russia. Jomini holds the rank of general in both armies. It's a conflict for anyone but a Swiss. He assigns himself to the rear battalions."

"Very believable."

"He stays clear of the battles of 1812, but during the retreat of 1813 he is accused of an error he feels he did not commit. Swiss don't mind criticism, only unjust criticism. He deserts to the Russians."

"Unbelievable."

"They welcome him with cries of joy," she continued, "and put him in charge of Russian troops hastening the ouster of the French. One would think Jomini eminently suited for this, since he knows the French plan of retreat. With his knowledge, Russian troops can cut the French to ribbons."

"Highly believable."

"No. Jomini says it would be against his honor to reveal the French master plan. It would be a betrayal of Napoleon. So the Russians have to chase the French without any help from Jomini. One would imagine this might sour the Tsar on his Swiss general."

"Most believable."

"Instead, once Napoleon's troops have been ousted, Jomini undertakes a whole new career as a Russian diplomat. He represents the Imperial Government of Russia at the Congress of Vienna and later founds the Tsar's military academy for him. In his memoirs, Napoleon goes out of his way to assure the world that he does not consider Jomini's desertion a betrayal. Being Swiss, he is free to go where he wishes."

"No, no, no way believable."

"Later Napoleon III calls Jomini to Paris for technical consultations. In his own good time, Jomini dies of old age, full of honors and awards. He has betrayed Napoleon twice and the Tsar once and remains till his death a perfect Swiss gentleman."

There was a long pause. Then Burris said: "You made that up. The whole thing with the funny name and all." He squeezed her shoulders. "Tell me you made it up."

"The stories of Swiss mercenaries are unbelievable, I will admit. Take your General Wirz."

"My General Wirz?"

"He certainly isn't mine. Heinrich Wirz, the Confederate major in charge of the Andersonville prison camp? The one the North shot for his brutality?"

"Hey, listen, let's neck a little."

She jumped up off the bed and started for the bathroom. "We simply cannot lie around this place all weekend. We're going to get dressed and get out of here, aren't we?"

"I guess we are, at that."

"Matt," she said, standing in the doorway. He rolled over to look at her, tall, long-legged, with neatly modeled flanks rising into a narrow waist. Her dark hair was in need of combing and most of the light make-up she used was gone. She looked beautiful, with her long neck and the fine flush across her high cheekbones.

"Yes?"

"This is the happiest summer of my life."

CHAPTER 45

Curtis had driven north to Geneva and turned in the Fiat at the airport. Aside from getting Palmer's okay to stop keeping close track of Matt Burris, the whole visit to Morcote had been an abort. He would take the late flight to Paris now and pick up the threads of more important UBCO affairs.

But the visit had left Curtis with a bad taste. Palmer's style on the tennis court, for instance. The man would do anything to win, and this was the wrong frame of mind for someone who claimed to have retired.

In itself, this would be a minor thought for Curtis to mull over, but finding this one crack in Palmer's façade, he could not help what his mind was now doing. It was a strange mind, and he knew it, but it was well suited to the job for which he was being paid. So it began to inspect other facets of the Palmer situation, like a diamond cutter examining an uncut stone for fault lines. Place the chisel here? Or here? Tap lightly with the mallet? Or give it a solid wham?

Finding Palmer more human and less divine, Curtis had begun to wonder about the various other works Palmer had caused to be created upon this earth. If he was not UBCO's Jehovah, then the mind of man had a clear license to ponder his motives.

For instance, bringing Burris to Basel. Why Burris? Was he that good? Was Palmer that fond of him? Was Palmer really fond of anyone but perhaps his daughter and his younger son? And the mysterious woman he referred to as his tennis partner? What had Gerri Palmer called her? "My future stepmother."

But why Burris to head up what would, at least in the beginning, be essentially an undercover job, hidden from the Swiss until it was too late for them to hamper its growth? Why not some real softshoe operator? Why a fullback who seemed to understand only the good old honest head-on line smash. Of course, Burris had proved brighter than that, as it turned out. His strategies for covert work were not bad. Curtis, uncharitably, began to wonder who had dreamed them up for him.

And that was another thing, damn Palmer. Bill Elston had gone to a lot of trouble and some risk, entrusting that little electronic machine to Gerri Palmer because he wanted Curtis to have it. Not to calculate his expense accounts, but for some other reason.

Elston was far from the center of the battle here, but his instincts were good. Why had Staeli come out with this essentially low-profit novelty, hardly worth even a blue chip in their scheme of things? When Staeli tooled up and moved, mountains shuddered. Heavy industry, machine tools, massive chemical production, intercontinental lending, funding of governments, of industrial giants, this was the normal Staeli work flow. Not dainty little gizmos that probably retailed for under a hundred bucks.

Bill Elston had wanted Curtis to have the machine but it was still in Morcote, with Palmer still teasing answers out of it, an overgrown kid with a sophisticated new toy.

As he waited for the late Paris flight, Curtis found himself glad to be out of Palmer's reach for a while. The man worried him. And so did his overly complex UBCO-Basel project. When a strategy got that sophisticated it was bound to have flaws no one yet suspected.

CHAPTER 46

One gets to the Schützenhaus by various means. The Number 18 streetcar tracks run right past it, the Number 6 tram drops one off a block away, and the Number 33 bus also goes by the small triangular piece of parkland in which the restaurant is situated.

The young men attending tonight's dinner in one of the large private halls of the ancient building came either by chauffeured car or drove themselves. This was why, in the parking lot to the rear of the large T-shaped restaurant, there was such a diverse mixture of small Porsches and seven-passenger Mercedes limousines.

The scrap of park usurped by the Schützenhaus was snipped from the nearby Schützenmatt Park many decades before when Basel's street system was modernized and rerouted. The Schützenmatt itself was sliced neatly into two almost equal halves. One had a racing oval and something called, in German, the Old Boys Sportpalast. The other was a proper park with paths, beds of flowers and benches.

In the oldest perspective views of Basel, which date from the Renaissance, the artists have tried to show, outside the walled perimeter of the town, the building now called the Schützenhaus. The celebrated Merian map of 1615 depicts it so clearly that it has, of course, been incorporated into the restaurant's menu.

The celebrated woodcutter Hartmann Schedel, in his "Liber Chronicarum" of Europe's major cities printed in 1497, shows the Rhine flowing peacefully through Basilea, as it was then called, the cathedral with one spire still being built, several other churches, but no Schützenhaus. The perspective Schedel chose gave him no view of the squat building.

Erich Lorn had always disliked the place. The Schützenhaus had once been the hunting lodge of a noble family, one of the patrician Catholic lines which the Reformation eventually erased, century by century.

In the many struggles between the guilds of Basel and the bishops, the Schützenhaus had finally fallen to the burghers, who were predominantly Calvinist. In succeeding wars between the city of Basel and the canton around it, whose farmers were still largely Catholic, the stubborn burghers continued to hold the Schützenhaus, though it stood then on disputed land outside the city wall.

In Erich's opinion it was not worth fighting for. Nor was it now worth the tremendous word-of-mouth prestige (the Schützenhaus rarely advertised) it had among semiknowledgeable Baslers. The ones who really knew avoided it except for organizational dinners like tonight's, or official dinners staged by the government of the city. When no meal was served, the city fathers used *das Wild'sche Haus,* on the Peterplatz in town, once the home of the Wild family, now owned by the city for formal ceremonies.

By the time he had reached the Schützenhaus, at well after seven o'clock, the sun was low enough on the horizon that the air had cooled a little and the ancient building, surrounded by trees, was already sinking back into a kind of dark-green reverie.

Two and three stories high, it offered many doors through which its regular patrons might enter. One wall of its main dining room was glazed to display the garden. The dining room, of course, was for tourists and perhaps for Baslers holding smallish dinners of ten or twelve guests, suitable for the announcement of an engagement or a corporate merger of another kind.

Erich directed the taxi driver to drop him at one of the parking-lot entrances. As he let himself into the rear hall, he stared up the grand steps that led to second-floor rooms. With his usual irritation, he noted that there seemed to be absolutely no end of mounted weapons on the walls: crossbows such as the entirely imaginary William Tell might have used, pikes with nastily toothed points, flintlocks of dubious accuracy, and even a few Alpine breechloaders.

Among the many philosophical concepts which the Schützenhaus symbolized was the Swiss male's love of killing. Erich stood there for a moment, trying to shake off the illusion that in the year since he had last been here they had somehow doubled the number of homicidal instruments used as decor.

Like every other adult Swiss male, Erich had spent much time earning a sharpshooter's rating during his Army service. Unlike most other Swiss males, he had not kept up his expertise with the Sunday target-shooting events that normally filled the tiny country's day of rest with a perpetual crackle of rifle fire from the French border to the farthest reaches of the Austrian frontier.

The reason he had surrendered his inalienably Swiss right to spray the countryside with bullets—although he probably could still hit a target—was that it seemed to bring out the worst instincts of his fellow Swiss males, the fake-hearty, thigh-thwacking, beer-slurping, back-slapping camaraderie of scrawny bank clerks and ox-thewed mountaineers in a mindless display of sheer noise that was somehow supposed to reaffirm each weekend the inviolability of the Swiss borders from craven attack by its neighbors.

Erich walked into the bar, which lay between the area of private rooms and the public dining space. There were, even now that they had passed the thirty-year mark and were firmly stitched into the comforter quilt of their family's business and fortune, a few of Erich's childhood comrades who shared his own distaste for what they thought Switzerland had become.

If they ever attended these dinners, they could be found first in the bar taking on appropriate loads of beverages harder than Feldschlossen beer, or the Cardinal brew that was produced on the banks of the Rhine not far from Schloss Staeli.

A few local men sat at tables playing jass, Erich saw. He knew some of them but none were of his class. In a ruthlessly classless society like Switzerland, only a Swiss could distinguish levels of class distinction, and only a Basler could choose either to honor or ignore them.

Some of the jass players were from the neighborhood. To them the hallowed Schützenhaus was simply their local bar. Others, perhaps, used the bar for informal gatherings of their marching clique. It was typical, Erich thought, of Basler democracy that everyone had access to the Schützenhaus on the basis of whether they could afford only a small beer or a full dinner. In the end, and despite Byzantine twists of lineage, it was money that established class in Switzerland and always had.

Seeing none of his old classmates or cronies, Erich made his way to the private salon. He was a bit late, but not more than it took to miss the first course of the dinner, usually a decent enough soup, thick with puréed legumes. He opened the door and found that, indeed, the dinner had already begun.

This private dining room of the Schützenhaus ran the full width of the wing, perhaps fifty or sixty feet, the two outside walls laden with narrow windows of a glass that distorted but did not shut off any of the light passing through.

As Erich took his seat halfway down the long single table, he glanced out at the darkening twilight in which shrubbery and trees looked twisted, sinister, as if painted by a Swiss fantasist like Fuseli. He wondered what these thirty or thirty-five men seated at the table looked like to a passer-by. This flower of the Basler bourgeoisie, in business suits and white shirts, perhaps resembled twisted, doomed wraiths of the sort the Basler Holbein had painted in his "Dance of Death" their painful correctness astigmatized into ghastly fury.

Erich ordered a scotch and soda, with ice, to be put on his own bill. Then he turned to the man seated beside him. "Hansl, you've put on weight."

The chubby young man gave him a sour look. "I don't see you in God knows how long and this is how you greet me? And you looking as thin as a stork. That youth treatment. I understand it takes a lot out of you."

Erich grinned evilly at him, accentuating all the Satanic V's in his face. *"You'd* think it was a lot, Hansl," he said and turned rudely to his other dinner companion. *"Putzi, wie gehts?"*

Putzi Sigg was quite bald, although Erich's age. He had tried his best to compensate for this by cultivating a truly magnificent mustache, thick, black, glossy with pomades and stiff at its upturning ends with a wax that smelled strongly of pine. He eyed Erich with some caution. "What brings you here?" he asked gruffly. "Arny Euler's talk?"

"Precisely. We all know what a mind he has."

Knowing this to be sarcasm, Putzi produced a blank face in which only his colossus of a mustache quivered with any sign of life. Then, in a discreet croak: "I hear great things about you, you cur."

"What things?"

"How many of us would like to bathe in that fountain of eternal youth." The mustache dropped slightly. "At least, you dog, it was one of us who did the trick, eh?"

One of us, Erich repeated silently. Sweet Christ, was he one of them? He glanced around the room. There sat Walter Staeli, as effulgent with self-satisfaction as his moon-faced father, occasionally nodding deeply in what had become, for him, no longer a habit but a kind of tic.

Next to him, trying to get his ear, sat a junior member of the tribe, Paul Iselin, who had the name but not the money. He looked pale, caved-in, too small for the chair in which he sat. His days in Basel were numbered unless he married well. Every time Iselin tried to attract Walter's attention, the sandy-haired White Rat with his pale complexion and milky eyes seemed deliberately to cut him off and turn to his opposite dinner companion, none other than the speaker of the evening.

Erich found himself wondering to how many people, so far, Walter had already confided the edifying secret of his great business coup with the little hand calculators. Was he boring Arny Euler with it now?

The main course, when it arrived, proved to be as typical of Swiss cuisine as the gathering here was typical of Basler upper-class males. Erich finished his highball and, when he saw that the wine of the evening was to be a rather heavy *Gewürztztraminer,* secured for himself a full bottle of one of the light Neuchâtel reds.

He went through the form of offering some to his neighbors on either side, but like any real Swiss, they were making do with the inferior wine that was included in the charge for the dinner. It had been paid for and it would be consumed.

So would the *Schnitterei* that stared up at Erich from the plate now placed before him. It seemed to him that no matter what meat dish a Swiss chef attempted—and no matter how well he brought it off—each piece of meat had been cautiously cut to the size of a one-franc piece.

It made no difference if the dish were a veal piccata, a beef stroganoff, a pork goulash or even a velouté of boned chicken, the meat had been reduced to mini-schnitzels, each about as thick as a matchbook, but easily hidden beneath one.

In cheaper restaurants where students ate, this miniaturization seemed to have been carried on with the aid of a magnifying glass and a microtome. It had to do with the fact that cheaper cuts required the kitchen workers to slice tiny pieces to avoid less chewable gristle or the bigger chunks of fat.

But in what was probably Basel's most expensive restaurant, where the tourist diners in the other room stuffed themselves on beef fillets and veal schnitzels the size of a bootsole, this kind of atomization of meat was hard to understand.

Erich sipped his Pinot Noir. So, his affair with Michele was all over town, probably had been for months if deadheads like these had learned of it. Under ordinary circumstances, this would have amused Erich and influenced him subtly in bringing the affair to an abrupt end. With Michele, this wasn't possible. He found himself wondering what people were saying about the two of them.

300

The difference in ages, perhaps? The difference in classes? The scandal if she should somehow permanently win Erich away from his fiancée? The effect of this on the male Staeli's problems with Margit? The plausibility of an investment in Euromichele GmbH.?

Probably all of these delicious tidbits had occupied Basler society for the summer, together with some curiosity as to whether Erich Lorn had finally met his match.

Well, he had, Erich thought, his eyes on his half-finished food. He glanced at his bottle of Neuchâtel red and wondered if he were drinking too much and eating too little. Later he had to butter-up Walter, in the social drinking that followed the talk.

There was no question but that Michele had a hold over him no other woman had ever achieved. It might have been a matter of experience, but it was, more likely, the result of her complete self-confidence. Unlike most of the women with whom he'd had affairs —single, married, it made no difference—Michele had a rock-solid base in the great world and in Basler society.

She was a person in her own right. She was not a politician's bored wife, looking for excitement and a simple act of revenge on her husband, or a career girl working her way up in a profession. In many ways she was already what Margit Staeli wanted to be, her own master.

There was a novelty to this, in Switzerland, but there was more, power. It had a profound effect on Erich. Even sitting here, isolated from her in a way he hadn't been all summer, the thought of Michele remained uppermost in his mind, as though she were incense filling this room.

In a way he didn't understand, she had the power to give herself completely to him, over and over again, without losing a bit of herself. All of her was still in her own possession.

Erich had taken and taken, gourmandizing great chunks of her, and he was still as hungry as he had been in the beginning, still anxious for more, still jealous and upset if he sensed any of it being withheld, still groveling—that was clearly the word—for any scrap he could have, and willing to do anything to get it.

It just wasn't him, Erich decided sadly, staring into his glass of wine. It wasn't what he had been for the past twenty years.

The power she had over him had little to do with her base in society. If anything, Margit had an even stronger base, but she had never once in their lives attracted him sexually.

Oh, that time in Vienna, he would have gone through with it in the hotel suite because, after all, why not? It made sense, since they'd be man and wife eventually anyway. But there was something sexless about Margit, for him. Obviously not for someone else this summer.

It was a mark of how engrossed Erich had become with Michele that he hadn't the slightest idea who the man was, except that he wanted Margit to be discreet. He was sure she would do nothing reckless. A capital indiscretion, on her part, would play directly into her dear uncle's hands.

And those of her dear cousin. Erich looked up to stare across the table at Walter, who had begun to look even more like an albino rodent as Erich continued to drink. Finish the bottle, he told himself, and you'll find it impossible to talk to Walter without first spitting in his face.

He found young Iselin's maneuvering curious, as if he had grown tired of attracting the great man's attention, but had doggedly to pursue him nevertheless. The look on Iselin's face was tainted with disgust, possible self-disgust, Erich thought now. He knew the look.

With the dessert, and no further preamble—the *Jungführerschaftverein* prided itself on a certain starchy informality— Arny Euler now pushed back his heavy chair with a loud scrape across the polished wood floor that commanded attention.

Erich pushed the red wine from him and tried to concentrate on Euler's skinny frame, surmounted by the scraggly red beard he had affected in recent years. The Euler line went back to the original eighteenth-century mathematical genius, but Arny's family was a collateral branch that had made its fortune after World War II in the handling of the oil sheiks' gold hoards.

In those far-off days of innocence, the syphilitic, half-crazed Arab despots who drained the oil-producing lands of their profit were content with gold, bricks of it, or else English sterling in safe London banks until the spectacular fall of the pound had disenchanted them with sterling.

With a new generation of sheiks' sons free of eye cataracts, paresis and a taste for wholesale sodomy, most of them trained in

302

cutthroat financial warfare at Harvard, the investment horizon had expanded for the handful of families that owned Arabia. If anyone knew the ins and outs of their now more sophisticated investment demands, it might be Arny, who was himself so financially secure that, in addition to the beard, he was actually wearing a green-and-white striped shirt that clashed with his beard. And a tie, of course.

Erich loosened his own and sat back. "Gentlemen," Arny began. "As we all know, the American century proclaimed after World War II has now ended some seventy years ahead of time."

A sound of chuckles and snickering went around the room. Everyone relaxed. Arny was going to be entertaining, it seemed, at least by Basler standards.

"As a matter of fact," he went on, glancing at his notes, but extemporizing, "it came to an abrupt conclusion in early 1974 when the Persian Gulf price of oil quadrupled overnight. The sheiks used as their excuse the boycott of Israel, and this may have taken in a few governments around the world, but it certainly fooled no one in Basel."

The chuckles became downright mellow. It was pleasant to poke fun at the Americans, as always, but it was even more enjoyable to pat oneself on the back.

"Under cover of this transparent excuse, oil went from a little more than six Swiss francs a barrel to more than twenty-four. In some ways it ranks as the greatest fiscal theft in history. At a single stroke the sheiks levied a tax of two hundred and ten billion francs on the rest of the world . . . in a single year!"

There were no chuckles now, Erich noted. He cared nothing about the whole matter. Lorn et Cie. did very little business with the Arabs. But he recognized that he'd paid no attention to the oil crisis when it exploded. Arny was offering a so-far-painless catch-up course.

"The next year, 1975," the speaker went on, "the sheiks increased their take to about two hundred and seventy billion francs, worldwide. They continue to increase this each year that passes." He stopped and cleared his throat. The room was silent. Sums of money of that magnitude commanded, all by themselves, the strictest of attention.

"My sources at the World Bank," Arny Euler continued then

303

with a kind of offhand unction that made it clear he actually did have such sources, "tell me that, without the slightest doubt, by the year 1980 the sheiks will hold surplus profits amounting to over one trillion francs. The figure, to be precise, is forecast at one trillion, two hundred million."

In the distance, muffled by the distorting windows, a streetcar clanged its bell once. Erich blinked, something he rarely did. Even he was impressed by a trillion Swiss francs.

"Let me describe this hoard in another way," Euler said then. "By the year 1980, the Arab oil producers will hold more than seventy per cent of all the monetary reserves in the world."

Someone coughed. Then someone whistled softly.

"Yes," the speaker said, as if in response to the whistle. "Of course, this is a truly fantastic opportunity for Swiss financial institutions. The money must be invested and the sheiks have utter confidence in us, to the point where they disdain to use the banking facilities of even their Arabic brethren in Beirut."

To Erich's utter amazement, there was a round of applause for this statement, as if Arny Euler had suddenly produced the answer to a particularly difficult riddle.

"Thank you. But these opportunities come to us not without problems and risks. It is with these that I wish to treat tonight. We all realize that the price increase in oil is creating a phenomenal inflationary trend in all customer nations. These includ—"

Erich switched off the speech. The rest of it he knew. Lorn et Cie. were closer to the consumer level than many Swiss banks. The few meetings he had attended of his own family's institution had already acquainted Erich with the devastating effects of inflation.

He concentrated on Walter, trying to work out his approach to The White Rat after the speech and the question period had ended. Perhaps he should maneuver Walter into a group that contained the mustached Putzi, who had risen faster in his family bank than Walter. He was thus a good person to use in stirring Walter to some bragging gesture. Force Walter to play the role of decision-maker in front of Putzi Sigg. Yes.

". . . but of all the suffering industrial nations," Arny droned on, "the one with the most serious problem is neither the United States nor West Germany. It is Japan. I cannot impress too strongly on you the tremendous economic problems facing the industrialists of Japan who—"

In front of Putzi, Erich thought, I will ask Walter whether he's decided on that brilliant new loan proposal. Putzi will perk up his ears. "Why didn't you bring this to my bank, Erich?" he may ask. And Walter will want to cut a fine figure by committing himself to the loan on the spot.

"Putzi," Erich murmured, "after the talk—"

"Sh, yes-yes." Sigg's mustache bristled.

"Later," Erich promised, giving up for the moment. He sat back and pretended to listen to the speaker.

". . . knowing as we do the close relationship between leading elements of Japanese industry and those right-wing political configurations that include most of the nation's strongly organized criminal element, we have to beware the possib—"

Erich closed his eyes for a moment. He could visualize Michele, lying back on her many-pillowed bed. If he opened his eyes, the image remained. She was not the most beautiful woman in Europe. She was terribly arousing to Erich, but even in his most Michele-drunk state he knew she couldn't be as beautiful as he beheld her. Nor was she any more intelligent than, say, Margit. Or more sexually knowledgeable than half a dozen women he'd known in his life.

He supposed, sitting there with Arny Euler's muttering in his ears, that it was a matter of matching imprints. He'd read something about it, in relation to the way animals recognize other animals and distinguish friend from enemy, or family from prey. It was a matter of early mental imprinting. Something unique about Michele matched an inner pattern of womanhood that Erich had been carrying around with him all these years.

". . . and that in the national mood of desperation, certain elements of industry and certain elements of organized crime will merge interests to secure the kind of illegal commercial advantage that can elevate Japan out of its—"

Where had he gotten the pattern? Certainly not from his mother, or any of his aunts, nor from any of the girls he had seduced, or who had seduced him, in his early years. Neither of his grandmothers could he remember. Perhaps a family friend? An older woman, a distant cousin? A film star?

305

Could one ever fathom the mysteries of these inner patterns? How many did one carry around unknowingly, until one saw *the* house, *the* tree, *the* town or desk or painting. It was like the men in Plato's cave, trying to find the real world by viewing reflections of . . . what was the word? He'd had too much wine. Archetypes.

". . . caution those of you who will be dealing with the problem of Japanese investments and Japanese funding to examine with more than your usual caution the entire range of ancillary—"

And too much of Arny Euler. Yet it would be rude to get up and leave. How untypical of Erich Lorn had he become. The old Erich would have slipped away, or stalked out, it didn't matter which. And to hell with the *jeunesse dorée* of Old Basel. The new Erich sits and stews and frets his way through an interminable evening because he is trying to bring home a pitiful bone to a master who is demanding and difficult to please.

She will never be satisfied with anything I arrange through Walter, Erich told himself. She is really after Margit. There is another hand to be played in her game. Another round or two. She holds more cards and I don't even know which ones.

The round of applause was polite but sustained enough to make it clear, even to Erich who had stopped listening, that Arny Euler's speech was well received. A round of questions followed from the usual types of questioners, those very few who actually wanted more information and the many who simply wanted to be noticed, among them Walter.

". . . but surely," Walter was saying under the guise of asking Euler a question, "surely there is enough business acumen among us to detect even the hint of something unsavory in the—"

Erich switched him off, too. Walter's questions were designed only for advertising his own genius. The wine glass was empty. Erich filled it and sipped slowly.

Yes, there is more to Michele's game, he warned himself. She is looking for more from Staeli than a large loan. She is looking for something organic. There is no other reason why she keeps demanding Margit's participation.

Seven questions and answers later, Euler brought the dinner to a close. Some of the men stood up and began congregating in small groups, finishing their glasses of wine. Erich turned to Putzi Sigg. "Can you help me with Walter?" he asked.

"Staeli?" The mustache dropped. "He's beyond help."

"Let me bring us together for a moment. You don't have to do a thing but stand there, Putzi."

"Is this a trick on The White Rat?"

"Definitely."

"Then count me in."

But where was the rodent? Erich pushed his way past standing groups. Someone remembered Walter going to the w.c. Erich left the room and walked to the nearest toilet. He started to push open the door, but the sound of low voices stopped him. They were not coming from the w.c. at all, but from the darkened alcove next door which in winter served as a *garde-robe*. Normally there were lights inside to help the little *Lausbub* find your hat and coat. Now, from the recesses of this place, came the sound of Walter's voice, low but audible.

"You've found where she goes?"

Erich moved silently to one side of the checkroom's counter, getting closer to the voices without being seen. He hid under the stair rise. Someone answered Walter too quietly to be heard.

"Affidavits, eh? Good. And tapes?"

Murmur.

"I like it," Walter said in a louder voice. "Let me know the moment the case is airtight. No, nothing more here."

The White Rat himself then marched from the *garde-robe* into the w.c. without seeing Erich, who had moved further into the darkness under the stairwell. A moment later he watched Paul Iselin emerge from the checkroom, small and thin and furtive. As he returned to the private salon, Iselin looked upset, Erich thought, which he damned well should, considering what he was helping the Staelis do.

Erich walked slowly back into the dining room. He stood silently for a long while, his glance moving past the groups of standing and sitting men. This was his Basel, whether he wanted it or not. It was after a few moments that Putzi Sigg found him there.

"Where's Walter?" he demanded.

Erich glanced up at him and at first had no idea what he was talking about. He stared at Putzi's mustache for a moment, focusing and unfocusing. "Oh, that," he said at last.

"Well, let's get on with it."

"Putzi," Erich said slowly. He drew in a breath and found that he was shaking inside, but whether with anger at Walter and Iselin, or fear for Margit, he couldn't tell.

"Something's come up, Putzi. Let's forget it."

CHAPTER 47

The moon was rising. Half full, it seemed almost as bright in the clear August sky as if it had been round. It lanced down almost as strongly as sunlight on the fluttering leaves of the beech trees that stood around the edge of the small private park off the Gellert-strasse.

The house sat alone in the precise center of the tiny park, a square house made of three stories of gray stone with corner windows and a rather elaborate porte-cochere. The Jaguar had, in fact, been parked under cover of the porte-cochere, but at first glance there were no lights inside the house to indicate that anyone was home.

This was quite normal at the old Iselin mansion. Only Paul lived there now. His sister lived with her husband and children in Buenos Aires. His parents had died when he was still in his teens. The last of their lifelong employees, Mrs. Cron, the housekeeper, had been let go by Paul some six months before.

It was not as if Paul Iselin had no recourse from poverty. Family money had run out but several construction firms had offered him quite large sums of money for the property. The lovely old mansion, of course, would be razed. But the two acres of land, at such a prestigious address, was worth a lot to a builder of, let us say, a twelve-story apartment building, assuming he could bribe his way past the zoning officials. They were tough, but Basel officials were, after all, no better salaried than anywhere else in the world.

The last offer had been shattering to Paul. A million Swiss francs. He could have left Basel and started over again somewhere else, and done well at it, too. But that would have been the last of his branch of the Iselin line. There were others still in Basel, cousins and the like. It was not as if the name would vanish after so many centuries of prominence in Basel. Only the line represented by Paul's father, who had been perhaps the most respected and beloved of all the family. To sell his mansion, his park, his birthright . . . Paul had resisted.

He stared out the bedroom window at the moon. A small candle in a modern glass urn gave flickering substance to the room, but the moonlight was much more real.

He found himself picturing the way Shelter had looked, slumped behind the wheel of the beige Volkswagen. Protecting the Iselin birthright cost a lot more these days than anyone realized.

"What are you staring at?" Elfi asked from the bed.

Paul turned and rubbed the sparse hairs on his skinny chest, an idle gesture that gave him time to think. "It's the moon, *chérie.* Come and look at it."

"No. You come here."

"Demanding wench."

"It was you who demanded," she reminded him. "What you start, you must finish. I'm not finished." She giggled.

He lay down beside her and absent-mindedly began to scratch softly at the big, erect nipples of her breasts. He'd hoped to get one of the Uher M-7's from the electronics shop in Kleinbasel. It was the size of a cigarette pack. Instead he'd had no choice but to get the expensive Matsui 6001, which resembled a large black vitamin capsule. They both had fairly good microphones but the Matsui FM transmitter carried only up to one hundred meters.

"Is that the whole thing?" Elfi asked, shifting restlessly. "There are other parts that need scratching."

"I don't need reminding."

"You need to concentrate," she advised him. "Your mind isn't on it."

He sighed and applied himself to scratching her softly downward, across her belly, down her waist and into her pubis. She liked that. He liked her. He always enjoyed big girls, rather than ones his size. But at the moment he had too many other things to worry about, chiefly whether she would do for him what he wanted her to do.

"Did anyone ever tell you you were greedy?" he asked her then.

"For what?"

"For this." He took her hand and put it on his penis. "You girls are all the same, you know. You keep running away until you catch us. We are supposed to think it's all our idea, but in the end you can't get enough of it." He felt her begin to stroke him.

"In other words," Elfi said, her voice low, "you're doing us a favor, is that it?"

"In other words," he said, feeling the erection begin to build, "it's a matter of mutual trust. It's a two-way street."

"Oh," she said, rolling over on top of him, "I quite agree." She fitted him into her. "Absolutely mutual." She giggled again. "Is this the way your upper-class girlfriends do it, Pauli?"

She snatched up from a corner of the bed where she had thrown it the big floppy white straw hat she had been wearing at lunch yesterday and again when he picked her up tonight after the Schützenhaus dinner. Naked, she clapped it on her head now and began a slow, almost solemn up-and-back movement. The expensive hat flickered teasingly in the light of the candle.

"Ask me later on."

He rocked with her, catching her rhythm and reinforcing it. She'd have to be told some good lie. Spy stuff? But she'd never believe that of her own mistress. A romantic intrigue, then?

The idea was to tell her anything, promise her the moon, but get her to plant the Matsui 6001 where it would do its job best. He'd noticed a golden-tan flight bag Margit Staeli always carried with her. Perhaps that was the right place for the Matsui. But what would get Elfi to plant it there. This?

"Ah!" Her fingers dug into his shoulders. Her shudder was strong enough to shake him. Her eyes were clenched tight-shut. The straw hat shook wildly, as if in a high wind.

Then she sat motionless for a moment. Her eyelids fluttered, but stayed shut. "Is that how it's done," she asked then, "among your high-born ladies?"

"You have a lot to learn, *chérie*."

Her eyes opened with hurt. "What?"

"If we stay together long enough," Iselin murmured, "I think I can make quite a lady out of you. In and out of bed."

Elfi's eyes grew round with awe. "Yes?"

He nodded up and down several times, mimicking Walter Staeli's gesture. Almost without thinking about it, he's found the motivation that would get Elfi to do anything for him, even betray her mistress. She must have seen enough of upper-class life as Margit's maid to want some for herself. Well, why not? She was presentable enough. By the time he was finished dangling the rich life in front of her, she would kill for him.

"Elfi," he said then, "be a good girl. Get off me and go to the dresser. You see that little thing that looks like a shiny black capsule? Bring it here."

She yanked down the brim of the white straw hat and made a face. But she did what he asked.

CHAPTER 48

Her dark hair even blacker in the moonlight, Margit stood by the window and looked back into the small inn room at Matt Burris, who lay sleeping on the bed. The night had been too warm at first, but up here in the foothills of the Vosges it was now turning cool. In all her years of poking in and out of these Alsatian wine towns, Margit could never remember having found this one, called Lautenbachzell.

In the still night she could even hear the Zell, a narrow, rushing rivulet, sinking fast through the rocks to the Rhine's flat plain many kilometers below.

The restaurant, the rooms above it, all of Lautenbachzell was a surprise to Margit, as if it had been created just for her to find on this particular night with this particular man. A cool breeze pushed aside the thin curtains and brushed them against her flanks. She shivered for an instant. She had awakened at two in the morning and found it impossible to sleep.

She supposed she had been wrong at lunch to make a scene about what their choices were in this affair. Men didn't like to be faced with choices, especially masculine men like Matt, who conceived it their responsibility to make difficult decisions.

But the fact was that while there seemed to be a hundred baffling questions for them to answer, it was really much simpler than that. It came down to the question of what they wanted to do with their lives.

Matt seemed to have very little interest in the question. Like any man enjoying an intimate affair, he was content to drift along, as if her body were a raft on a pleasant stream, an enjoyable raft, but in essence a vehicle with its own steersman. The limbo in which they pleasured each other would go on for as long as she was able to keep it a secret. After that, Matt would have to face the decision of what he wanted to do with his life.

Her problem was the opposite. She was suffering because she already knew what to do with her life.

It was unfair. She moved impatiently in the moonlight, gesturing with one hand as if talking to a jury.

If it had been this good, this serious, six years ago in the States before she had seen how to be her own master, then she would have been content to become his dutiful wife, following him to Japan, anywhere, a good little UBCO wife and a helluva asset to hubby-poo. Say, and doesn't she come from some sort of banking background herself? I wouldn't be surprised. Swiss, you know.

But it hadn't worked that way. Her understanding of the power she had for the taking grew slowly during the past six years. She had never forgotten him, that was obvious to her now. But she herself had changed from what Matt had called her, a big overgrown girl, brought up in a family atmosphere in which power was only another element of the air. One breathed it, one exhaled it, one hardly noticed it.

But in six years, and because of the way her father had bequeathed his estate, this invisible, commonplace air suddenly had become fiery with meaning. Power was an unfused bomb. Her father's will had activated the fuse. He had then placed control of it in her hands.

She stared across the moonlight shining on the floor of the room to the bed beyond. She could see his chest rising and falling slowly, easily. She was very clear about her life. It was too late for her to become someone's dutiful wife. Would Matt become Prince Consort to her?

She found herself laughing softly, almost choking with the knowledge that there was no knowledge. Only the present existed, precariously. If there were a future, she had no control of it.

How different from other summers. Everything then had been

prearranged, known, under control. She and Erich and their friends would fly to Capri or lounge on the landing at Schloss Staeli overlooking the river. Small, warm, seamless days flowed into each other, predictable, comforting.

The breeze freshened. It sent a shiver through her. She felt chilled as much by the night air sweeping down from the mountains as by her crystalline view of the dilemma. To see it clearly, and yet not see it. What good was power if it left you this unsure?

If she could talk about it with Erich, the two of them might be able to puzzle it out. Perhaps the unthinkable was the answer, marry Erich and live with Matt. But by now she knew the man on the bed. After a summer of lying together, of hearing his life, of pouring out hers, she knew Matt could never handle anything as "European" as a marriage of convenience.

They had led completely different lives. What one did marked one's way of thinking forever. And Matt always had to be up and doing. There had been no leisure for him, nor was there now.

She hugged herself to keep from shivering, crossing her arms over her breasts and trying to still the quaver in her breathing. Erich would know about this. He'd been this close with many women outside his own class, outside Margit's class. Women who had had to cope with the rough part of life, as Matt had. Who had always to solve the series of dilemmas that life presented people like Matt. Who had never panicked in the face of one, as she was now.

But perhaps panic wasn't the word. She could never remember panicking. She could not recall Erich panicking, and he'd been deeper into the muck of the world than she. Even so, even now, even in the unforeseeable future, there was no need to panic. Matt loved her, and all the slowly starving peoples of a famine-haunted world could not change any of the joy she felt. She had reread those earlier jottings in her journal only a day or two ago, the questions she'd meant to look into after that British peer had made her feel that the death of half the world was imminent.

All summer she had not once looked into any of this. The thoughts were buried in her exercise book and she'd never found the time or the need to disinter them. She could have talked about them with Matt. He might have had some reassuring answers.

But it was simpler than that. She'd stopped worrying about people dying. She didn't need to be reassured that the banks who financed the companies were all part of a conspiracy of famine. The questions lay in her journal like those bacilli that become dormant and lie quietly for years before flaring again into infection and death.

These small hours of the night were made for despair.

One worried about everything, most especially things that had been buried because they didn't bear thinking about. She wished she could talk to someone other than her lover. One didn't bother one's lover with the churning of old despairs. One kept these to oneself. It wouldn't be right to bother even Erich with such thoughts.

Staring across at the man lying on the bed, Margit found herself wondering where Erich was lying tonight under this cruel moon. She hoped he was pleased with the woman. She hoped the woman would recognize how special Erich was. She doubted it, though. Who could appreciate his particular brand of being and thinking except someone who had shared it all her life?

Matt was a different kind of man. What he was showed openly. He had never had the leisure to cultivate subtlety, nor was subtlety what Margit wanted from him. But Erich . . . She missed him.

Realizing the inappropriateness of what she was thinking, Margit smiled crookedly in the darkness. She hurried back into bed and lay beside Matt, pulling the sheet over them both as if to shut out any further thoughts of Erich. Outside the wind moaned restlessly.

But it will all work out, she told herself firmly. And one doesn't need Erich to tell one that. One remains an optimist, yes? Anything else makes no sense. Things are always this dark in these small hours of the night.

In the sunlight, everything will work out perfectly.

CHAPTER 49

Erich ransacked the study desk on the top floor of his house. He carelessly looted the drawers, looking for a spare set of keys to the Bentley in the garage. He had handed over a set to Bunter this evening but it was too late to telephone him. The spare keys had to be in the desk.

He found them at last, thrown carelessly into a small tin box that had originally held slender Dutch cigars. He glanced aimlessly at the other keys there, recognizing one to the mailbox downstairs, another to the orange Magna, a pair that unlocked the front and back doors of his vacation cottage, even a spare kitchen key to Schloss Staeli that Margit had given him once, years ago, for some special reason now forgotten.

Funny how intimate they had been, without ever being intimate at all. It was a friendship of trust.

Erich's movements were uneven, almost uncontrolled. He could see the way he grasped and dropped keys, the tremor in his hand. It didn't matter.

He pocketed the keys to the Bentley and clattered down the main stairway to the ground floor, where he made himself as large a scotch as Bunter had given him earlier this evening. This seemed to be alcoholic night, he mused, sipping the drink. And, of course, just when he had to think.

He stared at his face in the mirror frame around the Urs Graf woodcut. First he showed his teeth, like an angry hound. Then he closed his mouth and studied its downturned corners, a clown's mouth. And tonight he had behaved like a clown.

All the better people who had his best interests at heart had been telling him for years that he wasn't serious. He knew he wasn't serious. Life wasn't serious, either, so what was there to be serious about?

Serious people bored him. They obviously didn't know what life really was. They thought there was meaning to life and if one remained sober and serious one could tease the meaning out into the open, like removing a snail from its shell, and then one would be in control of it. But this was nonsense. It led one to behaving nastily, like Walter, or cruelly like his father Dieter, or slimily, like Paul Iselin.

It led to being foolish, like Margit. To being vulnerable, to becoming a target for nastiness, to opening one's bare breast as a target, to being unaware one was doing it, and to letting all these fine Swiss marksmen fill one's heart with lead. Poor Margit.

Erich swallowed down the rest of his drink. He held the Bentley keys in his palm and made them jingle slightly by tossing them up and down. In the emptiness of the house the noise was louder than it should have been. Still watching the clown's face in the Venetian glass, he found himself wondering if Michele could help him protect Margit.

There was a mysterious purpose behind her demand that Margit be brought into an otherwise routine proposal. Did that give Michele a stake in saving Margit's skin? But, really, was this something someone could trust to a stranger? How dare he unburden this on an outsider? It was an appalling breach of his friendship with Margit.

He turned from the window and walked through the inner back door into the garage. The empty space for the L-2 Magna made him wonder where it was tonight. Who was using it with Margit? A decent sort of fiancé would want to know.

He opened the garage door. The moon sparkled on the hurrying Rhine, flaring on the crest of running ripples and waves. Erich breathed in the warm night air and decided he couldn't lay any of this before Michele. But he was already late returning to her villa.

He drove across the river, into and through the old part of Basel, steering quickly along deserted streets in a southwesterly direction through suburbs and nearby Swiss villages. Bruderholz, Binningen, Bottmingen. Something was wrong. Everything began with B. Was he that drunk? Bloody Bentley.

Bien, Benken, Battwil. A fine dew of perspiration broke out on his forehead and upper lip. He was imagining all of this.

He pulled the Bentley over to the shoulder of the two-lane country road and switched off the engine. The moonlight beat down on him. Lunacy. He was moonstruck. There were road signs ahead. He started the car and drove on.

To Borg, Blauen, Bärschwil.

He turned left toward the French border. Michele's villa had been built on a tiny peninsula of Switzerland that poked into the side of Alsatian France toward Bettlach. Or was it Biederthal? Stop all B's!

He knew this to be so. He knew where the villa was. He'd been there as recently as this afternoon. It existed. Forget the B's. The villa was there. She had built it on a fingertip of Switzerland surrounded by France, as if, by going out her own back door, she could emigrate. It was not the kind of island she usually chose, but it was a landlocked island nevertheless.

She was Circe on her island. There was nothing left to the ancient business of turning men to swine. Out of date. The thrill was gone. She turned them, instead, into clowns.

At last Erich found the gate that led, through a thicket of thorn roses, cultivated as a living fence around the property, to the villa. Circe was waiting alone.

And he was bringing her nothing. He hadn't even spoken to Walter. He hadn't trusted himself to speak. He was returning empty-handed and Circe would be angry with the clown. The clown would have to grovel for scraps.

Erich got out of the Bentley and almost ran toward the house. The windows were dark. She had fallen asleep waiting up this late. Clowns cannot be trusted. They are simply not serious.

He stooped and felt under the mat for the key, found it and let himself into the cool foyer. The house was thick-walled masonry that stayed cool even in August heat. It was isolated from everything except, of course, the three incoming telephone trunk lines she needed to maintain her domination of the other clowns.

He moved quietly through the center hall and into the bedroom. He approached the rose-colored bed. Moonlight streamed in through the windows that faced France.

The bed was empty.

He switched on the lamp. The dusky-rose pillows glowed warmly. On the center of the largest pillow lay a pale-pink envelope with his name on it. He tore it open.

"I am traveling," she had written in her tight looping hand, "and cannot be reached. In two weeks, when you have cleared it up, call me in Sardinia. Not before. Undying devotion. M."

Erich sat down on the edge of the bed and put the note to his face. He smelled her perfume. Undying devotion. He fell sideways, pressing his face into the pillow, kissing it until it was damp with his tears.

PART FIVE

The Swiss are the last word in history.
—Victor Hugo

CHAPTER 50

By September the weather had turned a bit cooler. In Colmar the Tanners' Quarter in the old part of town looked even more quaint than usual at this hour of the evening. The orange September sun had reached the horizon. It tinged the whitewashed plaster with a mellowing warmth and brightened the dull brown of cross timbers on the fifteenth-century buildings.

In a room across the square from the arched apartment rented to Berta Hütsch, Paul Iselin sat at the window, shielded by a thin scrim of curtain. The headphones clamped over his ears gave him the whole thing, more than he wanted, background noises, scrapes of chairs, even Burris' hearty sneeze which he could also hear directly through the open window across the Old Custom House square, without benefit of a listening device.

The Nagra tape recorder was reeling slowly, feeding from the sensitive FM receiver next to it on the floor. Iselin monitored the conversation, such as it was. Most of it was a waste of tape. Yet he was afraid to shut down the recorder for fear of missing even a syllable of incriminating material.

He had quite a bit, as it was. He had them calling each other by their first names, an important point of identification, and shortly thereafter producing words and sounds about which there could be no doubt that sexual intercourse was taking place.

He'd gotten this just last week, after two dull, patient weeks of recording useless material. He'd also gotten some very useful information about the UBCO operation. Burris trusted her completely. The Matsui 6001 was still in perfect working condition and its tiny integral battery had at least another month of use before it might begin to run down. It had been well worth the extra money. Iselin wasn't quite sure where Elfi had planted it.

She'd been very upset, at first, about the idea, but Iselin had worked on her for days, feeding her an overcomplicated story about trying to protect Margit Staeli against enemies within her own family. Apparently Elfi had hidden the Matsui 6001 exceedingly well because it had gone everywhere with Margit, tucked away in her golden-tan flight bag, a big shiny black capsule that might lie forever unnoticed in its dark inner recesses.

He listened to water running, typical of these covert surveillances. Once, on an Army assignment, he'd expertly bugged a hotel suite where two businessmen from Hamburg were entertaining not two but four expensive whores at the Drachen Hotel off the Aeschenvorstadt. They'd spent all weekend with the women and all Iselin had been able to produce was a long series of giggles and grunts, a few snatches of singing, long stretches of TV sound and a lot of ice tinkling in glasses. Eloquent, perhaps, but not evidence.

"Do I have to be there?" Margit's voice demanded then.

Iselin sat up straighter. "You don't, unless you want to," Burris responded from a distance, over running water.

"But I'm consumed with curiosity about him."

"Hah." Burris apparently shut off the water. "I'm not."

"So I'm coming, then," was her response after a full minute of silence.

"It would make me happy, anyway," Burris assured her.

The rest was footsteps and some low muttering that even the Matsui 6001 couldn't preserve intact as it transmitted across the Old Custom House square. At one point he seemed to hear Margit Staeli saying something about "stop supporting your weight," but it wasn't evidence of anything, really.

Silence over the headphones now. Iselin turned to a large black attaché case lying open on the bed. He had filled it with folders and tape cartridges. In his spare time he painstakingly edited and transcribed the tapes onto paper. The typed transcripts lay in folders, each marked for the week in which it had been monitored.

This was, if anything, an even more boring part of the assignment than the eavesdropping, but it was too confidential to entrust to a secretary. Besides, the fewer people involved the lower his costs. The mortgage Dieter Staeli had promised him—twenty years at an unheard of 3 per cent per annum and so-called "evergreen" terms—would be more than enough to keep the Iselin mansion from the wrecking crews. But Paul Iselin still had to live. The cash settlement Staeli had promised must be husbanded thriftily.

He checked idly back and forth through the contents of the black attaché case. Everything he had was here. There were no security copies in safe deposit boxes. Iselin had been taught to play this work close to the chest. The tapes were all here, with their transcripts, the affidavit from the waiter at the corner bar downstairs, the next door neighbor and not one but two extremely conscientious gendarmes who didn't really require that much in the way of cash to see their duty and sign affidavits of their own.

The only testimony he was lacking was that of the woman who had rented them the apartment. She also owned the studio-shop where ceramics and sculpture were sold and, for some reason, Iselin had the idea she was a friend of Margit's. It wouldn't do to alert the guilty pair by asking embarrassing questions of their landlady.

A long sigh from Margit. Silence. Rustle of bed linen. Silence. Then Burris: "Unfortunately, that has to keep us happy till tomorrow night."

"Impossible."

Burris: "I imagine the usual separate rooms will prevail."

She giggled. "I have to pack. What's happened to my—"

Background noises. Creak of bed. ". . . exercise book?"

Burris: "I saw it on the desk. Yes, it's—"

Footsteps. "You know," she said then, "our goodly host has the reputation of being a very wise man."

"Probably undeserved."

"He's the man I have to talk to about—"

Rustle of clothing. Murmuring. Burris: "What did you say?"

"Famine. The responsibility of the banks. What can be done. What should be done."

"By Staeli?" His voice indicated a mixture of disbelief and irritation.

"Yes, ultimately. But by every—" Background noise.

"Kee-rist," Burris said then.

"I beg your pardon?"

"Nothing. Let's go, honey."

Silence. Then the *snap!* of the golden leather bag's clasp being shut. Evidently their weekend plans involved visiting someone, but who? A moment later Iselin heard a door slam.

They appeared downstairs, moving toward the garage in the rear of the inner courtyard. Iselin began to pack up his equipment in a flurry of activity. But by the time he had finished, the orange car was nosing out into the square. When Iselin got to his cream-colored Jaguar, the little antique car had already left in the direction of Basel.

Iselin consoled himself with the fact that it would be easy enough to pick up on its trail on the Autobahn or back in his home city. Meanwhile—he patted the black attaché case on the seat next to him—he really had enough material right now. He'd check with Walter Staeli on Monday. A dull and not very pleasant job would soon be ended.

And the family honor would be upheld for all the world to see.

CHAPTER 51

Air connections into Lugano were particularly unreliable that Friday night, but Burris managed to land before the field closed down at 10 P.M. Palmer's chauffeured Daimler met the plane, and Burris, who had already started to resent this command-performance weekend, was somewhat mollified to find Palmer himself waiting patiently in the limousine. The plane had been an hour late, but Palmer had no complaint.

They hadn't met in months and Burris saw that the older man seemed to have lost too much weight. "You've been on some kind of diet?" he asked.

"It's the Palmer Double-T formula. Tennis and tension."

"Tension? What's a retired man doing with tension?"

"No lectures." Palmer's voice had gone cold in an instant. They sat back and watched the corniche lights along the coast of Lake

Lugano as the Daimler moved smoothly down the shoreline toward Morcote.

"That General Motors proposal," Palmer said at last. "What's the outcome?"

Burris tried to match his impersonal tone. He'd made a mistake starting the conversation with a personal remark. But, Christ, Palmer didn't look good. Probably too many people had been telling him that.

"We're accepting most of the paper," he said. "It's coming through Frankfurt but it'll be on Basel's books. By the way, I've combed the last of the old employees out of our hair. I've got a new crew."

"Swiss?" Palmer asked quickly.

"Some. But they're Italian Swiss from around here. I figure they'll stay clean for a while. It'll take the locals at least six months to corrupt them."

"You hope." Palmer sighed impatiently. "This will be our continuing problem with the Swiss operation, security. Until we get big enough and our people start getting premium salaries, we won't be able to keep them honest."

"Uh, look," Burris began with some hesitation, "I thought you knew. I'm paying them premium salaries right now."

A sharp sound escaped Palmer, but he said nothing for a long moment. The Daimler began its tortuous climb over hairpin switchbacks. Then: "Okay, Matt, you're the boss."

"That cost you something to say."

The minute Burris let the thought escape, he was sorry for it. Palmer's glance at him would have drilled a hole through his skull at fifty paces. But, again, the older man kept quiet until he was under control. "I'm jumpy tonight," he said then. "Don't press me."

"Right."

They sat in silence, Burris trying to keep from drifting against Palmer on the curves. The chauffeur knew this road so well that even in the dark he was taking it at a speed that required both passengers to hold onto the strap handles to keep from being thrown against each other.

"Anything I can help with?" Burris asked at last.

"What?"

325

"The problem for tonight."

"Oh." Palmer stared straight ahead at the pine forest illuminated by the Daimler's headlamps. "Disturbing call from Curtis. He's in Brussels. Nothing to do with our operation here, some problem with other branches in Europe. I told him to check it out and get back to me later." He turned to look at Burris. "When is your lady due here?"

"Tomorrow morning, by train."

"Arrival time?"

"It's the overnight sleeper from Strasbourg. Nine A.M."

Palmer leaned forward and spoke to the chauffeur. "Tomorrow morning at nine, Charles. At the *stazione ferrovia* you'll pick up a Miss, ah—" He paused. Burris was about to supply the name, but decided he'd let Palmer show off, if his mind was still up to it. "A Miss Hütsch," the older man said then. He grinned at Burris. "Not bad, eh?" Then, to the driver: "She'll be looking for you and carrying a light-tan leather flight bag." He sat back and produced a smile of self-congratulation.

The car continued to weave back and forth around the hairpin curves until it reached the heights. The driver got out to open one gate, then drove on until he reached the second. Burris saw that Palmer's eyes were shut. Was he asleep? After giving such a sensational performance as the Hawk of Morcote, with a memory that would put a computer to shame, he couldn't destroy the impression now by falling asleep like a tired old geezer.

The Daimler pulled to a halt in the paved parking area. Palmer's eyes opened slowly. "What did you do in the war, Matty?"

"I beg your pardon?"

They were walking to the house, its immense window wall lighted from within. The driver trotted behind them with Burris' overnight bag. "What were you in, Vietnam?" Palmer continued.

"Infantry," Burris said. "A million laughs."

"I'll bet."

They walked inside. Burris had expected to see one or more of the Palmer children—who were really quite adult by now—but then remembered that the school semester had already started back in the States. "Why did you ask?" he said then.

"Wondered if you might have been in Intelligence."

"Too dumb."

Palmer shook his head. "Your security arrangements for Basel show signs of real genius."

Burris wondered if he dared explain that the attractive Miss Hütsch had created all the complex but successful planning that had kept his Basel operation secret until now. With her background and her mind, Margit had found the problem almost elementary. She'd spent her life learning to solve such matters instinctively.

"Anyway," Palmer was saying as he made drinks, "we had a saying in G-2 during the big war." He paused. "Hear that? 'The big war.' I'm getting to sound like one of those beery American Legion drunks left over from the First World War. Anyway, Matty, we had a saying. The first time it happens, it's an accident. The second time, a coincidence. But the third time, it's enemy action."

"The first time what happens?"

"Anything inexplicable. That's what bothers me about this business Curtis has uncovered."

Burris had sunk into one of the leather-padded Barcelona chairs. He watched Palmer pace back and forth for a while holding two drinks, before the older man finally realized what he was doing and handed one over. The room had no single source of light like an overhead fixture, but was illuminated instead by six or seven lamps at table level here and there. Some of the light was focused on modern oil paintings Burris found quite repulsive.

The effect was not glaring, but it tended to pick out peculiar highlights in Palmer's eyes. As he bent over to give Burris his drink, the hot little points of flame burned so brightly for a moment that he looked like something in a chamber of horrors, with a skull-like face and blazing eyes.

"I got a call last week from Bill Elston in New York," Palmer said then, resuming his pacing. "You remember Bill?"

"Head UBCO spook?"

"Curtis' boss," Palmer said, by way of agreement. "It seems that two of our biggest Manhattan clients are getting ready to sue us on grounds of negligence and willful misuse of confidential information for our own profit."

"Huh?"

"Can you believe it? Jet-Tech, the big electronics and rocket company, with millions outstanding on our books? They claim confidential information they revealed to us in a New York meeting has been leaked to their chief competitor, who is proceeding to ruin them."

"I don't get it."

Palmer sipped quickly at his drink. Burris noticed that the level in the glass hadn't gone down at all. He took a healthy swallow of his own. If this was going to be Palmer's long-winded night, he was glad Margit wasn't here yet.

"It worked this way," Palmer was explaining. "The Jet-Tech team came in for a powwow on some new projects that needed financing. A very hush-hush deal involving the use of supercooled circuitry on high-efficiency magnets. Another one relating to quadrupling the number of telephone messages that can be sent simultaneously over one wire. Potentially big stuff. Profitable. And, of course, while we don't have to know where every nut and bolt fits, we do demand a fairly full idea of how far along they are and how they plan to spend our money. All of this information, they claim, we leaked or sold to Dynofarben Teknik of Düsseldorf, a recent purchase of the Kuwaitis."

"UBCO *sold* information?"

"That they'll never be able to prove," Palmer assured him, "but they make one hell of a case for the rest. The new projects were so secret not even their own people knew what was revealed in our conference room. And worse, some added wrinkles they unveiled only to us had been dreamed up just a day or two before this meeting. But Dynofarben had the new wrinkles, too."

"Sounds damaging."

"To the tune of twenty million dollars in damages."

"And they're really going ahead with the lawsuit?" Burris asked.

"But you haven't heard the other one." Again Palmer sipped without in any way lowering the level of his drink. Burris wondered if he really were ill. Had the doctor taken him off booze? Was he pretending to keep up his usual façade, at least in front of one of his own executives?

"This was a service-company client, one of the big car-rental outfits. They wanted to hit us for financing of a new approach to computerized reservations. Had their ad campaign all worked out, the hardware was on line ready to run if we'd pay for it. I'll be damned if their biggest competitor didn't uncork the same ad campaign before they ever got the chance to use it. Christ, they were mad. And at us, of course. Now you can see what I meant before?"

"About what?"

"The old saying we had in Army Intelligence?"

Burris nodded. "This is the second time and it's coincidence. Maybe."

"But!" Palmer produced the monosyllable with such force that Burris shifted uncomfortably in his chair. The old boy was not acting right, not himself. Too intense, too wrapped up in this.

"But," he exploded again. "What Curtis called from Brussels with is Incident Number Three. A copper-wire manufacturer discussed a new alloy with us less than a month ago. Today Watanabe, Ltd. of Osaka has come out with their own version, same alloy, same properties. You could call that sheer coincidence, and our Brussels people are doing just that. But with what I know from New York, Matty, I can no longer call it anything but enemy action."

Palmer resumed his pacing. Burris watched him. Was it possible, he found himself wondering, that the adage he'd been taught all his life in athletics was just not true? Healthy mind in a healthy body? Palmer's body was healthy enough, thin as spring steel and twice as flexible. He strode like a demon long-distance walker, like someone atoning for a sin, working his body to use up what must have been an awful overload of energy.

When the telephone rang, Palmer spun on one toe, as if about to smash a tennis ball. He had been holding his drink in his right hand. Now his right arm swiveled around, elbow crooked, wrist stiff and bent back for a forehand smash. Whisky and soda splashed soundlessly onto the heavy carpet.

"I'll get it," Palmer snapped. He leaped for the bar counter and had the telephone off the hook before the second ring.

Sound body, anyway, Burris thought.

"Okay, shoot," Palmer was saying. His dark-gray eyes searched the room as his mind took in what was being said over the telephone. "London? Yes, yes, I see." His glance darted wildly here

329

and there. He had begun to scare Burris a little. Then, suddenly, Palmer's lids went halfway down. *"What?"*

The silence in the room was abrupt. It seemed to carry even more tension than Palmer's words. Listening, eyes lidded, he vibrated a taut, coiled power more noticeably than when he snapped out his demands.

Finally he sat down against the counter and crossed his legs before him in their white duck trousers. "Is . . . that . . . so?" he said then, all calmness. "You're sure of it, Curtis?" He nodded once, then again.

"Good man! Good man! Christ, this complicates the hell out of it, eh? But at least I'm relieved. Yes, he's here. The lady arrives tomorrow. What?" Palmer chuckled slightly. "Just playing Cupid, as always," he said then in a tone Burris didn't like. Palmer finished talking and hung up.

"Well." The older man picked up his drink, half of which had spilled without his noticing. He frowned and carefully topped it up with more scotch and soda. Then he put it down on the counter and ignored it.

"Fascinating," he said then. "Our London office has had precisely the same problem with a Manchester rolled-steel client. They had divulged to us their marketing plans for Africa. Two weeks later, an Arab firm outbid them on each and every contract by undercutting a few cents a pound across the board. The Arabs seemed to know precisely what the Manchester prices had been. And the prices had been discussed in only one place, our London office."

"That's not three, it's four," Burris pointed out. "Enemy action twice."

"No, it's something else."

Palmer sat down opposite him and seemed to have not a care in the world. He looked suddenly younger, carefree, his arms out on each side of him lying easily along the back of the sofa on which he lounged. Burris had never seen such a change so quickly in anyone, let alone Palmer.

"Here's where an agent like Curtis earns his keep twice over," Palmer continued. "I know you don't like him. He's said as much, and I can't blame you because you know, if it came to it, he'd be spying on you. For the good of the cause. But Curtis is a real pro. Imagine what he's learned."

"Whatever it is, it's taken a load off your mind."

Palmer smiled sleekly. "He's learned that the Barclay's bank in London is already being sued on a similar charge by one of their clients. So is the Staeli bank in Lausanne, Bank of America's Los Angeles office and Chase Manhattan in Madrid. Isn't that interesting?"

"Interesting? It's frightening."

"But at least it isn't directed solely against UBCO."

"Some sort of industrial espionage system in banks, selling clients' secrets to business rivals?" Burris finished his drink and stood up. "I suppose it was only a matter of time," he added, going to the bar. "Too many juicy secrets get hashed over in bank conference rooms."

"But an espionage system with global connections," Palmer said. "A thing that takes a lot of people and a lot of money. Only one group could handle it, the Mafia, and it's beyond them. Their minds don't operate that way."

Burris made himself a new drink and saw Palmer's freshened one standing untouched. The old boy was definitely off the sauce. Medical reasons?

"They could handle a piece of it," Burris suggested. "They might not be able to collect information or evaluate it. But their contacts are terrific for peddling the stuff."

"Possibly."

Palmer's body, lounging at ease, began to tighten as he stood up. "I think I'm in good shape now for bed. I've been worrying about this all week." He indicated some books and magazines. "Stay up as late as you want. Watch the TV. Your room is the second down the hall on the right." He smiled pleasantly. "Too bad your lady couldn't make it here tonight."

"It's a security problem for her. In fact, I wasn't too happy about extending your invitation to her. But she wants to meet you."

Palmer nodded as if this were the most natural thing in the world. "You're good at handling security problems, Matty."

"So is she."

"What's the status of—? Well, perhaps that's an unfair question."

The two men stood facing each other for a moment. "What was that business you mentioned to Curtis on the phone," Burris heard himself saying. He could hear the edge of grievance in his voice. "That business about playing Cupid?"

Palmer's dark-gray eyes went wide with innocence. "It's a perfectly ordinary comment."

"Playing Cupid, as always," Burris repeated. "That's how you put it, wasn't it?"

"I'm sure there's nothing wrong with your recollection," the older man responded after a moment. His voice had gone cold again. "Good night, Matty. Sleep well." He turned and left without another word of explanation.

Jesus, Burris thought, nothing works with him. He's all wrapped up in his own cocoon of power and anxiety and plotting. But damned if I'm going to be part of his plots, some kind of chessman on his board. Or Margit, either, for that matter. If Palmer had been playing games with the two of them—

Burris suddenly sat down against the countertop. "Playing Cupid, as always?" Suppose . . . No, but suppose this whole assignment had . . . Suppose the only reason Palmer had brought him to Basel was because he'd once had an affair with the very powerful and very beleaguered Miss Staeli? Could Palmer be quite that cruel?

CHAPTER 52

That Saturday morning, early, Erich Lorn was already on the telephone. He called Schloss Staeli, not because he had anything definite to say to Margit. As a matter of fact, he had decided not to alarm her with what he had learned some time before about Paul Iselin and Walter Staeli. At least, not until he had to.

But Erich needed someone to talk to and Margit was possibly the only one in all of Basel with whom he felt comfortable any more. He had called to thank her for returning the little vintage sports car and to ask if she needed it any more. Uschi, the house-keeper, had told him that, yes, Miss Margit had been home all last night "for a change," she had added archly. "But before I wake up, Herr Lorn, she is gone. Pfüff! Vanished."

Erich hung up and stared at the top of his study desk. It was depressing up here. It hadn't been cleaned in months because he forbade Bunter to enter this third-floor retreat. He knew Bunter occasionally did, nevertheless, but there was no sign of any recent cleaning. Filthy sty. Speckled with debris. Crumpled sheets of paper. Broken pencils. An old sock. How had he managed to turn this into such a zoo? He hadn't even been here that much.

Two weeks ago, when Michele's ultimatum had expired, Erich had tried calling her in the small villa she owned off the Costa Smeralda shore of Sardinia. No one answered for days and then a cleaning woman, in barbarous Italian, had explained that Madame Michele was not expected until November.

The idea that she was hiding from him soon dawned on Erich. He had wasted a week getting through to a Sardinian maid. Now his mind began to revolve more rapidly, throwing off sparks like those little colored lights produced by the children's toys.

One pumped the handle, Erich remembered very clearly from his youth, and a tin wheel revolved against a flint and sparks showered behind windows of colored mica. Red, blue, yellow. Hoop-la!

He then spent a solid day in this study trying to get through to her cottage in the Hebrides, without success. He tried Malta, then Kos, then Sark. Days passed. He found trays of food left outside the study door. He nibbled, sipped, left most of the food, lived chiefly on scotch, neat.

He had shaved once, last week. His ideas were giving out. There were no more islands for him to telephone, either because they had no phone or because Michele had never revealed their exist-ence. Dozen of islands of which he knew nothing and on which platoons of young men were servicing her in relays.

Of course there might only be one island, one secret place and one young man. It really didn't matter. Daily he drove to the villa southwest of Basel. He even once managed to shave and spruce himself up and drive south to Michelebad for a directors' meeting. They had not only let him in, but he'd asked for a tour of the place and examined every laboratory, every office, every storeroom. No Michele.

It had been an embarrassing meeting because he had nothing to report on the Staeli loan. But he no longer worried about embarrassment.

It finally came to him that Michele really had not issued any orders barring him. It came to him, in the end, that he wasn't that important to her any more, now that he'd let the whole Staeli proposal hang fire. He hadn't called Walter once. He'd tried to talk to Margit, but the one time he'd managed to telephone her he couldn't bring himself to discuss it because he couldn't bring himself to talk about Michele.

Everything conspired against him. He couldn't move the proposal along because it reminded him of Michele and what she had done to him. And he couldn't think of Michele without being plunged into the most terrifying condition of his soul.

It wasn't depression, he thought now, staring at the telephone on his desk. It wasn't anger. It was . . . frenzy? She somehow inspired him to a quick, pointless, revolving, completely mad activity, the spastic jerking and strutting of a cock whose head had already been lopped off, lunging and twitching brilliantly in his own bright spout of life's blood.

Blindly. Because the blood blinded one. Because not having one's head deprived one of eyes.

He slammed out of his study and ran down the spiraling stairs two at a time until he reached the door to the garage.

"Master Erich, sir?"

Bunter's voice. To hell with Bunter. Erich ran into the garage, flung open the door, jumped over the door into the open L-2 Magna and roared out onto the Unterer Rhineweg in the direction of the main bridge that led across to Grossbasel. He was driving a bit carelessly, but not that much, as he drove over the bridge, narrowly missing the long slim snout of one of the electric streetcars rushing across in the opposite direction.

He shot down an incline toward the Barfusserplatz and happened to glance in the mirror in time to see a cream-colored Jaguar behind him. He frowned, pulled the Magna in a hard turn and headed southwest for his daily check of Michele's villa. The Jaguar stayed with him.

In Binningen, or perhaps it was Bien or Brüderholz, he realized that the damned Jag was really following him. He downshifted to second, tramped on the brakes and whipped the ancient sports car around a corner into a little alley. Then he hid the car behind a hedge. In a plume of dust and a squeal of brakes the cream-colored Jag hurtled around the corner and kept pelting along the alley.

Erich pulled the Magna out behind it and followed closely, wondering how long the idiot at the wheel would take to realize he'd been outfoxed. "Iselin!" he shouted over the roar of both engines. "Iselin, you fool!"

The Jaguar slowed to a halt and Erich braked behind him. Both men got out of their cars. Paul Iselin grinned half-heartedly. "I didn't realize it was you, Erich."

"You thought it was Margit in my car."

The shorter man said nothing. They had halted on a hedge-lined road that lay almost in deep country. The last suburban house had been passed several blocks back. In the distance a copse of oaks had already begun to shed its leaves. The September breeze was cool but pleasant. A bird sang in the hedge.

"Why?" Iselin asked then. "That is, I beg your pardon."

"I know about the whole thing," Erich said then. He found he was breathing hard, as if they had been pummeling each other. "Life is short. The Staelis all eat their young."

Iselin looked confused for a moment. "What, Erich?"

"Lie down with dogs, get up with fleas." Erich shook his head as if to clear it. He realized he wasn't making sense. Oh, it made sense to him. But he knew he was simply confusing this rotten lackey of an Iselin.

The bird chirruped merrily. He seemed to have no idea that summer was over. "Listen to me, Iselin," Erich said then. "You are a famous spy. We all know this. It was shameful enough of the Army to corrupt an Iselin into spying. But it is unforgivable that you do this for private gain. Even this is not the worst. Tell me, what in the name of God can Walter Staeli pay you to make you spy *on your own kind?*"

That did it, he noticed. That finally communicated clearly. Iselin glanced nervously at his car. "My own kind?" he fenced.

"You are betraying a girl we have both known since we were

babies together. A good girl. One who has never wronged you, Pauli. You know this. I who am her fiancé, I assure you she has never wronged you."

The color seemed to rise in Iselin's cheeks. "Me? Perhaps not. But are you foolish enough to think she hasn't wronged you?"

Erich shrugged. He felt suddenly hot in the cool breeze. He stared hard at the copse of trees, then at Iselin, then at his own thumbnail. Needs cleaning. "You and Margit and I, we are of one breed," he said then.

"And so is Walter."

"Walter is a turd that walks like a man."

For some reason Iselin smiled slightly. "Be that as it may," he said then, "you have no right to intrude on my business with him."

"Intrude?" Erich was horrified to notice that he had taken a long step forward and grasped Iselin's jacket by its lapels. He saw that he was pulling up on the jacket and lifting the little man off his feet. "You follow me at high speed and accuse me of intruding? You dirty, treacherous little spy."

He slammed Iselin down so hard he heard the man's teeth click. He stepped back and surveyed him. "There is nothing a Basler wouldn't do for money, is that it, Iselin?"

"Don't Basler me," the younger man said petulantly.

The bird twittered on. Go south, Erich thought. He turned to the bird. "Fly!" he called. "It's summer down there." He whirled on Iselin again. "Pauli," he said, "Baslers are not like that. Don't let them fool you. Baslers are not mercenaries for hire to the largest purse. We have a prouder history than that."

"Erich, I'm getting tired of this."

"In our city, when Europe crawled with barbarism, we once held up a torch of humanity," Erich said. He sighed heavily. Then, to the bird: "I told you what to do. Do it."

"Erich, enough."

"Pauli, there was a reason Erasmus fled from Rotterdam to Basel. Basel welcomed him, Pauli, just as we welcomed Nietzsche. Remember Jacob Burckhardt, Pauli? Remember Holbein and Paracelsus? We have a tradition, Pauli."

"Listen." Iselin turned and opened the door of his Jaguar. "I can see you're upset about being followed. All right. It was an honest mistake and I—"

"Honest?" Erich's voice clawed at his throat, turning it raw. "Honest?" he croaked. "You dishonor us all. You dishonor Erasmus and Burckhardt and Bernoulli and—"

Iselin got in the car and slammed the door. "Ancient history," he said, starting the engine. "Can you get back under your own power?"

"What?" Erich was shocked to hear the way the single syllable screamed in his ears. Had he shrieked it aloud? He saw that he had grabbed Iselin's left arm and was yanking on it.

The smaller man shrugged free, threw the Jaguar in gear and roared off, his rear wheels spinning up a great cloud of choking dust.

Under my own power. Erich repeated silently. What did that mean? Was Iselin implying that there was something wrong with him?

CHAPTER 53

By Sunday noon, everyone in Valangin had gotten church well out of the way.

Outside town, in the village whose factory sign still carried the name of a watch company, the six-wheeled motorized vans from the state television network had arrived and linked up to each other by massive cables as thick as a man's arm.

In one van, control studio monitors already displayed colorful test patterns. In another, the generators hummed, but not too loudly. Cameramen had begun to assemble dolly-trucks and mount color cameras on them.

The village, much smaller than Valangin, supplied most of the laborers for the watch factory. Today these men looked strangely pale, the result not so much of working indoors by artificial light but because they had scrubbed themselves down by several layers of skin and now glistened whitely like peeled grapes.

A contingent of villagers had elected to appear in traditional peasant costume. The rest were to dress in their Sunday best, direct from church, as if this were the way one always looked in a sleepy little hamlet.

The elderly mayor—whose office had nearly been eliminated some years ago when Valangin tried to incorporate the village—had gone to Neuchâtel the previous day to rent a complete father-of-the-bride outfit, gray striped morning coat with hammerclaw tails, boiled shirt, dark trousers with silk side stripes, patent-leather shoes, gray spats, a gray top hat and pretied bowtie which clipped on in a mysterious fashion the mayor's wife could not fathom.

Whatever she did, the tie hung there drunkenly. She was sure that when he began to orate—she had married a man who even now, in his sixties, had a full, strong, tireless voice—the tie would fly off and hit someone in the eye. On national television!

It had been suggested by the vague young man who taught the schoolchildren in the first three grades, before they were old enough to be bussed to Valangin each morning, that it might make a pretty scene to have a Maypole. The plant manager had telephoned Basel and the distant Herr Staeli, the kind gentleman with yellow hair and pale eyes, had said that a Maypole in September made very little sense. He suggested something to do with the forthcoming grape harvest.

As a matter of fact, more than a dozen of the vineyard wagons had been mobilized for the event. Most of Saturday had been spent decorating them with red and white crepe-paper bunting and small Swiss flags, all shipped down from Basel by Herr Staeli's office.

The kind gentleman himself arrived at Valangin about one in the afternoon, cast a quick glance over the wagons, checked the pseudo peasants in their costumes and beamed approval.

Then the plant manager took him on an inspection tour of the factory. Walter Staeli angrily ordered the remnants of the Japanese packing crates labeled "Auto Parts" and other misleading words to be daubed over with paint and rendered unreadable at once. They then set up high walls of Staelicomp cartons to shield the offending Japanese crates.

"It is too late to turn them," Walter growled. "But once the television crews leave, every one of these crates must go into the furnace. Understood?"

338

"Absolutely, Herr Staeli." The manager had never seen the kind gentleman angry before.

Now a second car arrived from faraway Basel with three of Herr Staeli's assistants. They called a meeting with the television producer, director, the village mayor and the vague schoolmaster. Wristwatches were consulted. The timepieces were reset to match the face of the electronic clock in the mobile control room.

"This will run under fifteen minutes, you understand," the television producer explained, "and we have to make use of every second. It's live, not tape." He wore a khaki safari jacket and chukka boots and looked terribly harassed.

The mayor nodded knowingly, but it was one of the Staeli assistants who spoke. "Then we have to omit the mayor's speech," he said. "Herr Staeli has five minutes of remarks. We need five minutes in the factory. The rest is local color, yes?"

"Just a moment," the mayor began, fingering his treacherous tie and thinking of the rental cost of his clothing.

"Better yet," the producer said, turning so that the mayor could not see his wink, "we end the transmission with the mayor's speech. That way, it can go on just as long as he wants. Good enough, sir?" he asked the mayor.

He nodded and began adjusting the tie again. The television director, a woman in a mauve jumpsuit, reached over and with two deft movements firmly anchored the tie. "Better?" She patted his cheek.

"Much better."

"We're going to have a wonderful celebration," she told him with a big smile. "Look, even the sun is shining."

CHAPTER 54

As he sat there after Sunday brunch, Burris began to understand a little better Palmer's style of living and entertaining.

A chef and his housekeeper wife lived beyond the tennis courts in their own house. They slipped into the main house each morning, silently cleaned up and left in the ovens and refrigerator the meals for the day. Then they vanished, perhaps even left the mountaintop aerie itself for a half day off. In any event, Palmer and his guests then heated and served to themselves what goodies had been left behind by the invisible elves. It gave life on top a fake do-it-yourself air that annoyed Burris. But he had already started being annoyed from the moment Margit had gotten there.

Palmer seemed to take particular delight in hanging the steamier jobs on Margit. It was she who was delegated the heating of the still-warm *quiche* and the crusty individual servings of country *pâté en croûte,* while Palmer mixed the Bloody Marys, involving much arcane nonsense with freshly squeezed limes and the reduction of a stalk of celery to liquid in a special machine. Burris was assigned the setting of the bar-counter table.

"And if anyone wants eggs, Margit, I'm sure you can handle the order." Palmer had smiled blandly.

He seemed quite different from the tightly strung, half-loony character of last night, Burris decided, or even the unnaturally calm half-loony he had become after the Curtis telephone call.

Palmer obviously had two distinct styles, one with men and another when attractive women were on hand. With male associates he really hid none of those inner frustrations that made him seem to vibrate at times like a diesel engine whose governor has broken. But as soon as the Daimler had arrived with Margit, Palmer had smoothed out, slowed down, perked up and become exactly what Margit had been interested in meeting, a rather attractive older man with quite a background, grown children, divorced first wife, and in-residence mistress whom no one had yet seen. And, through it all, he managed to suggest, subtly, that he was still the retired head of a bank somewhat bigger than even the Staeli bank, although smaller than the entire scope of Staeli holdings.

Power attracts power, Burris thought as he watched Margit and Palmer after brunch was over.

They liked each other, of course. The background was similar throughout and probably identical in some details. And they both cultivated that slightly bland, who-me? style, he noted, as if they earned their living like everyone else, perhaps at unimportant or academic jobs.

Palmer in this guise could probably pass as a professor in a very

340

high-class university, with a few books to his credit. Margit could have been anyone successful, underdecorated without being plain, an attorney in a prestigious partnership, possibly even a doctor.

You knew at a glance they didn't work with their hands, either of them. It was the way they used their fingers and wrists. There was something, Burris reflected, about manual labor that stiffened the joints and slowly, over the years, began to turn the manual laborer back into a primate that had lost thumb-finger opposition. He'd seen this first in his own father.

Even the way they sat, each neatly occupying just a certain amount of his or her own body territory, never moving over the line or shrinking back from filling what belonged to them, even this spoke of a similar class training. So did their equal ability to produce utterly seamless wall-to-wall conversation without a single awkward pause.

But the thing that offended Burris most—although he carefully reminded himself that he was in no way offended—was their constant efforts to *draw him into* their conversation. As if he had no way of breaching it himself. As if he were that interested. As if he hadn't thoughts of his own to mull over.

The fact that now and then one of them would look across to him and ask what he thought about something, instead of reassuring Burris, had finally begun to chase him up the wall. He was *not* subnormal. He was *not* a deaf-mute. He was perfectly capable of initiating a thought on his own.

Burris knew, as sure as he was sitting here, that Margit had been taught this kind of social grace, if that was the right name for it, as part of the responsibility someone as moneyed and powerful as she had to take seriously when mingling with her inferiors. Palmer had learned the knack, too, but was rustier at it. And the fact that Burris hadn't opened his mouth in half an hour had probably begun to worry Palmer, as it was meant to.

". . . reserving a great deal more oil for petrochemical use than as fuel," he was saying.

They had gone over the surprisingly long list of people they knew in common, drifted into discussing places they both liked and were now at the core of what interested bankers most, making more money. Burris was shocked at his own resentment. He was a banker, too, wasn't he? But not, he realized, born to it.

". . . and some of the Swiss energy companies," she was saying, "are moving into nuclear production of power to supplement hydroelectric means. Matt," she went on smoothly, "they tell me the U.S. oil companies are trying to diversify that way, too."

Burris sighed unhappily. "That's right," he said, breaking his long silence. "They're all afraid the government will take over oil production one way or another, starting with regulation of prices and profits."

A strained silence fell over all three of them. Margit glanced at her wristwatch. "You will have to excuse me, but at two o'clock we have our Sunday magazine of television. Something to do with Staeli is scheduled for today. You know how it is, one normally wouldn't notice, but as it's my name, it rather leaped out of the page at me yesterday. We still have a quarter of an hour to wait."

"Certainly," Palmer agreed. "And later, when the sun has lost its sting, perhaps we can have a game or two."

"Tennis?" she asked. "I've brought no clothes."

"We have them, and in your size, I think."

"That's very good of you." Her glance shifted sideways to Burris and he could see she was about to ask him whether he played tennis. But she didn't, fortunately.

Somehow, over the long summer, they had had other things on their mind than tennis. And yet, Burris realized, they knew each other well enough to know that she played and he didn't. And what's more, Burris told himself now, she also knows what I think about tennis players. It's a fake sport, like any game where you don't handle the ball yourself, where your own body isn't really a part of the dodging and shifting and head-on contact. Basketball he accepted, and soccer. Not tennis. He knew it was stupid of him, but he'd never shied at recognizing his own stupidities.

He settled back in the upholstered sofa and half-listened to their resumed conversation. He realized that among his other stupidities, he was jealous of Palmer, who seemed determined to win Margit to him as if he were a suitor. And had.

The older man got to his feet. "I'll see about something long and cool to drink during television. Any suggestions?"

Margit looked up at him. "Anything."

"Matt?"

"Beer."

"Yes, for me too, please," Margit added quickly.

Palmer left the living room. They could hear him far back in the rear of the kitchen, opening and closing doors. "I don't really have to watch television," Margit murmured just above the level of inaudibility. "But he is boring me to distraction, this man."

Burris stared at her. "Huh?"

"You didn't tell me," she said in a tiny mutter, "that he was so dull."

Burris got to his feet. He could feel the grin on his face growing so wide his cheek muscles hurt. "You see," he said in a carrying tone, "it's a matter of energy priorities. For example, it takes nearly twice as much energy to make a paper bag as a polyethylene bag. So why burn oil to make paper when you can convert oil directly into polyethylene?"

Margit placed her hand over her mouth and clamped it shut to keep from laughing. After a moment she slowly released the following statement: "Yes . . . quite."

"More than that," Burris continued loudly, "it takes over twice as much energy to make a no-return glass bottle than a bottle of polyvinyl chloride. You see the problem."

Palmer returned suddenly with three beers on a tray. "Stop boring the young lady," he said in a light tone. He held the tray for Margit. "I've been doing a better job of it than you ever could."

"Not boring," Margit demurred, "fascinating."

"Only if Matty is explaining it," Palmer said, handing Burris his beer. Burris accepted it, feeling better than he had all morning. He began to discern that there was something warped about his own powers of observation when it came to people outside his class. Palmer was not really a stuffed shirt, it seemed. He already knew Margit wasn't.

The older man had bent over a large Phillips color television set and was twiddling the dials. "Up this high we get the best reception in Europe," he was saying. "What channel is this program?"

"Four, I believe."

He clicked into the closing of a panel show in which three earnest men faced each other and pretended to be chatting while over them the credits for the program crawled slowly upward. Palmer adjusted the sound and came back to his beer. "It's almost two o'clock."

Margit glanced at Burris, but said nothing. Burris shifted in his chair and sipped the beer. "Does the Staeli section come on soon?" he asked then.

"Matt's bored already," Palmer interjected.

"Sunday afternoon television is the same all over the world," Burris responded. "It's created for people who aren't home to watch it."

Margit burst out laughing in a way that told Burris she was releasing a lot of pent-up tension. "But here we sit, and it's my fault. Matt, I should think you'd already be sick and tired of the Staeli name."

"It's selective," he said. "Some Staelis I can stand."

This convulsed Margit again. "There," she said at length, pointing to the television screen. "It's some sort of ship-launching ceremony in Basel."

"Is that the Staeli part of it?"

They watched a terribly chic but quite fat woman smash a champagne bottle on the prow of a long, low freighter bearing Swiss flags. The ship slid sideways with a great splash into the water and crowds cheered.

"Mattilda Fügli," Margit said. "This happened Thursday last at the shipyards north of Basel. All her clothes are Givenchy but she isn't allowed to say so. Givenchy won't let her."

"Understandable," Palmer murmured.

Margit sipped her beer while various officials expounded on the tremendous value to the national economy of the Swiss merchant fleet, plying the Rhine with bulging cargos of international amity and profit.

They sat in further silence through another feature in which a group of reservists in the white Alpine battalion uniforms demonstrated their prowess with Oerlikon submachine guns as they skied downhill past targets. The noise seemed faint and faraway, swallowed by immense stretches of Alpine snow. The troops produced an amazing record of accuracy. The targets showed the outline of a man's torso from groin to head. They managed to pepper it with holes until the paper started to shred.

"Neat," Palmer said then. "I mean the idea of staging this in the snow. We have no way of seeing how many rounds missed the target."

344

It was Burris who laughed at this. "You see," he told Margit, "the Swiss have to get up very early in the morning to fox Palmer."

"There," she said, pointing to the screen.

"What?"

"The man with the pale hair. My cousin Walter. Sh."

The announcer began at a high level of enthusiasm, which didn't quite match the idea of this little village plunged into economic disaster by the failure of its watch factory. Margit translated some of it in quick snatches. The cameras roved here and there among the gathered villagers, lingering on those in peasant costume and spending an inordinate amount of time on a parade of vineyard wagons, each pulled by a tiny mule.

"The savior comes," Margit murmured then as the cameras cut back to Walter, accepting the handshakes of several ancient citizens and leading the way into the factory.

Now the camera work grew more intricate, flashing from long views of the benches with men in their Sunday clothes working on the small calculators, to close-ups of Walter and the plant manager holding up one of the instruments and explaining not only how useful it was but how many had already been sold.

"That can't be where they're made," Palmer said. The upturn in his voice indicated a question of sorts.

"Why not?" Burris asked.

"That's just an assembly plant."

Walter closed by saying that as crucially important as this was to the economy of the village, Valangin and the Neuchâtel area, this brilliant commercial success would also spell salvation for the entire Swiss precision-parts industry.

He promised that the full technical and financial background of the amazing adventure would be disclosed in detail via a press conference tomorrow afternoon in Basel at which the press of the entire world would be present to witness this new triumph of Swiss determination and skill.

Margit had been translating the dialect as Walter rattled along. Now she stopped so that the mayor could be shown in all his glory.

"Could you do that part again?" Palmer asked. "A press conference in Basel when?"

"Tomorrow afternoon. At two-thirty, I believe."

The mayor was speaking in his full, deep voice. The camera panned from him past the shining, scrubbed faces of villagers and their children, none of whom were watching the mayor. All eyes were on Walter Staeli, who stood modestly a few yards away, beaming and patting down his blond hair. Something the plant manager whispered in his ear caused Walter to begin nodding slowly, steadily, judiciously. As he did so, the plant manager held out a Staelicomp calculator to him.

The director switched to a tight telephoto close-up of the plastic instrument. The focus was so sharp that the name Staelicomp could be read clearly on the television screen. Fade to black.

Fade in, grass-covered playing field near Zurich where a motorcycle meet was already in progress, the machines blatting noisily and churning up chunks of turf. Palmer reached over to switch off the set.

"I'm sorry, Margit," he said then. "I'm afraid I didn't follow your simultaneous translation that closely. Did he say they've already sold a lot of these things?"

"Thousands of them, as I understand it."

Palmer nodded thoughtfully. "That's why Bill Elston sent one t—" He jumped up and disappeared in the rear of the house.

Margit frowned at Burris. "How soon can we leave?" she asked in her best *sotto voce*.

"There's a plane out at five and a train at six."

"*Wunderbar*. You take the train, *chérie*. I've had enough of it."

"Fine."

"I thought I recognized the logotype," Palmer said, returning to the living room with the Staelicomp calculator Elston had sent to Curtis by Palmer's daughter. "I've been playing with it all this month. I understand we've bought dozens."

Margit took the machine and idly punched up some numbers. "I see."

"You don't sound that enthusiastic," Palmer went on. "This is a tremendous marketing coup for Staeli. Your cousin must be quite pleased with himself."

Margit's smile grew slightly off center. "Walter is always pleased with himself," she said then, "and in my experience he rarely

346

needs a reason." She handed the machine to Burris, who began testing its various built-in capabilities.

"There's one like this the Japanese introduced this spring, before I left Tokyo," he said then. "It does the same things, but the keyboard layout's a bit different."

"The surprising thing is that the Swiss can make these at a competitive price," Palmer suggested.

"When you live four years in Japan," Burris said then, "you get a kind of feel for the way they design things, how they finish off a product, even the Japanese style in this." He pointed to the simulated-leather look of the black plastic covering. "I imagine the Swiss based theirs on a Japanese original."

"Never," Margit stated flatly. "The Japanese copy. The Swiss invent."

"Hear, hear." Palmer smiled at her. "But I think this could be based on Japanese ideas. Not copied, but based on."

Burris was turning the instrument over in his hands. "It says 'Made in Switzerland,'" he mused. "Would you mind if I took a look inside?"

"Go ahead."

Burris kept turning the calculator in his hands until he found what he was looking for. He sank his thumbnails into a slot and carefully pried the two plastic halves open as if the instrument were a large clam. He stared at the circuits inside for a moment. Then he turned over the half that held them and shook gently. Everything slid out into his upturned palm.

"Three, no, four layers of printed circuitry," he said. "A lot of integrated and F.E.T. stuff. Cut-and-dried for the Japanese. It's even their kind of phenolic-based resin that supports the circuits."

Palmer had come over to look at the innards of the calculator. Now Margit joined them. All three stared down into the machine's guts. "No other legends of manufacture," Palmer said then. "Just the 'Made in Switzerland' on the case."

"It's not made in Japan," Burris assured him. "They're very proud of what they do. They label everything 'Made in Japan.' They'd never let someone buy the circuits from them and assemble the gizmo in another country and pretend it was his work. They're very touchy about that, so they always overlabel their stuff."

"None of that here," Palmer muttered. "It's free of labeling."

"This thing," Margit said then.

"What?"

Her long, narrow hand faltered for a moment. Then her index fingernail gently touched something black and shiny. "Can you let me see this more clearly?"

Burris carefully lifted the top layer of circuitry. The three of them stared at the large black plastic pill. Its size dwarfed the subminiaturized solid-state devices around it.

"Somebody lost a vitamin capsule," Palmer said then.

"Or a giant jelly bean," Burris guessed.

"Licorice," Palmer added.

"You—" Margit's voice stopped suddenly. "I th—" She stopped again.

Then she straightened up and went to her golden-tan flight bag. She delved inside. "Wait," she said. "This is utterly—" She pulled out a large cloisonné Easter egg. "My pillbox, I—" She stopped again and opened the egg, bringing it over to them. "Look," she said.

They peered down at a collection of small blue tablets, some long brown pills and one very large shiny black plastic capsule.

"What do you take it for?" Burris asked. "Vitamins?"

"It's not mine. I saw it in there just yesterday. It's a capsule I've never seen before. I thought at first, well, perhaps I've just forgotten. So I left it in there. Until now. Until today."

"And it's not yours?" Palmer asked. "May I?"

He picked the black capsule out of the pillbox. Holding it at some distance from his eyes, he rotated the thing slowly. "Here, look." He indicated two tiny slots, one next to the other. "These little slots."

Burris frowned down at the gutted calculator in his hand. He touched the black plastic capsule inside and slowly pulled it free. He rotated the capsule. "There," he said. "Two little slots. They connect with these prongs. They're sockets."

Margit's face went white. They stared at each other for a moment. Then Burris took the capsules and went over to the bar counter. He felt himself moving heavily, as if the two black plastic ovals weighed a thousand pounds.

He switched on the radio and clicked it over to FM reception.

Then, slowly, moving the knob very gently, he dialed down to the lower FM ranges around 90 megahertz and below. He placed the two capsules in front of the radio and kept dialing slowly. At once the radio began to howl.

Burris tuned closer to the howl, then picked up one of the capsules and moved it away from the receiver. The set continued to howl. He picked up the other capsule and moved it away. Slowly the howl diminished.

He carried the capsule closer to the radio and the howl grew louder. He snapped off the set and turned to Margit and Palmer.

"These are bugs," he said then.

"This one," he held up one, "only works when it's plugged into a source of electricity. It came from the hand calculator. It works off the same battery the rest of the instrument uses. Which means it'll work for years. It's got a tiny microphone and an FM transmitter that operates at about—" He squinted down at the radio. ". . . about 88 megahertz."

He held up the other shiny black capsule. "This one is the same, but it contains its own source of electricity, probably a tiny mercury cell with a life of a month or two." He waved it slightly in the air. "It's been living in the pillbox now for some time, broadcasting twenty-four hours a day."

Palmer slumped down on the sofa. "An espionage system operating inside the offices of banks," he said then, as if to himself. "Picking up confidential information to be sold to the highest bidder."

"That's the reason for bugging the calculator." Burris was talking to Margit, not Palmer. "Who would want to bug your pillbox?"

No one spoke. Then Palmer grunted. "Hell," he said, "this shoots our tennis game."

CHAPTER 55

Since someone had been listening to their most intimate moments for quite a while now, Margit had decided to throw away the last scrap of caution and fly back from Morcote with Matt.

349

The schedules were sparse, but there did seem to be a very late F-27 that went direct to the Basel-Mulhouse Airport. After an interminable delay at the Lugano Airport, during which Matt and Palmer had wanted to confer privately, Matt boarded in a foul humor and refused to explain what it was about.

"It's not necessary," Margit told him. "Palmer has said or done something."

"It's what he hasn't said," Burris grunted, slumping down in the smallish seat and ramming his knees so hard against the seat ahead that an elderly little man with fleecy white hair turned around and glared at him.

"Sorry," Burris growled. *"Enschuldig mir. Scusi. Pardonnez-moi.* And fuck off, okay?"

Whichever language the nice old man understood—probably all of them, Margit decided—Burris' truculent tone managed to convey his meaning even more strongly. The F-27 taxied down the runway in a roar of jet-prop noise and angled upward into the darkening sky.

"No drinks on board?" Burris complained. "Jee-sus!"

"Matt," she murmured, "stop it."

He grunted again and turned to stare out the window at darkness. Margit considered the new Matt Burris, or rather, she reminded herself, the old Burris under pressure for the first time, at least in her experience with him.

The shock of realizing that their affair had been eavesdropped on was only part of it. The rest of the pressure on Burris was coming, she surmised, from Palmer. Possibly Palmer had refused to issue instructions as to how to handle the Staelicomp scandal. Matt would want instructions but Palmer would want him to solve it alone. Palmer was an interesting man, she reflected, tense but interesting. He would want this to be a test of Matt Burris.

In any event, the combination of the two pressures was turning Matt nasty and uncommunicative. This was a bad time in their relationship for him to stop talking to her. Because of him, she had now apparently ruined her plans for Staeli Internationale, GmbH.

No, she corrected herself, that wasn't true. She was an adult. She had known from the beginning what use Uncle Dieter could make of such a clandestine affair. She had gone into it under no false understandings except, perhaps, her own overconfidence in her ability to keep the affair a secret.

"I wonder how long—?" She stopped herself.

He glanced sideways at her. The plane had leveled off. There was a peculiar look in his eye, as if he knew precisely what she had been about to ask, but he was hoping she might not ask it. Neither of them spoke for a moment. Then he reached out and covered her hand with his as it lay on the armrest. He stroked her hand for a while, then held it again.

"Listen," he said then, "it may not be as bad as it seems."

She produced what she knew was a bad imitation of a smile. "Maybe."

"No, I mean . . ." He sighed heavily. "I mean we have to assume that the goddamned thing has only been in your bag a day or two, right?" Even in his new mood of trying to cheer her up, it was obvious he had no faith in what he was saying. He paused a moment, then switched tactics. "Look at it another way, honey. How much damage can they do to you? I mean, what's yours is yours. The property can't be taken from you."

"Just control of it."

The bald truth of it destroyed the last of his ability to put a good face on what had happened. She watched him lapse back into his own troubles. His big hand, clasped over hers, relaxed its grip for a moment. She slid her hand out and brought it over his in order to give him a few comforting pats. "Listen," she mimicked, "it may not be as bad as it seems."

"A lot you know." His voice had the true Burris truculence, but he had a half-hearted grin on his face.

"Palmer won't quarterback your team, is that it?"

"Bastard won't even be coach."

She laughed quietly. "Excuse me, darling," she said after a while. "But, between the two of us, I somehow can't work up as much sympathy for you as I can for me."

This produced enough of an answering chuckle to make them both feel slightly better, or so it seemed to Margit. She really had no idea what she was doing trying to cheer up this man when her own world was in ruins.

Curious, she thought, that it doesn't *feel* as if it's in ruins. Perhaps she hadn't wanted control of the family holdings that much. Perhaps she'd once wanted full control, but had lost the edge of her need during this long and confusing summer.

She felt her mind shift sideways.

The gargoyle's laughter hissed in her inner ear. He knew her better than she did. She had been brought up to the responsibility of wealth and, at the same time, she had been shown that it was not womanly to want the power that went with the wealth. The gargoyle understood such contradictions. He knew all roads to madness.

He had known what would happen to her—what *had* to happen —after that first insane night in Burris' hotel suite at the Drei Könige. The gargoyle had also known, from the beginning, why Burris had been sent to her.

He had been sent to ruin her.

Margit took a quick, gasping breath, as if the aircraft had risen too high and the air was suddenly unable to support life.

"Honey?" he glanced questioningly at her.

"It's nothing."

The question was who. Who had sent Burris? But, of course, Palmer. Fascinating man, part chess player, part torturer. Margit realized that her breathing had grown harsher. She made a deliberate effort to slump back in the uncomfortable seat and relax her tensions.

But how can I, she wondered, when the author of them sits beside me *not even caring* what torments he's created for me? Not even *knowing*. Unaware of how he's been used to get at me and spoil everything.

After a while, however, she began to feel her chest muscles slacken and ease the terrible constriction around her heart and lungs. She glanced out of the corner of her eye at her lover and saw that he was sitting bolt upright, as uncomfortable as she if not more so, eyes fixed balefully on the innocent silvery hair of the little man in the seat ahead. The look on Matt's face, if converted to electrical energy, would have scorched a tunnel directly through the elderly gentleman's head.

Then, Matt was in torment, too, she decided. Good. Let's suffer together. Let's not have Matt Burris come out of this a hero and Margit Staeli a complete loser.

She found herself wondering how much she could count on

Matt for help. Oh, moral support, yes. A pat on the hand and a kiss on the cheek. But if she had to fight—and it seemed clear that she would—how much could she count on him? First of all, he had his own immediate problem to solve, with Walter's fatuous spying machines. And then, possibly, when all that dust had settled, *then* he might turn a hand to help her.

But Uncle Dieter would have slain and flayed her by then, cut her in strips and nailed her up to dry in the cruel west wind off the Vosges.

The trouble with Matt as an ally now was the same thing that had made him such a good choice as a lover before. There was never any question in her mind that Matt wanted her for her money. With someone as deep-down surly about the rich as Matt Burris, it was always quite clear that she was being made love to in spite of her wealth and not because of it. That had been obvious from the beginning, six years ago in the States.

By the same token, however, there was no way she could kindle in Matt the same kind of anger that filled her now at being deprived of control of her property. To him wealth was the last step. Control was a frill. She could almost hear his reaction.

"Christ, honey, you've got the stuff. Why worry who administers it?"

This was Dieter's cry, too, and Walter's, and that of every other male in the Staeli clan. Be content with ownership, stupid woman. Control of property is for wiser, stronger heads. In other words, for men.

Her training had been sadly amiss, then. She'd been taught the traditional womanly virtues, the standard female reactions and positions and ploys. Even now, this instant, eaten with anger at what was happening to her, her conditioned instincts urged her not to burden Matt with it. As if her petty problems were beneath his notice. As if his mental ease was the only thing she had been placed on earth to assure.

But, surely, Margit thought now, this is how love ends. It must die in an eye-blink under this kind of contradictory pressure. There had to be some sideways maneuver that kept them equals and allies. If not, then there was nothing to the affair at all, only illusions and the hot squirt of sex between them.

"I forgot to ask Palmer—" She stopped as abruptly as she had begun.

Burris turned toward her. "About what?"

"This famine thing. The responsibility of the banks for people starving when—"

"Oh, Christ, that." Burris produced a sound somewhere between a snort and a groan. "He wasn't in an answering mood," he said then. "Son of a bitch wasn't giving away anything tonight."

"Just as well. I can't be borrowing opinions from others. And this is something one has to make up one's own mind about."

"Right." It was obvious to her that his mind was elsewhere, but, realizing how snarly he'd been, he was now giving an imitation of a man paying attention to a woman. Quite a married pair, aren't we, Margit thought.

"It's distressing that I haven't even done the research," she went on then. "So I really don't have the information on which to base a judgment. And this says something terrible about me."

"Um."

"It says that, like everyone else, when my belly's full, I forget that other people are starving. The two of us at l'Auberge de L'Ill, stuffing ourselves with three-star food. My God."

"Yeh."

The noise of the engines had abated now as the plane gained altitude and flying speed. "But if I'm ever to take the full responsibility for Staeli," she said then, "I have to understand fully what the responsibility entails. Not just in percentages of interest or profit or volume, but in human terms."

"Right."

"Because this is always the trouble with bankers," she persisted. "This is why we have such a bad reputation for being heartless, for caring only for money. Precisely because we pay no attention to the hu—" She paused, thinking.

"Sure."

". . . the human condition," she went on then, aware that his responses were automatic, but not really caring. "You know, I've hit on it. It's not that inhuman people become bankers. Except perhaps for Walter, and he had no choice. No. It's that banking dehumanizes the banker. Look at Uncle Dieter. Look at Erich's father. Look at Palmer."

354

"Uh-huh."

"Look at you," she said then. "Producing dehumanized responses like a machine. You aren't listening. You're completely wrapped up in how you're going to blow this Staelicomp thing wide open."

"Yeh."

She let his ear rest for a while, wondering whether any of this had sunk in. He stirred uneasily. "I've heard every word," he said then. "There just isn't a damned thing I can do about hungry people, honey, and neither can you."

"There is quite a bit we can both do."

"Adopt a kid? Send Care packages? I mean there is nothing the banks can do."

She shook her head. "I was raised to believe otherwise. My father made it very clear that banks are the backbone of civilization and have the responsibility for financing everything, good and bad."

"Who am I to disagree with your father?" He stopped slumping and sat up in his cramped seat. "Let me give you a bit of unfatherly advice."

"Yes, of course."

"Have you ever looked at the balance sheet for a Mitsubishi or an ITT? Or familiarized yourself, let's say, with the corporate holdings of the brothers Rockefeller? Has it ever struck you that the gross sales of Dutch Shell can be compared to the gross national product of a country?"

"Um-hm."

"And that there are goddamned few nations on earth with a bigger GNP than General Motors or Exxon? Say a dozen countries that are bigger? Does that give a banker incentive? A banker goes where the action is. In the case of the Rockefeller-Morgan boys, they bank themselves, much the way your Uncle Dieter banks some of the industrial holdings of Staeli Internationale GmbH. Banks don't create business. Banks go where business is. Agreed?"

"Yeh."

He made a face at her. "Cut that out."

"Couldn't resist. You being serious all of a sudden."

"I'm serious about you making a fool of yourself," he said, twisting to find a comfortable way to sit. "It's all right to talk about this stuff with me, but don't open up with your own relatives."

"Erich warned me about that, too. He considers that I have a social conscience. Why is that something one must be warned about?"

Burris squirmed. "Christ, if these are First Class seats what is it like in Steerage?" He patted her hand. "As a banker, you ought to know by now that it isn't conscience that rules the world, it's profits."

She stared at him for a moment. "You're telling me there are no governments, just business?"

"Would I say something that goofy? Of course there are governments, just as there are armies. But the corporations tell them what to do."

She pulled her hand out from under his and crossed her arms over her breasts. There really was no sense in having their argument about this, when the real disagreement lay elsewhere. She'd made a mistake. There are no sideways maneuvers between men and women, only face-to-face confrontations. "But in the end," she said then in a deliberately casual voice, trying to calm the silly discussion, "it is the banks that tell the corporations what they can and can't do."

He stirred restlessly against his seat belt. "I know the logic. For every ITT replacing the Government of Chile with a military dictatorship, there's a bank doling out funds to ITT . . . or not doling them out." She watched him mull this over for another minute or two and found herself hoping he'd let it drop. This was not, after all, the real problem between them.

"Let's face it," he said then, "in Polacktown, behind the tracks back in Carbondale, Illinois, we not only knew about going hungry, we also knew who to blame for it."

Like a seismic shock beneath their feet, the aircraft lurched suddenly through a patch of turbulence. The seat belt pushed against Margit's midriff and turned her as breathless as she had felt before.

"Just remember," he rumbled on, oblivious to the turbulence, "there is no way your family will let you use Staeli money to feed starving people. There isn't a banker on earth, let alone in Basel, who'd let you do that."

"And now they have the perfect way to stop me," she burst out, the words running together in her haste to utter them. "They have the ultimate weapon and we've not only created it for them, we've put it in Dieter's hands and—"

A sharp upward lift of the F-27 cut herself short. The thing was poisoning her, the realization that she was helpless in Dieter's hands. It was poisoning her feelings for Matt. It was killing everything between them.

She watched his face go through several expressions: surprise first, then a kind of defensive who-me look, then one of compassion. Finally his face went blank. When he spoke she understood that he had fallen back on the truth and nothing but the truth.

"It was a dumb thing to do," he said, "thinking we could get away with it." He sighed. "I knew up front all the risk was on your side. I should have stopped us. But it was just too goddamned good." He glanced at her. "And I can see what you're thinking now. Nothing is *that* goddamned good, right?"

She started to laugh and then realized she was crying, softly, but steadily. The breathless feeling under her lungs was loosening. She kept her hand over her mouth to stifle the sound of her sobs. The only way anyone would know she was crying was if they were close enough to see the tears roll down her cheeks, a telltale overflow of the grief inside.

Burris' big, square face looked pinched. He fumbled for a handkerchief and began dabbing at her cheeks. She took it away from him and pressed it against her lips. After a while the tears subsided and the constriction inside her was gone.

"Look," he was saying. His voice seemed to come from far away. The plane had started its descent into Basel and the change of altitude was playing tricks with her ears.

"Look, honey," he was saying, "we have more leverage than you think. I can use my information about Walter to take his father off your back. It'd work."

Her head had started shaking even before he'd finished describing his idea. "You don't understand my uncle," she said then. "Even to save his son he won't give up the chance of finishing off his beloved niece."

"Hard to believe."

"He plays that way."

Burris nodded slowly. "The old no-lose game." He looked up as the NO SMOKING sign flashed on. "This is going to be worse than I thought."

Margit sank back into her seat and finished drying her tears. Perhaps she hadn't done anything more than make them both miserable, but at least they were now feeling miserable about the same thing.

CHAPTER 56

The Silver Fox had never been busier or happier.

Walter's Monday had begun at the office, as it always did, at 8 A.M. But this time it had begun differently, not with a recital by his father of what had been left undone, but with high praise. Dieter Staeli had asked to see the sheets on Staelicomp production, listened for a moment to the details of the price-cutting strategy, nodded and then beamed like the face of the sun.

"Very good, my boy. Excellent."

He turned and entered his office, not to be further disturbed that morning, but he had said his final words in a voice that every other officer on the floor had heard.

They had completed the joy of the morning by clustering around Walter and offering their congratulations, even those who had not seen the television broadcast but had read of it in the morning paper. By nine o'clock the telephone on his desk had started ringing without letup. Walter instructed his secretary to take messages during his meeting with the public-relations staff of Staeli International, GmbH.

The problem for the morning was simple: where to house a press conference as big as this one was threatening to become.

Reuters, Agence France Press, Associated Press, United Press International, even Tass had asked for tickets for reporters and photographers. Eurovision cameras would film it for continental television. BBC and the American networks planned to send camera crews. Clips of yesterday's broadcast had also been included on the early-morning news broadcast over state television. West

German, Italian and French film crews wanted to preserve today's conference for posterity and their own viewers. *Time, L'Express, Newsweek, Stern,* the Sunday *Times* of London Magazine, all the major financial newspapers of Europe . . . would there be enough tickets to go around?

"We printed two hundred," the public-relations director confessed. "We already need more."

"And don't forget other banks," Walter told him. He smoothed down his pale hair and wondered how long it would be before people stopped calling him The White Fox and began to see him as The Silver Fox.

"Do we want other banks there?"

"Certainly," he said. "Half our business is done with banks. I want all of them to come, listen, suffer with jealousy and send us even more of their business. And buy more Staelicomps."

The three-man public-relations crew chuckled appreciatively at this intuitive master stroke of marketing genius. They said so for quite a few minutes until Walter, who normally would never stem such a flow of eyewash, glanced at his watch.

"It is now nine-thirty and we have no suitable location."

"The board room here is too small," one p.r. man complained.

"What about the Mustermesse?" another suggested.

They mulled it over in silence. Across the river, in Kleinbasel, stood an immense compound of giant convention halls, designed to hold the many fairs, exhibitions, meetings and other international gatherings to which Basel continually played host. The Mustermesse was a building one square block in size, with a hollow core treated as an inner courtyard.

"In the *Rundhof?*" Walter asked. "But it's open to the sky."

"Better for television lighting."

"And if it rains?" he asked.

"The weather today will be brilliant," he was assured.

Walter thought for a moment. He disliked holding an event that far from Number 17 Aeschevorstadt, not because he couldn't get there handily, but because he had never lost sight of the fact that the entire Staelicomp dream, which he had so wisely and cleverly nursed into glorious reality, was designed solely to show the world —made up of his father and all his uncles and male cousins—that their heir apparent was Walter Staeli and no one else.

If he could have held the conference at Number 17, this would have most readily helped him to establish his hegemony. But moving to the other part of Basel, to an area so big and so thoroughly associated with fairs and exhibitions, would cause the conference to lose its human scale. In the towering rotundity of the Mustermesse *Rundhof,* its central courtyard, Walter would find it impossible to establish himself *physically* as monarch of all he surveyed.

No, he needed something plain, something uncommercial, something with a great deal of prestige, something that showed by its own stature how tall The Silver Fox stood.

He held up his hand to cap the mindless spouting of names being thrown out, restaurants, hotels and other unimaginative locales. "Please arrange," he said then, "for the courtyard of the Kunstmuseum starting at 2 P.M."

There was a shocked hush for a moment among the men sitting around his desk. "The Kunstmuseum?"

"Yes. I think the courtyard is perfect. If the weather is to be fair, then the sunlight will help the television people. And, best of all, it's just around the corner from this office."

He dismissed the meeting and watched his people leave in an almost reverent silence, as if filing out of a cathedral. Possibly they would not have been less shocked if he'd suggested the cathedral itself. After all, the Kunstmuseum was one of the handful of top-level art museums in the world.

And why not? Was there an expensive or well-known artist whose work wasn't represented there? And who had provided the grants, the endowments and the outright gifts to make this possible? The Staelis, of course. The Staelis, the La Roches, Geigy, the entire roll call of banking and chemical families, with perhaps a few Vischers and Iselins and Lorns and Burckhardts thrown in.

There was no other reason why the Kunstmuseum was renowned throughout the world. Therefore it was time that one Basler called due his promissory note. For something as earth-shattering as today's press conference, the museum would be pleased to provide its magnificent Roman-styled forecourt with all the free-standing modern sculpture, including Rodin's "Burghers of Calais." A fitting place for the conference, precisely what Walter had in mind.

Of course, he mused now, this would mean a painfully fat contribution to the fund drive. Might as well get it over with. He picked up his phone and asked his secretary to get him the director of the Kunstmuseum at once.

"There's a Paul Iselin who has called five times, Herr Staeli. And *Der Spiegel* has called twice from Munich, *Oggi* from Rome and—"

"Refer them to public relations. Get me Iselin and then get me the museum director."

He sat back and smiled softly. The Silver Fox had many important matters in motion this morning. Other men would be content to have one such day once in a lifetime, but The Silver Fox was not like other men. He nodded to himself confirmingly. The telephone rang.

"It's Paul Iselin. I think I have everyth—"

"Yes, good," Walter cut in. He didn't like the possibility of his secretary hearing anything incriminating. "Ready to go, is it?"

"Completely."

"Then so are we, Pauli. It isn't hard to do business with the House of Staeli." He chuckled grandly, as though there were decades of difference in their ages. Iselin was only perhaps three years his junior.

"When can I bring it to you?"

"Today is quite full for me, as you can imagine," Walter said. He waited for Iselin to indicate, with some token of praise, that he had heard the grand news. When the silence grew too long to sustain, Walter cleared his throat. "Perhaps at five. I have a very, very full day, but I can certainly handle something as important as this. And, Pauli . . ."

"Yes."

"I take you at your word, Pauli. Between us a word is a bond. You tell me everything is ready, yes? Then I activate the mortgage immediately. Evergreen clause and all."

Walter hung up, well aware that he had produced his second grand gesture of the morning. Holding the conference in the Kunstmuseum was several light years beyond this simple game he was playing with Iselin, but the stakes were even higher.

It was one thing to assure the world that The Silver Fox was the true heir apparent to Staeli Internationale, GmbH. It was another to destroy, utterly and forever, any claim Margit had to control of the family interests.

And *in one day,* he would do both!

Walter sighed with satisfaction and patted down his sandy hair. This was to be the first of many such days. The rest of his life had begun to look exceedingly pleasant.

CHAPTER 57

By 1 P.M. Monday, when Margit had finished going through her waiting correspondence, the long windowed room that had been her mother's was brilliant with sunshine. September had produced this one truly summer day. She got up from the refectory table at which she had been working and walked slowly around the room, trying to recapture her feeling for this place.

Nothing changes, she thought, and everything. The chaise longue sat in the corner. She was rarely here long enough any more to get back into the sweet, melancholy mood of this room. Life with Burris was so different. She seemed to have no time for contemplation and perhaps this was to the good.

The things she had brooded about in this room, her mother's death, her father's—suicide?—were thoughts she hadn't had all summer.

She moved toward the windows and gazed across the greensward, baking under the vertical power of the sun's rays, past little groves of spruce and yew, beyond the private chapel with its willows to the ship landing at the river, its dark-red roof looking burned in the white light.

And yet the day itself wasn't hot, merely warm and pleasant, really like a day in late June, bright but not oppressive. A day in which, somehow, she would have to pull herself together with Matt's help and try to stop whoever was spying on her.

It was, as Matt himself had pointed out, a rhetorical question. Her own family was spying on her. Dieter Staeli, her uncle, her own father's brother, would be the prime mover in such an affair.

362

His mind worked that way. And whatever he devised, Walter would be easily induced to execute.

Margit had returned by plane with Matt Burris late last night. They'd had a small dinner in full view of all the other guests at the Schlüsselzunft restaurant on the Freistrasse, a very old building that had once housed—and perhaps still did—the *Zunft,* or guild, of keymakers.

They'd decided it was clearly a delusion to keep meeting out of town, but perhaps not a bad idea to spend the night in separate places. Burris had slept in his suite at the hotel and she at Schloss Staeli, which she now had every intention of inviting him to visit one day soon.

Margit hadn't any idea of how to find out who was spying on her, but Matt had promised to devote his time to tracing and stopping the surveillance before it harmed her. Neither had any idea of how long it had been going on.

"I'd start now," Matt had said, "but this thing with the Staeli-comp calculator has to be handled. I'll be finished with it by four-thirty and we'll start coping with your problems over cocktails." They were to meet openly at the outdoor terrace of the Drei Könige overlooking the Rhine.

But that was hours from now, Margit thought, and meanwhile she must start somehow to pick apart the threads of this. She had thought perhaps that Elfi might help, might have noticed something, someone. But Elfi had not appeared at the Schloss this morning and was not at her apartment when telephoned. Later, just half an hour ago, an unknown man had called to say she was ill and would try to be in by midweek.

Margit's second hope was Erich, who was much more familiar with the underside of Basel life than she. He would know what private detectives were for hire and might be called on to conduct such a surveillance. But Erich hadn't answered her call last night. This morning his man, Bunter, had said only that Master Erich had been out of town overnight. He'd obviously wanted to talk to her, but she hadn't time.

Her only ally in this was Matt, and he was busy today trying to pull together whatever it was they hoped to do about The White Rat's incredible blunder. Even now Margit found it impossible to credit Walter with such devious cunning. And to take such a

chilling risk with the Staeli good name! To blazon it across his little spying devices and ruin the goodwill Staeli could claim to have
earned over the years. It was an unbelievable mess for Walter to
have created.

Matt had felt that if Walter were "buried," as he put it, the plot
to discredit Margit would fail, but Matt didn't know Dieter Staeli
that well. He might lose a son but he was perfectly capable of
sacrificing his niece an instant later, especially in such a worthy
cause.

"You know," Matt had said at dinner last night, "he'll never let
up. You can own your fifty-one per cent or whatever it is, honey,
but you'll never own the loyalty of the Staeli men. They'll be forever hatching plots to bring you down."

It was this part of it, more than the sudden shock of knowing
she was being spied on, that had brought Margit to a low ebb. The
Staeli house was divided, perhaps forever.

She stared across the flat dark green of the German *Schwarzwald* beyond the Rhine. From the direction of France, from Strasbourg or perhaps Colmar, a front of high clouds was building up.
The sunshine over Basel was brilliant, but Alsace lay under a
heavy burden that, even at this distance, looked leaden inside, ugly
with storm.

She turned away and picked up the exercise book to jot down
another entry.

"September transitional," she wrote now. "The reverse of spring
and just as unsettling. Everything perfect, but will soon die. The
lushness of summer but, inside, the death of winter is already
there.

"Everything is about to change, my life, my fate, an upheaval
such as I have never known. People like Matt have experience
with these things. Their lives have always been filled with ups and
downs. They understand the cyclical quality of it, swim naturally
with it.

"Until now my life has been one sunny day of summer, because
we had the power to keep it that way. How much more intelligent
Erich has been to take none of it seriously. How much more
crippled am I, who pretended this long summer's day was reality.
How lucky to have Matt, who 'rolls with the punches,' as he said
this morning. 'Street savvy,' he called it, the cunning of the street

364

urchin. And this is what is missing both from Erich and me. If I could—"

She broke off, hearing the brash, snoring sound of the Magna sports car outside. She closed the journal and ran back to the window. The little orange car rattled into view, swinging around the back of the house.

Erich levered himself up and over the closed side door, stumbled, fell on the gravel and, holding onto a mudguard, pulled himself to his feet again. He stood for a moment, swaying unsteadily, then seemed to straighten up and limp out of sight toward the kitchen entrance.

Margit ran to the door of the study and threw it open. Erich was exactly the person she needed at this hour of her life. She had been aching to talk to him all this long, endless summer.

"Darling?" she called, hearing him coming up the stairs.

He pulled himself up the last flight and Margit saw that something had happened. She rushed out to steady him as he clung to the railing. "Erich, what's the matter?"

"Nothing. Not a thing. Why?"

His breath stank of old whisky. She drew back and looked him over. His narrow Satanic face, once full of V's, had grown puffy. He had needed a shave for several days and a bath for even longer. He was wearing an odd combination of clothes that seemed to have been thrown on in the dark.

"You're elegance itself today," she murmured.

"To hell with that." He lunged past her into the study. "My God, this place is so neat!" he shouted. He took a swipe at the pile of letters on the corner of the table. He missed, frowned at it and lurched along the table to the chaise longue. He threw himself down with a gasp of relief.

"I'm hungry and I'm tired," he announced. "And I'm thirsty. Scotch will do. Winter is here. The ant will die. The ant saved all summer while the grasshopper fiddled his time away. The ant will go south for the winter to Kos or Sardinia. The grasshopper will die."

She sat down at the foot of the chaise and shook her head at him. "You don't get whisky. Uschi will send up milk and sandwiches. Yes?"

"Uschi the ant. Erich the grasshopper."

"And what about a bath?"

He shook his finger at her. She saw a faint red rim around his eyes. Together with the unshaven beard, he resembled a clown in tramp make-up. "Erich, darling, you look absurd."

"As do we all. Clowns are always absurd." He closed his eyes for a moment. "Margit," he said then in a lower tone, "it's all such shit, isn't it?"

"What is?"

"Everything."

"Sandwiches and milk, a bath and a nap. I'll phone down to Uschi."

"Keep Uschi out of it," he snapped. He started to sit up straight, but seemed to lose strength. "You can't trust her, and you know it."

"Can't trust Uschi?"

His red eyes widened. "Can you trust anybody? You're in a trap. You can trust no one. Life is a minefield. And if one doesn't step on a mine, one falls in shit."

Margit felt a faint line of cold across her shoulders. The gargoyle had returned, the gargoyle with his ugly stone grin that sat on her back and dug his talons into her whenever he felt like it. He had just done it again. Erich, of all people, knew she was being spied upon.

"What do you know?" she asked.

"They've hired the Iselin boy. Remember Pauli Iselin?"

"That lunch at the Auberge de L'Ill! He was sitting there in a corner with his back to us and I told Matt—"

"Matt? Is he your lover? Yes, I know about it, Margit. Not important. Can you trust him? How about me? Look at me and tell me how trustworthy I seem to you."

She stood up because the smell of him had become too much. "Erich, I trust Matt the way I trust you. Does that answer you?"

He snarled slightly and turned away from her, then his glance shifted back to her face, as if she had somehow trapped him. "You trust us all. You're a fool, Margit. You'll be destroyed."

"By Pauli Iselin?"

"I caught him following the Magna yesterday. He thought you still had the car. He's . . . he's crazy." Erich's glance turned away, then slowly came back, as if testing her reaction to this word. "I argued with him. Then I thought, if it's money he needs, I can buy him off. What does it matter whose money he takes?"

"Where is he?"

"He's not at the Iselin house. He's—" He suddenly broke into sobs. Great tears welled up in his bloodshot eyes and began to moisten his cheeks. "Margit," he moaned, "she has treated me so badly. You mustn't trust anyone."

"Who is it this time?"

"You don't know her. Michele."

"The youth clinic woman."

"She's not your kind," Erich said, snuffling. He rubbed at his eyes and was quiet for a moment. "She's not my kind. But I'm her kind."

"I know of her. I've met her, I believe, at a reception. She's lovely. A bit . . ." Margit stopped. There was no point in tearing Erich down any further. "Quite successful, too, I understand."

"She wanted me to get to you," Erich said. "That's what it was all about." He sighed, pulled himself together and stood up, moving listlessly here and there, touching the surfaces of things as if to reassure himself that their texture hadn't changed, a chair, a picture on the wall, the glass of a window.

"There's a proposal for a major lending program," he said then. "She wanted it placed before you. I couldn't find you. I placed it before Walter. And that, dear Margit, is the last I've seen of her."

Margit nodded. "You were on intimate terms?"

He whirled on her. "I loved her!" he shouted.

Margit put her hand over his mouth. "Sh, yes. Yes, I know. Sh."

He shared gloomily out the windows. "Look at those clouds. And me in an open car. I'll have to put up the top."

"Erich, sit down and take some lunch. Have a bath. You're very tired. Your mind hops around like a sparrow. It's disconcerting."

"Isn't it?" He laughed loudly, a short barking sound. "I've become quite a shell of my former self, eh, Margit?" He glowered at the approaching storm. "This wasn't forecast. It was supposed to be fair all day."

"It may pass Basel by."

"I'm heading south now, with the birds. Winter's almost here."

"Erich, please." She took his hand and pulled him back to the chaise longue. "Lie here. I'll be back in a moment with a . . . a washcloth, a drink, whatever you wish."

"Scotch, neat."

"Yes, Erich," she said dutifully. "Try to relax. I'll only be a minute."

She hurried out of the room and down the back stairs to the kitchen. Uschi was lying down somewhere for her own nap. Quickly, Margit loaded a tray with cheese, some crackers and a glass half filled with whisky. She rushed back upstairs. The study was empty. What had he done now?

Carrying the tray, she walked down the hall, then stopped as she heard the water running in her own bathroom. She knocked on the door and, when there was no answer, opened it and walked in, still carrying the tray.

Erich lay back in the tub as the water filled it. He had dumped his clothes in an evil-smelling heap on the floor.

"Just leave it, miss," he said. "Oh, and take a tip out of my trouser pocket, there's a good girl."

Margit put the tray on a bench and stood over the tub, watching his naked body. She had seen him this way a few times in their life, usually when he and a few of their friends decided to go swimming in the Rhine by moonlight.

She found herself comparing him to Matt, whose body was equally broad through the shoulders and chest and tapered very slightly at the hips before reaching thick thighs and calves. Erich's body, like his face, was V-shaped, tapering quickly from the shoulders down. He had livid bruises on his shins and kneecaps. He worked up a handful of lather now and carefully plastered it over his penis. The incoming water instantly washed it away.

"You have me at a disadvantage, miss. I am an engaged man."

"I have a razor in the cabinet. Will you please shave?"

"Thank you, miss. As long as you're here, would you do my back?"

She grinned at him and began soaping a loofah sponge. "Hold still." The coarse fibers rasped at his skin.

"Easy! Is this the kind of thing Matt enjoys?"

"I'll have to try it on him."

Erich nodded and patted her cheek. She felt the water slowly

368

rolling down her face like tears. "Ah, my God, Erich, we've been through so much together and it's so little."

He nodded solemnly. "Babes in the woods, Margit. Things happen in the great world, people come along. Michele is a creature from another planet. And the name of the planet is Earth."

"We've been fraternizing with other species, is that it?"

He touched a drop on her cheek. "I hope your experience is better than mine." His eyes slowly closed under the steady stroking of the sponge. "Babes in the woods. And the birds . . . cover them up . . . with leaves."

The moment she stopped sponging his back, he snapped awake. "What can I do for clothes?" he asked, suddenly very alert. "You don't have a shirt I could wear?"

"I may. Finish your bath and shave."

She searched methodically through one of the high armoires in what had been her father's suite of rooms. Most of his clothes had been given away, but some packages had arrived long after the funeral from a men's tailor on St. James's Street in London. She found the box and carried it, unopened, to her bathroom.

Erich had finished shaving, but was now trying to find a styptic pencil to stem the four or five gashes he had made in his cheeks and chin. Margit watched him looting her medicine cabinet, shoving bottles aside, knocking combs to the floor.

"Erich!"

"Sweet Christ, I'm bleeding to death."

She applied the styptic pencil and he winced twice, then calmed down. "They're only superficial wounds," she said comfortingly.

He eyed her at close range, their faces inches apart. "Since when do you and I sustain anything but superficial wounds? Other people starve, grow sick, die. You and I . . . heal."

He pulled her to him and kissed her. She backed away after a moment and stared at her face in the mirror. One of his cuts had transferred a faint line of blood to her cheek. She rubbed at it thoughtfully. "A fake wound," she said then. "Is this the fate of the Staelis and the Lorns? We bleed but it's nothing serious?"

His face grew somber. "There is always internal bleeding." He made his devil's face for her, but neither of them found it funny this time. He stared at the shirt box from London. "Never opened?"

"You're about his size."

"But these were custom-made." He broke open the box and a faint smell of lavender rose from the pale shirts. Erich lifted one out, white with a very faint beige pattern that only showed in a certain light. He unbuttoned it slowly, watching her face. "Like robbing a grave."

"I don't want you tearing around Basel looking the way you did."

He pulled on the shirt and examined himself in the mirror. "Not bad." He lifted his chin, made a fiercely proud face and preened for her. "The eagle awakes. Onward and upward! Excelsior!"

"Where are you going from here?"

"I have to see . . . somebody."

He frowned at her. They were watching each other in the mirror, standing side by side. "You're going to try paying off Pauli Iselin?" she asked.

"Nasty little man. Did you ever like him? The size of a lizard, and just as tricky. I am a firm believer in size." He rose up on his toes until he towered over her. "We tall ones, we uphold the honor of our family and class. It's the little lizards who betray their class. How tall is Matt?"

"Taller than you, even on tiptoe."

His eyes had started to flare again, as if he were somehow getting a reverberation from his face in the mirror. It occurred to her that, without his reflection to reinforce him, he might fade away. Both of them might. There was something insubstantial about the two of them standing there like children playing games.

"What if you can't buy Pauli?"

"It's only a matter of money."

"Take any of mine you need."

He grinned Satanically. "Staeli money against Staeli money. Grrf!" He turned and stared at the pile of clothing on the floor. "Keep my underwear," he said then. "I can get by with just the trousers and shoes. Elegance is all in the frame upon which it hangs, after all."

"Erich?"

"Yes, miss?" He was pulling on the trousers.

"You will be careful with him?"

"Yes, miss." He reached for the glass of scotch and swallowed it in one gulp. "Yowr. Summer has returned. Here, miss," he rooted in his trousers and came up with a one-franc piece. "I'm sorry it isn't more. You have a firm touch with the sponge."

She took the coin. "You look like a different person," she said then. "On just a bath and a shave."

"And a London shirt. Class will tell." He turned and started out of the room, then stopped in the doorway and glanced back at her. "Do you remember the summer we—?" He stopped.

"What summer?"

He laughed softly. "All the summers of our life." He straightened up and strode out of the room.

She listened to his footsteps. Then to a door closing somewhere. Then to the raucous put-put-rowr of the little vintage car being started. Then to the sound of gravel churning up and falling.

Then to silence.

CHAPTER 58

At a quarter to two, the forecourt of the Kunstmuseum was already in an advanced state of chaos. People ran in different directions, Burris noticed, somewhat the way ants did when a stone was dropped in the mouth of their anthole. But, like ants, the scurrying people he was watching had a purpose.

He wasn't sure what it was, whether the greater glory of Walter Staeli or the daily need to fill columns of space in newspapers and magazines, hours of time on television. As far as Burris was concerned, the news had been yesterday. Today would be a nonevent. Until he showed his hand, that is.

He frowned at the big, rawboned figures sculpted by Rodin, and tried to remember the story behind them. Now capped by mantles of bright aquamarine corrosion, the somber bronze figures told a story of sacrifice, the burghers offering themselves as hostages for the town of Calais in some ancient war. The old leadership-through-sacrifice theme. The king must die. Walter wasn't king yet, but he was already dead.

The stolid burghers were the only human forms at rest in this antheap of activity. Burris stood off to one side and watched workmen in Staeli uniforms bolt together the last supports for a sort of dais, while others fastened long rows of folding seats to make a curving audience area for, perhaps, one hundred people. The rest was tangled in thick television cables. Crews checked recorders, film magazines, battery power sources and their own fill-in lights. Assistants ran about importantly.

Burris glanced up at the intense blue of the sky. One didn't expect such a Mediterranean blue this far north. It was a trick of the sun and the humidity or something. He'd have to ask Margit, the weatherbird, why Walter Staeli had won for himself such a gorgeous day to die. Lives right?

His attention was attracted by a still knot of figures across the courtyard. He wondered why they weren't moving, then realized they were part of another free-standing sculpture, slightly elevated, of three children with their arms upraised as if shouting joyfully into the sun.

Burris closed his eyes against the glare. The hubbub reduced itself to sounds now, the fast crackle of hasty German, the looping smoothness of hurried Italian, the clatter of the Basler dialect, someone repeating over and over again in English: "No room presence Harry. Give me room presence. I need room presence."

Burris glanced at his watch. Almost two. He had half an hour or less to make up his mind. Damn Palmer for throwing this into his lap. He would always remember that scene at the Lugano Airport last night.

Sensing that the two men wanted privacy, Margit had taken herself off to the newspaper counter and was spending a long time deciding whether to buy something. Palmer's eyes, the dark gray of gun muzzles, darted to her, back to Burris, then swept the nearly empty waiting room.

"Well, Matty, it's all in your hands."

"No way," Burris backed off. "This has to be a corporate decision."

"You *are* UBCO in Basel."

"This is an international decision. We have these bastards dead to rights. We can ruin them cold in ten minutes. I have the stuff to do it."

"Yes." Palmer eyed him almost as if he were a stranger. "And

372

Curtis will be wiring you additional material tomorrow morning in Basel. You'll have a dossier than can destroy Walter Staeli."

"And Staelicomp. And Staeli Internationale."

"And Margit Staeli," Palmer added quietly. "We've already let her see too much."

"What's she got to do with it? They hate her guts."

"No," Palmer insisted, "she's got the wrong name. Anything named Staeli is going to hurt a lot once you uncork your little A-bomb."

"Is that what you want me to do?" Burris demanded.

"I didn't say that." Palmer grinned maliciously. "As an old-timer, a banker's banker, my advice might be to close ranks and keep the faith. Let Staeli off the hook. What's bad for one bank is bad for all. If Staeli totters, banking totters. You've seen it happen before, Matty. One big bank goes bad and we have to live with the damage for years afterward."

"You're telling me to sit on it? Do a cover-up?"

"I didn't say that, either." Palmer's grin widened. "You're the boss, Matty. This is your hot potato."

"Shit it is," Burris burst out.

Palmer slapped him on the shoulder. "As we say in Illinois, Matty, shit it ain't. Have fun." He turned and left the terminal.

That had been yesterday evening and the issue hadn't yet resolved itself in Burris' mind. He began strolling through the scurrying anthill that occupied the open area of the courtyard. With any luck, the press would fill this place to bursting, giving him precisely the audience he needed to destroy Walter Staeli with a few quick questions from the floor.

"Can you tell me, Mr. Staeli, why all your little calculators contain a bugging device?"

"Can you explain, Mr. Staeli, why banks that use your calculators are now being sued for breach of confidential information?"

"Can your firm be that hungry, Mr. Staeli, that it has branched out into industrial espionage on a global scale?"

Oh, Walter was a fish in a rain barrel. You couldn't miss. He'd set himself up for this. His worst enemies couldn't have asked for a better or more lethal shot at him. Was he stupid, as Margit had hinted, or so determined to become the next head of Staeli that he'd thrown every caution away?

Whatever his reasons, he'd opened himself up wide. Under his arm, Burris carried a manila folder containing enough information to fill Walter as full of arrows as St. Sebastian. In Paris, Curtis had worked overtime to be able to report seven more cases of banks being sued by their irate clients.

He'd even given Burris the name of the bugging device, a Matsui 6001. And he'd been able to find an electronics expert who could identify the calculator circuitry as among the components of three well-known Japanese hand calculators, common subassemblies produced by a fourth Japanese concern.

Burris walked up the broad stairs from the courtyard into the entrance hall of the Kunstmuseum. The guards eyed him curiously as he paused for a moment inside the hall, the cloakroom to his right, to his left the counter that sold postcard reproductions. Ahead stretched a long flight of stairs leading upward.

To the right of the stairway stood an immense placard that Burris found was a sort of table of contents to the museum. The artists were listed alphabetically over color-coded drawings of the plan for each floor. If you wanted to sample the Gustave Klimts, you looked for space E-4. Burris saw from the floor plans that the space devoted to Paul Klee was quite large, but Klee was Swiss, of course.

He walked to one of the guards. "Is the museum open now?"

"*Ja*, of course."

"But with all the excitement outside . . ."

"It makes no difference, sir."

Burris nodded, pleased with the absolute sureness of response. How about trying him with a tougher question? "What should I do about this Staeli mess, eh?" The man exuded great authority. Let him try his hand at a real ball-buster.

"Tell me," Burris asked, "should I lay waste to them or let them live?"

"Pardon?" The guard blinked twice.

"*Danke schön*." Burris nodded pleasantly and left the museum lobby for the brilliant sun outside again.

No sense burdening the poor guy with somebody else's problems. No sense asking anybody. If Palmer wouldn't take charge of it, who was left? Just lucky old Matt Burris himself. He couldn't

374

even ask Margit for help because, as Palmer had so nastily indicated, she had the wrong last name. Bastard.

He found himself standing next to the sculptured group of three children, arms outstretched to the sky. They were nude, two boys and a girl, one boy perhaps ten years old, the others much younger. The bronze had been pitted and blotched in a strange way, perhaps by the artist, perhaps by weather. Burris bent over the inscribed slip of metal attached to the base of the statues.

"Seekers," it read, in English. The artist was someone called Hannah Kurd and the sculpture was on revolving loan from the Cultural Section, Department of State, Government of the United States of America.

A very brief statement on Hannah Kurd, who had died some years before, called her one of the leading American sculptors. She had been born in Basel in 1898. The work in question had been done from live models, the children of the private collector who still owned this sculpture. His name seemed to be Woods Palmer, Jr.

Burris made a face. He backed away from the statues as if they had suddenly begun to radiate heat.

Why hadn't anyone told him? Somebody had to know the damned thing was here in Basel. Palmer knew, didn't he? If only for the public relations of it, the bank could have—. Christ, Palmer played it close to the chest. A shadow fell over the busy people scurrying around the courtyard. Each of them lifted their heads to peer at the sky. Ugly clouds were rolling in.

Burris was peculiarly shocked by the sculpture. He knew Palmer collected art. Anybody who had been to the Morcote villa or even the main office on Fifth Avenue in Manhattan in the years when Palmer ruled the roost, would know that the colorful daubs on the walls were his personal property and worth millions. But this statue of his kids. Why did it have to intrude on him when he was trying to be his own man? Palmer had said it. "You're the boss, Matty." Nobody knew what it cost the man to say it, but he obviously meant it.

Yet there was a Palmer way to decide this thing, and a way Palmer wouldn't like. Giving Burris free rein was the same as letting him hang himself. Why did Palmer have to play everything this sideways, mysterious way? Why couldn't he just come right out and say—?

"Harry, gimme more room presence. More presence, Harry."

"The light's bad. I have to take new readings."

Burris wandered around the perimeter of the courtyard, strolling under the arcade formed by the Roman peristyle plan of the place. He watched the technicians finishing their work and saw that the first of the press had started to file in past the guard at the outer gate checking admission tickets. He found himself doubting the word of the authoritative guard inside the museum that it was, in fact, open to the public today.

But Burris saw that people who had come just for the museum were being shunted along a flanking path protected by ropes on stanchions. They eyed the press preparations with some interest, but they marched dutifully along into the museum.

". . . nothing new expected," a man was telling a colleague.

"Nuts and bolts details, huh?"

Burris moved toward the outer gate. He checked his watch. Two-ten. He felt the bulk of the folder of damaging material under his arm. Before he'd come over here, he'd taken the material into the UBCO office on the Aeschenvorstadt and carefully reproduced all of it on a copying machine. The copies had been locked away in the safe-deposit vault. Now what?

"Can you enlighten us, Mr. Staeli, as to how you merchandised the commercial secrets gleaned by your eavesdropping devices?"

"Can you estimate, Mr. Staeli, under the Swiss criminal code against revealing commercial secrets, what your jail sentence will be?"

"Can you give us an idea, Mr. Staeli, of how much in total damages your company expects to pay out over the next five years? Ten years?"

"Can you tell us, Mr. Staeli, how destructive the effect of this will be on the main corpus of the Staeli holdings?"

Damn Palmer. Damn all bankers. Damn the greedy, conniving lot of them for putting him in this position. He was a team player. Margit had been right about that. He wasn't the coach. He wasn't even the quarterback. Damn them all for forcing him to make such decisions.

376

CHAPTER 59

By two-fifteen the skies over Basel had turned almost black. Erich sat in the front seat of the orange sports car and shivered.

He had parked in the small garage turnaround space behind the almost-deserted Iselin mansion. He pulled himself up from the slump in which he had been sitting, got out of the car and began putting up the canvas top. It took a while because he couldn't seem to co-ordinate his seeing with his thinking and the two of them with his fingers. And his teeth chattered with cold. Also, there had usually been a girl with him in this car to help raise the top and clamp it in place. There had always been a girl.

He got back inside the car and huddled down in the abrupt darkness of its covered interior. He didn't like the look of the Magna with its top up. The English idea of a drophead coupe design only allowed for it looking good with the top down, which was the way Erich usually kept it.

He glanced at the sky. Winter. So fast. But he'd warned everyone. The bird, Margit, everyone who counted. They'd been warned.

He could hear the Jaguar's velvety twelve-cylinder purr before it rounded the corner and paused, then advanced and parked beside him. Iselin hadn't put up the top yet. Foolish Iselin.

"Pauli," he called. Catch more flies with sugar than—. "Pauli, I've been looking all over for you. I have wonderful news."

Both men got out of the car with a certain wariness. In Erich's case it was stiffened somewhat because he had been taking falls these last few days. He wasn't sure why but he'd been stumbling and falling. His shins showed black-and-blue marks. Iselin was carrying a large black attaché case, which he now shifted to the side away from Erich. "Pauli," he reiterated. "Great news."

The shorter man eyed him with distaste. "What have you been doing to your face? It's all cut up."

"Let me explain."

Iselin glanced up at the windows of his family mansion. "Explain out here, then," he said.

"Great news about your immortal soul," Erich told him.

His hands moved out sideways, as if demonstrating the length of a fish he had caught, or perhaps sketching the sentence as a mighty newspaper headline. He could see the way Iselin was watching him and it was worse than looking into a mirror, but just as cruel. To hell with it.

"I have a way for you to get all the money you want, more than Staeli is paying you. Seriously. And without jeopardizing your immortal soul. Seriously."

Iselin sighed impatiently. "Erich, you're drunk."

"Cold sober. Whatever Staeli will pay you, Pauli, I will pay plus two bonuses. Money, yes. That's the first, a money bonus. And the second bonus is spiritual. I will destroy every scrap of the material you have collected, thus saving the Iselin name from total degradation."

A faint smile crossed the small man's face. "You're crazy, Erich," he said then. "Anyway, I already have what I want from Staeli. They've already written a mortgage on this place. It has an evergreen clause. You know the form?"

Erich nodded. "You pay only the interest. Such a mortgage hasn't been written since we were boys in school." He shook his head sadly. "They have you, then? They own this place?"

"I own it."

"You're a fool. Staeli owns it the moment you default." Erich turned away as if to get back in the car.

"But, look, it isn't too late," he said then, wheeling back to face Iselin. "I can help you. I will help you. And I ask nothing in return except the filth you've scraped together about Margit."

The shorter man glanced up again at the windows above them. He shifted the attaché case to his other hand. Erich got the feeling they were being watched, but it didn't matter. None of it mattered if he could get this idiot to agree. "What do you say, Pauli? Play both ends against the middle, eh? You're not only tapping the till at Staeli, but I'm opening the spigot at Lorn et Cie. You ask, you get. Name your price."

"No good."

Iselin moved toward the back door of the mansion. Erich

snatched at his arm. They froze for a moment, motionless, staring at each other in a way they had never looked through the years they'd grown up together. "Pauli, there is a clean way to do this," Erich said. "There is an honorable way."

"Where there is no honor?" Iselin asked.

"We create it again."

"No good," Iselin repeated. "Staeli would never let me get away with this. If I have any hope of making a go of things now, it would be crushed by them. The money, the career, everything because of your crazy notion of honor. And for a whore who's betrayed you a hundred times this summer."

Erich's knuckles snapped against the bone of Iselin's cheek. The small man recoiled, touched his face. "All right," he said sullenly. "Perhaps I owe you that. Now get out of here."

Erich began to step about in a peculiar way, lifting his bruised knees high, tapping his feet on the pavement. He turned this way and that like one of those mechanized animals in a shooting gallery, left, right, front, back. "Erich," Iselin said with some alarm. "Erich, stop this."

"It's a trap," Erich muttered. "I must go south. Winter is here."

"Yes, go, Erich. Go south."

"You owe me more than a slap in the face," Erich shouted, his voice suddenly rising from a rumble to a yelp in a tearing rush that burned his throat raw in an instant. "You owe me a chance. Yes, that's it, Pauli. You surely cannot deny me this one thing." He coughed. "Do you like my shirt?"

He began to close his fists and huff into them, as if he were freezing cold. He continued stamping about in a tiny circle, imitating a man who was trying to stay warm in deep winter.

"You can do this," Erich insisted. "I won't stop you from going to Staeli with the information. Fair enough? I won't stop you. But you owe me this one thing, that I come with you. That I have the chance to argue Walter out of this. Isn't that fair? Surely you can't object. Pauli, we were all boys together. It was warm then, summer all the time. You must see that you owe me this very small, tiny little thing. Give all of it to Walter. I won't stop you. But give me also the chance to make him see that he can't use this kind of filth. Isn't that fair? I'll even drive you there, Pauli. We can take my car, it's right here. The top is up against winter."

"Walter wouldn't be happy, I can assure you."

"Happy? Which of us is happy? The clowns always cry, Pauli. The clowns always cry." He coughed again. "Do you like the shirt? It's a dead man's shirt."

CHAPTER 60

Margit held the exercise book in her lap. She glanced over the entries of the past spring and summer.

At first she had found a pleasant bench in the leafy courtyard of the cathedral, but the lowering skies had sent her inside, past the clutter of scaffolding and plastic sheets that seemed to mask most of the cathedrals of Europe these days.

In the half-dark of the church she sat in a back pew and glanced up now and then from her exercise book to the crisscrossed maze of timber that supported, far over her head, two young men with beards. They were measuring a rotted piece of Gothic carved stone with calipers. From time to time they murmured to each other. At a distance, they sounded like doves muttering.

This peaceful scene, Margit decided, was not typical of the day itself. Erich was off somewhere—dressed in her father's shirt—on another of his Quixotic missions, doomed to failure. Matt, too, was entangled in the lies and plots of the Staeli clan, with what luck? And here she sat, while the sky outside darkened like a bruise, listening to the faint coo of human doves in their cote high above.

One of them made a clucking noise now, as if disapproving the sloth of the woman on the bench far below.

Margit looked down at her journal again. "Check famine statistics," she read with a pang. "Check whether increase in price of oil has put cheap fertilizers and pesticides out of the reach of underdeveloped countries."

She almost winced, remembering these strong concerns of hers which she had all but forgotten over the long summer. Her eye skipped down the page. "Whose responsibility?" she read. "Big manufacturers for monop—?"

She closed the book, but held the place with her finger. She had really grown quite irresponsible. She was no better than Erich, with his self-destructive love affairs. There had always been that streak in him that attracted women. "Watch me blow myself apart," he seemed to be saying.

But she had been the Good Basler Daughter, the responsible one who built instead of destroying. Erich had his downhill ski racing and his sports car rallies. She had her studies, her university degrees, her titles at the bank, her steady acquisition of knowledge and power and experience, quite like Germaine de Staël, in fact. But, really, so different.

She hadn't thought of her ancestor in some time now. Love had eventually destroyed Germaine. She had been an extremely serious woman, as befitted the daughter of the Swiss financial wizard Jacques Necker, not only Minister of Finance to Louis XVI, but later called in by Robespierre to straighten out France's money mess after the Revolution.

A serious woman, Germaine, student of social problems, author of criticism, reportage, novels and, finally, the book that so angered Napoleon he had the entire edition seized and pulped, *De l'Allemagne,* her celebration of German liberal romanticism over the dictatorial ambition of Bonaparte.

And yet, her high achievements were to be undone by love, first for the writer Benjamin Constant (Inconstant Ben, Margit thought), who left her for a younger woman. Then, nearing fifty, she married a twenty-seven-year-old Swiss officer and died a year later. Germaine had never learned to keep love in its place. But yet she had achieved greatness.

I haven't learned, either, Margit thought now, nor achieved anything at all. And worse, through love, to drop all responsibilities completely. To drift through a summer, never once to come to grips with the problems of her responsibility. She opened her journal at the same entry.

"Big manufacturers for monopolizing world's supply? Big banks for financing monopolists?" she read.

High overhead, one of the men laughed. She peered up at him. The laugh had sounded derisive, as if from his perch he could read not only her journal but her mind. No, the bearded man who had laughed was not even looking at her.

"Check whether," she continued reading, "increasing mechanization makes redundant nearly half the people on earth."

She'd never even looked it up. There were libraries all over town. The library at Schloss Staeli would have told her what she needed to know. How redundant a summer could one spend?

And only in affluence could able-bodied young men while away the long years restoring fourteenth-century stone fretwork. In Laos, in Zaire, in Udaipur, they would be dying in the fields, scratching a subsistence from dry stone. Which job was redundant, to keep oneself and family alive, or to restore a detail no visitor would ever see except with binoculars?

And laugh and chat on one's scaffolding, doing one's redundant job? While people obscenely bloated with famine died in gutters? Or was it more redundant to sit like a worshiper in the pew of a church one never attended, a faith one didn't believe in, and stir over notes of past problems? And chide oneself lightly for letting a physical love take precedence over the real concerns of the world? Surely, the worry of an utterly redundant woman.

A fool about men, Germaine de Staël had always had money, had always known how to use it for good. She had been foolish about men, but not about the serious responsibilities of her age. When she wasn't taking direct action, through her books, she used her salon, indirectly, to influence the opinion of the world. Through it passed the great of her age, as they had a generation earlier through her mother's salon. And Stendhal himself had called Germaine's salon "the States-General of European public opinion."

While here she sat, Germaine's pitiful relation, the same kind of fool as Germaine, but without her ability to overreach personal emotion and achieve something far beyond it.

Margit closed the journal with a snap that echoed through the empty cathedral. If only she could pull her life together with such precision, she thought. Everything was finished now, and all for love.

The information Dieter needed to destroy her grip on the Staeli empire was almost in his hands. Margit understood that by wasting away the summer she had let her opportunity pass. Worse, the way she had wasted it had created the weapon that would now be used against her.

All these fine questions in her journal. All these world problems which were her responsibility shortly would become as redundant as she. Once Dieter took away her chance of control, he removed any opportunity she had to do something useful, something good, with this vast empire of money, something practical about the problems she had so glibly jotted down in a book she neglected to reread. A journal of futility now, eh?

She glanced at her watch. She had two hours before meeting Matt. Her life was now pivoting around his. She had lost her own center, surrendered it to him. Their rendezvous was five minutes' walk from here, which meant she had two hours to kill. How to fill the interim?

This was going to be her life now, wasn't it? Finding time-wasting make-work? The university had libraries near here. Perhaps she could go to one and . . . and what?

Far above her, someone laughed again. She sat down.

CHAPTER 61

At two-thirty the rain began.

It fell upon Basel with the force of an avalanche, warm rain pelting the city from one end to the other, sending strollers running for cover, hammering the face of the Rhine to a seething flatness, as if it were simmering beneath the surface.

In the courtyard of the Kunstmuseum, umbrellas went up hurriedly. Camera crews dollied their equipment back under the overhanging arcades. Lights were switched off and electricians gravely eyed the shuddering puddles of water forming around the long snaking power cables. Everyone, nevertheless, awaited the momentary arrival of Walter Staeli.

On the Aeschenvorstadt, rain pounded down into the steel tracks of the streetcar lines, turning them into long running rivers of silver. Someone on the second floor at Number 17 twitched aside a curtain for a moment at twenty minutes to three, then twitched it back again with an impatient flick.

At the Drei Könige, waiters on the outdoor terrace had cranked down a sweeping spread of red-and-white striped awning at the first sign of clouds. They stood under it now, listening to the drumming of rain on canvas and watching the Rhine sizzle with exploding droplets from above. Unbelievable! Out of a clear blue sky!

At three, the door of Erich Lorn's house across the way from the hotel opened for a moment. Bunter put his head out and withdrew it almost at once. From inside the doorway he frowned at the rain, then closed the door.

* * *

At the same time, three o'clock, Dieter Staeli's voice, a trumpet of anguish, could be clearly heard throughout the entire second floor of Number 17.

His words came spaced out almost evenly, as if the anger inside was forcing him to take a separate breath for each agonized syllable. "God . . . damned . . . piece . . . of . . . shit!" he bellowed.

Under his pale-blond hair, Walter's face had already turned the color of dead cigar ash. Now, like ash, it was breaking in strange crisscross lines, as if the flesh beneath had begun to wither in the blast of his father's wrath.

Burris had, until this moment, been standing directly in front of Dieter's desk. He now stepped aside, out of the immediate area of howling. His report had been brief, almost a model of conciseness during which Staeli had interrupted him several times while he summoned Walter and half a dozen other ranking officers to his desk, each time apologizing politely to Burris for the interruption, as if what the younger man had to say, while interesting, was more or less routine.

It was only when Burris concluded his report, mentioning the duplicate set of evidence locked in his own office safe, and all the Staeli officers had by now gathered around Dieter's desk, that the older man's lungs filled, his sunlike face began to radiate dangerously intense heat, his glance fixed his son like two flaming javelins and he began to howl obscenities. Walter's was not the only face that had paled, but it was the only one that had started to crumble.

"Did . . . I . . . *warn* . . . you?" Dieter was screaming now. "Out . . . smart . . . Jap . . . anese . . . *du Hundt?*"

"Let's hear what he has to say," Burris suggested in a mild tone reasonable enough to set Dieter off on new flights of stentorian cursing.

"P-papa, I had n-no idea they would—"

"Shut . . . up . . . *scum!*" Dieter was breathing easily now, like a pro boxer in an early round, pacing himself, or a character actor with a lot more lines to deliver *en haut*. "Brain . . . less . . . *Scheiss . . . fresser!*"

On the last German word, spittle flew. Perhaps some hit his son's face, perhaps not. Walter recoiled, at any rate, and put his hand to his eye. His father had worked up a good glow now, Burris noticed, and was keeping his throat clear and his lungs filled, but he couldn't be allowed to dominate the scene forever.

"I'm sure Walter didn't know the things were bugged," he insinuated smoothly.

"This . . . *weiss* . . . *Ratte* . . . never . . . knows . . . anything!"

Out of the corner of his eye, Burris could see that, as upset as they were by the screaming, the Staeli officers were not that disturbed. Walter had never won any popularity contests in his years here, Burris thought, but what boss's son does?

"Listen," he said in a helpful undertone to the man nearest him. "One of you ought to run over to the Kunstmuseum and cancel that press conference. Wouldn't that be a terrific idea?"

No one moved. Burris wasn't giving any of them orders . . . yet. At last Dieter Staeli, in a perfectly calm voice, said: "Hans, you go. No reasons. No comment. Dismiss everyone."

Then, filling his lungs, he bellowed at Walter: "How . . . does . . . a . . . man . . . dismiss . . . a son?" He slammed one meaty hand down on his desk. "*Schluss!* You're finished in Basel." His voice slid down to conversational level. "If I cannot fire you outright, you will be transferred to . . . to . . . to the Antarctic." His little eyes in their puffy beds of flesh swiveled sideways to gauge the effect of this deportation order on Burris.

"That's a start," the American agreed equably. "Anybody who thinks he can play games with the Japanese Mafia and come up winners isn't my idea of prime executive material."

He paused for a moment because his heart had begun to beat so heavily he was sure it could be heard by others in the room. Dieter Staeli might hope this was the end, but Burris knew it was only the beginning. The pressure in the room was fierce now. They all suspected he was about to name his price for silence.

He took a calming breath. "You know," he said then, "I've been very impressed by your operation . . . up till now."

Dieter produced a sound halfway between an anguished laugh and a groan of pain. "Until now, yes."

"It occurred to me," Burris continued, feeling everyone's glance locked on him, "that every week, every month, your chemical and metallurgical operations secure new financing commitments. Not always with the Staeli bank."

Someone farther from the desk cleared his throat. The pressure seemed to mount now that Burris' drift had been perceived.

"My dear friend," Dieter began, widening his eyes in an expansive blaze of pure generosity, "let me save you words. When next we seek financing for a project, Dear Burris, be assured we will immediately think of the man who saved us all from disgrace. Yes. Yes."

Burris held out his hands as if to produce a clapping sound. His motion had the effect of cutting off Dieter's third "yes." The room was utterly silent. Burris shook his hands up and down twice. "No good," he said.

Walter blinked as if spat on again. His father's eyes narrowed to slits. Behind the thin, horizontal openings, Burris could see a faint, flickering glint, as if lighted from within.

"No good," he repeated firmly.

One of the Staeli officers sneezed out of sheer nervousness, and so tense was the moment that no one muttered a *gesundheit*.

Burris planted his right hand, palm down, on Staeli's desk. "From today forward," he said in a slow, measured voice, "UBCO-Basel will assume *all* your new financing."

In the thick silence, the sound of rain could be heard drumming on the window glass. In the distance a telephone rang and rang.

"I beg your pardon?" Dieter's voice was just above a whisper.

"All your new financing. Every part of it. Leasing. Factoring. Plant expansion. R and D. Accounts receivable in all currencies. Revolving credit. Forward commodity hedging. Arbitrage. Anything Staelifer and Staelichem need of a bank. From now on, they come to UBCO-Basel, your friendly neighbor across the street."

He beamed at Staeli. The older man's lips moved twice before he managed to say: "But you couldn't poss—"

"Yes, we can handle it. I plan to take personal charge. You'll have a friend at UBCO-Basel."

"I don't see h—"

"You will."

Now the Staeli executives began to mutter among themselves. Dieter stood motionless. Burris raised his hand and was pleased to see the men knew enough to fall silent. "Is one of you gentlemen a corporate counsel? We need a simple letter of agreement both of us can sign."

When Dieter stirred, it was as if from a trance. His eyes were almost shut. He rounded his desk suddenly, blindly, stumbling, reaching out, spittle fizzing at the corners of his mouth.

He threw himself at Burris, his butcher's hands outstretched. He began to claw for the throat, grabbing, slipping. Burris swiveled sideways and caught the older man across his hip. He sent Staeli pitching forward toward the floor. Two executives caught him and held him upright.

Staeli's face was crimson. He seemed to be choking on his own spittle. He was trying to say something but the words couldn't get past an obstruction in his throat.

Not that it matters, Burris thought somberly. He has nothing more to say.

The two men forced Dieter to sit in a chair. Burris watched them prying open his collar. Was it worth giving a man a stroke? Mr. No-Lose? Dieter was thrashing now against the restraint applied by his own men. Burris felt ashamed of himself. Nobody had the right to put another man through this.

Burris shifted his glance to Walter, not because he was interested in that pale, cracked face, but because he was ashamed to look at The White Rat's father.

Walter's idea, bugging Margit? Or had the idea come from the father of The Rat?

"Oh, yes, something else," Burris said then.

Dieter Staeli's eyes rolled up in his head. One of the men holding him looked up. "Mr. Burris," he said in a grave tone. "Nothing more."

Burris watched the old man. He was quite an actor, but the dangerously heightened color hadn't come from make-up. Perhaps now wasn't the time to bring up the question of bugging Margit. One more thing to swallow and Dieter might choke to death.

"There is another thing," he told the man who had pleaded with him. "But it can wait till tomorrow."

The man nodded. "Thank you." He winced as Dieter Staeli grunted something unintelligible.

Staeli's meaty hand quavered in midair, pointing a pudgy finger first at Burris, then at two of his men who were silently drafting an agreement on a pad of paper. Words gargled from his mouth. The attending officer looked up at Burris.

"Anything signed today," he said in a tone of uncertainty, as if probing for a soft spot, "has been agreed to under duress. It cannot be valid in a court of law."

Burris nodded. He wondered what the Swiss law really said. It was quite archaic here, no habeas corpus. People spent months in jail without being charged with any crime.

"Which of you has the balls to bring it into court?" he asked then, his eyes on the face of the older lawyer. "Legal or not, the agreement will be honored because you won't sue to break it and have the whole story exposed, will you? And as long as you honor the agreement, I keep the story to myself."

The elderly attorney sidled over to Dieter Staeli. Guttural Schweizerdeutsch rose and fell harshly. *"Ja!"* the lawyer said then, on an inward gasp of air, as if burying the agreement within himself. He glanced at Burris. "It is duress. But we do not sue. So." He returned to the desk and finished writing on a long pad of yellow foolscap.

Burris and everyone else watched him, except Dieter, whose eyes were now closed. The scratch of the lawyer's fountain pen stopped, started, each stroke clear in the complete silence of the room. The elderly attorney looked up suddenly. "This will be a forward commitment of one year only, Herr Burris. We cannot spend the rest of our corporate life coming to UBCO for money."

Burris' nose wrinkled. He plunked his rear end down on the edge of Dieter Staeli's desk next to the pad of foolscap. "A year?"

He thought for a moment. "Make it three and we have a deal. No sense me being a hog."

* * *

At four o'clock the rain shut off, as by a turn of some Olympian faucet in the heavens. The afternoon sun poured down upon Basel with such force that in a few minutes the edges of puddles had begun to steam as they dried.

At four-thirty, when Matthew Burris arrived on foot at the Drei Könige, the waiters had already cranked the awning back out of the way. He sat in a sunny corner table, the round one usually reserved at lunch for Dieter Staeli. The maître d' approaching, bowing.

"The usual, Herr Burris?"

"For two."

Abasing himself, the man withdrew. Burris glanced at the river, sparkling in the sun. Then his attention was caught by the orange L-2 Magna parked in front of Erich's house. He smiled. It was Margit's signal, reassuring him that she would be there for their drink.

Burris' smile tightened. He dropped it. He still felt unable to relax. Perhaps Margit could help him when she got there. Two hours in the lion's den was a bit too much, especially as he'd more or less improvised the whole thing. If he'd carefully premeditated it, Burris knew, he'd never have had the nerve to carry it out properly.

As it was, he'd intercepted the Staeli party as they were leaving for the Kunstmuseum press conference of the century, both Walter and his father in dark-gray Homburg hats the color of Palmer's eyes. Burris, remembering, laughed abruptly.

One of the waiters started forward expectantly, then fell back.

In the old devil's office they had moved stiffly like deep-sea divers under hundreds of fathoms of pressure. The air had been thick with hatred, burning out of the old man like malign radiation.

Burris blew out his cheeks and let air escape. The waiter brought a small glass pitcher in which ice cubes and vodka tinkled. He placed next to the pitcher two chilled cocktail glasses and a tiny china pitcher of the size sometimes used back in the States for individual servings of pancake syrup. "The vermouth, Herr Burris."

"*Sehr schön.*" Burris grinned at him and tried again to relax.

What the hell, he thought, I've pulled off the trick. Gone into the deepest den of the thickest thieves and blackmailed them into elevating UBCO-Basel from a midget to a prime lender. Wasn't this what Palmer had wanted? UBCO-Basel had achieved critical mass with one stroke of Dieter Staeli's pen, and the old devil still didn't know what had hit him.

". . . you realize we can never explain this to our stockh—"

"Forget the stockholders. Someone better get on the telex and start recalling every one of those damned little calculators."

Burris' grin broadened for an instant. Across the Rhine, the little sports car produced a startling noise that carried over the river. He wondered if, before Margit returned the car to her fiancé, they shouldn't have the muffler replaced. But Erich Lorn was probably an antique-car nut who'd insist on original English equipment.

Burris wanted to wave to Margit, but he couldn't see her. The cloth top of the Magna was in place and its small isinglass windows hid the driver from view.

The car shot forward a few feet, then slammed to a stop with a squeal that carried across the broad river. Another start-stop-squeal. The little car shot forward along the Unterer Rheinweg.

Margit shouldn't mistreat it, Burris mused. He'd have to mention it to her. Funny position, him protecting the fiancé's car. Funny relationship to begin with. European.

The orange car rocketed ahead, accelerating with a harsh whine of gears. Then, suddenly, the front wheels swiveled left and the entire car lifted up on one side as Margit put it into a tight U-turn.

Now the car accelerated again, whining like a gigantic mosquito as it howled back in the opposite direction, flashed past Erich's house, screamed up an incline and swerved wildly onto the Mittlererhein Bridge, thick now with late afternoon traffic.

Burris jumped to his feet.

He'd never seen Margit drive this wildly. The car was wobbling unsteadily in the streetcar tracks.

It swerved to avoid a woman, bounced sideways up over the sidewalk and scattered half a dozen pedestrians who jumped for cover.

390

Burris ran to the railing. On the bridge, the Magna was speeding up in a deafening churning of gears. The roar of its engine filled the air.

Horns began blowing. A woman screamed. Burris saw one of the long green double streetcars racing up the bridge from his side of the river.

The streetcar bell clanged. The orange car slammed a few yards further along the sidewalk, right-hand wheels on the curb. Then it twisted hard to the left, as if the driver had yanked the steering wheel with one powerful motion.

"Margit!"

Traveling at about fifty miles an hour, the low-slung Magna plowed head on into the pointed nose of the streetcar.

Burris' ears filled with the rending crash of steel. Something flew out through the windshield of the car where it met the canvas top.

Sparks showered up from the center of the explosion. A great white fountain of electrical discharge spurted upwards out of the smoking heart of the crash.

Burris was running. He tore through the hotel lobby, swung left and dashed around the corner onto the bridge. Sirens whooped in the distance.

People were clustering about the body on the street. Police came running. Burris shouldered his way through to the crumpled body.

Police were shouting, trying to keep people back. An emergency truck had pulled up. Burris stared down in horror at the body.

It was a bright mass of red. The windshield or the canvas had cut it to shreds as the collision catapulted it through the air. Burris knelt. He started to reach for the body.

Someone was shouting about electricity. Voices took up the cry, warning people back. Sparks shot up out of the collision. Then Burris felt the ground shake under his knees.

A roar slammed into his ears. He slitted his eyes against a wave of heat and saw a puffball of scarlet-orange flame burst from the ruined Magna.

Greasy smoke billowed across the pavement. Sirens rose and fell. Burris reached for the bloody body to turn it face up.

"Erich!"

His glanced jumped. Margit was running toward him. The body

wasn't Margit. Her mouth was wide, eyes staring. The body was Erich.

She dropped to her knees beside Burris. The bridge shook with people running, trucks rumbling. Someone shouted for chemical foam.

An ambulance pulled up beside Burris. In the distance a woman was screaming wordlessly. Burris gritted his teeth against the high, piercing voice.

An interne shoved a stethoscope under the body. Margit's hand went out to touch a scrap of white shirting with a faint pattern of beige to it.

The interne listened, shifted the stethoscope, listened again. Sparks rattled and shot from under the burning wreck of the Magna. Its long hood had crumpled into the slender snout of the streetcar, smeared sideways like a smashed nose.

Someone was shouting about switching off the power. The woman kept screaming something at the top of her voice.

"Is he—?" Margit's voice choked off.

The interne waved over an orderly. The two men gently rolled Erich's body onto a stretcher. "Is he alive?" Margit begged.

Burris watched the interne's glance switch suddenly in the direction of the screaming woman. Then he started running toward the burning wreck.

"This man," Margit said to the orderly. She pointed to Erich.

"Sh." The orderly held up a hand. "She says—" He stopped and listened to the screaming. "She says there is someone."

"This man here," Margit insisted.

"Someone else," the orderly said, "inside the car."

PART SIX

Switzerland is a country where very few things start, but many things end.

—F. Scott Fitzgerald

CHAPTER 62

"Miss Margit is very lucky with weather," Uschi said in her most formal manner. "Tonight you would almost think was midsummer."

"Along the river," Bunter responded with equal judicious heaviness. "April evenings are often cold. But not tonight, *Gott sei dank.*"

He stood in the large kitchen of Schloss Staeli, near the staff of caterer's people at work, and stared out the windows at the lawn beyond the shrubbery that sloped gently down to the river below. Behind him, Bodo watched the guests strolling on the new grass.

"We have time yet," he murmured, "before the midnight refreshments." He nudged Bunter in the back. "In the pantry sits Maxl waiting to play jass."

Bunter frowned to show that the nudge was a mark of disrespect. Nevertheless, he followed the younger man into the pantry. Maxl, the assistant gardener, nodded politely to him. Through an open window they could hear the dance band playing *"Wiener Blut."*

The three men sat at a table Bodo had moved in from the wine cellar. Normally it was used to open and decant bottles. It had been scrubbed of old stains and did well enough as a spare table now. Maxl produced an ordinary deck of cards and began stripping it to a jass deck.

He put aside everything between the six and the ace, reshuffled the thirty-six remaining cards and dealt them three at a time until each player had nine. Then he turned up the twenty-eighth card, a queen of clubs, to indicate the trump suit, and set aside the remainder of the deck. Bodo grunted softly, removed the six of clubs from his hand and exchanged it for the queen.

"Funny," Bunter mused, arranging his hand, "to be playing jass with queens."

* * *

The gazebo stood to one side of the immense lawn that ran from the house to the very bank of the Rhine. It had been Lucas Staeli, before he became a virtual hermit, who had enlarged the structure from a small French *folie* only big enough for a party of four into the present gazebo, a roomy octagon with slender Ionic pillars supporting a circular dome sheathed in copper.

The gazebo was now large enough not only for the seven-piece band but the bar where waiters filled their trays before circulating among the guests. The caterers were already setting up a long table draped in shimmering damask on which the midnight buffet would be served.

The band finished *"Wiener Blut."* The leader noted that, although there were plenty of old folks who enjoyed a waltz, they hadn't been out on the floor. He muttered something to the cornet and drummer. A moment later the band swung into its usual tepid medley of elderly Beatles' numbers. This, the leader felt, would bring the younger people out on the floor.

The floor itself had hardly gotten much of a workout. It had been laid down in sections of polished maple, bolted together over a plastic sheet that protected it from wet grass. Maxl's boss, the head gardener, had protested that the grass was too young for this treatment. It had only just begun to sprout in delicate shades of yellow-green.

He'd been overruled by Miss Margit. This was a major social event. There would be dancing and it would be out of doors.

The band leader watched one middle-aged couple begin to foxtrot sedately. No one joined them.

* * *

Across from the gazebo, Herr und Frau Stöcklin frowned first at the dance band and then at the middle-aged couple dancing. They turned to Herr und Frau Grütli and Herr und Frau Schtumpf, all of them in their seventies. The waltzes had been excellent. What was this trashy noise now from the band?

"However," Frau Schtumpf added, "a lovely party."

Herr Grütli nodded. "But not as lively as the old days, eh? We should all be out there, waltzing."

Frau Stöcklin sighed heavily. "Dancing is for the younger ones. And where are they? Talking business."

Frau Schtumpf sniffed. "Not the same without a few young bachelors. They make a difference. Erich Lorn used to ask me to dance."

Her husband emitted a short bark of a laugh. "He's doing damned little dancing these days."

His wife frowned at him. "And young Pauli Iselin," she added in a better-not-make-a-joke tone.

Herr Stöcklin made a grunting noise to Herr Schtumpf, by way of rescuing him. "I understand the Iselin house is being torn down, eh? Quite a real estate windfall. I hear it went for—"

His wife cut him short with a glare. "Talking business?"

* * *

Elfi stood quite alone in the second-floor sitting room. Through the windows she watched the party shift here and there in the amber light of candles set around the edge of the lawn. Everyone looked so fine, the women in their ball gowns, the men in dinner jackets and black ties.

She had never seen Pauli in a tuxedo. He would have looked marvelous, of course.

Miss Margit had invited her to enjoy dinner with the other servants in the kitchen, but Elfi stayed out of kitchens. She was not a cook, nor a scullery maid. She was Miss Margit's personal maid. Her official domain was this suite of rooms. The rest of the house was limbo for Elfi. And so, too, was the party.

Ladies' maids didn't attend such grand affairs, even those that once, for a brief moment, might have been made into more than they were.

To make everything even harder to endure, Elfi had been able to follow the party's progress by its sounds from the floor below. Promptly at seven, for example, the septet from the Munich Philharmonic had begun to play Mozart and Albinoni in the conservatory. Elfi had never seen the great corner room open before, much less decorated as it now was with potted ferns.

She had seen the septet alight from its bus, two violinists, two violists, two cellists and the only woman, who must be the player of the harpsichord that Bodo and Maxl had wheeled into the house.

Haydn, Vivaldi, Bach were played to greet the guests as they arrived through the main entrance of Schloss Staeli, the great porte-cochere, newly reopened for the party. Pauli had wanted to give her a party. They would have unwrapped all the dust cloths and opened the Iselins' own porte-cochere to . . .

Elfi's mouth pressed into a straight line. She had had no more than a bad dream. It was fading slowly. She would never forget it, but she would work to dull down the details, one by one.

* * *

In the years since Lucas Staeli's death, this was the first time the schloss had been opened for a party. Remembering when she had stood beside her father on the receiving stairway, Margit had asked Matt Burris to stand by her and help greet guests. He had no official status, other than friend, but everyone in Basel knew him and would find his big, smiling presence reassuring as they arrived. So would Margit.

Burris had firmly joined the home team and settled so well into the routine of Basel business life that he had been forced to maintain several tuxedos, pairs of dancing slippers and the like. It was not a life he had originally foreseen for himself, but it was a life into which he fitted very smoothly.

Standing near Margit at the top of the stairway, smiling and bowing and smiling again, he quickly met, or remet, a Herr Eggers, a Herr und Frau Hüpli, Herr von Arx, Frau Rot, Herr und Frau Wo, Frau Ru, three Fräuleins Finckh, Magistrate Lu, Archbishop Klat, Advocate Flüm, Colonel und Frau Nafer, Herr Kratsch and Herr und Frau Dieter Staeli.

Dieter avoided Burris' hand, although he drily pecked his niece on the cheek. Resentment of Burris hadn't died away, even though the last of the fatal Staelicomps had been recalled, the company phased out of existence, its assets transferred to a Panamanian shell, and Walter ignominiously transferred to Beirut.

Even now Dieter Staeli avoided Burris. He seemed still to command his usual formidable spy network, which warned him when Burris was planning to attend a business or social function. Staeli would rather ostentatiously stay away.

It was a strange way for the acting head of Staeli Internationale, GmbH. to behave toward the manager of the bank that financed so many of his newer industrial activities.

In other ways, the business relationship had been flawless; both companies continued to abide by the rather unprecedented agreement signed that day last September, when, out of a blue sky, the heavens had poured down upon Basel, Baslers and all their works. But it was equally unprecedented that the heads of the two concerns had never again met . . . until tonight.

Burris hoped to confront the old man at some point, but not in the reception area. He had too lively a respect for Dieter's ability to spoil the whole party.

"And many happy wishes, dear Margit, for the day," Dieter's small, frail wife added as they moved into the hall.

Burris eyed Margit. "What was that? This isn't your birthday."

Margit nodded. "And Auntie remembered."

His voice dropped to an undertone. "Your thirtieth birthday?"

"Afraid so."

"Then Uncle remembered, too."

Margit smiled crookedly. *"Natürlich."*

Burris patted her shoulder discreetly. "Honey, this is Liberation Day."

"Not a word to anyone."

"But when they leave, this calls for a real celebration."

Margit glanced around her. "Some would call this celebration real enough," she remarked drily.

"You know what I mean. Just the two of us."

She nodded. "After they leave."

Then she changed her half-smile into a broad one of welcome as the next guests mounted the staircase. "So good to see you again," she began in a high, carrying voice.

* * *

By the time the medium-tempo Beatles' medley had ended, three couples were on the floor. The band leader felt he had somehow broken the ice. He could give them any style of music they wanted, but the trick was to find the kind that made them dance. Otherwise the hostess would be unhappy.

Appearances were everything in these affairs, the band leader knew. The music could be junk, but the people had to be dancing. Why, even the appearance of the band was vital. They had three changes of costume: black, red and white.

It was a mark of the leader's approach to the art of music that the cost of dry-cleaning uniforms was ten times what he paid each year for musical arrangements.

But it was worth it. Anything was if it got the people dancing.

* * *

Margit stood beside one of the Burckhardt girls her age and a young couple name Pik, recently returned to Basel. They had been chatting of skiing and Margit had remarked that the whole winter had slipped past without her once putting on skis.

"And do you know, I have just this moment realized it?"

"It hasn't perhaps been a completely joyous winter for you," Frau Pik murmured sympathetically.

Margit's face, blank for a moment, shone faintly in the illumination of candles in amber hurricane glasses at intervals around the garden. The light flickered, but Margit's expression didn't change. This was not the first time someone had referred, even so diplomatically, to Erich Lorn.

Although the event had had all the makings of a prime scandal, witnesses at the inquest had told a story that, despite the questions it raised, could lead only to a verdict of accidental death.

There had been nothing left of poor Iselin but ashes. The same was true for anything else that had been in the car with him. With Erich unable for so long even to answer questions, the identity of the body had been established only by dental records.

"Not completely joyous," Margit echoed then. These were some of her oldest friends. They had grown up with Iselin and, of course—

"What do you hear from Erich?" Frau Pik asked brightly.

Again Margit was slow to respond. The Lorns had closed ranks rather formidably after the accident. Erich's married sisters, in particular, had gone out of their way to shut Margit off. They seemed to feel that if she had set a wedding date several years earlier, none of this would have happened. Clearly, they were right.

As a result, news of Erich was hard to come by, even for the woman who was still, officially, engaged to marry him. He lived—precariously—in a sanitarium near Zurich, where surgeons put him through their grisly twentieth-century version of medieval torture. For all his wealth, he had become something of a guinea pig for the doctors.

The series of skin and bone grafts proceeded slowly. Rumors varied. He might walk; he would never walk. He had lost the power of speech; he could grunt words. His brain was that of a vegetable; his mind was unimpaired.

The Lorns had shut him off from the rest of the world quite as if he had been committed to a subterranean dungeon where, in secret, these nameless tortures were performed over and over again, as if there were something they wanted to hear him confess.

"Not enough," Margit said at last. "The Lorns are very . . . possessive."

Almost, she had blurted the truth of the matter, that the family had forbidden even her to see him. Was he that hideously marred? She had gone several times to Zurich, used all sorts of influence, but the doctors had their orders and not even a Staeli could countermand them.

Oddly, she had once run into Michele there, sitting outside the sanitarium in her black Lincoln limousine, waiting like any other petitioner for an audience. The two women had sat in the car for an hour but, of course, neither had been allowed in to see Erich.

"But, surely, as the fiancée," the Burckhardt girl was suggesting.

"They've been quite extraordinary about the whole thing," Margit said. She used the English word "extraordinary," pronouncing it in the British manner, to try to make light of the matter. She had no wish to expose any more of the hurt, including the lecture Erich's father had given her about leading his poor lamb down the garden path, complete with tears.

It had never been clear to Margit how the Lorns had contrived to confuse Erich's adventure with Michele and his Quixotic, destructive defense of Margit, but they had. "Tell me," she said, struggling to change the subject. "How was Gstaad this season?"

"Dull. Dull."

As the rest joined in the general celebration of the season's dullness, Margit thought of Erich again. She had often written him over the winter. The letters hadn't been returned. Nor had they been answered. She assumed he had read them, or had them read to him.

Not being able to communicate had only sharpened her need to. If one counted the year since Matt had arrived in Basel, she'd seen Erich only a few hurried times. Suddenly, in the middle of the party, she found herself wondering if the Lorns hadn't simply destroyed her letters. They would do that. Oh, yes. Once a Swiss family got something in its head—

"Don't you agree, Margit?" the Burckhardt girl was asking.

"Sorry. Mind on a million things."

"This Michele woman. She's become quite respectable with that new spa of hers in Gstaad."

Margit's smile was a bit off center. How Erich would laugh to hear of it. If he could still laugh. "As a matter of fact," she said then, "I expect her tonight."

"Here? Surely you didn—"

"Yes. It's too bad she's missed the concert and dinner."

"And what a gorgeous dinner," Frau Pik hastened to add, smoothing over the mild sensation. The resources of the Staeli kitchen, with caterers, had produced a formidable array of soups and pâtés, pheasants, racks of lamb and profiteroles of unearthly lightness drowning in dark, fiercely sweet chocolate. Of course, Margit mused, with her figure, someone like Michele would have to be careful about profiteroles.

"It's all such a lovely party," Frau Pik continued. "You can be proud to have reopened the schloss so brilliantly." The Piks had spent the past two years in New York and couldn't be expected to have mastered all the ins and outs of Basel scandal yet.

* * *

Burris had spotted Dieter Staeli huddled on some cast-iron lawn chairs with the Archbishop. It seemed an auspicious moment to renew an old acquaintance under the imprimatur, if not the *nihil obstat,* of Mother Church.

When he saw Burris approach, Dieter's round face turned sour.

"Good evening," Burris began. "You must formally introduce us, Herr Staeli."

A gasp of exasperation escaped the older man. "Bishop Klat, Herr Burris." Dieter's mouth sealed shut with an audible snap.

"Wasn't it brilliant of your niece," Burris went on quickly, "to import such lovely music for tonight?"

"A lovely occasion," the Archbishop said. "Lovely music."

Staeli got to his feet. "You must excuse me."

Burris took the older man's elbow. "I'll walk with you." He half led him along the edge of the height above the river to a point where the nearest guest was out of earshot. "Stop acting like a child," Burris murmured.

Dieter pulled his elbow free. "Stop behaving like a rugby player. Anyone can see you outweigh me."

"I've enjoyed the whole winter without your company. It's not for that pleasure I'm here. But, eventually, I must talk to you."

"I don't talk to blackmailers."

"Normally I avoid spymasters. And don't tell me you didn't know what Iselin was bringing you that day."

"Is that why he was murdered?" Dieter's face looked raw, burning with hatred. "You Americans with your portable, disposable consciences. Corrupt the world and call it democracy." He spit the word out like a worm on his tongue. "Corrupt our women with dreams of equality. Churn their brains and make them unhappy. Turn them into harlots and our young men into murderers. And now, the supreme hypocrisy: I must *talk* to you? Talk to your harlot-queen. I choose my company more carefully."

The skin across Burris' cheeks felt as if it was burning. "I didn't realize how much pus was left in you." He stared at Dieter with a somber look. "And to think, I tried to open the door between us." He turned to walk away and had actually taken a step.

"You hold the trumps, of course," Staeli said.

Burris paused. "Yes. In my vault."

"You can blackmail me into talking to you." There was a strange, masochistic note of complacency in Staeli's voice, as if submitting to superior force. Burris picked up the meaning at once. Since the old devil knew he had to talk eventually, he pretended to have no other choice.

Staeli's head shook heavily from side to side. "Someday you'll

403

be too old to fight back." His small eyes hooded. His small mouth flattened. "And that . . . is old."

Burris had always recognized Staeli as a dangerous opponent. Watching his old-man act, he realized just how dangerous Staeli could still be.

* * *

In the pantry, Bunter swept the cards into a neat deck and glanced at his watch. "Have we time for another?"

The three men listened to the faraway sounds of another waltz. Bunter had twice melded the four *Unders,* the highest meld count in the game. It said something particularly Swiss for jass, didn't it, that the lowly *Unders* counted for more than any other meld?

He'd done well, but playing with queens instead of *Obers* was still disturbing. Bunter normally used a real jass deck, not one stripped from a poker or bridge deck. The sight of the ladies in their finery disturbed him.

Jass wasn't jass if played with queens, was it? But what was anything these days? Basel wasn't Basel, a job wasn't a job. A good family of long standing like the Lorns could turn into parvenus overnight. How else to explain their cheapness when, forty-eight hours after the accident, they'd closed the poor boy's house and put Bunter on what they called "extended leave"?

As if Bunter hadn't done his best all that summer, to keep track of Master Erich and feed him and try to get him to rest. But Miss Margit had risen grandly to the occasion.

The job he had at Schloss Staeli was actually a tremendous one, sorting out the cellar. Lucas Staeli had bought only the finest wines but they hadn't been turned, restacked, inspected or even catalogued. This Bunter was thankful to be doing. In this sad matter, with its hints of scandal no God-fearing Swiss would give credence to, Margit Staeli had behaved like a Queen.

* * *

At eleven-thirty, looking a bit harassed, but otherwise impeccable, Woods Palmer arrived from the airport. "Forgive me for being this late," he begged Margit. "The plane from Lugano simply didn't take off. I had to find an UBCO jet."

He had swept her onto the dance floor as the band struck up

404

one of the slower and more melancholy waltzes by the least-known Strauss, Edouard. Spinning slowly in his arms, Margit said: "I feel quite like a puppet."

"Surely not."

"And you the puppetmaster. You have completely altered my life," she told him, circling endlessly. Her head was whirling, not at all unpleasantly. "Suddenly you pulled the strings and changed everything."

"I did?"

"And now that it's come full circle, *Herr Puppetmeister,* tell me what it was all about? Why did you assign Matt to Basel?" She smiled tauntingly. "Because he was so familiar with Switzerland? Or with me?"

Palmer's skull-like face had gone quite blank, his dark-gray eyes searching hers. "My dear girl . . ."

"We've thought of you often with your little bow and arrow," she said. "What is it in English? Cupidity?" She smiled even more broadly at him. "Like so much of English, it doesn't mean what it seems to mean. Not playing Cupid. Just a synonym for greed."

The music grew faster and more somber, the chords fantastic. They were spinning in a tighter circle and her breath came more quickly now.

Palmer returned the smile. "I hope, at least, it was interesting for you."

"Such a cynical man. So like a banker." Margit closed her eyes for a moment. The dance floor was spinning. "To think on what slender support one's happiness rests. The greed of another is responsible for my happiness."

She wondered who had told the band to play anything this unhappy. "I'm dizzy," she said. She opened her eyes and stopped their pirouetting. They left the floor and walked toward Burris.

"Don't quit now," he said. "You have the silver cup cinched."

"Is that a surly Illinois voice I hear?" Palmer wondered.

Margit tried to catch her breath. "I know you have a lot to talk about."

"Not really," Palmer assured her, but she had run off.

* * *

The waltzes were really catching on now, the band leader noted. The older folks had the stamina. Automatically playing his mindless violin arpeggios, he reminded himself that in Basel the old people had firm control of things and the waltz was theirs.

That was why he'd never leave this town. He'd had offers from ski resorts, other posh jet-set places. Never. Give him Basel, every time. He hadn't bought a new piece of music in years.

* * *

"I see our friend, Dieter," Palmer murmured. "Got him on the team yet?"

"No way."

"How's his volume?"

Burris shrugged. "Can't complain. Listen, it's a party. No business."

"A scrap. I got a final report from Brussels, a sort of narrative of how Staelicomp happened."

"What's it to be, a Literary Guild selection?"

"It does fill in the gaps, Matty. Did you know, for instance, that Iselin got to her maid?"

"Elfi? She's still on the payroll."

Palmer looked grave for a moment. "Curtis has also substantiated our guess that Walter had no idea the calculators were bugged."

He turned to watch a long black Lincoln Continental limousine pull around the driveway. "It was a desperate move," he said then, "collusion between a few Japanese contractors and their own mafia. That's why the innards didn't say 'Made in Japan.' If anybody found the bug, he would blame the Swiss, not the Japanese. You can see why, with that protection, they had to try their luck."

Burris shook his head. "I could never see why they took such a chance to begin with."

"What chance? With Walter Staeli fronting for them?"

"Even so, most of the Japanese I knew wouldn't go for anything that raw. They're sharp, but not criminal."

Palmer glanced around for eavesdroppers, but found none. "This was an extremist fringe of Japan, Inc.," he explained, "right-wingers who hooked up with their own underworld and the P.L.O. It's the bunch who supplied Japanese gunmen for the Lod Airport massacre in Tel Aviv."

"I know. But who needs oil that badly?"

"They were trying their luck with the Arab terror groups. It looked like a smart move—Arab oil and gold, combined with Japanese industrial knowhow. Of course, in this case, the ultimate knowhow was to be supplied by the bugged calculators. It was this sort of advance confidential information they were peddling. It gave them an ear on the entire West and they were hoping to use Arab clout to cash in on—"

Palmer stopped suddenly. "You think it's a fairy story?"

"Can't we talk about it later?"

"Sure. But, meanwhile, think about what the Arabs lack that the Japanese could give them. And vice versa." He shrugged lightly. "Meanwhile we're trying to figure out their next move, now that the Staelicomp thing blew up. A group like that doesn't say die. They'll be back with another lulu. Let's just hope they don't find another Walter."

"And he thought he was outsmarting them," Burris mused.

"Now we know why he found it so easy."

Both men laughed quietly.

* * *

Margit, too, had seen the Lincoln limousine. She'd returned to the schloss in time to greet Michele as her chauffeur ushered her from the long black auto.

The scene reminded Margit of a seller of expensive antiques carefully removing a fully refurbished masterpiece of great age from its dust-free enclosure. The chauffeur's solicitous way of holding Michele's arm indicated that, in addition to being very expensive, she was also quite fragile.

In the lights of the porte-cochere, Michele looked costly enough in a floor-length gown of something knitted with strands of gold that clung to her breasts and hips and shot out faint muted beams of smoldering yellow flame. Her broad Magyar face with its high cheekbones was in perfect repose and, at the same time, somehow seemed full of anticipation for a party to which she had arrived almost too late.

"So delighted you could come," Margit said.

"So sorry to be this late, darling," Michele replied.

They were edging near each other in the manner of a luxury

liner tying up at a dock. They shook hands somewhat formally. It would be years, if ever, before they kissed each other's cheek.

* * *

The small group was spread out, the men not bothering to close ranks as they talked privately.

Palmer eyed them. Dieter Staeli occupied the precise center, with someone who resembled him, a cousin perhaps, on one side. The gentleman in the rusty dinner jacket with the decorations was a colonel, the highest-ranking army officer in time of peace.

Palmer recognized the fourth man as the President of Switzerland, something many Swiss would have been unable to do. The President was simply one of the seven members of the Federal Council. Each year the Council elected a chairman from its ranks who had the title of President but was lucky if even his next-door neighbor knew it.

The fifth and sixth men were younger. They stood silently, openly drinking in wisdom in the manner all ambitious young men cultivate in Switzerland, and everywhere else, for that matter.

"Herr Staeli." Palmer tried a frontal attack. "We've never met. Woods Palmer." He held out his hand.

The atmosphere chilled alarmingly. The two younger men stood in frozen shock. The colonel and the President, innocent of anything, merely blinked pleasantly. Staeli and his kinsman looked wooden with surprise. A long moment passed. Then, jerkily, as if worked by badly oiled pulleys, Dieter Staeli's hand came slowly up, blunt, squat of finger.

It felt dry in Palmer's hand. He pumped it ceremoniously and, when nothing further was said, went on: "We're pleased to be sharing in your tremendous industrial advances."

Dieter's little eyes hooded slightly. By now, Palmer knew, the entire strategy of UBCO-Basel was exposed for anyone to see, but too late for anyone to hamper.

"You . . ." Dieter faltered an instant. "You are . . ." The silence was complete. "You are too kind," he concluded then.

Although the younger men relaxed, the kinsman did not. Apparently neither the colonel nor the President had felt the tension. They continued to provide free samples of a patented noncommittal political smile.

408

"Matthew Burris," Palmer said then, "has told me wonderful things about you. And Staeli Internationale."

Dieter's eyes, half imbedded in fat, grew even smaller. "Herr Palmer," he said, releasing his hand, "you can perhaps gladden an old man's heart?"

"With pleasure, sir."

"Your Herr Burris."

"Yes?"

"Promote him."

"Yes?"

"He would make you a fine, ah, European manager. Based in some other country, no doubt."

The band played a flourish and the leader stood up. "Ladies and gentlemen," he purred into the microphone, "supper is served."

* * *

Elfi watched people moving in twos and fours toward the buffet set up under the dome of the gazebo. Even at this distance she admired the leisurely way they moved. These people had all the time in the world.

Elfi herself hadn't eaten tonight. She dreaded going down to the kitchen. Bodo would resume his crude sexual teasing, this time in front of others. It wasn't that she disliked Bodo. Men like him were her fate and she had often told herself, of late, that she might as well get used to them.

But Bodo reminded her much too painfully of what her fate might have been, if Iselin had lived. At the same time, she realized she was being foolish, that Iselin had only been using her. But, foolish or not, she couldn't help the way she felt.

Elfi frowned. She'd been insane to dream of becoming something more than a lady's maid. Iselin had planted that thought in her head, for his own reasons. She was what she was, and worse: she was in a dead-end job that eternally rubbed her nose in the fact of being the maid, not the lady. If only she'd never met Iselin.

* * *

"Madame Michele, this is Woods Palmer."

Margit took a step back out of the combined aura of the meeting she had just arranged. Both of these people had powerful personalities and it was needless to wonder if they'd heard of each other. Of course, in Palmer's case, while he may have heard of Michele through her business triumphs, this was his first head-on blast of her as a woman.

Margit found her impossible to dislike. Yes, she'd put Erich through a lot, but Erich was no stranger himself to the cruel side of these affairs. But Michele transcended individual affairs. She was unique.

Other women, like Margit, might work hard to train themselves in professions, or protect their rights and liberty. Not Michele. She had obviously never doubted that a woman's chief function was to ensnare, arouse, upset and use men beyond endurance. In the life-long war of the sexes, she was a one-woman commando brigade.

She was establishing a beachhead now on Palmer, listening attentively, eyes bright with interest, breasts in their golden sheath moving infinitesimally closer to him as he talked, and talked.

". . . Burris has mentioned your franchising plans for Europe and the States."

"Mm." She indicated that this was not really a topic she was dying to discuss with a man like Palmer.

"I don't suppose our bank cou—"

She smiled at him, which had the effect of cutting him off in mid-word. "They are playing a Lehar waltz from *Paganini*."

"I beg your pardon?"

"The music." She took his arm and turned him toward the band. "It's the tenor aria, *'Gern hab' ich die Frau'n geküsst.'* You've heard it so often. It made Richard Tauber famous, singing it."

Palmer listened for a moment. "Charming. What's it mean?"

"Oh, something about loving to kiss women."

"But, you know," he said, "it's not a waltz."

She smiled up at him. "Really?" she asked as they strolled toward the dance floor.

* * *

Once supper ended, a lot of the older guests began to leave. The caterer's people, swooping in on the gazebo, began to pack and clear off equipment. The band remained, playing softly, sticking to the old tunes. Some of the candles in their hurricane glasses had burned out. The rest flickered low. A few of the younger couples danced or sipped champagne.

Most of the guests who remained were of Margit's age, or younger, only too pleased to extend, even for a little longer, this bright spot in the wall-to-wall family gray of Basel's normal social life. The party had reached a pause now. It could, at this point, go in one of two directions. The younger people could decide to leave, or they could decide to force new life into things.

Dieter Staeli had left with his age group, pausing neither to bid his niece adieu nor even to nod at Palmer, much less Burris. The two Americans, with their ladies, were now gathered on the edge of the lawn near the house while Margit tried to convince Palmer and Michele that, if they stayed, the party would "pick up."

The younger Burckhardt girl joined them, possibly out of malicious curiosity as to what Margit and Michele would have to say to each other. "Yes, yes, by all means," she broke in at last. "You must stay. Margit, it's a grand idea. Let's keep the party going till dawn, *nicht wahr?*"

Margit looked past her to Burris for help in time to see him stifle a yawn. "Come on, Matt," she said. "Are we keeping you up?"

He blinked lazily. "No, I'd have to be up anyway," he said with a slight grin. Then, to Palmer: "Stay a bit."

"Michele's offered me a lift to my hotel."

Burris turned to her. "Don't whisk him away just yet."

"Mein Gott!"

The man who had spoken was halfway across the lawn, his voice high with shock. Everyone turned to look at him. Then they turned to see what he was staring at with such surprise.

As they looked, a large white ambulance van, roof lamp twirling long scarlet spokes of light, moved very slowly around the sweep of the driveway and began to edge its way carefully over the grass.

The great ghostly white van was heading inexorably toward the gazebo. So shocking was this apparition that the dance music died in midchord, as if produced by mechanical musicians whose plug had just been pulled.

"Here!" someone shouted. "The fool's ruining the lawn."

"Stop!"

There was something ominous about the slowness with which

the ambulance made its way unswervingly to the very center of the lawn. Holding Margit's arm, Burris felt her muscles tense.

Now the white ghost was turning in a tight curve. It pulled around so that its rear doors were facing the guests, revealing nothing more of its identity than this rude backside view.

"Here, you!" someone shouted.

The driver hopped out, dashed to the rear doors and swung them open. He reached inside and pulled down an inclined ramp that ran from the ambulance down to the grass.

"Was gibt?" the Burckhardt girl asked in a near-scream.

A thin, mosquitolike whine of electric motors came from inside the ambulance. A moment later, a self-propelled wheelchair moved like a robot visitor into view, paused for a moment in the doorway of the van and nosed carefully down the runway.

In it, dressed in a black dinner jacket and evening shirt of resplendent white ruching that frothed at neck and cuffs, sat Erich Lorn.

The sheer silence was hardly broken by the whine of wheelchair motors, muffled now in the grass. Erich steered himself on a collision course for Margit.

He stopped the wheelchair a few feet from her and produced his usual Satanic smile, filled with V's that flickered in the uncertain light of the guttering candles.

Long red spokes of light twiddled back and forth, crisscrossing his face and hers. Red. White. Red. She dropped to her knees in the grass beside his wheelchair.

"Happy birthday, Margit," Erich said.

*　*　*

It was one-thirty. Burris found himself at the landing that overlooked the river, standing alone. The last of the guests, chattering madly over this juicy new story, had finally left after assuring themselves that good old Erich was not only alive and well but, with the aid of two aluminum crutches, could walk well enough.

And talk. Quite his old, unblinking self.

The bastard could have come by cab, Burris found himself thinking. He could have walked across the lawn. No grand, spotlighted entrance, the lousy hambo.

Burris laughed, unable to help it. This had been his first experience with the fabled Erich Lorn and, despite the odds, he found himself liking the man.

He decided now that, ambulance or no ambulance, the return would have been just as dramatic. Erich Lorn couldn't have returned to the land of the living—ostensibly for Margit's birthday —any other way but spectacularly.

They'd done a fair enough job on him in Zurich. Maybe now Margit could stop brooding over him. His legs were knitting. His face looked pretty good, minus a few of the old V's, as Margit had pointed out, and plus a few new ones. Naturally, such an unveiling had to be stagey.

And Margit! Almost hysterical. Burris had never seen her carry on this way, laughing and crying at the same time, kissing Erich's hand, introducing him not once but four times to Burris.

"Matt, this is—. Oh, but you—"

And yammering away in Schweizerdeutsch, the lot of them, like the old schoolmates they were, crowding around the wheelchair, laughing and screaming and—

There had only been that one awkward moment.

In her confusion and near-hysteria, Margit had introduced Erich to a number of people he'd known for years, but this only drew good-natured laughs. Then she introduced him to a stranger, Woods Palmer.

In the most natural manner possible, Palmer had turned and introduced Erich to Michele. There had been a longish pause. Thinking back over it now, Burris found it impossible to believe that Palmer hadn't known what he was doing.

All over the lawn, guests froze into attention. This was perhaps the confrontation they had been hanging around to witness. Tomorrow morning all Basel would be buzzing.

Erich had, after a moment, reached out a hand and Michele had taken it. *"Enchanté, Madame,"* he had murmured. They shook hands once. But then she had not let his hand go.

Bending over him in the wheelchair, her broad face absolutely placid in the uncertain candlelight, she had turned his palm up to stare at it.

"A bad scar. New?"

"Cut several nerves, they tell me," Erich had replied.

"It lies directly across the life line."

Her voice was low. Her other hand came forward and she touched the scar gently with her index finger, slowly stroking it.

Erich nodded. "But I've always had a rather ominous break in that line. Remember?"

They eyed each other silently. "Early death," she said then. "By violence."

Her voice had been almost a whisper. Then she smiled brilliantly at Erich, the full thousand-watt Michele smile, and spoke more loudly, carryingly. "You needn't worry about *that* any more, eh?"

He didn't reply for a long moment. When he did it was gravely, with no answering smile. "Yes," he said. "I'm quite a new man, it seems."

Burris stood on the landing over the river. He could see the lights of a lone car across the Rhine, its headlights moving slowly along the road that paralleled the river. He wanted to be in it. He wanted to be alone and out of this abruptly complicated triangle in which he found himself. Here, on this landing where Margit said she and Erich had lazed away so many summers, the complexities of everything seemed too much for him.

He made a face. He had never been one for quick reactions. It took a long time to know how he really felt about something. But he was really uneasy about what had happened tonight. He realized he was being hypocritical. Erich had always been part of the triangle. But his dramatic return, as it were, from the dead, had spotlighted the whole dilemma. *His* dilemma.

Margit could not be counted on for any help. She was too wrapped up in Erich's return even to tie off the loose strings of the party, tipping the bandleader and the caterer's supervisor. Burris had done this for her.

The Prodigal's return. And not to his family, whom he seemed to dislike more than ever, but to his own true love. All Basel would be talking of nothing else for days. By and large, all Basel would approve. And, pretty soon, all Basel would remember the interloper, the American. And then?

Burris frowned at the night and the river. He wanted to be away from this place and these people.

"Matt?"

He saw Margit moving toward him across the darkness of the lawn. The candles, one by one, had died. Only a few still flickered. She smiled at him. "We're deserted here," she said. "Everyone's left."

"Yes. I told your staff to hit the hay."

"Good."

"And tipped the visiting talent."

"Thank you."

She hugged his arm against the chill of the river. "That was thoughtful of you. I haven't been much help."

"Mm."

She nodded to herself. "And you're miffed, yes? But I couldn't help myself, Matt. He's still not recovered and it was insane for him to come here tonight. The hospital found his bed empty. He'd run away from Zurich for my birthday. And he doesn't intend to return there."

"Mm."

"I thanked you for your help. I'm grateful that you dealt with the staff for me. It wasn't an effort for you, anyway. They're already part of the Burris team." She turned and stared back over her shoulder at the schloss, a huge black shape, darker than the night itself.

"There's a light in my study," she said then. "Earlier in the evening Elfi was up there. She's gone now."

A faint aroma, not unpleasant, came to them, mingling the smell of the river and the garden. "Are you very attached to her?" Burris asked then.

"Elfi? Why?"

When he failed to answer, she put her arm around his waist. Across the Rhine, the headlights of the moving car were gone and Burris felt, unreasonably, as if his last chance of escape had vanished.

"You've found out," Margit said then, "about Elfi and Iselin?"

"You figured it out, too?"

"No. She came to me and confessed." Margit sighed. "She expected to be sacked, but I didn't see it that way."

"She did betray you."

"The Swiss have different meanings for such great concepts." He felt the chill river air thicken as she spoke. "I told you the story of General Jomini, the bank clerk who betrayed Napoleon and the Tsar? We don't call it betrayal. And I don't choose to call it that with Elfi."

Burris said nothing. It was not, he thought, as if this side of the Swiss character was unknown to him. But, apparently, he'd had enough of ambiguities for now. His own position here was ambiguous enough since the amazing resurrection of Erich Lorn.

After a while Margit said: "Did you notice what was going on between our two unescorted celebrities?"

"Which two?"

"Your Palmer and my Michele."

Burris said nothing for a moment, the air thick and humid in his nostrils. He wasn't at all sure he liked any of these people, Palmer included. He needed a vacation from sophistication.

"Your Michele," he said then. "I gather she's no longer Erich's Michele." Making the snide remark didn't seem to relieve his feelings.

Her arm tightened around his waist. "You didn't like him."

"I liked him. What the hell, it's hard not to."

"The dramatic return." She began to laugh softly, fondly. "There are three ways to do a thing: right, wrong and Erich Lorn's way."

Burris nodded stiffly. "The way he picked to chill Iselin wasn—"

"Please, Matt."

"Sorry. If it'd been me, I'd have punched out the little roach and destroyed th—"

"Please. You don't know Pauli Iselin. He was caught in a trap from which there was only one escape."

"Conveniently provided by Er—"

"Please, Matt."

Burris fell silent again. These people. It wasn't that he hadn't pulled fast ones in his time. The blackmail of Dieter Staeli hadn't been your average Boy Scout Merit Badge examination. But there was something so bent . . . strangely bent, about chancing suicide to finish off Iselin.

Not devious. Laying your life on the line was anything but. The idea was a warped one, though. There were other ways of handling Iselin, unless you really wanted to die in the attempt. Perhaps that had affected Erich's choice of action. Perhaps.

416

The right word for the whole thing was . . . Swiss. Right. Burris would never understand it, any more than he'd understand keeping Elfi on the payroll. Swiss was the word for it. And now she'd installed the runaway lad in her own home.

"What's he doing upstairs?" Burris blurted out then.

"Sleeping. Heavy drama takes it out of a fellow."

"I noticed the ambulance is gone."

She didn't answer for a moment. Then: "Yes, I sent it away."

Her arm tightened about his waist for a moment, as if to say: "Come on, take it easy." Having a fiancé of doubtful health and future hidden away in a remote sanitarium was one thing, Burris thought. Having him home, free and clear, was another. Hell, next week the attorneys would officially convey Margit's inheritance to her. An hour later she could get married if she felt like it.

"I noticed," she said, breaking the growing silence, "that you'd sent your own car home when you arrived. Is your driver coming back?"

"I hadn't—"

"I'm just kidding you," she interrupted. "Poor Matt." She kissed him lightly on the mouth. "It can't be very jolly, this sudden vision of Erich popping up like a magician's rabbit."

"Not jolly."

"Poor Matt," she repeated.

"You get such a kick out of saying that. Try 'poor Erich.' He's got a year of mending ahead of him."

"What about 'poor Margit'? It's even closer to the realities."

He touched her cheek gently, then tipped up her head. "Poor Margit. Next week a multimillionaire with only two eligible men panting over her. There isn't a woman in Europe who wouldn't feel sorry for you."

"I'm not sure I like the new, sarcastic Matt Burris."

"I never had this kind of material to work with before."

They eyed each other warily for a moment. Then he nodded. "You're still not finished with him. We both know that."

"Finished? I'm haunted."

The river damp swirled around them like a low-lying mist, shredding itself against shrubbery and trees. "I don't think you understand it from my viewpoint," Margit said then. "Once I thought Erich and I were level. We felt the same way about each other, detached, or as they say in the U.S., cool. That was a mistake on my part. What he did for me was the act of someone who . . ." Her voice died away and she stared at the river mists. "Someone who loved me much more than I loved him. And I never knew it."

She broke away from him and turned to look back at the house. "That girl in the window haunts me, too. Why didn't I dismiss her? I'm not yet finished with that September, Matt."

"Of course you are."

"Because I can give this party? If I'd let them, every newspaper would have sent reporters. Schloss Staeli returns to the land of the living. Margit Staeli is still haunted by ghosts."

He drew her back to him again. "You're tired. Let's talk about it tomorrow."

She pulled away. "Don't humor me."

"Still the captain of the opposing team?"

She nodded. "And the score is even worse now: fourteen for you and nothing for me. I can't seem to get my backfield in motion."

Burris grinned. "Watch the way Michele does it."

"I did. Matt, do you realize that after all of this, the tragedies and the comedies, the intrigues and the betrayals, even this smashing party tonight *with* the Munich baroque septet *and* the schmalz band, *plus* the resurrection of Erich Lorn, nothing has really changed?"

She shook her head in disbelief at what she was saying. "It's just come full circle. It needed only Erich to close the ring." She kept shaking her head. "Not fair, Matt. You get what you want. Palmer gets what he wants. Even Michele . . . whatever in God's name she wants, she gets. While I—" She broke off.

"Next week the lawyers give you what you want."

"Is that meant to be humorous?"

The chill in her voice was colder than the mist off the river. "Wasn't that what you wanted all along?" Burris snapped back.

"Never!" She paused. "Well. That's not true, is it?" She gave him a rueful look. "You see? I'm starting to tell myself lies."

"What do you want, then?"

She stared at him. "The age-old question. All of you have what you want, even Erich, I suppose, although—"

"Stop keeping score," Burris cut in. "There have been plenty of losers in this game, starting with Iselin."

Her eyes went wide, the irises darker in the uncertain light. She nodded. "And Elfi."

"What do you want, Margit?"

Her glance shifted to the night beyond the river, on the other side of the Rhine. "What indeed. You see, I'm really too Swiss for my own good. Swiss to the core, Matt, Swiss enough to realize that what the lawyers sign over to me next week I will one day bequeath to another. The conveyance of the estate, Matt. It's an article of Swiss faith. So, being Swiss, I must insure that there is another to whom I can bequeath what has been left to me. So . . ."

When she failed to go on he finished the thought for her. "So you have to marry and have children. It isn't all that hard to say, is it?"

"It is if one prizes one's freedom."

"Okay. Let's leave aside the question of whether you've ever been free," Burris told her. "What happens between now and when you feel you have to get married?"

"How long is that?" Her smile came and went so quickly Burris almost missed it. "Sooner than any of us would wish. I'm tired of fighting Dieter. The whole dead weight of the male Staelis presses me down. Their hatred is very tiring. A husband will deflect that hatred. You see? Eventually they win. And they knew they would."

She shivered, then put both arms around him. "Keep me warm." They embraced. His kissed her slowly, feeling her lips tense, then slowly relax. "It doesn't have to get that lousy," he said then.

"They don't leave me any options."

"Not if you think Swiss, no."

She looked up at him. "You've got an idea."

"You won't like it."

"Marry you?" Her glance moved back and forth across his face. "I'd give it a year, darling, maybe two."

Burris shook his head. "Sell out."

"What?"

"Liquidate."

"I don't understand."

"Sure you do. When they convey your inheritance to you, transfer it into one of those closed-off Liechstenstein *Stiftungs*. Then start to sell. Sell it all, shares, bonds, debentures, commercial paper, even titles to Staeli property. Sell it fast, before anyone catches on. Sell it for Swiss francs. Cash it all in."

"I don't—. It's too much cash."

"And then," he chuckled, "start your own bank."

"I don't—"

"Honey," he cut in, "stop saying 'I don't.' Just think of basing a newly formed Swiss bank on all those cash assets."

"It's unheard of."

"Sure, if you keep thinking Swiss. But look beyond it. This would be the last goddamned time you'd ever have to go to Staeli for anything. No family conferences. No foot-dragging. No back-stabbing. No intrigue. Just you, in your own name, operating your own bank."

"You realize . . ." Her voice died away for a moment. "You realize what this would do to the Staeli bank?"

"Start a run? It'll weather the storm. Forget them. A clean break is your only hope."

She stood there in his arms, silent again, eyes half closed in thought. Burris could see that her mind had already jumped ahead to the possibilities of what he had suggested. "But, still," she said then, "don't you see, Matt? This doesn't relieve me, it only piles more responsibility on me. And I still, someday, must pass this on to an heir."

"You seem to be stuck on that thought."

"Marriage and children? Yes."

"Think about it for a while. You've got time. Think in terms of getting a divorce from your family. Does that ring any bell? Think about the fact that you've always wanted to be free to do something like this."

"Like what?"

"Christ, I don't know, call it . . . call it a women's bank. The only one in Switzerland where a shopgirl can get a small loan to furnish her apartment."

Her glance lifted. "Or start her own shop?"

"Or finance a vacation."

"Matt!"

"I finally rang a bell, huh?"

"And if I made loans to famine areas? Who could tell me to stop?"

"Nobody."

"And if the loan went bad, who could tell me to stop?"

"Nobody."

"It wouldn't all be going out," she went on quickly, her Swiss mind looping back on itself. "I could cover that kind of loan by financing people like Michele."

"Honey, there are dozens of Micheles. Some bank is going to get fat helping them become millionaires. If you want to plow your profits from rich ladies into feeding poor ladies, nobody can stop you."

In an entire night of hostessy smiling, Margit had failed to produce anything like the smile she now gave Burris. "It's worthy of a Harvard M.B.A.," she said, hugging him fiercely. "Matt, I love you."

He stared over her shoulder at the schloss, dark now except for a row of windows on the second floor where her sitting room lay. The vision he had opened up for them now unfolded before his eyes in a quick, bright flash, the combination of women like Michele with women like Margit, the same combination men had been putting together for hundreds of years, business brains melded to banking brains. A combination like that was unstoppable, and there were fifty more Margit could put together just as profitably. It needed nothing else, this female combination, and certainly it didn't need him.

Her arms tightened around him, slacked off, tightened again. "You've gone all rigid."

"Yeh."

"Paralyzed?"

"By a vision of the future."

"Oh, no." She hugged him more tightly now. "By what you should say next. That's what's turned you into a stick. There is no torture so horrible as the inability to say what must be said." She stepped back and watched his face. "Bull's-eye. You really can't bring yourself to propose marriage, can you."

"Right. You know why."

"But you're no longer the poor boy from the wrong side of the tracks. My God, you're a roaring success."

The light of a few dying candles was too dim for him to see her face clearly. Her voice had gone a bit hoarse in the chill night air of the river. As he stood there, he understood that she was proposing marriage to him, or would. Or could.

He could hear the purling sound of the river at their feet, rushing past rocks and snags. They'd had one hell of a summer and a pretty good winter. Erich was back. The affair had taken a new and abrupt turn. And now?

She was already one of the wealthiest women in the world. She had the ability, one day, to become one of the most powerful. Her husband would have to be someone rather special. Matt Burris had never been someone special, and he knew it.

After a while she cleared her throat. "It's cold," she said.

"Let's get inside."

She took his hand as they walked the upgrade, through dew-damp grass, toward the dark hulk of the house. He stopped a moment on the lawn. "And Erich?"

"Sleeping in a guest bedroom."

"Is he back in Basel for good, then?"

She shrugged. Burris glanced at his watch. "After 2 A.M. Is there a cab I can call at this hour?"

"Nonsense. We have plenty of guest bedrooms."

* * *

Bunter was alone in the kitchen. He shivered in the night chill and carefully shut all the windows. He had not yet grown used to this strange old schloss and now, soon perhaps, he'd be leaving it for Master Erich's house in town. Bunter shivered again, but this time it was an echo of the same shock of excitement he had felt as Master Erich had appeared tonight, as if from the grave.

What a spectacle! Just to see him again made an old man young!

Briskly, Bunter picked up the table on which they had played jass and carried it back to the cellar. He put back on the table the racks and corkscrews he normally kept there. He eyed a Graacher Himmelreich '59 he'd been about to test when preparations for the party had overtaken him.

And what a party! The President himself, whichever one he'd been. And Colonel Nafer! And Archbishop Klat! Even that woman whose face had been on magazine covers, Madame Michele, the one they said had been hopelessly in love with Master Erich when—

Ach. Old gossip.

He turned the Himmelreich in his hands, gently. While 1959 had been the Year of the Century, the trouble with even a quality Moselle was that no white wine kept well this long.

So thinking, he pulled the cork on the long, slim bottle. The cork was damp and smelled fresh enough. He poured a quarter of a *Pokal* and sniffed it. Still firm. He sipped it. *Mein Gott,* still perfect.

And three dozen more in the racks! He'd report this find to Miss Margit in the morning. But, meanwhile, the bottle was open, yes? And what better way to celebrate the triumphant return of Erich Lorn? Bunter filled his glass to the brim and lifted it in silent tribute.

Over his head he heard footsteps, two sets. She had come in from the river, then. And with the big American. *Schade.* When she had Master Erich, she had no need of newcomers.

What an entrance! Like a soccer star, a conquering hero. This would end the American's chances, of course. Bunter had never pretended to be shocked by Miss Margit's being seen with Herr Burris. She was a healthy young woman, although much too thin, and the good Lord knew her financé had never hesitated to play her false.

No, Bunter hadn't found it in his heart to make conventional noises of dismay over the relationship with the American. But now that the master was home, well.

As soon as his health was up to it, the women would be flocking in and out of the house on the Unterer Rheinweg again, just as in the old days. Bunter filled his glass again. And then, in the fullness of time, the master would settle down and marry Miss Margit.

Bunter's imagination never reached beyond that point. Being Swiss, he would find it hard to envision anything beyond marriage. It would take a while, though. When he'd helped Master Erich upstairs and put him to bed he'd seen the little capsules he took to help him sleep. Bunter had been shocked at the various pills his master now took.

"Pain killers, Bunterli," Erich had said. "The finest Staelipharm concocts."

"But only for a little while?"

Master Erich hadn't replied.

Bunter sighed now and helped himself to a third glass of the Moselle. It had stayed fresh and light and *herp* after being open to the air this long, but one couldn't be too careful. He'd have to finish testing it. Overhead the footsteps stopped.

The American had never been at Schloss Staeli this late before. He came for Sunday lunch quite often, but had never before been above the ground floor. Bunter sipped thoughtfully. This sort of situation was more like what he was used to in the house on the Unterer Rheinweg, women hiding, doorbells ringing, desperate midnight flights, irate husbands. Quite scandalous.

Bunter smiled.

"Dreaming, Herr Bunter?"

He turned, startled but slow to react. Margit Staeli was watching him with a half-smile. "Fräulein Margit, this Graacher Him—"

"Tell me tomorrow." They were exchanging Schweizerdeutsch, the choppy syllables like someone in wooden shoes climbing an uneven flight of cobblestone steps. "Is there any champagne left?"

Flustered, Bunter stared at the cooler, unable to move without revealing the nearly empty wine bottle behind him. "I'll get it," she said.

There was something new in her voice that froze his blood. He sensed that it wasn't directed entirely at him, but there was a force he had never heard before and, already washed with waves of guilt about the '59 Moselle, he stood rooted to the spot. She picked out a bottle of Dom Ruinart and two glasses, then started to leave the kitchen.

"Bunter."

"Yes, Fräulein Margit?"

"Enjoy it. Fifty-nine was a good year."

She disappeared, leaving him with his back to the table on which the bottle of Himmelreich stood. What eyes! X-rays!

* * *

Margit settled Burris on the wicker chaise longue of her mother's. She poured champagne for both of them and they touched glasses.

"Happy birthday."

424

"Mm." She put the glass down on the long refectory table. "Sit there. I won't be a moment." She left the room and moved swiftly through the dark along corridors she had known since first she had learned to walk. Erich's bedroom was next to the suite in the far corner which her father had once used.

She opened the door and listened to Erich's slow, even breathing. In all their years together, she had never heard him sleep. An odd, sexless relationship to have with such a celebrated seducer as Erich.

Margit stepped into the room. A faint light outside, not the moon or stars but a lamp kept burning in the delivery yard, showed her Erich's profile as he lay on his back, chest slowly rising and falling.

The sleep of the just. Nothing troubled his conscience. In that one insane act of self-destruction, launched to free her of Iselin, he had apparently cleared all his sins away. Marvelous to be able to do that.

Clear away his sins and demonstrate his devotion. One mad act, one heavy stone that crushed two birds.

Even by the romantic candlelight on the lawn, she had seen the new seams in his face where they had managed to save both eyes, and the scars on his neck where he had been extraordinarily lucky with the carotid artery. Now, in this near-dark, none of the patchwork was visible. Nor were any of the lines life had placed on his face.

He was a boy again, still unmarked, a privileged boy for whom there would always be the means to hold life at bay. Just as there always would for her.

A boy who had shown how much he loved her, when what she felt for him was not love. A boy who had turned the tables on her.

She picked up his hand and turned it over to glance at the palm. Even in this dim light the scar looked raw. Early death. By violence.

Margit believed in none of the occult arts but, as for the scar, she read it exactly as Michele had, visual assurance that the early death foretold by his palm had been cheated. He would live a long time, she decided now.

She looked past his calm young profile to the bedside table where a water carafe and several bottles of pills stood. Being forced to pay close attention now to his health, he would live to be a very old man . . . and a very attractive one. She pressed her lips to the scar on his palm and set his hand down on the coverlet.

He muttered something through drugged sleep. Some woman's name, Margit thought, smiling in the dark. Possibly mine. Possibly not.

She moved thoughtfully along the dark hall toward the lighted room where Burris waited. Happy birthday. She felt no different. The full weight of being thirty would not fall on her until Monday, at the office of the law firm that had served as her father's counsel.

Now it had no weight. She was in her own castle with her financé and her lover. Everything was still make-believe.

She came to the doorway of the sitting room and saw that Burris had kicked off his patent-leather slippers, loosened his tie and looked terribly at home. He was staring deeply into his glass of champagne, as if counting bubbles.

He really did seem to be getting together a trial balance, so many bubbles per second. At Harvard he'd been a new and unexpected sensation. In the interim they'd both changed, Burris much more than she. He'd become a—what was the American word?

Glad-hander? No, subtler than that. Any good banker—and he was a superior one—could fake affability when it suited him. Not glad-hander . . . *booster*. That terrifying American hypocrisy, reeking of sales conventions staged like Miss America contests, of an eternity of Rotary-luncheon optimism and Kiwanis Christmas handouts to poor children, flesh-colored Band-aids on open sores.

"I expect a final audit of those bubbles," she said from across the long room, "complete with bar charts."

"How's Erich?"

"Sleeping."

He nodded gloomily. "How are you?"

"Thirty."

"How am I?"

"Sleek."

She picked up her glass from the refectory table. "Fat cat," she said, raising it to him. "Have they proposed you yet for the *Jungführerschaftverein*?"

"What's that supposed to mean?"

"Some terrible insult. I'll have to figure out why I said it." She saluted him with her glass. "In the other room lies a noble lad whom life has creased—but only creased—with experience and a faint sketch of pain. And here you lie, Mr. Chamber of Commerce." She raised her glass a bit higher. "And here stand I. Here's to me."

"No fun, is it?"

"Mm?"

"Being thirty."

* * *

It was scandalous, a girl alone upstairs with two men, *nicht wahr?* Bunter sipped his wine. In the silence of the night he could hear the easy creaking of the old house. A brisk spring wind swirled outside. It was April. Everything was starting up again as it always did.

Bunter caught sight of the stripped jass deck on the sink counter. It had been thrown there carelessly, perhaps by Bodo. The face of the queen of spades stared commandingly at Bunter. He frowned. He would never get used to playing jass with queens.